THE LAST HOPE

Also by Krista & Becca Ritchie

The Raging Ones

THE
LAST
HOPE

KRISTA & BECCA
RITCHIE

WEDNESDAY BOOKS
NEW YORK

First published in the United States by Wednesday Books, an imprint of St. Martin's Publishing Group

THE LAST HOPE. Copyright © 2019 by K. B. Ritchie.
All rights reserved. Printed in the United States of America.
For information, address St. Martin's Publishing Group,
120 Broadway, New York, NY 10271.

www.wednesdaybooks.com

Designed by Devan Norman

Library of Congress Cataloging-in-Publication Data

Names: Ritchie, Krista, author. | Ritchie, Becca, author.
Title: The last hope / Krista & Becca Ritchie.
Description: First edition. | New York : Wednesday Books, 2019. |
    Sequel to: The raging ones. | Summary: Franny, Court, and
    Mykal escape prison with the help of a mysterious stranger and
    join him on a mission that will determine the fate of humanity.
Identifiers: LCCN 2019008125| ISBN 9781250128737 (hardcover) |
    ISBN 9781250128744 (ebook)
Subjects: | CYAC: Science fiction. | Survival—Fiction. | Love—Fiction.
Classification: LCC PZ7.1.R5756 Las 2019 | DDC [Fic]—dc23
LC record available at https://lccn.loc.gov/2019008125

Our books may be purchased in bulk for promotional, educational, or business use. Please contact your local bookseller or the Macmillan Corporate and Premium Sales Department at 1-800-221-7945, extension 5442, or by email at MacmillanSpecialMarkets@macmillan.com.

First Edition: August 2019

10 9 8 7 6 5 4 3 2 1

For our brother and dad,
who sail into the stars

ACKNOWLEDGMENTS

BOUNDLESS THANKS TO:

Our superhero agent, Kimberly Brower, for an incredible amount of belief in this sci-fi world, these three (now four) main characters, and in us—you have been one of the biggest, most magical blessings in our lives. We are forever grateful to have you in our corner and that the world we've landed on has you here.

Tiffany Shelton, for helping us shape up *The Last Hope* into a sparkling beauty that we could only dream it'd become. And to Eileen Rothschild, for loving Franny, Court, and Mykal from the start and paving the way for our childhood dream to be tangible.

The Wednesday Books team, for all the hard work and dedication in making our work come to life. Seeing these books on a shelf in a bookstore and holding them in our hands has been the most surreal moment of our lives. Thank you so very much for making this dreamlike thing possible.

Our mom, for being a backbone, a cheerleader, a fellow dreamer, a light in a dark place, and the kindest heart we've ever known—we don't need a link to know how much you love us, and in turn, we can only hope you know how much we love you. Thank you for being the first to listen when we spout off our wild ideas about a world where everyone knows the day they'll die, triple helixes, and a myth baby. Thank you for always reading our work, even in the toughest times.

Our dad and our brother, for your endless encouragement in

this sci-fi world, for all those space and sailing talks, for so much love and support surrounding our childhood goal—and we're in tears knowing you both could see and hold this one.

Jenn Rohrbach and Lanie Lan, for being our shining sea stars from now until forever. In our eyes, you're what makes humanity so immensely beautiful. Thank you for the unconditional love throughout so many wonderful years and for championing these books as if they exist inside your soul—you two are simply incredible.

Our family, for always being there with pom-poms and confetti cannons and the deepest of love—we are so lucky to have so many aunts, uncles, and cousins. Our hearts sailed through oceans seeing you run out to bookstores just to see the book on the shelf.

The Fizzle Force family, again you are powerful. And rare and beautiful. You have given us hope and light when we needed it most. Thank you for taking a chance on these books, for celebrating them, for loving these characters enough to encourage others to read about them too. Simply, thankyouthankyouthankyou.

Lastly, to all of you dear readers who've read both books. Thank you for not only picking up the first but finishing with the second—we are so very honored that you've stuck with us and these characters. *The Raging Ones* and *The Last Hope* are a combination of everything we love in young adult novels, and to be able to give you Court, Mykal, Franny, and Stork has been a dream and a real feat. Thank you for traveling through galaxies with us and feeling the strength of humanity.

For any aspiring writer reading these acknowledgments as we often did as young girls, know that we believe in you. Never lose hope.

THE
LAST
HOPE

ONE

Court

Y ou've escaped one prison before, so you'll be escaping another in no time." Mykal spoke those optimistic words thirty-one days ago, but I didn't have the heart to remind him that it took me five years to flee Vorkter Prison.

Now that we're trapped aboard an enemy starcraft and only fed scraps every three days, we don't have five years to spare.

Our bodies heave in miserable hunger and pain, and I'm in far worse shape.

With time running out, I refuse to lie on the only cot, our only comfort, and I sit on the hard floor.

Slumping against the firm wall, my spine aches, and a sharp *pang* in my hip radiates like hot agony throughout my rigid bones. I breathe shallow breaths between dry lips, and my shaking hand constantly hovers near my hip. As though I can fix what's wrong, but the only remedy is outside this brig. Medicine, antiseptic, *water*.

I have none.

We're all together, but there is nothing here besides a single cot. There are no bars to peer out of, like at my last cell. This is just a tiny, bare, enclosed room inside a starcraft. Clean with polished floors, sterile walls, and a spotless padlocked door, all bathed in soft pink hues from an overhead rouge light.

Mykal hunches as he stands, the ceilings too low, and since I'm much taller, I spend most of my time sitting or crouching.

Franny squats next to a hatch on the cumbersome door. No

windows, the hatch has been our sole view outside the brig, but it only opens when they feed us.

She presses her cheek against the chilly pink metal. Listening.

With our linked emotions and senses, I try to concentrate on Franny. Just for a reprieve from my own torment. I wouldn't be able to hear what she hears or see what she sees; we still only share touch and taste and smell. I can barely feel the bite of the cold door against my jaw and ear.

Her senses, *his* senses—they both sweep past me as another pang of misery scratches at my flesh.

I look down.

Crude, gnarled stitches weave jaggedly along my lower abdomen. My golden-brown skin is sickly green and inflamed. I resist the urge to itch.

Franny scratches her own hip—*she feels my pain.*

I shut my eyes for a long moment. Hating that they both *feel* the deep cuts from a man I loathe. From Bastell: the man I shared a Vorkter Prison cell with, the one who relentlessly hunted me until he attacked me at Yamafort's museum.

We may've left Bastell behind on our home planet, we may've stolen the *Saga* starcraft and reached space, but he left real wounds that can't disappear easily—*focus.*

I open my eyes and try to focus on our plans of escape. Though we've failed each and every day. I try to think of anything to forget that last encounter in the museum.

We're out of Bastell's reach.

I try to breathe stronger, and then I wince and shift, a stabbing pain shooting up my side. *Gods be damned.*

Mykal swings his head back, his hard-hearted blue eyes meeting my grim grays. If he could beat down the door with his fists alone, I'm certain he would.

Because he's already tried. Until the skin on his knuckles busted and bled, and sores formed.

"What are you moving for, Court?" Mykal asks. "Rest yourself. You've hardly slept one blink of an eye."

"It's not so easy when we need to leave," I say in a single breath. I sink my head back to the wall, our eyes not detaching.

Mykal.

I asked him to fly away with me, and I've led him to a prison. No apology I speak can erase the guilt. I just need to free Mykal and Franny from this place.

I have to.

"There's no time," I say with another wince.

Franny stiffens and cautiously glances back at me. I don't know how to ease her worry.

Mykal takes a step toward my spot on the floor. I don't know how to ease his either.

"Don't," I say weakly, stopping him.

He scratches his jaw. Frustration burrowing through his body and mine. He stays an arm's distance away and gestures to me. "I may not be a physician like you, but once upon an era, I nursed you from the brink of something foul. I can do it again, you realize?"

It's too late for that.

His muscles flex. "Court?"

He can't read my mind, and so I'm left to wonder what emotion accompanied my thought. What did he sense?

I blink a few times. Unsure of what I felt. But I want him to know something. "I still remember . . ." I swallow hard and fight to speak louder. "I still remember the winter wood."

His eyes redden. "Yer telling me this now?" His northern lilt breaks through. I'm truly happy to hear it again.

In a whisper, I clarify, "I know what you've done for me."

"Court—"

"I wouldn't have survived without you." My voice cracks, days and months and years rushing toward me. Frostbitten skin and the crackle of fire and his impossibly bright laughter. I remember the moments after I escaped Vorkter.

Where Mykal brought me to his warm hut out of the wet

snow. Hovering over my gaunt frame, nearly nose-to-nose, he lathered mud and herbs on my wounds. Grenpale remedies.

He was a wild Hinterlander.

I was a lost boy of fifteen, and years later, we've found ourselves in a similar position. I'm on the brink of something foul again, but there are no trees, no mud, no plants, nothing that can save me by his hands.

I'm afraid.

I take in a breath, finally understanding my emotions, and I do everything I can to contain them. Bottle them. Swallow them. So they won't know this fear.

Let me suffer alone.

Mykal bends low to be at eye level, palm on the floor. "I don't want yer praise. I got you in this mess—"

"No." I cut him off.

He's still kicking himself for not stopping Bastell. In his mind, he broke a devout promise. He swore that I'd never encounter that cruel bastard again, but I did.

I already forgave Mykal a hundred times, even when he didn't need to be forgiven. He's just not ready to absolve himself yet.

He reaches out his hand to me . . .

"I don't want your guilt," I say, more strictly than I intend. Purposefully pushing him away, and it works.

He retracts his callused palm. And he flicks his forefinger in a vulgar Grenpalish gesture. Rising to a hunched stance again.

I try to bury my disappointment. Because I long for Mykal. I want him closer and closer, our chests pressing together and the heat of our bodies easing us into a contented sleep. I'm called toward him. Every minute of every day.

Toward his kindness and fortitude and foolish optimism. A great pull beckons me into his arms, but in the same breath, I'd rather Mykal be far, far away from my suffering.

If we touch skin-to-skin, the link will make him feel what I feel tenfold, and since we've kissed, we've already heightened this bond between us a significant amount. He's noticed the shortness of my breath, whereas Franny can't distinguish the subtleties as well.

He's even started recognizing emotion in me that I can't even name.

"I'll just be standing right here," Mykal says, angling toward me, "where I can stare at your handsome face."

I roll my eyes, but I don't mind him staring at all. I want to smile, but it seems like an impossible feat.

Quietly, his gaze slides down my weakened frame. Inspecting me from afar.

I do the same to him. Sweat builds up on his pale skin and drenches his wheat-blond hair.

All we've ever known was the ice and snow on our frozen planet of Saltare-3. None of us are used to the sweltering room temps here.

The brig stinks badly of a musky odor, our stench the obvious culprit.

We've all shed our onyx-and-gold StarDust uniforms to combat the scorch. No slacks, no cloaks, and Franny slung off her bra. Left only in black underwear, we sweat through those and make the best out of the absolute worst.

Beads roll off Mykal's sideburns and slip down his stubbly jaw. I watch his eyes lower to the tangled scars and ink over my heart, and then I scrutinize his brawn. Bands of his muscle have begun to lose their tautness, not as carved or cut as they once were.

My squared jaw tightens, and a rock lodges in my throat. I want to believe that he's fine. That he's not hurting, but I can feel him starving. I can feel his stomach gnawing on itself and his body withering away.

Franny is worse. Her rib cage is visible and juts in and out as she breathes, more skin and bones than either him or me.

My concern for her grows and grows every day.

She refuses to eat our rations. No one is willing to take more than our share, but we've all volunteered to take less.

Mykal fixates on my stitches. He grumbles a harsh curse and grinds his molars. More guilt cinching his features.

"You're not to blame," I say while trying to sit more upright. I can't pull myself up without angering the wound, so I stay mostly slumped.

"I *am* to blame," Mykal growls. "I sewed you up poorly—"

"No," I interject again, my heart pounding. "Your sewing is what's kept me alive, Mykal. If we hadn't been taken as their prisoners, I would've healed properly."

But our *Saga* starcraft had been roped in by the *Romulus,* and the cadets physically pummeled us as we struggled and fought to run. All the while, their commander of some twenty years looked on. Leering with no ounce of sympathy, he ordered us to be locked away, and later, we learned his name.

Commander Theron.

"Court is right," Franny chimes in from the door. "He could've been eating a hearty meal if we weren't stuck here. One made for the gods. Not the little bits of bread we've been given for supper."

At the mention of food, our stomachs collectively groan.

"Mayday," Franny curses and rests her forehead on the shut hatch.

I suddenly shiver.

Cold ripples through me, and my arms and shoulders quake vehemently.

Their heads swerve to me, and they stare me down as though I let out a dying wheeze.

"Why are you cold?" Mykal asks. "Aren't you sweating? Isn't he sweating?" He looks to Franny for confirmation.

"He's dripping sweat." She nods. "Maybe there's a draft over there." But she doesn't believe her own words. I can tell as her stomach flips. I think she wishes it were just a draft.

I don't want to alarm either of them, but all I know is how to prepare them for the worst. How to help them survive in foreign places.

My pulse speeds as their panic sets in, and I try not to tremble again. Biting down hard, my teeth throb. "Franny," I say slowly. "You can ask me anything."

She's quiet.

Mykal starts pushing at the flat ceiling for any exits. He does this every hour, but urgency floods him more than ever before. He shoves harder. Faster.

I think he feels my fear.

Franny stays in a crouch and presses her ear back to the padlocked door. Concentrating.

I lick my dry lips. "You've been wanting to talk for weeks on end," I remind her.

Her brows scrunch. "I know I've been harping on about what the *Romulus* commander told us, but it's not important right now." She unconsciously touches her hip, scratching.

I'm fine.

I'm fine.

I swallow and say, "You mean that we're human."

I don't know what a human is.

I don't know what or who we are, but I haven't known that for years. Now is no different. Learning that we're *human* has only left us with more questions that need greater explanations.

"There's nothing to talk about," she mutters, unmoving. "You know nothing just like the rest of us." Worry undercuts her snappy tone, and I'm not good at figuring out the origin of emotion. But I assume her worry is about me.

Franny has already asked if Andola, also called Earth, is shaded pink. She theorized that the cadets placed us in a pink-shaded room to make us feel at home.

But Commander Theron hasn't seemed to care about our comfort. Clearly. What makes me even more nervous: they had separated us at first. But only minutes later, they threw us in the same brig together. I'm not sure why.

I answered Franny, *I don't know what Earth looks like.* We

only know that Saltarians were forcibly exiled from Earth thousands of years ago.

Franny asked how we can be human if we look Saltarian.

I answered, *humans must look like Saltarians.* She snorted and said, *that, I could've figured out on my own.* It made Mykal laugh. One of the few times we've heard the lively sound.

She asked what a Helix Reader is, the device that blinked orange and told us we're human. Which, we've discovered, is why we were able to dodge our deathdays unlike everyone else.

I answered, *I don't know.*

She asked if all humans are linked together by senses and emotions. Like us.

I answered, *I don't know.*

She asked what makes us human.

I don't know.

At the door, Franny mutters to herself, "After all that we've been through, we deserve a better ending." The heat in her voice is far away, barely inflaming me.

I gather my strength to say, ". . . talking is important."

Franny is motionless, but her pulse pounds and pounds. I want her to ask me whatever she needs to ask. Tomorrow, I may be gone.

"Franny—"

"You're *dying,*" she shoots back and swerves around to face me. Her eyes sting.

My eyes burn, and Mykal wipes his runny nose, all of us on the verge of tears. He shoves the ceiling more forcefully. Urgently. Until he's banging his fists for an escape.

It hurts more to watch him bash his knuckles. His skin splits open again, and I grimace.

Franny shakes her hand out, feeling Mykal's pain too.

I need him and her to survive. They must. So I dig into my last reserves of energy, and I reach for the heap of clothing. I grab my black slacks. Slowly rising, I brace most of my weight against the wall. Creeping upward.

Mykal drops his arm and spins on me. "What are you doing? What—have you gone mad? You—"

"I'm fine," I interject and force my leg into one of the slack holes.

Mykal tenses, boiling hot. He bows toward me, putting a callused palm on the ceiling. "Then tell me you aren't dyin' right in front of me."

They can sense when I lie.

I fight back tears. Stomping on emotion. But I'm afraid. I'm angry. I'm wading in despair. I'm so many things at once, and all I want to be is at peace with them. And it's over.

It's over for me.

I run the heel of my palm beneath my watering eyes. Shivering.

Mykal steps forward. "Court—"

"I'm not dying," I retort.

A burning tear scalds his cheek. He wipes it roughly away. "My pa is rollin' in his grave, the one that I dug, just hearing the boy that I've been loving *lie* to my crooked-nosed face."

My chest tightens in a different kind of agony, and I struggle to step into my slacks. Teeth chattering and clanking. Hands vibrating.

"How are you cold?" Franny questions.

"I have a fever."

"A what?" Mykal asks.

I don't answer. Gently, I lift the hem of my slacks to my waist. The fabric brushes harshly against my inflamed wound. I inhale a sharp breath. Blood rushes out of my head. Light bursts in my vision. Faint, I start to slide down the wall.

Mykal instantly catches me beneath my arm and supports me upright.

I place my hand to his chest. And I try to push him back.

His hurt flares in me. "What are you doin'?" He sways slightly, even with my weak force. Clearly he's depleted too. More than I've ever seen him.

Mykal.

I have to hang on to his shoulder to stand. He lets me, and he brushes my dark hair out of my lashes with an aggressive hand. Rarely gentle, on any occasion.

Our eyes meet.

"I'm fine," I protest.

"You know you're not," Mykal growls. "I know you're not. Franny knows. We all damned well *know*. So stop pushing me away, Court."

I suck in emotion, but water pricks my eyes. I shudder. "You don't deserve to feel what I feel. Like Franny said, you both deserve a better ending—"

"*We*," Franny spits back. "I said *we*. That includes you."

I hang my head. "Just let me die," I mumble.

Mykal's chest rises and falls heavily, and his palm encases my jaw, clasping my face. "What was that?" he asks.

But Mykal can read my lips from any distance, anyplace, after doing it so often at StarDust. They both can.

He knows what I said.

Franny screams at the locked hatch, "Help us! *Anybody* out there!! Please, *gods*, help!"

No one has been able to hear our pleas. We don't know where the *Romulus* crew took our friends from the *Saga* starcraft. Including my older brother.

Kinden, the Soarcastle sisters, and Zimmer have been missing ever since we were thrown into the brig. The last we saw of them was on the observation deck. When we learned we're human.

If we want to escape, we have to do it ourselves.

I'm going to die.

Tears threaten to well again.

Mykal taps my cheek. Twice. Trying to show affection and get me to lift my head.

I don't.

"Court."

My throat almost swells closed. Finally, I look up at Mykal.

And I choke out, "I'm afraid to die." I don't know how both sentiments can be true. I don't understand what I'm feeling. Death is more complex than it's supposed to be.

Only love makes sense.

Forcefully, Mykal says, "You won't be dyin' anytime soon."

I blink and tears fall. "You and your fantasies."

He cries, "I promise you."

Both of us hunching, I tug him closer, gripping his bicep for dear life. His bare chest pushes up against mine, an electric spark zipping through my veins.

We inhale.

"I promise you," he repeats, wrapping his burly arms around my shivering body.

Warmth kisses my flesh. I hold on to him, and the more Franny calls for help, the more I think of Kinden.

"Mykal," I whisper. "If you see my brother again, tell Kinden I'm sorry . . ." I take a second. "I'm sorry . . . I couldn't give him longer."

All my brother wanted was more time with me.

And I've lost him again.

Mykal pulls back and stares deep in my eyes. "You'll be telling him yourself."

I doubt. "I have one day left. If that."

He pats my cheek again. "Today is the day of freedom then." Mykal wears a halfhearted smile.

I'm about to mention how every day our plan of escape wields the same desolate result, but Franny speaks first.

"It's different now," she says, voice raspy from shouting. But she's settled back into a crouch, ear to the door.

"How so?" I wonder.

Purpose locks her shoulders. And lights her eyes on fire. "We're more desperate than ever before."

TWO

Franny

Court will not die here.

We will *not* die here. Gods, do you hear me? I scorch from the inside out, not just from the fykking heat of this bare-bones room that smells like piss. A fiery scream scratches my throat, aching to be freed.

Because I'm so tired of fearing death, and I've started replacing those grand, overwhelming fears with one of Court's big words.

Indignation.

A noun. In-dig-na-tion. Defined as *anger provoked by a special something that is unjust, warty, or downright mean.*

I may've added some flair to that, but my definition still carries the same meaning.

I keep my ear pressed to the pink metal door. With no time left to dwell, I focus on our plan. Every few days, a cadet has been giving us a small portion of bread and an even smaller canister of water.

So I listen for footsteps.

Mykal and Court separate behind me. Hands lowering from each other, Court fishes his slacks' button through a loop and carefully takes a seat on the cot. His bones wail at every little movement, and mine start aching badly if I concentrate too long and hard on him.

So I train my mind elsewhere.

The door.

The door.

The door.

"Ready, little love?" Mykal pants and sweats, crouching down on the other side of our soon-to-be exit. Hopefully. He looks graver than Court, and that's saying something.

I nod, and while we wait in silence, I only break the quiet to whisper, "Do you think the gods are on our side?" Sometimes I think they've abandoned us.

Maybe because we're human. They hate what we are as much as the Saltarians do.

Mykal grinds down like he was chewing dry root. He has none here. "My pa used to say that the gods will be believing in you if you just believe in them, and that's all there is to it."

I tuck more belief close to my chest. Back home in Bartholo, maybe I'd be called a chump for questioning such certain things. Death and gods. Or maybe I'd still be a *no one* to most everybody.

Just the girl behind the wheel of a battered Purple Coach. Driving people to wherever they need to be.

I don't care what I'm called. All I know is that I'm not ready to let Court die, and I'm not ready to give up on the gods. I pray and hope that they're not ready to give up on me.

Clap.

Mykal and I exchange a readied look at the sudden noise.

Clap, clap . . .

Our pulses speed in sync. Court freezes on the cot, his concern an undercurrent to our anticipation.

Untroubled footsteps grow louder and louder.

And then they fall quiet again. He or she is right up against the door. I ease back from the squared hatch and hear a brutish snicker.

"Day thirty-one, vermin."

I bite my tongue as hard as Mykal bites his. We've spat back nasty insults before, but for Court's sake, we're doing our best not to lash out.

The hatch screeches. About to open.

I bristle and breathe heavier. *Don't botch this, Franny. Don't botch this.*

And I watch the hatch slide to the right. I don't peek through the sudden opening. Quickly, I reach my bony arm through the slot and try to grab the cadet. His wrist. His shirt.

Anything.

Not able to see, I feel around for his body. Snatching air and air. And more air.

Come on.

Come on—the sharpest *zap* sears my arm. I cringe as the shock spindles through my veins like I rolled in hot casia. My body cramps up and rattles.

Mayday.

I fall backward on my bottom. Shaking. I've felt this painful jolt time and time again, and it always hurts. Always burns like heat I've never known.

"Heya!" Mykal roars at the cadet.

He laughs. "Pathetic little weaklings."

I brace myself on my elbows, and the cadet bends and peers at us through the hatch. Spiky brown hair, a smug snarl that I'd like to tear off with Mykal, and a red birthmark shaped like an eye patch—I've never seen this cadet until now, but it doesn't make a difference.

I still don't like him.

Not one bit.

Mykal spits. "You snot-nosed goat! I'll be tearing you limb from limb and then we'll see who'll be laughing—"

"Oh shut up—"

"We did *nothing* to you!" I scream, a blaze bursting inside my chest. I push back up to my knees. "Let us out!" I stick my arm through the hatch again.

I desperately grab at anything, but I only close my fingers over air.

His cruel laughter echoes shrilly.

Mykal growls in frustration. "I hate people."

"Likewise, *human*," the cadet snarls.

"He's toying with you . . . both," Court whispers with clattering teeth.

My fingers graze something.

I think I feel . . . the metal of the canteen. It slips out of reach—a second zap sends me flying backward. *Fyke.* I land hard on my back and wince through my teeth.

My body contracts in agonizing positions. I heave for breath, and Mykal rushes forward, his blond hair matted back with sweat. He almost hesitates, wanting to help me, but he knows he can't waste time.

This is our last chance. And so he takes my place at the hatch and shoves his arm through the opening.

I gasp for air.

Court—*Court* is suddenly hovering over me. Pieces of his dark brown hair fall to his lashes. Knelt above my writhing body, he looks down at me.

I look up at him.

He shouldn't have left the cot. I try expressing that in my eyes, but I choke.

Court places his clammy hand . . . on my forehead.

I don't understand until his senses race toward me, more powerful with touch, and an abrupt wave of pain radiates around my hip.

His pain.

His hip.

I inhale a lung full, and my body slackens. So sluggish and heavy and cold. I wonder how he can even move if he feels like solid ice.

As I battle to breathe normally, he scrutinizes my rib cage that moves up and down. I can count each rib bone by sight. Starving. But my hunger can't be resolved now. He should know that, being a doctor and a good planner of plans.

I wish he'd stop staring at my bones. I snap at him, "I'm *fine.*"

Sternness narrows his eyes. "You realize you're lying like I was." Court's worry washes over my body like warm bathwater.

A part of me is surprised that he cares about me. The other part is sad that I'm surprised at all.

"I'm not the one dying," I say with less bite and roll away from him. Nearing the door. I appreciate his help, but we can't bicker. Not now.

I kneel and train my concentration on Mykal. Heightening the link, I soon lose sense of the sting in my hip and feel the quickened *thump thump* of Mykal's heart in my chest. Beads of sweat pouring down his pale skin.

His strength is my strength.

My hand is his hand.

I'm no longer afraid of feeling his unrestrained, furious fortitude that could injure and maim any foe.

His enemies are my enemies.

And we owe this cadet *nothing*.

"I can see your arm wailing around." The cadet chuckles. "You're pitiful."

Mykal grunts, stretching his arm farther out and pressing his cheek up against the metal door. He fists clothing.

The cadet jerks back. "Too slow—"

Mykal seizes a bony wrist. His fingers wrap tightly around the cadet's limb.

"You don't want to do that," the cadet warns.

"Yeah, I fucking do." Mykal squeezes his wrist—I squeeze in violent desperation.

Mykal never lets go.

I never let go.

The cadet zaps Mykal twice. We all breathe through our noses. *Don't fall. Don't fall, Mykal.* The shock scalds Court and me.

We rattle.

Another zap.

Mykal screams through the pain. Spit flying. Muscles twitching.

His scream rumbles inside my lungs, and suddenly, all of our anger explodes to the surface. Thirty-one days of confinement and punishment. For no good or justifiable reason.

I yell with snot and blistering tears. Court yells with the last of his breath. And Mykal wrenches the cadet forcefully against the door. *Thwack!*

It sounds like skull hitting metal.

The cadet lets out a guttural groan.

Mykal pulls back and yanks again and again. Slamming the cadet into the door that imprisons us.

"Stop," the cadet moans.

I can't see any of this. I can only hear it and feel what Mykal feels.

I stumble to my feet, standing, and lean on the door while the cadet zaps Mykal repeatedly. Until Mykal involuntarily releases his clutch. He trips backward. Falling down next to Court.

Me again.

I stick my arm through the hatch and immediately clasp a rod. *The zapper thing.* I fight with the woozy cadet. "We did nothing wrong!" I scream, wrenching the rod with everything I have in me.

We did nothing to deserve this.

Sizzling maddened tears prickle my eyes, and I yell and yank and I must press a button because I hear another zap and his garbled voice.

What sounds like a body hits the floor with a loud, echoing *thump.*

My brows spike.

I stay very still.

Waiting.

And the cadet goes completely quiet.

"Franny, bring it inside," Court says quickly, referring to the weapon. He slowly rises with Mykal, both hunching with the low ceiling.

I maneuver the rod long-ways and carefully slip it into the brig. I cradle the sleek light weapon that appears more like a blue broomstick with no bristles. Each end is flat and identical.

Mykal sidles next to me. "What in three hells is that?" He tilts his head and inspects the zapper thing.

"I haven't seen anything like it before." I pant, still catching my breath. I run my fingers down the smooth rod. I can't find the button that I pressed. "Maybe it's an Influential weapon." I look to Court, who'd know best about Influential business.

Court wipes his damp forehead. "Most likely, it's a Saltare-1 weapon."

I nod. Our icy home planet, Saltare-3, wasn't as technologically advanced as our sister planets. While we lived in perpetual winter, others in our galaxy had better climates. Especially the largest planet of all: Saltare-1.

I never needed to think much of our four sister planets. Not when I thought I'd die at seventeen. But in StarDust, I learned to read and I did discover a bit more than the tales I heard.

I discovered that Saltare-1 has the most technology and sent our planet aerospace training machines, holograms, and the *Saga* starcraft. All in hopes that Saltare-3 would join Saltarians in a war against Andola. Earth.

For Court, Mykal, and I—all we wanted was to find peace. And safety.

"So Saltare-1 may have more of these zappy things?" I ask Court.

He cringes. "Why must you use slang?"

That's what he's so worried about? Really? "What harm is there in talking how I like? We're not pretending to be Influentials anymore. They know our *real* names."

We told Commander Theron who we are. I didn't bother saying that I'm Wilafran Elcastle when I could be Franny Bluecastle. Court didn't chide me either. We all believed it'd help free us.

Obviously, we were wrong. It wouldn't be the first time.

Before Court responds, Mykal nods at the rod. "Let me see the funny-looking stick." He reaches for the weapon, and I tuck the rod to my chest.

"I think I should hold on to the funny-looking stick," I say.

Court tells Mykal, "You'll break it."

He scratches the light stubble along his hard jaw. "You're telling me these wondrous ladies and men from this forward-thinking planet didn't *think* to make an unbreakable stick?"

My brows pinch. Could the *Romulus* crew possess unbreakable, undefeatable weapons? I guess I wouldn't know. But at least we have one to use against them.

Court takes a measured breath. "We don't know what any weapon is capable of." More sweat trickles down his temple, and another shiver disrupts his no-nonsense posture.

Mykal hangs a heavy arm over Court's taut shoulders and draws him close. Warming him. They share a look of longing before Court turns his head and stares gravely upon me. His back and neck are irritatingly sore.

I wouldn't be able to tell this if we weren't linked, and I crave to stretch my arms and spine. Just to stretch *his*. But it wouldn't help much. It'd just drive me mad.

"What?" I ask Court.

"We don't know who we need to pretend to be in order to survive," he says with great severity.

My lips part. *Court wants to survive.* I think it a hundred times. Because it means that he believes an escape is possible.

For all three of us.

I start to smile.

A crooked one crosses Mykal's face. He messes Court's hair and says, "Looks like we have our Court back."

Court nods stiffly, and just as he begins to lean his weight on Mykal, we hear new noises outside our brig. We freeze and listen to the slap of soles on metal floor and muffled chatter and gruffer curses.

"Someone's coming," Court says. A surge of panic collectively storms us.

THREE

Franny

Standing a few feet away, we watch the open hatch and wait. A friend could be arriving, but most likely, it's a foe. And we're too cautious to stick our noses out and yell.

Tightening my grip around the rod, I stay one step in front of Court and Mykal. I'm not surprised when Mykal tries to change that. Barreling forward, he aims to block Court and me from harm.

Court captures his shoulder. "She has the weapon."

"My fists are stronger than a stick," Mykal counters.

Court goes to speak and then coughs in his fist. My throat tickles, followed by stabbing pain in my hip.

Mykal changes course. Returning to Court's side, he rubs his back in comfort. Mykal pats too hard at times, but Court doesn't seem to mind.

The brig rumbles. We tense, apprehension passed between us like a bad offering of spoiled milk. Mykal breathes harder as Court cages his own breath, and I aim a flat end of the rod at the padlocked door.

An unseen force lifts the low ceilings higher and higher. Granting us more room to stretch and stand. My eyes sweep our surroundings that haven't altered until now.

Court rises fully for the first time in thirty-one days. He rotates his aching shoulders, the relief as pleasant as lying on the softest bed underneath the wooliest blankets.

Mykal stares openmouthed at the ceiling. "Why would they do that?"

"I'm uncertain," Court whispers, his lips becoming a hard line.

"Maybe they want to talk," I theorize.

Court frowns more. "They had their chance many times before. It makes no sense."

We go quiet and watch the front wall and door change color from opaque pink to transparent glass. Gods, I can clearly see what lies outside the brig.

My gaze widens at the motionless body of the spiky-haired cadet. Lying on the starcraft's metal floor.

Behind the unconscious cadet, a sleet-gray empty corridor seems to travel endlessly. Blue-green lights line and illuminate the walkway. But I can't even dream of an escape. Not when two young and unfamiliar men stand on the other side of the wall.

The footsteps and chatter we heard—they must belong to them.

One looks more like me than like Court or Mykal. Same black hair, shape of our eyes, and beige skin, but I'd never go as far as to say we're related. The burgundy Saltare-1 cloak that I've come to hate hangs off his wiry shoulders, and a triangular Star-Dust brooch is pinned at the hollow of his long neck. He's a *Romulus* cadet.

He nudges the limp body with his boot.

I study the second young man, who cares nothing for the unconscious cadet. Longish snowy-blond hair is tucked behind his ears, a vibrant jeweled earring dangling on his right lobe. An odd piece of bronze armor covers his chest—armor that I've only ever heard of in tales—and a leather skirt ends just above his knees.

The symbol on his breast is nothing I've seen before.

"What's on that strange one's feet?" Mykal whispers. "I can see his damned *toes.*"

None of us know the name of his footwear.

"It's not important," Court says, but his curiosity joins ours

THE LAST HOPE 23

like we're feverishly catching stars in a bottle. Before each one vanishes and we're left in the dark once again.

I direct the rod at his face. With the *Romulus* cadet, I at least know his malicious intentions. This one is an unnerving mystery.

His frosty blue eyes drift across the brig and our bodies. My breathing deepens when his gaze lands on me, and his jaw locks.

With haste, he turns to the *Romulus* cadet. "You stripped her?"

"I stripped myself!" I shout and steal their gazes in a single heartbeat.

The *Romulus* cadet ogles me crudely from toe to head, but that says more about him, less about me.

I don't falter.

The strange one blinks away the heat in his eyes. Holding my gaze, he cocks his head like I'm a sad little chump.

"I have a tongue," I retort. "If you wish to ask questions about me, speak to me."

"Oh trust me, dove, I'll speak to you in no time, but see, there's a wall separating you and me and you're more than indisposed at the moment."

I scowl, my guards still high. I can't tell if he truly cares whether I'm sick or well. Whether I'm satiated or starved. Why would he care at all? No one does.

Barely anyone ever has. He's not linked to us. He has no reason to help us.

These facts arch my shoulders.

Court raises his voice. "What do you two want?"

"Don't speak, *human*," the *Romulus* cadet chides, and he taps on a handheld device.

Mykal points a threatening finger. "You'll both be letting us out of here. Or we'll be putting you on the ground like your friend."

"By all means," the blond-haired one says and jerks his head toward the *Romulus* cadet. "Have at him. Aim for the kidney."

The cadet whips around and glares at the blond. "Bludrader." He spits a wad on the blond's exposed toes. *What a strange name . . .*

Bludrader hardly blinks at the spit or the caustic look being slung his way. "Open the door."

The cadet grumbles and spits again, but for some reason, he obeys. Punching another button on his device, the door lets out a heavy groan and a *click*.

Unlocking.

And in one swift movement, Bludrader pinches the back of the cadet's neck and slams his forehead into the wall. *Oh gods . . .*

The *Romulus* cadet falls backward like a stiff board.

Bludrader yanks open the translucent door and marches into our brig. We could run, but Court is too weak and this person could restrain us too easily.

We'll need to tie him up somehow.

Knock him out. And then we can go.

He steps near, his fingers to his nose, and he squints like his eyes sting from the putrid smell.

"Stop!" I shout and raise the tip of the rod to his throat. Not letting him get far. Not without answers. My pulse thumps in my ears, and I bark, "Show us your identification."

His mouth quirks with a short laugh. "You've got to be shitting me."

I cringe at that gross-sounding phrase. "What?"

Mykal glowers and pushes forward like a hunter on attack. "What'd you just say to her?"

Court clasps his shoulder to calm him.

"Take it back," Mykal warns. "Take it back right now."

Bludrader stands still but searches the brig with his eyes alone. "It's a harmless expression—where are your clothes?"

In a heap near the cot.

I wave the rod at his gaze. Capturing his attention. What feels like eons ago, I held an iron poker at a stranger's throat.

That stranger turned out to be Court Icecastle.

That stranger became one of my greatest friends.

But I can't sense Bludrader's lies from truths and truths from lies. Right now I can't take a chance on someone who could trick us.

"You're not touching *any* of our belongings," I say. "We don't know who you are. You could be a thief, a stalker, someone who wants us dead—"

"A murderer," he adds. The word is completely foreign. Mykal frowns.

Court shivers behind me, and I try not to tremble. "Say that again," I demand. "With the definition."

Bludrader tilts his head, his earring swaying. "*Murderer.* A person who kills another person. Also known as a killer. Saltarians cannot be murdered, but you three can be."

His speech leaves me feeling defenseless and bare. If I had a choice, I wouldn't be human. I'd know my deathday and remind him that I won't die for another so-and-so years.

I lift my chin. "You could be a murderer, come here to murder us," I retort, trying to appear as indestructible as I once did, and I push the tip of the rod at his throat.

He doesn't stiffen. Doesn't balk or recoil. "I'm the guy who's going to get you off this bloody ship."

What?

Our confusion escalates at his odd words. Court keeps shaking his head, not understanding.

"What's a ship?" I ask.

Bludrader stares more keenly at the rod. "It's what you call a starcraft."

"What's the meaning of a *guy*?" Court questions.

"A man . . ." He almost rolls his eyes in thought. "A boy."

"All right man-boy," Mykal says gruffly, not fond of this person. "Step aside and we'll be on our way without you accompanying us."

Court and Mykal don't trust anyone easily, and their distrust of Bludrader burrows inside my heart, resurrecting caution and barriers. Adding to my own suspicions.

I take note that Bludrader never showed us identification. He just *said* what he planned to do. Maybe he said what he knew we wanted to hear.

It could be a trap.

"No, you won't," Bludrader says matter-of-factly. "The three of you aren't going anywhere without me."

I bristle. "We're making the demands here. We're the ones with the weapon."

Court swallows a cough, doing his best to hide his sickness.

I speak more urgently. "You're going to show us to an escape pod—"

"You're holding it backward." Bludrader nods to my hands. "Your weapon. It's backward, dove. The electric end is pointed at your breast."

I go cold. "No, it's not," I combat, afraid to take my eyes off him and inspect the rod.

He nearly laughs into a groan like he's found himself in the worst situation. He's not the one who's been imprisoned and starved. "Lord have mercy," he says. "Do you even know where the trigger is?"

"She does," Mykal says with certainty.

I'm not so sure. "Sure I do," I lie, feeling more exposed than ever. My stomach curdles. Confidence wanes with the rise of insecurities. I'm not holding the weapon right.

I'm not clothed right.

I'm not right at all.

Court bends carefully to our pile of clothes, and I feel the damp fabric of shirts, slacks, and cloaks as he digs through our belongings. Returning with Mykal's shirt, he stands poised behind me and wraps the black baggy cloth around my flat chest and knots the fabric at my spine. Court cements a warning glare on Bludrader.

All the while, I never drop the weapon.

Bludrader studies my friend's commanding presence.

But as Court's fingers brush my bare shoulder, a stormy wave of uncertainty and unease crashes against me. And so I know, his self-assurance is just a well-worn costume shrouding his scars and wounds.

"Tell us your full name," Court says with sharp intensity, "your place of origin, and who or what you're loyal to."

Bludrader looks him over with interest. "That's a lot of requests for a guy in a brig."

"An unlocked brig," Court corrects. "You have one minute to answer."

"Or what?" Bludrader wonders. "Your only weapon is useless in her hands."

A bad taste drips in my throat. "I said I know how to use it," I retort.

"*It* is an electrowand—"

His words halt as I swiftly adjust my grip like I clutch a bat. And I swing the rod at the back of his head.

I strike him just as he ducks, and a grunt expels from his lips. He holds the spot, and as he checks his palm for blood, only a little dot of red on his skin, Mykal barrels forward and slams a hard fist at his jaw.

Bludrader shoves him, and Mykal seizes his wrist while he stumbles backward. They both topple to the floor. Wrestling.

Throwing punches.

Blood spews from mouths and noses.

I shake out my hand again as the sores reopen on Mykal's knuckles. Stinging. He's not winning easily like he usually would. I've heard so many grand and beautiful tales of Mykal fighting wolves and bears with nothing but his hands.

He should be able to overpower this wart.

But he's spent thirty-one days confined, starved, and weakened.

I've come to know that Mykal hates when he lets bigger men make him feel small, and he growls curses from his homeland.

Clawing and beating at a person in armor. He can't seem to grab hold of Bludrader for long.

He loses his grip.

Court looks grave at the scene, and he turns to me with urgency. "Give it to me, please."

I hand him the rod.

He searches the weapon for the trigger, and then Bludrader pins Mykal to the floor. His metal armor crushes against Mykal's bare chest, the weight unbearable.

Court chokes next to me, his eyes flaring, the link between him and Mykal too heightened. He pushes the rod to me about the same time I steal it back.

Feverishly, I hunt for the trigger.

Mykal elbows Bludrader in the jaw, the impact throbbing my bone. And then the weight releases off Mykal's chest.

I look up and see Bludrader straddling him.

Mykal breathes in a lungful of air and launches another fist— Bludrader socks him back in the face. I hear and feel and see the *crack*. Blood gushes out of his nostrils. Pain stabs our noses.

Mykal groans.

"*Stop!*" Court yells between his teeth, his distress spiking his pulse. He runs to Mykal, wincing through both of their pain, and I whack Bludrader on the back of the head with the rod. Over and over and—

He blocks my attack with his forearm, sheathed in the same bronze metal as his broad chest. The rod breaks cleanly in half.

"Mayday," I mutter and watch Bludrader stand.

Mykal rolls out underneath him, and Court helps Mykal to his feet and tries to quickly set the bone straight on his nose. His hands move with such familiarity that I guess they've done this before.

Bludrader spins around on me. "Franny."

He knows my name.

Sickness rises and burns my throat. Wordless, though I crave to question why and how. As Court would say, *there's no time.*

I aim half a rod at him.

No fear wells in his icy blues, despite redness blooming around his eye, blood drizzling out of his lip, and his blond hair knotted and stained crimson.

He's not afraid of us.

As though he already knows that he can't die today.

"You're Saltarian," I say.

He presses his thumb to his cut lip, wincing slightly, and then he stalks forward. "And what would you do if I said that I am what you think I am?"

I walk backward. "Saltarians are natural-born enemies to humans." It's what I've learned, and he has to know I'm human. "So I'd have no choice . . ." I let my voice die out, not about to tell our foe the plan.

We'll have to fight him until he passes out, and then we'll run.

We'll run.

We'll run.

Gods, let us run.

And we'll find an escape pod on our own, and be free.

He keeps edging forward. "What if I told you that I'm human?"

"Are you?" I ask and my spine suddenly hits the wall. Trapped here, I toss the half-a-rod at his face.

He blocks the attack but gives me time to run. I sprint toward the door.

"Wait!" he shouts. "Bloody hell." He chases after me, gains speed, and as he surpasses my stride, he pushes me into the corner.

Breath ejects from my lips, and in one blink, he reaches over his shoulder and clasps a handle attached to his back. He draws a long glinting blade to the front of his body. Holding the sharp side perilously at my throat, his armor pushes up against my bony build.

My eyes grow big. *He has a weapon.* This whole time, a sword was strapped on his back.

Maybe he truly doesn't wish to hurt us.

Court tries to come near me.

Bludrader glances over his shoulder. "You move, I cut her neck."

Maybe he does.

Court goes rigid, and he battles another incoming cough. He loses this time and hacks into his fist. Doubling over.

Mykal puts a hand on Court's back and roars something at our enemy, but his words are muffled with blood.

"Everyone, just calm down," Bludrader says with heavy breath, looking between our raging eyes. "You don't need to fight me to the death."

Fight to the death. I've never heard that saying before.

"Why won't you show us your identification?" I ask heatedly. "Why won't you tell us who you are?" I need answers. I need answers to everything. Anything.

I need them so badly, I could scream and scream and *scream.*

He smiles weakly. "Because, dove, I have no ID on me, and saying my full name isn't as simple as I wish it were. I will tell you. Just not here. Not now."

Patience, is that it?

It's what I've been. It's what I've been continuously instructed to be.

Patient little Franny. Don't ask questions.

I rumble inside, but I know that now is truly, *truly* not the time. Court isn't well.

Court.

I suddenly remember what he once did as I held an iron poker to his throat. In a snap-second, I decide to take the biggest risk.

And I step into the blade.

Fear, for the first time, flickers in Bludrader's gaze. He instantly retracts the blade, not drawing any blood from my neck. *He doesn't want to hurt me.*

He spins the sword in his hand, looking miffed.

Court shakes his head. "You don't want to hurt her, yet you *threaten* to slit her throat and you hurt my . . ." His voice catches, hesitating to tell Bludrader what Mykal is to him. He simply nods to Mykal.

I don't want anyone to use their coupling against them either. It'd be worse than cruel.

With a staunched nose, Mykal tells Bludrader, "Court is mine."

"Mykal," Court hisses, his face burning.

"I said nothing wrong." Mykal rubs blood from his nose. "We're a couple, you and I."

Court looks like he could cry. "Please, *stop.*" He's scared for his safety.

Mykal is hurt, his shoulders dropping. He doesn't understand that Court is trying to protect him.

Gods, this is a big bad mess.

Bludrader watches on with too much intrigue.

"You shouldn't stare at them so hard," I tell Bludrader, attempting to steal his attention. When it works, I add, "It's not kind."

He tips his head at me again. "Kindness is considered an uncommon trait for Saltarians."

My eyes glide across the sharp carve of his jaw and the glimmering sadness in his gaze. "So you are Saltarian."

He pauses, scrutinizing me in search of something. "You're not scared of Saltarians." He lets out a soft laugh. "No, I guess you wouldn't be."

I'm about to question him for what feels like the hundredth time, but he speaks again.

"A human who isn't afraid of Saltarians is rare."

"So you are—"

"I am Saltarian," he affirms. And he sheathes the blade in its leather casing on his back. He pulls his weight off me and rotates to Court. "I threatened to cut her neck, not slit her throat. I would've only nicked her if it came to that. As for Mykal—"

"You know our names?" Court questions.

"You told the *Romulus* commander your names. Nearly everyone aboard this ship knows."

I sigh into a scowl.

We've done a poor job at secrecy, but that part isn't so much our fault. At least we've been able to hide our link from everyone. Even our friends from the *Saga* starcraft have no idea. Though I'm not so sure we'll ever see them again.

I try not to think about that.

"As for me?" Mykal cuts in, pinching his nose to staunch the blood flow.

"As for you," Bludrader continues, "I was *defending* myself. From being knocked unconscious. I need to stay awake as much as you three need to stay alive."

I take a stronger breath.

Trusting him more.

Court sends me a strict look like, *be cautious, Franny. It's too soon.*

I think it's almost too late. "We need to leave," I tell Court, the band of his slacks cutting painfully into his wound. He's been ignoring the anguish. "What if more cadets arrive and lock us back up?"

And he's dying.

He can barely stand upright. Mykal has his arm around Court's waist, supporting most of his body.

Bludrader starts to notice his weak shape. "There's a med kit on my ship."

Mykal perks up. "Court."

He's afraid—I think Court is so afraid that he'll send Mykal and me to our doom, that this could be a life-ending trap, but we're not leaving without him. And we're not letting him die.

It's a risk that Court would've taken for Mykal and for me. So we're taking it for him.

Court swallows hard, maybe feeling our concrete decision, but he turns to Bludrader. And he asks once more, "Who or what are you loyal to?"

Bludrader clips a loose buckle of his chest armor. "I willingly serve the Republic of Gaia, which means nothing to you because you've never heard of it before. Honest to the grave, I'm going to help you leave, but you *have* to come with me."

Court lets out a breath of annoyance.

"Look, I don't like the *Romulus* any more than you do."

Court thinks and then asks, "How are we escaping?"

"We're walking out."

I snort. "We're just *walking* out?"

His brows rise as mine arch at him. "Yeah, I'm not joking," he replies. "There's been a trade, and you've been released into my custody. I know it's difficult to answer to a stranger, but you need to follow my lead."

I know Court would rather die than have us all return to the place and people we escaped, but I want to believe that the gods are taking us where we should be.

So I nod.

Mykal nods, and we wait for Court.

He blinks and blinks, as though he's remembering his haunted past and the horrors that could await outside the brig, and Mykal whispers in his ear. I can feel the words on his lips.

I'll be keeping you safe. Until my very last breath.

Court inhales, looks up at Bludrader, and he nods.

Ready to live.

FOUR

Franny

We dress in our black-and-gold rancid StarDust uniforms, and Bludrader ushers us down the sleek-gray empty corridor.

Before we left the brig, Mykal rifled through the cloak of the unconscious, spiky-haired cadet. Searching for his confiscated hunting knife, something that the *Romulus* crew had taken on day three. When Mykal tried to cut the cadet's finger off through the hatch.

He found the weapon in the wart's back pocket. Grenpale emblem still etched on the rosy hilt.

With the knife tucked safely in his boot, Mykal trudges onward, and he keeps an arm around Court to brace him from stumbling. From sight, it'd be hard to tell that's the reason he holds him. They just appear fond of one another.

Which is true too.

Though I hear Court and Mykal bickering about it behind me, they quiet as Bludrader instructs, "Stay calm, don't fight anyone, and try not to look at their ugly mugs."

I make a scrunched face. "Why would we want to stare at their drinks?"

Bludrader almost falters a step, and he peers over his shoulder to give me a look like I'm impossibly dumb. And he nearly laughs. I can't tell if he's laughing at me or at the situation.

I cross my arms.

He may be helping us escape, but I'm beginning to dislike him very much.

"A mug is a *face*," he defines.

"What do you drink out of then?" I snap back.

His lip quirks in a semi-smile. "A mug."

Gods. "I loathe your slang."

"I find yours charming."

I frown, wondering if he heard me say *mayday*. "You're a Fast-Tracker?" I wonder when he'll die. He doesn't look any older than twenty years of age.

He turns a corner into another identical corridor. "I'm well-educated in Saltarian culture, especially language."

I hate how he didn't really answer me.

We all walk in silence now, and our muscles shriek at the first lengthy movement in days. I peruse our surroundings, most of which were a blur when we were first brought into the brig. Since we were dragged and half-conscious.

The *Romulus* starcraft is similar to the *Saga* with metallic walls, dizzying hallways, and lit corridors. Bigger, more cavernous, it would've been harder to pass the StarDust starcraft exam if we were tested with this vessel.

Court scans each passing door. "Are other prisoners held here?"

I've forgotten our morbid theory. That Zimmer, Padgett, Gem, and Kinden were thrown in a brig too.

Bludrader keeps the same pace. "No one is here you'd want to see."

Court clarifies, "The people we arrived with, do you know where they are?"

Leather strips of his skirt flap as he rounds a corner, and we follow step-for-step. Foot-for-foot. "The four Saltarians who stole a ship from Saltare-3," Bludrader says, sounding indifferent. "Yeah, I've heard of them and their fate."

Court jails his breath.

I sense Mykal, the coil of his muscles as they tighten.

We all nearly stop in place, but Bludrader adds, "The *Romulus* commander let them go the same day that you were put in the brig."

"Let them go," Court repeats, blinking slowly.

I picture Zimmer sighing a breath of relief, safely back on the *Saga* without us. Laughing at the beauty of the stars.

It's a better way to die than being stuck here.

Yet sadness creeps up, clouding my eyes. I don't think this emotion belongs to me.

Court drops his head while we walk.

"They have no use for Saltarian traitors," Bludrader explains. "The *Romulus* crew didn't trust them enough to let them stay on their ship, so they let them go. They're probably sunbathing on a far-away tropical planet by now."

Mykal growls a curse, mumbling, "They left us to rot."

I feel Court pushing against hurt. Attempting to thwart emotion from compounding.

Should I be briny? Should I want to scream? But all I think . . . "They owed us nothing," I mutter.

Court says beneath his breath, "He's my brother."

I don't know what that means. Sure, I've seen siblings before, but brothers and sisters aren't obligated to aid one another just because of their parentage. One of my Fast-Tracker friends had an Influential brother, a fancy engineer, and he didn't give his sister a single bill for food or clothing.

She resorted to thievery.

But I can't deny that Kinden's fondness for Court—the lengths he went to seek out his brother—was beyond any kind of devotion I'd witnessed before.

Bludrader pauses, causing us to halt in the middle of a corridor. He turns to Court. "Whoever you think is your brother *learned* that you're human. You care about him because it's in your nature. He couldn't care less about you because it's in his."

Court layers a dark glare. "You know nothing."

He lets out a fading laugh. "I know too much. Definitely more than you." His odd footwear squeaks as he spins around and moves along. "Keep up, you three."

Court swallows his distaste.

Another left turn and we approach a burgundy rectangular door. A *Romulus* cadet guards the entrance. She doesn't speak, but when she recognizes Bludrader, she sets her hand on a screen.

The door slinks open horizontally, and we breach what looks like the main crew quarters. Twelve levels rise with the vaulted, domed ceilings.

My feet slow. At the sheer size of the room. At the sheer number of people.

Thousands of bodies crowd the banisters, some people sitting on the railing, others hunched casually over. Almost like they knew we'd be passing through. Waiting to catch a glimpse of us, to point and stare.

My back bumps into Mykal's firm chest.

Something hot wells in my eyes. Overwhelmed. Choked. I'm certain these are my emotions. Not Court's. Not Mykal's. The longer I see the loathing behind thousands of eyes, the more sickness rises and I want to puke.

I've met disgust and animosity before. There are plenty of people on Saltare-3 who thought I wasn't good for much because I was a Fast-Tracker.

But I've never met this kind of universal hatred. Until now.

Mykal leans down, his mouth brushing my ear. "Pay them no notice, Franny."

It's difficult.

Court reaches out and clasps my hand in his, and I breathe stronger.

Bludrader braves a glance back at us. "Ignore them and move forward."

I can't help it.

I am looking. On the first floor where we walk, people stand too close. They've created a small path for us to pass through, but their breath blazes against the side of my cheek.

Someone spits.

But the aim isn't for me or for Court or Mykal.

The gross wad lands on Bludrader. *Splat* on his temple. He treks forward, not breaking speed. We head to another burgundy door.

A short-haired girl sticks out her foot to trip him.

He stumbles and then catches himself. Walking again like nothing happened.

I look to Court, and he's fixated on the same scene as me.

"Be careful," Court whispers to me and Mykal. He must think there's a chance others will target us next.

But the farther we go, every onslaught, every wad of spit and curse word is directed at *him*. From the balcony, someone tosses an empty can, and the metal bounces off his shoulder armor.

"Bludrader!" a man sneers.

"*Bludrader.*" A girl spits at his face.

He wipes off the wad and says nothing. Does nothing but moves forward, as he instructed us to do.

Another person launches a shoe but misses Bludrader and smacks Mykal in the jaw.

Anger surges, *his* anger, and he whips harshly toward the crowd. Court lets go of my hand and clasps Mykal's, pulling him back onto the path.

"Stay with me," he urges.

Mykal looks every which way, hearing *Bludrader!* echoing around us, and confusion replaces his fury.

As we approach the burgundy exit, I pick up my pace and ask Bludrader in a quiet breath, "How do they all know your name?"

I don't hear him answer over the cacophony. "What?" I ask, pushing so close that my arm skims the cold metal of his bronze breastplate.

"I said *that's not my name.*"

I frown. "Then what are they calling you?"

He peers over his shoulder.

Meeting my eyes, he says, "Blood traitor."

FIVE

Mykal

A whole lot of fools allow us to leave the *Romulus* without any show of valor. We prance on out as though we hadn't been sitting lazily in a room. As though we weren't famished for so many wretched days with nothing to do or see.

The man-boy guides us onto another starcraft: one much smaller than the *Romulus*, even tinier than the *Saga*, but wide enough to comfortably fit all four of us.

We strap into jump chairs, and the man-boy settles his ass in the single-pilot cockpit. He flies us somewhere.

None of us are liking that he's in control of our destination. Of what we know, he's Saltarian and loyal to some odd-sounding land.

He's given us nearly nothing, and we're trusting him with our lives.

But anything's better than having Court die in a prison. I dunno much, but I do know that.

Soaring through dark space, the starcraft begins to hum like the hush of winds sweeping coolly through a mountainside. As though letting us know it's safe to move about.

Court, Franny, and I leave our jump chairs and gather around a midnight-blue corner booth, located in the bridge along with the cockpit.

We have our eyes on the man-boy.

Even as I tend to Court's stitches with the med kit. Even as we fill our bellies with packaged meals in tin trays. Looks like brown mush. Tastes like soured potatoes and dry mystery meat.

The lack of freshness doesn't bother me. I lick my thumb. Scarfing down the meal.

Court is slower. Meticulous. Setting his fork down often and staring out the round window more than he eats. His head is churning with thoughts. Could be, he's planning our next move.

Next escape.

I'm just glad he's not shivering with a fever anymore.

Franny shoves her food down as fast as I. But she scowls every now and again at the man-boy. Who has taken us for a ride, and I know she'd rather be in his seat.

Once I lick my tray clean, I push the tin aside and stare hard at the cockpit.

I lean into Court's shoulder. "We outnumber him," I whisper to them both. "I can take him from behind."

Franny, on the other side of Court, pops her spoon out of her mouth and angles toward me. Elbow to the round table, she says hushed, "He just rescued us."

I grunt. "You had the electro-whatcha-call-it. We were freeing ourselves no matter what."

Court reroutes his attention to us. "Can you take him out alone?" he asks me.

"He's no match for I," I assure him, though my sore nose says otherwise. "Now that I'm fed," I add.

Court nods, urgency narrowing his eyes.

Franny gapes. "You two can't be serious."

I eat a bit of meat underneath my thumbnail. "Serious as a ram on a ridge-wall." He's far from a friend of ours. Our best bet is to aim this starcraft at a world we want to go to. And *talking* to the man-boy won't be helping us achieve that.

Anyway, I prefer not speaking to people.

Court frowns. "Why wouldn't we be serious?"

Her eyes dart between us, and realization eases her bones. "You two have always run from people. For survival. Haven't you? Your distrust for *everyone* stems from longer than I've been linked to either of you." She stretches forward, more excitable. "But can't you see that he could have answers?" She lowers her voice even more. "Like why we're human. What that even means."

I don't care much about that.

I just want to find a safe place to settle down. Wake up before the light bathes the land, and hear the wind whistle through rustling trees. Hunt for a good feast. Warm my skin with a wood fire. Hold the boy I love in my arms. Go to bed.

Fall to gentle sleep.

I'm about to shrug, but Franny says passionately, "I'd like to know. I'd like to understand why we're linked. Why we ended up on a planet that was never our home."

Her fraught need and plea for answers strikes me like ten quivers of arrows. Shot at my wild heart, and I rub my rough jaw and look to Court.

He stares unblinkingly at the table, emotion too muddled to make sense of. I'm supposing he's confused.

"You're bleeding," Court says, not picking up his gaze.

Since he feels me more strongly than Franny, I know he's speaking about me. I run my coarse fingers over my crooked nose. Dried blood is flowing out of my nostrils again.

"Gods bless." I stand from the booth, turn to face the cushion, and kneel on the ground. Forearms set against the seat.

Court and Franny let me be.

I have no eyes on the man-boy, but I trust them to keep a lookout while I pray.

When I was a boy of five years, a little lady fought me for a snow leopard that I had killed and lugged across my shoulders. She pushed me in knee-deep snow, and people in my village trickled out of their warmth to watch.

I'd spent two days hunting that animal and had quiet pains that no man or lady could see.

She punched. I clawed.

She beat. I howled.

And when I couldn't stand up on my own two feet with my own two hands to help me, she proudly won my snow leopard.

My eye bled badly for two straight nights. My pa told me to go to the village sanctuary. Losing the snow leopard dishonored the God of Victory, and so I knelt in front of the sorcerer. She performed a familiar ritual, and the next morning, blood finally dried.

In the starcraft, I can almost taste and feel the ritual. Like only just yesterday I hiked through my village with the crunch of snow beneath my boots and with a friendly gust blowing my unruly hair.

I whisper a blessing in my head.

I shall do good, be good, and honor thee in greatness and glory. For ye shall know the mighty winds do sing songs of Wonder, of Victory, of Death.

Dipping my fingers in my blood, I draw a line from my forehead, down my nose, lips, chin, and neck. I mark three scarlet lines beneath my eyes.

"Let the gods hear my roar," I pray and touch my right hand to my right shoulder, left hand to my left shoulder. Right hand to my mouth and then up to the sky.

As I stand, Court eyes my face and shakes his head stiffly. "You should staunch your nose with gauze."

I smile crookedly. "Are you doctoring me?"

He sweeps my gaze, almost asking if he's reading into my words right.

I nod to him.

His lip hikes. "Would you like me to?"

"I think my prayers will be working all right," I tease.

He rolls his eyes.

I add, "I'd like to do a lot of things with you."

Court subtly checks the cockpit, and his body tenses. "We should be more careful."

I see what he means.

The man-boy is spying on *me*. Studying the red markings on my face with too much hidden in his eyes.

I stare him down, and he only stares harder at me.

So I take a seat next to Court and grind my teeth. "Holy Wonders, what I'd give for dry root."

"Your ear?" Franny jests.

"I could spare one," I smile.

"Court's ear—"

"*Never.*"

We look to Court to see if he's smiling.

He's watching the cockpit. Lips not lifting, but his stomach flutters and he breathes deeper than before.

I grin.

Franny swallows the last bite of her food and asks me, "How come you never taught me that prayer to stop my nosebleeds?"

I check my nails for any more meat bits. "Because you never disgraced a god." I tell her how I lost the fight in the brig, and clearly the loss mattered to the God of Victory. Or else my nose wouldn't be dripping.

Frustration crosses her brows.

We still don't know why her nose has been bleeding on and off, and I suspect that's another question she craves answered.

I turn back to the man-boy.

He's still looking at me funny. His blue eyes could sketch my features for how long and deep he observes. Tracing all my brawn, all my crooked bones and gnarled hairs.

I lean into Court, arm against arm, our touch hitching our breath. And I ask in a coarse pant, "You think he wants to romance me?" I don't know the signs as well as Court.

Something jumps into his throat. Swallowing hard, he tries to subdue his firm protectiveness. "I'm uncertain," he admits.

I grimace. "But he knows I belong to you." I said as much in the brig.

Court licks his lips. "He may be Saltarian, but we don't know where he was raised, Mykal, or who he really is."

I lean my head back. "You won't be letting him try anything—"

"He'll never," Court says powerfully, looking me right in the eye with forceful promise. "I can't even bear the thought."

He speaks truth. His muscles clench, and hot breath expels from his nose. He's been grinding his teeth more than I.

I find myself smiling, and I'm not sure why.

He rolls his eyes, but they drift over to the cockpit. The man-boy has suddenly unclipped his straps, and he's standing out of his pilot seat.

Franny raises her fork like a weapon. "What are you doing?"

He saunters over to us. Finally taking his beady eyes off me. "I need the med kit." Where Franny hit him, dried clumps of blood tangle in his blond hair.

He looks all right to me.

"Heya, man-boy," I call out and point to the empty cockpit. "Who's flying the starcraft while you're walking about?"

"It's on autopilot." He approaches the corner booth and nears Franny's end.

She scoots closer to Court. Giving the man-boy room at our table. Which is the only table. Maybe she thinks if we're kind to him, he'll be granting us answers. I trust her with her own plans, but my guards are still mountains high around him.

He stays standing for a moment. And he massages his jaw with a wince. We watch as he sticks two fingers in his mouth. In a hard tug, he yanks out a molar.

I must've knocked it loose.

I grin wider at Court. "Power of the gods."

Court rolls his eyes again. Morose in thought.

As the man-boy slides in, I hold out my hand to him. "In battle, we take what we earn," I say.

A dry smile hoists his mouth, but he's lost in my bloody markings and eyes again. "You think you earned my tooth?"

"I loosened it."

"I pulled it out myself," he combats.

"Doesn't matter." I wag my fingers for the molar.

He blinks a few times and shakes his head. "No." He tucks the tooth in a pouch on his waist. His skirt has no pockets. "You're not taking anything else of mine."

I dunno what he's talking about. "I've taken nothing from you. *Yet.*"

He unbuckles his heavy-looking armor in silence. Pulling off the bronze breastplate, letting it clunk to the floor. "We're on a straight course to the *Lucretzia.*"

Court watches him with a keen eye. Which is making me feel better. Court can outwit any man, lady, and person alive.

Court taps his thumb to the table. "The *Lucretzia*?"

From the med kit on our table, the man-boy removes gauze, tubes of ointment, and pills, and he says, "A ship that belongs to the Earthen Fleet."

Franny flinches. "You work for Earth?"

He laughs shortly, their gazes latching. "Lord, I've never heard anyone say it like that. I do more than *work* for Earth. I'm devoted to the planet and the people."

"Bludrader," Court says in thought. "Saltarians call you a blood traitor because you're against your own people."

He's quiet to answer. I see the look in his eyes. Staring at us with as much caution as we brandish for him. Prey, we each are, circling one another.

Unfreezing, he untwists a pill bottle. "That doesn't alarm any of you? That I'd betray my own people?"

We each shake our heads. Him being a blood traitor holds no heavy weight.

Not long ago, we stole the *Saga* starcraft from StarDust. From our planet. In an act of treason. We became enemies of Saltare-3 before we even knew we were human.

Before we even knew we were born enemies.

"Fascinating," he says, and he doles pills into his palm. And he's realizing the label on the bottle is written in a language we can't read. "Do you want a painkiller?" He rattles the bottle at Court. "You don't look so hot."

"No. I don't trust you."

He throws back the pills in his mouth and swigs from a leather flask. "That's fair," he says after swallowing. "But let me remind you, *I'm* the one who risked my limbs to retrieve you three."

"And we're risking more than our *limbs*," Court says smoothly.

Franny has lowered her fork. "Why'd you help us?" she asks.

He swishes his flask. "I already told you, there was a trade—"

"What kind of trade?" Court asks. "You may believe we're intellectually inferior, but we've all noticed how you walk around answers."

"It's aggravating," Franny points out.

The man-boy leans back and looks to each of us. "You want answers, I get that. But they don't come for free."

My pulse ratchets up, and I realize the source is *Franny*. Heart beating faster.

Court and I set withering glares on this man-boy's head.

His brows rise. "What? You think I don't see how this ends? Me, giving you every harrowing answer you've ever searched for. You, stealing this ship and flying away. But not before you shove me out so I can float endlessly in a wasteland of *space*." He takes a swig and licks liquid off his pink lips. "I'm not that bloody naïve."

Court stops drumming the table. "You're bluffing. You don't know anything."

"On the contrary, mate." *I don't like the sound of that word.* "I know everything." He caps his flask. "Like how three humans ended up on Saltare-3. I even know the day you were born. Let's just say that I carry every answer you've ever sought, and since it's my only leverage, you can believe that I'm not giving a single detail to you without something in return."

Hells.

Court glares darkly. "What makes you think we care about answers to any of those questions? We've moved on. We don't need to know."

The man-boy sways back in soundless worry. Uncapping his flask, he takes a larger swig.

Silence ekes, and I sense a brutal pressure sitting on my chest. Mixed with heavier breathing. Franny—she hangs her head. Gazing haunted at the table.

Something's not right.

"Here's what's going to happen," Court says to the man-boy. "We're going to take this starcraft. We're going to fly out of here. Now, you can either—" He stops short, quiet.

We're both choking on breath. Trying our best not to show it. *Distress* constricts my throat like a damned beast landing on my neck.

Stomach curdling next.

Court's hand slowly rises to his heart as though he feels a great pain.

I try to inhale for all three of us.

The agony . . .

Court grits out, "Franny—"

"I want to know these things," she says from the core of her being. It grips me.

Rips me open.

Tries to cut me in three. *I won't be letting it. I won't.*

"I can't bear the thought of walking away from these answers," she professes. "Even if I'm indebted to someone for something. To this wart." She gestures to the man-boy on her right.

He's eyeing Franny with too much curiosity.

"A life lived without knowing where I came from, who I am," she says, "it'll tear at me every day. I would've searched for centuries for these answers. You know that? And someone is *right here* offering them to us. I can't let that go. *I can't.*"

I want to reach out.

Hold her hand.

Something.

Anything, but I'm left suffocating beneath her riled emotion. It's always been Court and me. From the start, it was us, and it's not fair to her—but I won't be leaving him.

I can't.

But I don't want to leave her either.

I can't.

My heart is already broken. I'm fearful of Court's answer. He can be stubborn, and I'm not sure I can convince him otherwise.

Court's face contorts, trying to shield her emotion.

It hurts feeling it.

But I think it's supposed to hurt.

Franny doesn't wait for Court. She sniffs loudly and asks the man-boy, "How many bills for the answers? I don't have much . . ."

"You don't have anything," Court says like a real crank, but his remorse comes quick. Sinking in my gut.

Franny makes no qualms about his words.

His eyes sear the longer she ignores him.

The man-boy focuses on Franny. "Lucky for you, I'm not looking for money. I need your help with a mission. It's the last one. If unsuccessful, the Earthen Fleet will have no choice but to go to war with Saltare." He adds, "Earth is your rightful home, whether you've been there or not. You're human. Protecting the planet is in your best interest."

"We're looking for a peaceful planet. Not a war zone," Court shoots back.

I jump in, "We're not fighting for a whole lot of people we've never met. Never known. Could be a whole lot of foul-mouthed goats." Who said humans are worth fighting for?

Not I.

He looks me over with more bitterness. "I don't give a shit what you want to fight for, whether it's for your boyfriend or your religion."

I laugh hard. He's not so wise. "I have no Boy Friend."

"Court is your boyfriend."

My grin fades. "No." I expel a gruff breath. "Court is more than just a friend."

Court stands like a pillar. Wholly guarded.

The man-boy flashes an irritated smile. "Just listen," he says, "the mission has *nothing* to do with fighting. We're trying to prevent a war from even happening."

Court holds his hip, pain flaring. He clears his throat. "And let me guess, you'll refuse to offer us the details regarding this *mystical* mission. Just like everything that comes out of your mouth could be a lie."

My pulse is slamming in my chest.

Franny.

Court is unwilling to trust a soul. Franny trusts too easily. And I'm stuck head-and-foot in the fucking middle.

Being shred apart.

The man-boy takes a pause and then edges closer to the table. "It's a retrieval operation."

We listen.

"We have to recover *something* that's on Saltare-1," he continues. "That's all I can say right now. I'm many things, but a liar is not one of them. It's why I'm evasive. I could have lied from the jump and saved myself the trouble." He pushes himself to his feet and walks to a comms unit. Opening a cabinet, he grabs a bottle of amber liquid. "Scotch." He smiles dryly and bites off the cork with his teeth. Taking a gulp.

While he collects four glasses, Franny spins to us, eyes reddened. Mine burn with hers. "You can leave," she tells us, her voice cracking. "I'll find you after—"

"Stop," Court interrupts.

I shake my head at Franny so hard it may fly off my neck.

Pain balls up in her lungs. "I can't . . . I can't put you two in danger." She almost chokes.

We're all caught between each other's needs.

Court suddenly extends his arm across the table. Toward Franny. He opens his hand.

She fights tears. "What are you doing, Court?"

"Will you take my hand?"

"Court—"

"Will you please take my hand?" he repeats in the softest voice he can muster.

Thank the gods. I see what's happening. I put my arm around Court. I could kiss this handsome crook. I could cry.

She places her hand in his, and she breathes in what I already feel.

Calmness whirls tenderly inside Court. He's made peace with this decision.

Gently, he tells Franny, "You chose us once upon an era. You chose our grand, delusional plan to flee your home when we asked. And now, you're asking us." He nods twice. "This time, we're choosing you."

Tears prick her eyes. And mine and his.

"Are you sure?" she asks us both, wiping her nose.

I reach out and put my hand atop theirs. "Yeh, little love." Not worrying about concealing my lilt.

Truth being, I can't stop looking at Court. My pride for him surges in my bones, my veins, my blood. I know how much strength this took him. How much strength exists. We've spent our life surviving, and returning to a Saltare planet, just for a bit of knowledge, is everything Court had run from.

Court nods to Franny again. "I can do this. You've both taken care of me, and it's time I take care of you."

"I'll never forget this," she whispers—but our heads turn. Hushing quickly as the man-boy returns to our table.

Bottle wedged in the crook of his arm, he places four crystal glasses down. "When the crew on the *Lucretzia* make deals, we end them with scotch."

Franny pushes the glass away. Her eyes scorching his face. "We do this," she says with bite, "and you give us our answers each step of the way. Starting *now*. Tell us something we don't know. Like your name."

He pours amber liquid in only one glass and leaves the bottle on the table. Clutching the crystal, he takes a single step backward.

And he says, "I'm the son of Kian and Briana Kickcastle."

I recoil. Not breathing.

That's my pa.

My ma.

"You're my brother," I choke out, staring him up and down. Down and up.

He has lighter blue eyes, lighter blond hair. I'm shorter but more muscular. Pale, the two of us, but his chalky white skin isn't weather-beaten from the slap of cold wind. He has no lines in the creases of his eyes. No noticeable scars.

Still, we look alike.

We're brothers.

I have a brother. Just like Court has a brother.

"No," he says.

And he takes another step back.

I shoot up. "What do you mean, *no*?"

Court stands, grasps my waist. "Mykal." He knows. He's smart enough to see what I'm missing.

I'm left wading head-deep in snow.

His fingers tighten on his glass. "My mother only had one child. She died giving birth to me in Grenpale. My name is Stork Kickfall." He raises his glass to his lips. "Cheers."

SIX

Mykal

My mind lags behind my body, and I charge. Ripping out of the hands of the boy I love, I *charge* toward another who I don't understand.

Stork has been stepping back, expecting my outburst, but he only tries to protect his liquor from harm. About to shield the crystal behind him.

I smack the scotch out of his hand.

Glass shatters at his feet, and he huffs out an irked breath. A chill reaching his gaze. "You're confused, I reckon, and dim—"

"You make no damned sense," I say between gritted molars.

"Dim is another word for—"

I shove him against the cabinets and comms station, a headset falling off a hook. Dangling by a cord. Stork is bare-chested. No longer hiding behind his strange armor.

But the knowledge of the day he'll be dying protects him better than any metal could.

He's not shaking or wide-eyed or frightened like a lamb. Even though his eye is puffed and reddened, mouth split from my earlier fist. Jaw swollen.

I close in on him, my hand to his collar. Trapping him.

And he takes a better look at my features. At the blood I drew along my cheeks and lips and neck.

"I know what *dim* means all right," I growl. "You aren't the first boy who's ever called me dim-witted and dumb. But you still make no damned sense. My ma died giving birth to *me*."

I'm Mykal Kick*fall* for that very reason. Unlike Court and

Franny, I was never adopted and I always knew who my birth parents were.

"No, see, you're human," Stork says plainly. "Briana Kickcastle can't be your mother."

"Briana could've been human."

"She was *Saltarian*," he emphasizes. "I have her ID card in my barracks on the *Lucretzia*."

My world is overturning. I feel like I'm falling face-first in three hells.

I lick blood off my lips. "No . . ."

No.

"My pa," I say slowly, "he said a villager stole her identification after she died."

This near, I eye Stork as he eyes me, and I meet his bitter sorrow. Lifting the corner of his lip, almost rolling and glassing his gaze. No link needed to spot the icy rawness.

"He was my father," Stork says, "and he probably believed whatever he told you. He couldn't have known the truth any more than you could've."

I release my hand off his chest. "And what's the truth?"

"His baby was taken—*I* was taken, and a human baby of the same age was swapped in place of me. *You* were swapped . . ." He loses his voice while staring at my worn face, nicked with scars and cragged from blizzards.

I sense Court shaking his head, and he asks, "Why would anyone put a human baby on a Saltare planet in a Saltarian galaxy?"

Stork looks away from me and then bends down to collect the glass at our feet. "That's enough answers for the day."

Does he know who birthed me? Who would've raised me if we hadn't been swapped? But I know, well and good, that my pa is still my pa. No blood relation and dead—he will always be *my* pa.

He raised me. Taught me most of what I know. How to spear, how to shoot an arrow off a bow. How to whittle and how to respect the gods. How to howl at the wild so the wild will be howling back.

But he's not just *my* pa now.

He's someone else's.

I squat and help pick up glass with Stork. Looking at him, mostly. "Do you want to hear about our pa?"

Stork just places more large shards, dripping in liquor, in his palm. "Why would I want to hear about the life you lived that could've been mine?"

I hear his nasty tone, but I press onward. "He would've wanted you to know him. That's why."

Stork blinks a few times, then slams a fist into the cabinet. The silver metal pops open. Sliding far out to reveal a bin, and as he rises, he dumps broken glass in the squared compartment.

I do the same, though fumbling a lot more, and I watch him ignore me. He seizes his armor and then treks to the cockpit.

Can't be too surprised that didn't go right. I'm bad with words and with people.

SEVEN

Court

The starcraft rattles from passing space debris, and we strap into our jump seats for the duration of our travel. I stare out at the vast darkness of space through the bridge window. And obsess over the pieces of information I've gathered:

We were released from a brig because we were traded for something.

The Earthen Fleet is planning a retrieval operation on Saltare-1.

Which they need us for.

Stork willingly serves the Republic of Gaia.

Mykal and Stork were swapped as babies.

And we fly toward the Lucretzia, *a starcraft of the Earthen Fleet.*

I want to stay ten steps ahead of Stork, but I'm at a great disadvantage. Earth and humanity couldn't be more foreign to me. The best I can do is remain alert and steadfast. So if he ever tries to pull wool over our eyes, I'll notice the ruse before he even starts.

Mykal and Franny try to stay awake, both weary-eyed from the hours-long voyage. They shove each other's arms every time slumber sweeps them.

My brain won't sleep.

I can't sleep.

Stork is sharp—I see how he observes Mykal and Franny and me every chance he can. He takes notice of how I'm unblinkingly studying him and our journey while Mykal and Franny grow comfortable enough to shut their eyes.

"You're an Icecastle," Stork says to me while he reaches up into a compartment above his pilot seat, "a Saltare-3 criminal." He's showing me how much he knows. "What'd you do, mate?" He tethers a headset to an outlet. "Steal a snow cone?"

I can touch the memories of Vorkter more than I used to, but I'm not diving deep and retrieving them for Stork.

I simply reply, "Snow cones don't exist on Saltare-3." *Whatever those are.* "You want us for a Saltare-1 retrieval operation, but do you even know that the five Saltare planets are very different from one another?"

"I studied all five from the moment I could read," Stork says, his brows lifting in challenge at me. "I'm aware."

I can't say I've read the same. Very few books mentioned our sister planets. We had a map of our galaxy and vague atmospheric conditions, enough to cause resentment. Our frozen planet could never thaw after the Great Freeze, and Saltare-1 was always said to have the "perfect" temperate climate.

Holding my tongue, I say nothing in reply.

So Stork faces the bridge window and fits on his headset, the comms comparable to Saltare starcrafts. I've noticed *many* similarities between this vessel and the *Romulus* and *Saga*, which only makes me believe that the technology between Earth and Saltare can't be too different.

I raise my voice. "Is Earth's technology comparable to Saltare?"

"Yes and no," Stork says. "It depends on which Saltare planet you're referencing." He grips a joystick and talks into a microphone at his lips. Speaking a foreign language.

I stop asking questions as we approach the massive hull and gray shell of the *Lucretzia*. Shaped like a dart with wings, the durable body stretches infinitely. In comparison, what we're currently flying is the size of a transport vessel.

I start to lean forward, but the leather buckle digs into my hip. My inflamed wound, cleaned and bandaged, wails in protest.

"We're here?" Franny asks, rubbing her eyes and pushing Mykal awake, both having dozed off for a minute.

"We're here," I confirm. Nerves flip my stomach. Tripled senses, all three of us feeling the onslaught of anxiety as the *Lucretzia* opens its hull for us to enter.

Scratches, divots, and dings mar the *Lucretzia*'s exterior shell, and more than just robust engines sit beneath the wings.

Weaponry.

Cylindrical artillery is mounted to the starcraft. "Is the *Lucretzia* a battlecraft?"

Stork pulls his headset to his neck. "What did you ask?"

I repeat my question.

"Not exactly." He flicks a switch and releases the joystick. Our transport starcraft begins insertion into the larger vessel. On autopilot. "The *Lucretzia* is a carrier ship," he explains, unbuckling. "It houses the fleet's combat jets. You'll notice that most of the crew onboard are C-Jays." He stands. "Also known as combat pilots."

Franny smooths her lips together. I can only assume she's trying not to proudly state she's a driver and a pilot. I'm certain she would if our circumstances were different. But her skill set behind any wheel could benefit us more if it's kept secret.

She knows this.

I don't need to remind her.

Mykal mutters something about senseless technology, and then Franny stares bright-eyed at the sheer enormity of the *Lucretzia*. Which swallows our transport starcraft.

Wheels retract, and we land on what Stork says is a *tarmac*. Rows and rows of various-sized vessels line the docking bay. As far as the eye can reach, and some are only outfitted for two seats.

The hull shuts, enclosing us inside the *Lucretzia*.

Stork is turned toward our jump seats, and with the cock of

his head and carefree wave of his hand, he tells us, "Welcome home."

And I recognize that I am human on a human starcraft.

So many times I've felt out of place and wrong and I've begged for a world where people can be saved and not left to die. And I know this is the world I never thought possible. Never believed could exist.

You belong here, Court.

Yet everything feels foreign to me.

EIGHT

Stork

Eighteen years alive, and not a single one went by without being reminded that I'm Saltarian living among humans. Raised by humans. Raised *like* a human.

I should be bitter, maybe. Or resentful.

But I'm not a prisoner. I'm not chained here or coerced. I serve the Republic of Gaia, Earth's government, by my own free will. It hasn't been all sunshine and kittens. I'm the only Saltarian to ever step foot on the *Lucretzia*. My presence on this ship is a grisly reminder of why humans fight. Why they're sitting in a different galaxy light-years away from their home.

It took *years* to gain the respect of some of the crew. Admiral Moura says I would have earned it faster if it weren't for my lack of charisma. On the contrary, I am very charismatic.

At seven years old, I played with children my age in the galley of a first-class starcraft. Pots and metal bowls on our heads, we pretended we were C-Jays. Chasing one another like we flew combat jets, I grinned and laughed.

"Have at me!" I roared. "If you think you can catch me!"

I was a boastful kid.

Still am. Though now I'm more of a man.

We'd aim our cooking utensils at the enemy starcraft: an enormous icebox that stored the fleet's poultry.

"On the count of three!" a child shouted. "One!"

I raced ahead. Unafraid.

Thrill inside of me burst vividly. And I thought: *nothing in this universe could truly hurt me.*

The people who raised me from infancy—they often said that I have a choice, and the choices I make will ultimately define who I'll come to be.

So when a pair of harsh hands shoved my shoulders—not for the first time, not for the last time—I had a choice to make. I tripped from the force, soup ladle spilling out of my palms, and I landed on my knees.

Right then, I chose to turn my head, knowing what I'd meet.

A hateful fist slammed in my soft cheek, and the boy screamed, "Go back to where you came from, knave!"

Blood pooled in my mouth, and I smiled with a soft laugh, ignoring the pang of hurt. Honest to the grave, I didn't *need* to be admired or revered or liked by anyone, but I was seven. I didn't exactly love the wads of spit in my hair and on my face.

Years would pass, and I'd be pushed down again and again.

At eleven years old, I was on my knees in the dining hall. Tray of beans, apples, and chicken thighs spilled onto mosaic tile.

I staggered to my feet, brushed the beans off my kneecaps, and I gestured the older boy toward me. "Come here, then." I sported another wily grin. "You want at me; I'm all yours."

He yelled between his teeth and shoved forcefully.

I fell again, and I stood once more.

His anger burned through two narrowed eyes and tried to impale me hot.

He couldn't kill me, and he knew it. The next time he tried to push me down, I caught his wrist and whispered, "We're on the same side, mate."

At fourteen years old, I thought I knew everything there was to know and learn.

Naïve. *Probably.* Cocky. *Most definitely.*

I stood on the training deck inside an Earthen starcraft and finished buckling my bronze breastplate and metal armguards. The lightweight bronze was an alien metal mined off the planet of Gigadon and one of Earth's major imports, and even though

I didn't really need protection from fatal injuries, I chose to wear it to seem more like them.

More like humans.

Inside the docking bay, fifty sleek combat jets were parked. One would become mine after academy graduation. The pretty one—I'd hoped.

A drill sergeant cautioned me, "Head down, guards up."

Standing tall, I pushed my blond hair back and said, "Or better yet: head up, guards down."

She rolled her eyes and stepped to the side. "Turn on your mic and listen for instructions, knave. Unfortunately for me, I'll be in your ear."

I whispered under my breath, "The misfortune is all mine." I fit on my bronze helmet, metal plates shielding my nose and jawline.

After adjusting the small microphone that brushed my pink lips, I began to climb into the cockpit. I wore the customary fleet skirt: made of midnight-blue leather strips.

Unconstricting, weightless. I could easily move. And as I hiked up the jet, the leather skimmed the gray metal shell, and I settled in my seat.

Strapping in, I listened to the crackling voice in my ear. "Drill 508: abandonment protocol. Trainee, do you copy?"

"Copy," I replied. Normally I'd reach for the thrusters, but to pass this specific drill and become a C-Jay, I wasn't supposed to fly the jet.

She started describing the simulation. "You've been attacked by a Saltarian starcraft. It doubles the size of your jet. Your command functions are disabled. The enemy starcraft is pulling your jet aboard. You are their prisoner. What is human protocol? *Begin.*"

Quickly, I unstrapped myself from the seat. Jumping out of the cockpit, I slid down the body of the jet and landed on the training floor.

The *thump* of my leather boots echoed in the cavernous docking bay, and I watched three men march forward to apprehend me. Their wool cloaks billowed behind hurried feet, and their triangular StarDust brooches gleamed at their throats.

Pulse pounding, I reached behind my armored chest and gripped a rigid hilt. Unsheathing a long two-edged sword with a tapered point, I braced myself and twirled the weapon. More flourish than purpose, I could already picture the points being deducted for my bravado.

As the cloaked men reached me, I instantly ducked and sliced their Achilles tendons. Blood spewed, and each body fell.

I stabbed them in the gut for precaution. But heavy footsteps resounded, and I spun to find seven more Saltarians running toward me.

This time, they were armed.

I clutched my weapon with two hands and chased down the barrel of seven guns. Sprinting, alert, and ready.

I knew my strengths.

I couldn't tackle seven people. I wasn't a muscular fourteen-year-old. Hell, I probably weighed a buck-fifteen back then, but I was fearless, especially.

Some would say careless.

Whatever the truth, I still moved toward danger. I could wield a sword better than they could aim their firearms, but humans have an archaic joke that I had read in too many books.

Don't bring a knife to a gunfight.

And yet, blades are a better defense against Saltarians.

Guns jam.

So I ran straight for them.

"Follow protocol!" the drill sergeant shouted in my ear.

"I have them," I assured, more than confident.

Triggers were pulled, and guns blasted with a violent pop of bullets. The hot metal whizzed past me; some struck my armor with a powerful *thunk*.

I rocked back twice and then plowed ahead. Two more purposeful strides and I came upon them, gracefully swinging my blade. I slashed the arms off four Saltarians.

Limbs and weapons greeted the floor with a sickening noise. My nose flared, and I reminded myself, *this is the only way.*

I had an overarching purpose to protect the human race.

And no matter if I cut a hand off or took a leg, these people that I fought would still survive. In training for war, we're taught there'd be casualties.

But the death toll only rises on one side.

Humans die.

Saltarians live.

I bent low and sliced two calves, and as I rose, a bullet pierced the pale flesh of my neck. Suddenly every enemy and gun flickered out like a technological glitch.

I breathed hard, the holograms gone. I cursed beneath my breath, sweat dripping down my temples inside the stuffy helmet.

The drill shouldn't have ended that abruptly. I slid my sword into its sheath on my back.

As the drill sergeant neared, I removed my helmet and said with hot, panting breath, "I could've gone on longer. I had them overrun—"

"The task was to follow the abandonment protocol."

I let out a short laugh and wiped sweat off my face. "I know the protocol. Never aim for their heads." It'd be a waste to try to slit a Saltarian's throat. It would, at best, cause a paper cut. It would, at worst, break a blade in half.

Aim for their vulnerabilities: spots that can cause injury but not death. Saltarians can't die unless it's their deathday, which renders them nearly invincible to attacks.

"And when you find yourself outnumbered?" she rebutted. "What is the protocol then, knave?"

Radio for help.

Or surrender.

Communications were disabled, so the only answer had been to surrender myself for capture.

"I'm no one's prisoner," I said plainly. "I'll take my chances. They're bound to be light-years better than yours."

She grunted, "Arrogant bastard," and made me retake the drill the next month and then the next month after. Every time, I refused to surrender. I only graduated the academy because the admirals signed off my paperwork, despite the fact that I never completed Drill 508.

Admiral Moura sat me down after graduation and she said, "Your training will never quite end, Stork. Every so often, you'll find yourself in situations you aren't ready for, and you'll feel like you've returned to the beginning again."

Four years have passed since that day, and now I feel like I'm at the beginning again.

Never did I dream about someday, *one day*, coming face-to-face with these three humans. Who are, for better or worse, entwined messily in my history.

I considered them dead and buried.

I moved on with my life without them.

No thought. No care.

Never even imagined what their fate was like. Never predicted what age they reached before a cold planet and misfortune stole their lives.

Why would I?

Meeting three humans who should've died on a Saltare planet that I should've called home was never in the cards.

Today wasn't supposed to happen. How they managed to stay alive, how they even left Saltare-3—the least developed and most deficient Saltare planet of all five—is nothing short of a miracle. Or so the fleet admirals told me.

I don't see the miracle in their survival.

I just see an undisputable testament to the human spirit.

But I reckon none of that matters. Not me being whiplashed and thrown figuratively overboard while I try to come to terms with two guys named Mykal and Court and a girl named Franny.

I have a job.

A bloody purpose, and there is no braking. No stopping or slowing down to gather my *feelings*. At the end of the day, what I feel is trivial.

Especially in comparison to the many human lives on the *Lucretzia*.

Once Court, Mykal, Franny, and I are off the ship and safely inside the silent docking bay, I turn to them, walking backward so I can see their faces. "I know what you're thinking. *Why'd this guy bring us to an eerily quiet docking bay?*"

I mean, I can't name a time where it's been *this* quiet on the tarmac.

"I wasn't thinking it, but now I am," Court tells me sharply.

"Good," I say, brushing off the coldness in his tone. "Because all you need to know is that it's late here. Usually, there are more people around."

The difference, for me at least, is startling. No rev of engines, no Catapult Officers in mustard-yellow tunics darting back and forth, signaling to pilots. No loud crash crew in red tunics, yelling at one another, or the even rowdier maintenance in purple.

Destroyers, battle cruisers, and combat jets are stationary. Noiseless, statuesque, and recently buffed like they're on display in a spacefleet museum. Eerie. If I didn't know where everyone was, maybe the hairs on my arms would be standing straight up.

Good thing I know what's going on. *They don't.* And I know what it may seem like, but I take zero pleasure in keeping information from them.

Franny scopes out her new surroundings. Black hair oily and unwashed, and face dirtied from weeks in the brig. She inhales the magnitude of the docking bay.

I skim her once and twice over, not able to tame my curiosity. A human raised as a Saltarian is a uniqueness that only these three share.

Bitterness twitches my lips.

I am a Saltarian raised as a human who has never stepped foot on a Saltare planet, and I share this in common with me, myself, and I. What I would've given for one to become three.

"Is that why no one is here?" Franny asks me, voice flaming like she's constantly set on fire. "Everyone goes to sleep early?"

I pause, considering my choice of words. If I scare them, they could become overwhelmed and form an outrageous plan. Like stealing a ship and flying to a toxic or dangerous planet where they'll *die*.

Humans are scrappy but they're also startlingly dim when spooked.

"Some of the crew are sleeping," I say, skirting around the answer. *Evasiveness*: some might say I'm a master at it.

Mykal cracks his neck and scrutinizes the roof. Staring at him too long is a bad idea. I start ruminating over a life forgotten, and I'd rather chew on a pack of nails and yank out another molar or five. Grenpale, my birthplace, and all my long-ago history is *off-limits*. I'm putting it there. For my own sanity.

Court has been eagle-eyeing me this entire time. Trying to excavate my intentions.

What I'd give to just look at him and say, *we're on the same side, mate,* and for him to believe me without a second thought. But I've said those words too many times and to too many people to know that they carry little weight. I've come to realize many things on this ship. One being: actions mean more here. More than *my* words, at least.

Off to the right, the control window has been blacked out with dark linen. Just so Court, Mykal, and Franny are unable to spot any people behind the glass. Before docking, I was told that Captain Venita and a few lieutenants would be observing us from the control room's camera monitors.

My orders were simple: *rescue the humans and put them to bed.*

Easy enough.

With the snap of my fingers and a curt wave, I gather their attention. "I'm about to bring you to the main deck." I point out the spiral staircase several yards away. "You can't gallivant around the ship tonight. You need water wings before you can jump into the deep end. Stay by my side. Don't touch anything."

"Water wings?" Franny makes a face.

I rub my mouth with a weak laugh. "You don't know what water wings are." I nod, remembering.

Terrific.

At five, ten, fourteen, and on—I was extensively trained in language, and I'd boast about being fluent in Saltarian to really everyone, classmates and superiors. Chuckling when C-Jays maimed the dialect. Smirking at captains who begrudgingly asked for my services.

And here I am, ironically only "somewhat" able to communicate with these three.

Even as a kid, I consumed every piece of literature and online text about Saltare-3 with an unrelenting ferocity. Knowing I was born there, I thought the knowledge would connect me to the faraway world. But no page, no word could bridge that distance.

So the next time I read about Saltare planets, it was with the purpose to defend Earth. And prepare for war.

It's not like there are whole encyclopedias about Saltare-3. I'd be lucky to find a paragraph. In history, the planet has scarce documented information due to its regressive technology and detachment from its sister planets—no exports, few imports, almost solely autonomous.

What I know for a fact: Saltare-3 is a frozen planet. No one would swim in an iced lake. Assuming indoor pools exist, swimming could've easily been a luxury. Intended for the rich or Influentials only.

Plastic also isn't a resource on Saltare-3. So water wings—definitely bad on me.

I tie my hair back with an elastic band, a small ponytail at my neck. "Forget the metaphor," I say. "Let's go."

I warn them that the *Lucretzia* is unlike Saltarian ships.

Stepping off the staircase onto the main deck, I'm interested in what draws their eye first. These are the three people I heard about in stories, after all. Like fabled characters come to life. Abruptly, they roll to a stop.

The three of them are struck silent beneath the first towering archway, staring at the long length of a shallow pool. Steam skates across the calm surface, water murky green from a mix of perfumes.

No thyme and daffodil aroma can mask their stink.

Hours earlier, I pressed my body against Franny while holding a blade to her throat, and her pungent odor still clings to my skin.

I've almost grown used to the smell. No longer tingling my eyes or ransacking my nostrils.

Shockingly.

Court unfreezes and strolls warily along the walkways around the pool. Mykal and Franny close behind.

The domed glass ceiling reveals an expansive, boundless view of the star-speckled *Dis Pater* Galaxy. Looking up, I sometimes feel like I'm back home. Lying on the earth after fleet class and relishing in the crescent moon. Laughing as I spot the Big Dipper.

But we're far from Earth's galaxy.

Dis Pater is a tumultuous location where a quarter of the Earthen Fleet has remained for a decade. The *Lucretzia* is the most important ship here, residing in a threatening range to the Saltarian Fleet so we can protect our civilians back home from possible invasion.

Earth is a honey pot to Saltarians, and humans are wingless, stinger-less bees defending their hard-earned home from undying bears.

As the crew always tells me, in this scenario, I am the undying bear willing to protect the bees.

"What is this room?" Court asks me.

I stay on the opposite side of the pool. Giving them space to explore this part, and I track their intrigue to the tile beneath their boots. Pieces of fine, lightweight artificial marble create an intricate mosaic, and oak benches hug the walls.

"The atrium," I say. "Crew lounges here. Similar to your parlors." *I'm assuming.*

Franny skims her fingers along the wispy midnight-blue curtains that drape along arched doors. "This is nothing like a parlor. It's more like a common room."

Close enough, I guess.

Our eyes meet across the pool, walking with unhurriedness. I motion to the closed rooms along each side. "Crew barracks are here."

She stares too hard at the next towering archway. Silver flowing drapes sweep the floor and conceal the other side. Light streaks through little star-shaped holes in the fabric.

Put them to bed.

Yeah, I thought that would be easy.

"I'll show you to your beds," I continue, "you can wash—"

"What's *that* noise?" Mykal cuts in and whips his head around, searching for the source of the faint croaks of bullfrogs and chirps of crickets.

I tip my head. "Lions, tigers, and bears." I flash big mocking eyes at him, but I'm positive he won't catch the joke. "Oh my."

Franny notices, though, and shoots me a fiery scowl.

Mykal peers calmly at me. "Your lion sounds like it's choking on your bear."

I let out a short laugh. *He's not afraid of a lion or a tiger or a bear.* I'm glued in surprise, and to unglue my bloody self I laugh again and say, "It was a joke."

"A bad one," Franny snaps.

I smile wryly and explain the bullfrog and cricket noises. Adding, "It's electronic."

Mykal groans. "Is anythin' real?" He kicks the leg of a wooden bench that breaks.

"That was," Court says plainly. He's been quietly studying the stained-glass patterned walls, along with framed motion-picture portraits. Still examining the photos, he asks, "And these are?"

"Pictures. You have films on Saltare-3; these are similar. Think of them as tiny movies on one-minute loops." I catch a glimpse of one nearest me.

Grayscale, the motion-picture portrait showcases three young guys and four girls in military skirts, seven jets parked behind them. Laughing, pride sparkling their eyes, they applaud each other and hug.

I read the etched inscription on the silver frame: CLASS OF 3017. Every portrait is of C-Jay academy graduations.

Mine is hung in the dining hall.

Quickening my pace, I cut off Franny from potentially racing through the silver-draped archway. She skids to a halt a few feet from me. Skepticism bunching her brows.

"Heya, I know this animal."

Our heads turn.

Mykal gestures to the mosaic tiles. Brown and beige pieces depict a furry, tusked creature. "Woolly mammoths, aren't they? I heard stories."

"As did I," Franny chimes in. "My mother used to say they went extinct on our planet because of the Great Freeze."

Lord have mercy. I only realize Court is watching me *after* I've already made a face like these two are discussing flying pigs.

"Unlucky beasts." Mykal bends and touches the marble. "Pelts woulda been nice during a blizzard."

Court saunters closer to me. Noticing how I shield the archway.

I raise a hand. "Look, there's no way to sugarcoat this. You three look and smell like shit."

"No one asked you," Franny slings back.

Desperately, I try not to smile. "You three need to wash. Fresh tunics are on your beds. Showers are in your barracks—" I cut myself off at their confusion.

They've never had a shower.

I have a feeling they'll trust the showers even less than they're trusting me. "Or you can bathe here." I gesture to the pool. "No crew is around—"

"Why is that?" Court commands an answer more than asks, but his hand is planted on his hip. Sweat builds up on his brow. Clearly, he's in the worst condition of the three. Mykal and Franny often turn to him, half out of respect and the other half out of worry.

I stand just as tall. "No one wants to overwhelm you three. They were ordered to stay in their barracks for your *homecoming*."

"By who?" Court steps closer.

I cup my fingers, expecting a bottle to be in hand, but I have none at the current second. "By the fleet admirals."

"Why can't we see more of the ship?"

"Because you need *rest*. You're emaciated. Starved." I speak hushed but forcefully. "No one wants to add more stress on you." I had orders to *not* take them on a *Lucretzia* Worldwide Ship Tour for this reason.

Franny pokes a finger toward the pool. "Does Earth look like this?"

I shift my weight. Opening my mouth, meaningful words are trapped violently in my lungs, and I can't purge them.

I have orders.

A list of things that I cannot, under any circumstances, share with Court, Mykal, and Franny. Even if they're on the brink of death, I've been told: *let them die with the history they've understood to be theirs.*

Only when Earth is safe can I immediately tell them what I know.

The fleet admirals' wishes:

Do not describe Earth.

Do not speak of their parentage.

Do not explain how they arrived on Saltare-3.

They let me share my name and origin because they knew it'd be impossible to keep secret once onboard the *Lucretzia*.

There was no day, no second, where I believed I was human. I was told that I was Saltarian. I was given choices and freedom. Now I'm ordered to deny these three what I was rightfully handed—and there is no easy path around this bitter avenue.

If I mention my orders, they'll blame the admirals for making them and then distrust the Republic of Gaia.

With every question they ask, I trek, head held high and fist in throat, through thorns and razored walls.

So that's what I do now.

I sigh out this metaphorical sharp-edged *thing* that's stabbing me in every direction. Raking my hair back, I laugh lightly. "New plan: forget about what Earth is or isn't. Instead, clean under your arms, behind your ears, between your—"

"That's the same plan," Franny retorts.

She's definitely cross with me. "Is it?" I tease and walk forward, causing Franny and Court to walk backward. Heels edging toward the pool. I gesture to the water. "One dip?"

Her brows spring. "You don't even know what Earth looks like, do you? You've never been there, admit it."

"I've lived on and off Earth, dove." I stop once steam licks their feet, closing in on the lip of the pool.

"Dove," she snaps hotly. "It's soft but the way you say it, it sounds more like you're caressing a bed of nails."

Lord. I struggle not to laugh, not be completely enamored with what she thinks of me. Honestly, I don't even know why

I chose to use the term of endearment for her. On Earth, it can be mocking or sweet. I suppose I've landed somewhere between the two.

"It fits you," is all I say to Franny.

Her brows furrow. Mykal is trying to pry a picture frame off its mount. Using all his strength, he braces his boot on the wall and heaves and grunts.

He's definitely different.

I could mention how the picture is attached by talyglue, similar to cement, but Mykal being occupied frees me to deal with these two.

Court asks, "How did you end up here?"

"I was found on Earth in a small pod." *No Earth details. No details.* I lick my lips and add, "Under the Republic of Gaia, all lost kids must be turned over to the fleet." Briefly, I explain how the fleet helps place these kids with their families. I had no family on Earth. So I was allowed to either join the military or be put in a foster household. I chose the military.

"Why didn't they send you back to Saltare-3?" Franny asks like that's the logical choice.

The question drills into my eardrums and pierces my brain in a million excruciating ways. I can't answer. I offer her a half-smile and motion to the pool. "Scared of the water?"

"I see what you're doing—"

I push Franny.

Her voice dies, breath jettisoning out of her lips as she falls backward—but Court is swift and his seamless movements catch me off guard. He clutches her wrist and tugs Franny back upright. In another split second, he shifts to the left.

And he grabs on to me and pulls forward. *Hard.*

Gravity propels me down and I splash into the warmth of the shallow pool. And I stand, dripping wet. Water stops at my knees, and I look Court over, seeing more of him than I had before.

We all breathe heavily.

Mykal bears a murderous expression. Like he could disembowel me and feed me to his pet wolf.

"You wart," Franny sneers.

I smile, loving that insult more than any other. I wipe water off my face, beads rolling down my breastplate. And I nod to Court and guess, "You were a thief."

He glares.

I laugh. *I guessed right.* Won't be the last time. My laughter fades as Mykal completely angles toward his boyfriend. His kill-or-be-killed face changes to heart-pounding concern.

I don't see what's wrong.

"Court!" Mykal shouts, and then he charges for him.

Franny yells Court's name, but only after his eyes flutter and his body slackens. His weight plunges toward the pool—I run through water. Franny seizes his wrist, too weakened to support him upright, and Court falls into my outstretched arms.

She doesn't let go of him.

"I have him," I assure her.

Mykal almost jumps into the pool, not thinking twice, but then he stumbles backward. Tripping over an unseen force, eyes heavy-lidded, he fights faintness and falls back onto the mosaic tile.

"Mykal, don't!" Franny yells.

He pants and curses.

She hesitates between helping Court and aiding Mykal.

I adjust Court against my chest. Tall and a little muscular, but I've carried heavier artillery into my combat jet. "Go," I say.

"No," Mykal chokes. "Franny, stay with Court." He struggles to a stance. She won't let go of his wrist.

Humans. "Look at me," I tell Franny sincerely. "I need you three alive. I'm taking him to the sick bay where he needs to be treated. You both should come. I reckon that's a win-win for everyone."

She nods tensely but only shifts her grip to his palm. She's holding his hand, but it offers me room to step out of the pool.

I climb out.

Mykal keeps his distance, taking a knife from his boot. "We may share the same pa . . ." He aims the blade at my eyes. ". . . but you hurt even a *hair* on his head, I'll be gutting you inside out."

Yeah, I can't die.

Today is not my deathday.

But I enjoy my intestines inside my body. I nod. "Follow me."

I head toward the silver drapes, and Franny is slack-jawed in shock before she passes beneath the archway. Surprised that I'm allowing them through.

I have to bring them to the sick bay. The captains will understand.

We emerge into an office for all crew, including high-ranking officials: the captains and the admirals. Instead of a pool, a glossy oak desk is the focal point. A few hardbacks are stacked next to a hologram computer screen. Starry constellations shimmer in gold paint along the dark blue walls.

Franny momentarily ogles the third towering archway. More silver drapes block her view of the courtyard, but as the fabric gusts, I make out the fountain: water lilies entwined in long dark hair, a woman chiseled out of marble. Head raised, eyes pointed to the sky. An effigy of Reva Woncu, a thirty-second-century war hero, has been in the *Lucretzia* for as long as I can remember.

I leave the courtyard alone. The sick bay is accessible from the office, and I hurry to an arched door on our left.

Propping Court more against my body, I free one arm so I can open the door—

"Mykal, you can't." Franny panics, letting go of Court's hand. She restrains Mykal, palms to his broad chest, and I look back.

His eyes are reddened in pure frustration. He growls into a scream between his teeth, battling an invisible enemy. Grappling to move forward . . . blinking repeatedly.

He wants to hold and carry Court.

Desperately . . .

"Why are you looking at him?" Franny snaps and waves her hand in my face. Forcing my gaze onto her. "*Open the door.*"

I whisper under my breath, "As you wish."

NINE

Court

I wake to a fusion of combative sensations: a dreamy light-headedness, a rank stench of body odor, bare feet pacing on warm mosaic tile, and most clearly, an ass on a hard seat, tingling and sore from not moving, and a knife between coarse fingers: chipping at wood.

And *smoke*, seeping down and scratching my esophagus.

Eyes still shut, I cough lightly. "Mykal."

"Court?" He plucks something out of his mouth.

I cough again as my gaze opens onto him.

Mykal is hovering over me.

He always says that I'm a beautiful sight, but when I awake to Mykal and his lopsided smile and the rigorous drumbeat of his kind heart, the sun has kissed me. And I feel unbelievably whole again.

The corner of his mouth lifts higher, brightening the grave, dark places inside of me. "Well, aren't you mighty pleased and satisfied." He eyes my lips. "I'll be taking credit for that."

I almost smile. "You should," I whisper.

He pats my cheek twice and then holds my jaw—but our reality suddenly rushes toward me.

How I fainted in front of *Stork*. How we're no longer in our familiar snow-covered country. Up above through a round sky port, a star-blanketed galaxy stares back. How, at any second, we could lose sight of the dangers and be taken from each other.

Split apart or worse.

I refuse to lead him or Franny into peril again, and that means staying focused on the task at hand.

So I start to make sense of where I am. My back lies on what appears to be a dark-blue cushioned bench. A plush circular pillow beneath my head.

Mykal balances his hunting knife and a whittled piece of wood on his lap. Sitting on a stool next to me, he says, "You're glaring at me, you realize." His crooked smile remains, even as he sticks what appears to be a lit cigarette back between his lips. "You have that cross face about you. Like you enjoy wringing *happiness* by the neck."

"I don't enjoy it," I say curtly, and in all the gods-forsaken places I could rest my narrowed eyes, they fall to his mouth.

Mykal mumbles with his cigarette, "Ah, so you're looking to be kissed then." He runs his thumb along my squared jawline.

My nose flares, a sweltering intensity lighting my nerve endings. This close, I can only truly sense him and me. Embers eat the end of his cig, and smoke spills into the air like a tender wisp.

I remind Mykal, "It has to be done."

"Kissing?" He plucks his cigarette out and blows a gust of smoke off to the side. Out of my eyes.

"Staying focused."

Mykal sucks his cig again and cups my face. "Can't we do both?"

We can't.

It's better to be cautious. To be alert. To be maddeningly strict and survive than to be starry-eyed in love and perish.

His thumb glides roughly across my cheek and mouth with keen desire. Heat gathers. Pleasure rousing, and then stirring a need that should be kept dormant for his sake.

He's more overeager than shy, as I always thought he would be if we coupled. I could happily envelop myself in these feelings with him.

But I caution myself again. And again. *I can't put him at risk.*

I try to set my stern gaze on his hard-hearted blues. His thumb parts my lips, and a wild, torrid fire ignites across my limbs—as though reminding me that this is life. I am alive. I inhale, breath pouring into my lungs.

His chest rises, and he clasps my jaw, primal and rugged movements aching to swathe me. I feel his need grow stronger, and with a ragged exhale, his hand clenches the bench beside my head.

Mykal craves to roll on top and tangle together like two young lovers in his village. All raw strength and wanting breath and uninhibited things.

He resists the pull. Combatting his yearning for my sake.

Our lips haven't even touched, a single breath away, and I'm wrapped *fully* in his essence. Falling further away from focus.

Focus.

Abruptly, with my palm to his bare chest, I push him back and sit up. Gasping like I breached the surface of a pool. Undone. Air colder than his warmth. I comb my hair out of my face with two hands.

Frustration springs into my muscles. I try to exhale *his* frustration.

Leaning back farther, Mykal taps ash. "I think you love nurturing misery like a baby. Cradling the tot all day, all night. Letting it suckle your—"

"Will you ever shut up?" I retort.

Irritation flares madly in both of us, and he takes a harsher drag from the cig.

I cough into my fist, stifling a glare.

"I hate when you two fight," Franny mutters from across the small room. She's peering into the glass cabinets that contain medical instruments.

"Court started it," Mykal mumbles, picking up his hunting knife and wood.

I do glare, this time at the sky port. "How long have I been in the sick bay?" I ask, hurrying to take note of our new setting. A row of seven cushioned benches, including the one I'm on, line one side of the room. Cabinetry on the other.

Dotted squiggles and calligraphy are scrawled in ink on each tawny wall. Possibly an ancient, decorative map.

"About five hours, I think," Franny answers.

"You think?" I crane my neck over my shoulder. Behind me, a wide, silver-framed screen is hung. Much like the ones in the atrium, but instead of moving photographs, I trace the vivid blue outline of a male body that rotates slowly.

My body.

Familiar numbers flash in a column to the right of the silhouette.

118/73. *Must be blood pressure. Stable.*

84. *Heart rate. Stable.*

Though, my medical knowledge is based on a Saltarian. Not a human. I can only assume that biologically, we're very similar. But this monitor is far more advanced than the equipment in Yamafort's hospital. Where I once walked the halls as a physician.

"We only found a clock in the sick bay an hour ago," Franny explains. "We didn't want to wake you."

Mykal snuffs out his cigarette with the heel of his boot. "You weren't tossing or turning. You felt . . . at peace."

Did I?

I unconsciously touch my chest and solidify at the sight of my clothes. What . . . is this? I'm wearing a short-sleeved, high-collared white cloth that ends at my thighs, my tattoos peeking out on my quads. A leather belt is tied at my waist.

"That's a tunic apparently," Franny explains, taking a seat on the closest bench.

"It's odd-looking," Mykal mentions, carving a chunk out of the wood. "But you make it look handsome." His neck reddens, and I feel the flush ascend his face, as though the heat belongs to me.

I swallow my feelings.

"Mykal undressed you," Franny says, catching my gaze. "He made everyone leave the room." She smiles at that. "I only took off your socks."

I'm appreciative. For both of them. I should say this aloud, but I find myself on a mission to loosen the leather belt.

I've been in insurmountable pain, and now I feel none.

Careful, I lift only a corner of the tunic up to my waist. The *Lucretzia* crew must not wear undergarments beneath tunics because I clearly wasn't supplied any. Some kind of medical dressing is clinging to my hip.

"He said it's a Band-Aid," Mykal tells me, flaking wood. I don't ask where he found the material to whittle. A stool near the door is missing a leg and leans askew.

I peel the sticky bandage off my hip. Stitches removed, they cauterized the cut. My golden-brown skin appears less aggravated and exponentially healthier.

Yet I slept . . . almost too well. "What medicine did they give me?"

"Something to rid your infection," Franny says, "and painkillers. Stork told us that humans can die too easily from infections if we're not careful."

I inspect my arms for bruising, for any intravenous fluids, but I'm not covered in cords or wires. All I discover are two translucent, thin dots stuck to my wrist.

I rip one off, and the monitor behind me beeps aggressively in warning before the screen blinks to black.

"Heya." Mykal points the tip of his hunting knife at me. "Put that back. It's been helping you."

I stick the clear dot back to my wrist, and the monitor flashes to life once again. This is technology that I can't comprehend.

"And there are such things as *diseases*," Franny proclaims dramatically.

Mykal cringes. "Sounded real nasty. So we let them prick us."

I freeze. "You let them *what*?"

Franny crosses her legs beneath her bottom. "We had a stew first."

I would imagine Mykal quarreling about medical tests. More so, I'm in utter disbelief that they allowed Stork to test them for *diseases*. "You trust Stork?" I ask, voice strict.

"He has answers, and he needs us alive," Franny defends. "But he's still a wart who tried to shove me into a pool."

Mykal mumbles something about fatherhood, but then he shakes his head and expels a gruff breath. "I dunno what to think, Court."

Every time their guards dip, mine shoot upward. The last person I trusted unconditionally, who wasn't linked to me, had been my cell mate in Vorkter—a man who tried to cut out my heart.

The last thing I want is for Mykal or Franny to meet that callous betrayal and gut-wrenching agony. They've already sensed enough through me.

"Don't open your arms too wide yet," I caution.

"You'll be *happy* to know," Franny snaps back, "that we're all disease-free."

"Wondrous," I say dryly. "Did he tell you why you have random nosebleeds then? Or is he withholding that knowledge for a time that benefits him?"

She bristles. "Maybe he knows nothing about my nosebleeds."

That's only one possibility, and a slim one. He said he knows *everything*. And if that's true, he's a bastard for letting her wade in uncertainty. The kind that will plague her day and night.

I know this because I was that bastard. Before StarDust, she'd pleaded to retest her deathday, and I kept telling her to *wait*. Saying *now's not the time*.

And I'll regret it for the rest of my gods-damned life.

She needs answers, and she deserves them. Sometimes the truth is more painful, and maybe that's why I've been content to never discover our origins. Our history.

But I'm willing to confront these answers for Franny.

I swing my legs off the bench, facing her more. "Obviously he's withholding a vast amount of information." *All so we'll help him with his retrieval operation.* I continue, "But if you want answers, Franny, you don't need to wait."

Back when we met in Bartholo, Franny never pressured me to open up about myself because she was being kind. I could barely return to my past without becoming ill. But Stork is being tight-lipped as leverage. Using his knowledge to exercise power over us.

"You can trick him," I clarify, "or talk his ear off until he lets something slip." She fooled many StarDust candidates with the indigo cards, and though he seems clever, his guards seem to lower around Franny. He smiles more, teases only her, and so there's a possibility that he'll falter.

Her brows jump. "You trust me to do that?"

"Yes." I nod. "Just be careful." *Please be careful.* I shut my eyes tightly, already partly regretting this idea.

I feel her smile before I even open my eyes.

"I will," she says quietly. "And I'll wait for the day where you say it's *too dangerous* and then I'll continue on anyway."

Mykal laughs. "Predictable." He reaches for a carton of something.

"No more than you," I say distantly. "What are those?"

"Human cigarettes." He hoists the pack at my eyes. "Not too strong, but they do the job all right."

Franny motions to the cabinetry. "Mykal found them in a cabinet drawer. We were joking earlier how the *Lucretzia*'s sick bay looks like a Bartholo cigar parlor."

They have been here for a while. I comb another hand through my dark hair. Kicking myself for fainting and risking their health.

I go rigid. "Did either of you faint after me?" I should've asked this first.

"No." Mykal shakes his head, but a sort of brawling torment

festers and scalds his eyes. He sucks deeply on a newly lit cigarette. Smoke glides down my lungs, feeling Mykal, and aggra-
vation swirls angrily inside him.

I don't understand the source of his emotion. "It feels like a
yes."

"Well it's not," he retorts.

He's not lying.

I'm sorry. I must've put him in a position that hurt him
somehow—

"You don't need to be apologizing." Mykal points at me with
the cig between his fingers.

"I didn't say anything," I tell him smoothly.

He jabs at his chest. "I felt it in my soul."

I roll my eyes and let them land on Franny. "Did Stork seem
suspicious about us?"

"No." She picks at a frayed hole in her slacks, ripped at her
knee. "He didn't seem to know about our link."

I nod. "Good. Let's keep it that way." The less he knows
about us, the better, and our link may be our last well-kept
secret.

TEN

Franny

I whip up a plan: find someone else on this starcraft who speaks Saltarian.

So far, no one we've met except Stork has spoken our native tongue. Not being able to communicate with anyone else is a bothersome fact. Stork may have carried Court to the sick bay and helped us escape the *Romulus* brig, but I can't forget that he needs us for the fleet's retrieval operation. Without that, he may not even care whether we live or die.

I search for a handle or knob to the sick bay's door. *Gods.* I should've paid sharper attention to how the nurses exited. The metal door sparkles metallic silver, and four diamond pegs slide along crisscrossing tracks.

I shift one peg and wait for the door to open.

Nothing.

Nothing happens. Who'd think to transform a door into an elaborate puzzle? Albeit I only spot four pieces, but a four-piece puzzle is more than any door should have.

It is a beauty, though. Just like the rest of the doors on the *Lucretzia.* Midnight-blue drapes frame the arched entryway, drawn and pinned on either wall.

I reach out to attempt the puzzle again, and the pegs suddenly slither rapidly. All on their own.

I fast lose sight of which pegs end where, but as soon as the door whooshes open vertically, I step forward—*holy hells.*

I bump into a hard chest, and I quickly catch the door frame to stop from stumbling backward. He must've opened the door on his side.

He being . . .

Oh.

No.

Mykal and Court go quiet, but their heads whip around. Concern cramps their limbs, but I start to concentrate elsewhere and their senses drift further and further away. Becoming faint.

I'm staring at silver-laced open-toed footwear, up higher to a pair of muscular thighs that peek beneath a leather skirt. Blondish hairs on chalky skin.

Stop looking.

Higher, against better judgment, I ogle the leather strap across an armor-less chest. A sword sheathed across a broad back and a leather band twisted along a chiseled bicep, spiraling down a strong forearm.

I lived my Fast-Tracker life with simple pleasures: the laughs of a few long-gone friends, the rush and high of drugs, the heat of tangling up in limbs, the rumble while behind a Purple Coach wheel, and the marvelous tales that my mom whispered at night.

I was told I could not attend school.

I could not be a person of influence.

I could not become old.

But I basked in the grandeur of stories. All sorts of whimsical tales. I don't believe fairy tales are real. They live in the air after they're told from ear to ear and on pages in old Influential storybooks.

My mom spoke of knights and queens. *So regal,* she said, *they stand tall and proud, my little Franny.* She'd brush my nose with her nose. I smiled as she whispered, *All the people in the faraway lands revere the queen and her knights.*

Why? I asked.

Because they're good and just.

I can't say the body I bumped into is good or just, but his

posture is straight with purpose and pride. Stork Kickfall refuses to budge and let me through, a black leather satchel in his left hand and a squared bottle of amber liquor in his right.

I arch a brow at him, but a sweat breaks beneath my armpits. Since I barely sense Court or Mykal, this has to be real sweat building. *My sweat.*

Why am I hot? I try to subtly waft my putrid-smelling Star-Dust shirt.

All I know for sure is that I'm far from afraid, and I wish my eyes would stop traveling all around Stork and his knightly body—*gods*, I wish I wouldn't call him knightly. My mom would be mortified. Namely if she found out he wasn't good-hearted.

Hopefully her spirit has better things to do than watch me tumble face-first through the extra life I've been granted.

His pink lips hike up. My roaming gaze has triggered his amusement.

I simmer. Mad at myself, at first.

Curiosity glitters in his blue eyes. He dips his head, his breath warming my cheek. "My advice," he tells me, "if you want to go on a scavenger hunt around the ship, bring a map. There are people who've lived here for five years, and they still get lost belowdecks."

"*Perfect*," I say in my finest Influential voice. "I'd like a map, please." I outstretch a palm. "And thank you." I expect a warty roll of the eyes. Like Court would do.

But he's certainly not Court.

And he certainly doesn't care whether I'm proper or not.

Stork smiles with a curt laugh. As though I'm an amusing *child*. He raises the bag and bottle. "My hands are full, dove. Perhaps later." We lock eyes.

For a long beat.

He asks, "Are you moving?"

I'd much rather annoy him than entertain any of his irritating desires. But I also have plans of my own. Lofty plans that I refuse to botch. Like prying my way toward more answers.

I cross my arms. "Will you make me move?"

"Like I said before, my hands are full."

"If they weren't?"

"If they weren't, I would've found you a map." He tilts his head. "You're not my prisoner. I'm not your captor. If you ever want to leave, you can walk out of your own accord. I'll encourage you to stay. It'd be the smarter choice, but I'll never force you to remain here."

I like his words.

Maybe he knew I would, and that's what concerns me and Court and Mykal most of all.

I reach out and grip the doorway again. Not letting him pass. "What's in the satchel?" I ask.

Stork lowers the bag behind his back. "Are you always this forward?"

"Maybe I am. Maybe I'm not."

A laugh sticks to his throat, followed by a briny smile.

"See how it feels when someone has too many answers and refuses to share? It's not pleasant."

He makes a noise that sounds cross, agitated, and haughty all at once. "This is going to be fun," he states like it'll be anything but fun. He suddenly wraps a powerful arm around my waist and hoists me like a storeowner adjusting a mannequin.

"Heya!" Mykal yells.

I kick Stork's shins, but he's already setting me down. Moving me only far enough so he could enter the sick bay.

I swat and spit flyaway hair out of my mouth. Wafting my shirt again, I adjust my stance to appear as dignified and knightly as any Fast-Tracker can be. "I'm no fan of etiquette—"

"I hadn't noticed," he quips, eyes dripping down my body.

I try not to unravel. "But that was rude."

"Which part?" he asks, nearing the cushioned benches where Court and Mykal have sprung to their feet. Both spearing stormy threats into Stork.

He acknowledges them with a brisk nod.

"You, lifting me up without a warning."

Stork tosses the satchel on a bench and mulls this over for half a second. "We were at a standstill." He turns to me while I approach them. "If I didn't move you, then you would've slipped between my legs. I cut to the chase."

My face scrunches. "Who says I would've slipped between your legs? Maybe I would've moved you too."

Stork swishes his bottle and appraises my outward ire that cinches my brows. "If you can pick me up off the floor for five seconds, I'll answer any question you ask."

Any question.

He's dangling what I hunger after most of all, right in front of me.

Any question.

Any answer.

Please.

Court glares. "Don't do this to her."

Stork holds my gaze, waiting for my response. "She can say no if she wants."

Their discourse confuses Mykal, who picks at the dried blood on his cheeks. Bruises blemish the skin beneath his eyes, but his nose looks no more crooked than before.

Court is trying to tell me not to do this. I could embarrass myself with the attempt. Clearly I see that Stork has given me an opportunity with no real chance to succeed.

And I know who I am.

I can do a lot of things terribly and a whole lot of things decently and then very few things miraculously.

There's a great big chance that I botch this, but maybe Gem Soarcastle, the fearlessly prideful and confident Soarcastle sister, rubbed off on me at StarDust. Because as soon as Stork acts as though I *can't,* I ache to prove him wrong.

Even knowing he's probably right.

I clamp my hand around his wrist. He lets me.

He also lets me guide him to the end of the bench. More room here, I clear my throat and shake out my arms. Preparing.

Stork removes his sword and throws the sheathed weapon on the same bench as his satchel. And then he positions himself like a stone wall. Limbs hanging at his sides. "My sandals have to be off the floor."

Sandals. We all eye his footwear. "They will be," I say.

Mykal hollers out an encouragement between cupped hands, and Court stands gravely.

I think of all the questions I want answered. All the mysteries and uncertainties. Where was I born? Why am I human? And the one I can't even ask Stork: how can we be linked together?

With a determined inhale, I curve my arms around his bare waist. Pushing my breasts up against his chest, I cling sturdily like I'm hugging a heavy chiseled statue.

Stork raises his arms a bit, elbows bent, all so I can have a better grip without his limbs flailing in my way.

One breath out, I heave upward. Imagining I'm lifting a Purple Coach off an icy patch. My arms shake madly, and my legs quiver beneath me. His body weight seeking to drag me down.

Lift him up, Franny.

Taking a peek, I see Stork is firmly grounded. Not dislodged one bit. His sandals might as well be stuck permanently to the mosaic tile.

Stork whispers with strange gentleness, "What were you saying about moving me?" Sounding less cocky, I hear his disappointment.

As though he's wishing I could win this silly bet. And he can give me more.

Maybe he's not in charge here. He hinted at the regimented military having a hierarchy. Maybe he's just adhering to a command and shielding all of these answers from us because another person told him so—but what can be harder: knowing everything or knowing nothing at all?

I try again. With all my might.

I grit down. Veins pumping hard with blood, heat exploding across my face, I scream between my teeth and try and try and *try*.

Squeezing him tightly, I pull up and his heels lift off the tiles for half a second. Not nearly long enough. I pull up and up and up but only frustrated, hells-bent tears threaten to rise.

All humor has evaporated, sucked brutally out of the room, and on my umpteenth try, Stork rests his hand atop my head. "It's over."

"*Wait!*" I exclaim in a short breath, hugging him harder. "Let me try again. *Please.*" I'm begging. I fykking hate that I'm begging, but the chance at knowing more is an uncontrollable high-speed force that can't be stopped easily.

I think I spot remorse reddening his eyes. Sharpening his features. But I can't be sure. He drops his head a fraction. "No, that's it, dove."

I detach from him swiftly this time, wiping at my face, but no tears have fallen. I shake my hands, clenching them into fists.

Roasting inside out.

I'm not sure where to look. I know I've unraveled a little. My throat closes, and I bite the inside of my mouth. Drifting silently until I plop down on a bench.

Botched it good.

Mykal is fast. He's sitting next to me, and he sweeps his brawny arm around my shoulders. Tucking me to his chest. "You did your best, that's what'll be mattering tomorrow." He messes my hair with a playful hand.

His compassion cloaks my being. Resting my cheek on his collar, I try to simmer down.

"Congratulations, you're crueler than you realize," Court tells Stork, both boys still standing.

Stork laughs lightly while strapping his sword to his back. "No, I'm very aware of how cruel I can be."

ELEVEN

Franny

Before we start a stew with Stork, he does something less cruel and shows us to a new room just across from the sick bay. Not a single soul is here, but he calls it the "strategy room" and the way he says those words, we know it's important. Court meanders around the room and scopes the surroundings, while Mykal hovers close.

I stand in the center, taking in the sights. A large squared table is illuminated with neon pieces like a game. Starcrafts and planets line the board. Stork already told us it's a map of the galaxy that the *Lucretzia* currently resides in. *Dis Pater*. The admirals use the board to plot the fleet's next movements.

It only takes a couple seconds to realize the true reason Stork brought us here. The back of the room has a long slender bar with deep-green cushioned stools. He goes directly for the glass cabinets behind the bar. His satchel, now hooked over his shoulder, bounces off his hip as he walks. Bottles of liquor sit prettily on the shelves, and Stork removes the slender emerald one. We all watch as he spins off the crystal top and takes a swig.

Before I truly start a stew for wasting our time, he unbuttons his leather satchel with his free hand. Digging, he procures three tiny discs the size of a thimble.

"What are those?" I ask and take a seat at the bar.

Like a bartender passing us ale, he slides each of us a single disc. "Translators called EonInterpreters, EI for short. Place the EIs behind your ear and you'll be able to understand and communicate in all human languages. Tap the translator and an ocular function will engage and help you read."

My mouth is on the floor. "Why?" *Why is Stork offering this to us?*

Mykal sinks down to the barstool beside mine and puts the disc up to his eyeball.

Court asks more skeptically, "Why wait until now? This could've been useful to us *before* we boarded the *Lucretzia*."

Stork loosely grips the neck of the bottle. "You fainted only a few minutes into boarding the ship. Unless you dream in a human language, impressive but unlikely, an EI would've been *useless* to you."

"On our way to the *Lucretzia*—"

"I didn't bring any with me," Stork interjects, and to me, he answers, "Like I said before, you're not a prisoner—"

"I couldn't even open the puzzle-door," I admit.

His lip rises. "I'll show you later. It's not difficult." His smirk fades quickly, and he drags his gaze along the ground before eyeing each of us. "The crew has nothing to hide, but of course, I do." He downs a gulp of liquor, faster and harsher. Wiping his mouth with his forearm, he adds, "You need the EIs to communicate with the crew, and they want you to be able to understand them."

Court inspects the tiny disc on his fingertip.

"If you want to have full conversations with more than just me and each other," Stork says, "you'll have to wear those. Only a handful of people on this ship can speak Saltarian, and the few linguistic specialists and two lieutenants who learned the language can barely string together four sentences." He rounds the corner of the bar and leans against the wall, a silver-framed picture above his head.

Mykal spins a new, unlit cigarette between his fingers and mumbles something about the disc blowing our heads clean off our necks.

I try not to visualize that gore.

Court hesitates. "Why not have the crew wear EIs and understand Saltarian?"

Stork places his sandaled foot on a cushioned bench, balancing his forearm on his bent knee. "I can't decide who asks more asinine questions, you or her." He aims his bottle at me.

I flash a cringe at him.

He smiles into his next swig.

Court is all no-nonsense. "I'm starting to believe you call questions *stupid* just to avoid answering them."

My face breaks into a grin.

Stork sighs, nearly smiling as he eyes me, and he drops his foot. "EIs are created by humans. As you three should know, the Saltarian language has a variety of dialects and slang, and it's complex. There's more inaccuracy when the translators try to interpret Saltarian languages than you trying to understand humans."

I suddenly feel something behind my ear—*not my ear.* I turn to Mykal. He just placed the disc on his skin.

"Mykal." Court glares.

"Better my head blown off than yours," Mykal says with a cigarette between his lips. "Nothing's changed. Must be broken."

Stork speaks in a throaty language that has some flair and flourish. But his words make no sense to me.

Mykal feels the opposite of confused, and then he starts replying in the *same* language Stork used—Court rocks back. My mouth unhinges again.

Mykal must feel our shock. He swerves to us, frowning. He plucks his cigarette out of his mouth and says words that we can't understand.

Court cuts him off. "You're not speaking Saltarian."

Mykal laughs heartily and gestures for us to try the EIs. He also offers me the cigarette, but I decline. Not as interested in smoking. At least not now.

I fumble with the disc, and I stick the device behind my ear. Court is faster than me, already putting his on.

"What'd you say to Mykal?" I ask Stork.

"That the discs are waterproof and can be worn at all times. If the adhesion wears off, spit and reapply." His lips are moving oddly, but I understand each and every word now.

And what he said sounded like a fib. "Really?"

"That was a joke." He laughs with a shake of his head and reaches back into his satchel, setting his bottle on the bar. "EIs are expensive. They take a big chunk out of the fleet's budget, so treat them like they're your favorite pet."

I crane my neck to see into the satchel.

"No one has pets on Saltare-3," Court tells Stork in a tone that very much says, *you're not as smart as you believe.*

Stork glances back. "It was a figure of speech." He snatches a *book* out of the bag and tosses the hardback to Court. "Here you go."

Mykal slumps at the sight and curses under his breath. Grabbing his wood and knife from his pocket, he complains, "No one said this mission involved reading."

"It doesn't, but this book is the key to everything," Stork says.

We all tap the disc behind our ear so we can read the human language.

Court angles the worn hardback toward us. I mouth the words as I read: *The Greatest True Myths of the 36th Century,* by Sean Cavalletti.

"There is no such thing as a *true* myth," Court says flatly.

Stork subconsciously touches his sapphire earring, shaped like some sort of bluebird. "There is, actually. Some myths that were believed to be false have been proven true."

Court's interest piques, but his features don't change. I suppose he wants to keep Stork further than arm's length and not be reeled in too easily.

As they face one another, both assertive, both domineering, and both dressed in Earthen clothes—military skirt for Stork and simple tunic for Court—at more than a glance, I'd think Court has belonged on the *Lucretzia* for years.

He's good at seamlessly fitting into new environments. A skill that extends beyond our planet.

"What myths were proven true?" Court questions, disbelieving, but he silently thumbs through the book and begins to pace slowly around the strategy room.

"Just last month," Stork says, "a new mineral was discovered on the planet Prydorium. A pliable powder-blue rock, which has become one of the universe's first naturally occurring fertilizers in over a century. That book described the mineral in detail *years* before it was ever found." He points at the hardback in Court's hands. "And there are two other myths inside those pages that have come true."

Fighting the urge to smile, I ask, "So Court is wrong?"

Court flips a page. "I'm not wrong."

"Haven't we just decided?" I wonder. "Myths can be true." I lean my shoulder into Mykal while he whittles.

Court stops in place near the map that's shaped like a game board. "I'm not having this argument."

"Read up." Stork nods to him. "You might enjoy what you find."

Mykal wears a lopsided grin. "Hear that, Court? You might enjoy something."

Court licks his thumb and turns another page, but I catch his lip ticking upward.

I'm about to ask Mykal if Court just smiled at his joke, but I sense Mykal: the sudden swell of his chest. He stares at Court for a long, long while, almost like he's replaying the moment.

Stork hops up on the countertop behind the bar and sits there. Right across from Mykal and me. "Saltarians want a fight," he explains like we're a little slow to catch on.

"That part has been obvious," I snap.

"Well, let this sink in, dove. Humans can die. *You* can die."

I shiver, trying not to fear that uncertainty. Not again. *Please,* not again.

"Saltarians fight without any shields," Stork continues, "while you have humans walking into combat in full-metal armor." Before I ask why *he'd* wear protective gear if he's Saltarian, he tells me, "Armor is customary in the Earthen Fleet."

"But you don't need it," I state.

"Accurate." He nods and licks his lips. "Saltarians know that the Earthen Fleet has no real chance if we go to war. We can't kill them, and so for the past decade, the majority of the fleet has been avoiding their ships and trying to devise alternative strategies."

He really loves Earth, but I don't understand why the planet is so special besides being the motherland for humans. "Is Earth beautiful?" I wonder.

Stork cocks his head, sloshes his liquor in its bottle. "What do you define as beauty?"

I think about the Catherina Hotel. All the gold and grandeur. A kind of beauty I dreamed to die inside, but nothing compared to seeing the stars. "I find all sorts of things beautiful, I suppose."

"Trees," Mykal pipes in. "There's no better beauty than a sturdy tree."

Stork frosts, rubbing his knuckles, and he appraises Mykal without a word. Again, Stork has skipped over my answer. Not providing *any* detail about Earth.

Mykal brushes wood shavings off his legs. Finished whittling, he displays a beautifully carved snow leopard between two fingers to Stork. "For you—"

"No—"

"Our pa—"

"He's dead," Stork says with an uncaring shrug. "He died."

Mykal runs his tongue along his sharp molars. "Yeah, he died, but he's still watching."

"I don't believe in your gods," Stork proclaims.

Mykal grunts something and pulls at his hair, finding words. "Then believe that he'd want you to know about him, and *this*"—he chucks the snow leopard and Stork catches it quickly— "is somethin' a pa crafts for his newborn. Supposed to represent the wild inside of his child."

I've heard this story before. How Mykal lost his wooden sculpture when he was nine and wandering the Free Lands. He accidentally dropped the white bear figurine in an ice fissure while fishing. Sunk to the bottom. When he realized he couldn't retrieve the carving, he said he cried until he passed out.

Stork brushes his thumb over the edges of the snow leopard. He inhales, then ejects a forceful sigh. "I don't care about him."

He looks like he cares. "You're lying?" I ask.

"Am I?" An icy smile crosses his mouth, and I remember how he said he doesn't lie.

Maybe he's lying to himself.

Stork swigs another big gulp, and then holds the bottle limply. "You want to know something? If you and I"—he gestures to Mykal, then to himself—"if we *hadn't* been swapped, if instead I grew up on Saltare-3 . . . then I still would've *never* known my father." He tosses the snow leopard in his palm and then throws the statuette at Mykal's chest. "So, really, this is yours. Not mine."

I'm confused, but Mykal isn't.

He scratches his neck. "You're an Influential then."

Oh. I should've remembered. There are no Influentials in Grenpale. If Stork has a deathday that is later in life, he would've been sent to another country. Instantly. As a newborn.

Stork nods.

"What's your deathday?" I ask.

"Not for another one hundred and thirty-two years."

I try not to gawk. "You're living to be . . . one hundred and fifty?" That's one of the longer life expectancies. Anything past one-fifty-five is rare and starts feeling like tall tales. A girl at the orphanage said her brother would die at one-sixty, but I thought that was a bold-faced lie.

"With certainty," Stork says with an arrogant smile.

Jealousy nips at me like a cold draft.

Mykal is rolling the snow leopard in his palm. "He's fallen into luck." I hadn't thought about that . . . how Mykal isn't the lucky one since his ma never died giving birth to him. She died giving birth to someone else.

Stork is the true Kick*fall*, blessed by the gods.

He tosses the statuette back to Stork, and before he protests, Mykal says, "A pa still crafts one for his Influential newborn. It's yours."

Stork opens his mouth to reply.

"It's the baby," Court interrupts us. We all turn to look at him. He's wandering back and flipping the *last* page in a hefty-sized book.

"What?" Mykal and I say together.

"There's a myth about a baby." Court reaches the bar and still scans the end of the hardback. "Said to be the first of her kind, neither human nor Saltarian. A new species. She carries the ability to both teleport and cloak items." Court plants his sternness on Stork. "You want her to hide Earth. Your retrieval operation—you're not planning to retrieve a *something*. You want to retrieve a *someone*."

A baby?

Stork rubs his mouth, shock parting his lips.

Mykal points his knife at Stork. "Never underestimate our Court. He's smarter than the best of anyone on any damned planet."

Court doesn't roll his eyes or say he's not good. He breathes deeply, letting himself soak up the praise for once.

Stork recovers by jumping off the countertop, his sandaled feet hitting the ground with a *thud*. "Yeah, *that's* the mission.

Because if we bring her to Earth, she'll keep everyone out of a war that we can't win."

Strained silence bleeds into the strategy room.

He outstretches his arm. "This kid . . ." He pauses. "This *child*. She is Earth's last hope. Otherwise, Saltarians will find us sooner than later and overrun the planet."

I slowly stand to my feet.

Mykal follows. "I'm just going to come out and say it." He smacks his lips. "What's teleporting?"

Court shuts the book hard. "It's made up. Fictional. Like a fairy tale."

Stork laughs curtly. "We've been through this. Myths can be true. And teleporting is the ability to transport objects, including people, from one place to another."

Mykal shakes his head. "No, that doesn't sound right. Seems made up."

Stork turns to me. "Do you think this is make-believe?" He's asking because I've kept my mouth shut.

Teleportation? I can barely picture a person with an ability to move objects, but if anyone asked me to imagine and believe our *link*—I'd call them mad.

I exchange a look with Court and Mykal, and they must remember our strange, *unreal* connection because their skepticism begins to subside and their stressed shoulders drop.

I shrug at Stork, keeping my thoughts close.

Stork nods and then his eyes drift to each of us. "Look, there are certain species in this universe with abilities, but this baby is the only one I've heard of that can both cloak and teleport objects as large as an entire planet. And at the end of the day"— he shoves the book in the satchel, also slipping in the snow leopard—"I'm not asking for your permission. I'm telling you this is the op. You're either in or out. It's your choice, but if you choose not to do this, you don't get the information you want."

Before any of us can answer, the door whooshes vertically open, and a young girl in a military skirt and armor emerges, panting and out of breath. Footsteps pound frantically behind her, and I catch a glimpse of people running in the same direction.

"Stork," she says, face flushed. "It's happening."

TWELVE

Franny

W hy are they gathering 'round like this?" Mykal asks. Stork leads our way, fisting a new bulbous bottle with darker liquor. "You'll see."

We've followed the frantic footsteps inside the divine courtyard. Rivaling the unique splendor of the atrium, the courtyard is like being transported into an Influential storybook.

Foliage and budding pink flowers spindle up humongous marble columns that pillar eight wraparound balconies. *Upper observational decks,* Stork called them, and we climb a spiral staircase to the fourth level.

As we ascend, the gushing fountain hooks my attention. Right in the courtyard's center, a lovely stone-carved woman gazes powerfully at the sky port, petal blossoms adrift in the pool at her sturdy feet. Continuous streams of water burst from her palm and trickle down her curves.

With the lush greenery, fancy columns, a starry sky port, and midnight drapes blowing like wind exists indoors, I would've happily died in this beauty. At least back when I was preparing poorly for my deathday.

Now my stomach lurches at the mere thought of dying.

Don't think about death.

I try.

We gather around a balcony railing, and I spy crew accumulating on each observational deck. Their wide eyes fix on the stone fountain down below. The rush of water and cool mist cuts into the uncomfortable air.

Nothing is happening that I can see.

Stork guzzles a mouthful of liquor. Drinking more than any Fast-Tracker friend I had, and most spent all of their bills on ale.

Court braces his forearms on the banister, his intense focus pumping adrenaline more than I really like.

Pacing back and forth, I try to free myself from the prickly energy. I rotate on my heels and stumble toward an anxious cluster of boys and girls my age. Pooling onto the fourth upper-deck, all sport military leather, armor, and archaic weapons like javelins and clubs.

Their whispers fade and their probing eyes poke at my Star-Dust slacks and shirt. Most gawk but meander right on past. Going to another balcony section.

But three stay put.

I latch eyes with each. Trying to emphasize that I'm not afraid. *I'm not afraid of you.*

Stork mentioned that he's the only Saltarian onboard.

These must be humans.

Real-life living, walking, talking humans, and I crave to hear what they have to say. With the translator behind my ear, I can finally understand them.

The petite girl with tightly coiled curls—she drops her crossed dark-brown arms to her armored sides, battle-ax strapped to her back. Head turning fast, she plugs her nose. And cringes.

A towering boy whiffs the air, a scar cut along his sculpted cheekbone. He has reddish-gold skin that complements his bronze shield, his woody-brown hair shaved on each side. A mop of curls on top. Silver bow and quiver slung over his shoulder.

His face bunches up. "What's that smell?"

"Piss," I say bluntly. "I took a piss on myself." In the brig, I thought I could hold my pee until we were freed.

I was wrong.

Waiting for his snide remark, I try not to feel as pathetic as the *Romulus* cadets said we are.

Mykal lounges against the railing beside Court, but he faces the military-clad people like me. His flexed muscles tensing mine.

The towering boy looks to the third person, a steely-eyed one, who holds him dotingly around the waist. *Coupling.*

Humans must couple too.

The steely-eyed boy has cropped black hair and a rich blend of olive and copper skin, and like the others, his weapon, a spear, is situated on his back. He moves his hand in a variety of ways. Signing something to *Stork.*

And strangely, I understand the gesticulation. The EonInterpreters must be translating his finger motions into words, and the answer just breezes to mind.

He signs, *"Why didn't you bathe them?"*

Stork props his shoulder against a column. Cocking his head at me.

I flush hot in remembrance of how he tried to shove me into the atrium pool. To clean me up.

"See," Stork tells me, "I told you, you stink like you've been sitting in your own shi—"

"I can bathe myself," I cut him off.

Behind me, Mykal says huskily, "You tell them, Franny."

I nearly smile.

The girl unplugs her nose. "It's unsanitary to be in soiled linens. You'll get *sick.*"

"She knows," Stork says to the girl but keeps his eyes on me, and then on Mykal. "They both do."

"Then why hasn't she changed yet?" the girl asks, soon after pinpointing Mykal. "Why hasn't he?"

Court was sponge-bathed and dressed in a tunic. Though, he had no real choice. His wound needed to be properly cleaned.

"Why do you care?" I ask, not too snippy.

She frowns. "Why don't *you*?"

I do. I try not to take offense, but wordless sound scratches my throat.

At the start, I didn't. I had no desire to take care of myself. Not my cracked lips, not my aches and pains. Not my headaches or chills. But I've come *far*.

I'm certain I have.

I care.

So deeply, so impossibly about my little life. I've done *everything* I can to stay alive. How is that not proof? Why do these dirty clothes tell a different story?

Court rubs his face, attempting to soothe the fire that scorches me. His hand is my hand. His palm, marred with old scars, pauses on his mouth. He struggles against the impulse to peer over his shoulder at me.

I find my voice. "I care."

I care.

No one can tell me otherwise.

The steely-eyed boy signs to the girl, *"They don't trust us enough to bathe here."*

Sympathy lowers her shoulders. Realizing why we've risked our health and stayed in rancid clothes.

"You can trust us," the towering boy says, brows cinched like he can't believe in a reality where we *wouldn't* trust in them.

I shift uneasily and shake my head. "I don't even know who you are."

Stork pushes off the column. Sidling next to me, so near that I smell the sharp liquor off his breath, he introduces them with a casual point of a finger. First to the steely-eyed boy. "Barrett Daybreak." Next to the towering boy. "Arden Shipwreck." And then to the girl. "Nia Hopscotch."

Daybreak? Shipwreck? *Hopscotch?* "Are all human surnames that odd?"

Hand over nose and mouth, Arden muffles out, "All Saltarians taking *castle* as a suffix is weirder."

Not to me. So it goes: we're all one people, together—or I was once a part of those people. I still feel like a Franny Bluecastle. I don't know who else I'm supposed to be.

Barrett signs, *"Those aren't our surnames."*

"What?"

"Those are our C-Jay call signs," Arden replies, still muffled.

Stork pays little attention to them, checking more on the state of the balconies that are filling up rapidly.

Nia puts the tiniest stick in her mouth. "We belong to the Knave Squadron."

The Knave Squadron.

At StarDust, no one grouped off like that. We just had the *Saga 5,* which became the *Saga 7,* and I guess it's now the *Saga 4.* Just Kinden, Zimmer, Padgett, and Gem. Off somewhere in space or docked on a new planet.

Mykal eases forward to Nia. "Can I have a stick?"

She quickly plugs her nose and tosses him a pack. "They're toothpicks. Keep it."

He mumbles a tongue-tied *thanks* and starts chewing on a toothpick.

I start to connect the military attire to C-Jays. So Stork must be one, and instead of asking outright, I jump ahead and question, "What's your call sign?"

Stork jerks in surprise, and his blue eyes sparkle down at me. But he's not answering. *Of course.*

"Tight-Lipped?" I guess.

He smirks. "Try again."

He's too pleased. I shut this down. "It has to be that."

"It's not."

"It is."

"It's Knave."

Cold spurts up and ices my brain. This is *his* squadron?

He mockingly lifts his brows as mine arch at him—I hate when he does that—and he brings the bottle to his lips.

I see more than his cocky attitude. I see how there's a chance to find information from *new* sources. No longer needing to rely on Stork, I ask the other three C-Jays, "What does the Knave Squadron do, exactly?"

Each one turns to Stork.

Un-fykking-believable.

Stork nearly laughs, but the gathering crowds seem to pre-occupy half his mind.

"Are they not allowed to answer without your permission?" I question.

"There's a hierarchy, dove. Certain information is classified." To the C-Jays, he adds, "The human rescues are being granted two-stripe clearance." He explains that a two-stripe clearance is equivalent to a combat pilot, the same as Daybreak, Ship-wreck, and Hopscotch.

So if they want, they can tell me anything they know. He spoke true when he said that the crew had nothing to hide from us. I prod Stork for more. "How many people are above you, then? Fifty? A hundred?"

"Four," he says, a gloating smile on the rise. "Venus Squad-ron is a first-defender. Mine is second. I'm a rank below Cap-tain Venita."

Still plugging her nose, Nia says nasally, "And the three admirals of the Earthen Fleet."

Stork takes the biggest swig yet.

To save the C-Jays from my smell, I shuffle backward. Until my hip bumps into the railing next to Mykal, and I rotate to discover more and more bodies on balconies, fretful whispers and nervous eyes.

No one is dressed in regal gowns or classic suits. Here, people either wear tunics, the military skirt and armor, or draped lin-ens with an Earthen brooch: three concentric circles with a leaf in the middle.

Stork approaches me.

I think he has something to say, but he bypasses me with a knowing once-over and he clamps a hand on the railing. Dan-gerously, he hikes his leg over the banister and straddles it. One more swing of the other leg, and he faces forward, both limbs dangling carelessly off the observational deck.

Four stories off the ground.

One wrong move and he'll plummet. *Not to his death.* Gods, what I'd do to be certain that I wouldn't die if I mimicked him.

I hang back, loosely holding the railing. Once upon an era, I would've been just as fearless, and that change inside me stings bitterly. I loved who I was as a Fast-Tracker, and I want to love who I am as a human.

But I'm not sure how.

Stork pats the railing. "Hop up if you want."

Court and Mykal are whispering to one another. Hugging close, but both eye Stork skeptically.

They're not why I falter. My belly up against the banister, I hone in on the terrifying plunge, and who knows? Maybe Stork will push me just for kicks.

I keep my boots on the deck, but more brazenly, I peel off the tiny EI disc so we can speak in private. "You don't act like an Influential," I tell him.

Sharp glances pierce us since I just spoke Saltarian.

Stork pays them no mind. "That's because I was raised by humans." Voice clipped at the end, he downs another gulp. Knowing the day he'll die, that has to change him. He has no hands on the railing and such little regard for personal injury. Willingly hanging off the balcony.

FTs would love the thrill.

"You're more like a Fast-Tracker," I mention.

He tips his head in thought, but then he gestures his bottle to the other balconies. "I reckon they are too."

Handfuls of people sit leisurely on the railings. Some even lounge across the banisters, backs propped up against the columns. Legs dangling everywhere. Hardly batting an eye at the death they could meet below.

"These are humans?" I ask in disbelief.

He soaks in my reaction before nodding, "Yeah. All of them."

I blink back maddened tears.

Why aren't they afraid to die? And why am I so *petrified*? Shame weighs my head down.

I only look up again when whispering escalates. Placing the disc behind my ear, I translate a nearby conversation. Someone says that the entire crew is here.

Only about two hundred bodies have spilled into the courtyard, which seems so small in comparison to StarDust. There, we roomed with over a thousand candidates.

With a passing hush, the courtyard goes eerily still. All eyes descend to the stone-carved woman.

"What's happenin'?" Mykal whispers to us.

Court is unblinking. "I'm unsure."

The statue suddenly glints and flickers out, and the woman in all her glory just *vanishes*. Leaving behind the fountain's base, petals floating in a tiny pool.

"Knew it was a fake," Mykal whispers proudly. "Was too pretty-looking to be real."

"It's a hologram," Court murmurs.

One that can produce mist and sound. And soon, a new image replaces the stone-carved woman, light beaming up from the fountain's base. Static crackles the picture. Less lifelike, the projection resembles a three-dimensional film and shows a starcraft viewing bay—a *familiar* viewing bay.

The *Romulus*.

Where we once stood against a long metal railing. Where we once glanced out the enormous window that oversaw the galaxy. Where we were told we're human.

Court stands more upright.

Mykal grinds his toothpick, all three of us recognizing the location and the cadets in sleek burgundy uniforms. Hands cupped out in front, the image halts on the young brassy-haired commander.

Theron and his brisk authority. He snaps his fingers and the picture zooms on his intimidating face: slanted forehead, hooked nose, and dark eyes lost within black pupils.

Lucretzia's crew sucks in apprehensive breaths, others huff out angrily. Strain wrenching the air.

"Humans," Commander Theron says, voice unreadable. "We're broadcasting live from the *Romulus*. To remind you that we will take what is rightfully ours. Andola belongs to Saltarians, and nothing will stand in our way. Not your starcrafts, not your armor, and not your leaders."

He snaps.

The hologram swerves, and the *Lucretzia* crew jolts, everyone rousing like they've been rattled awake from a deep stupor. Voices and small cries in the courtyard intensify like a sickening chorus.

I can't look away.

Two women and one man are blindfolded, gagged, and kneeling on the *Romulus* viewing bay. All three seem young from my vantage point. Wrists cuffed and an iron collar locked around their throats, bronze armor still protecting their chests, they breathe raggedly but stay calm. And motionless.

None of them yank at their chains.

None of them scream through their gags.

On their breastplates, I can read the symbol using the EI. Tapping the disc once, I realize that the letter *A* stands on five lines.

The admirals of the Earthen Fleet.

I'm so confused. Looking to the *Lucretzia* crew to the C-Jays behind me to *Stork*—I expect a readiness, a fight to go rescue their leaders. But no one moves.

Stork chugs liquor to the bottom of the bottle. Dulling a pain in his eyes.

I lean forward. Watching the admirals do nothing, not even as Theron loads a gun, and I think, *run*.

Stand.

Stand.

Run.

"Look away."

It takes me a second to realize that Stork is speaking to me, Court, and Mykal.

"Why?" Mykal asks like it's a dumb request.

And all four of us are staring at one another as violent gunshots ring out, three rapid-fire *pops*. The *Lucretzia* crew screams into guttural sobs. Wailing like *nothing* I've ever heard.

I open my mouth, baffled as the people on the balconies cry and embrace, arms wrapped tightly around each other. Hands tangled comfortingly in hair.

I focus back on the hologram: three bodies crumpled together, blood soaked beneath their lifeless limbs.

Lifeless.

What . . . "What just happened?" I ask, just as the hologram recedes and the stone-carved woman returns, the rushing water more ominous.

Court pries his methodical gaze off the fountain. "They're dead."

Stork hops back onto the observational deck. "They were killed."

Killed.

Life can't be taken like that on Saltare . . . from Saltarians. I've never seen anyone be killed before, but when Bastell was hunting Court, I feared that ending.

I stare off, unsure of what I feel, and I mutter, "Let their souls find peace."

Mykal nods wholeheartedly, and he brings his hands together in robust applause. I would've joined too, so I could respect the dead, but the noise drops uncomfortably.

He stops.

And a dense air compounds, tears sniffed back, and the crew's anguish morphs to enraged horror.

"What's wrong with you?!" a girl screeches.

Mykal is hot all over, and Court wraps a firm arm around his waist and whispers in his ear.

She wails again. "WHAT'S WRONG WITH—"

"He meant no offense to you!" I holler back over the balcony. Not against spitting if I have to. I will toss a wad if someone means to shame him again.

"Knave!" a few people shout, as though telling Stork to wrangle us.

Stork motions an *okay* to a young woman down at the fountain's base. Fiery red braids line her scalp, inked rings tattooed around her tawny-olive biceps. I read CAPT over four lines on her breastplate.

I figure she must be Captain Venita.

Court drops his arm from Mykal and then seizes Stork by the elbow.

"Mate—"

"Tell me they didn't give their lives for ours," Court says urgently. "Tell me that wasn't the *trade*."

Oh.

Gods.

To help free us from the brig, the admirals let the Saltarians murder them.

Sickness churns, and I wait on edge for Stork to shake his head and say *never*. Because who would ever do such an irrational thing?

He doesn't shake his head.

Doesn't deny.

He just says, "Follow me."

Stork brings us inside a stuffy storage pantry. Boxed and canned foods teeter on tall, uneven metallic shelves, hundreds of provisions enclosing us. I skim the labels: *marshmallow cereal, honey beans, peaches, coconut milk*—and once the door is locked, Court and Stork are in a standoff. Glares puncturing glares.

"You shouldn't have done that trade," Court says coldly.

Stork rests an elbow on the shelf. "There is a much bigger picture here."

"*Your* bigger picture," Court corrects. "I'm not indebted to anyone. We want no part in whatever you and your dead admirals have orchestrated—"

"They died *for you*." Stork sneers, stepping forward. Blond tendrils slip out of his hair tie and fall in his infuriated face.

"Heya!" Mykal wedges between their fuming stances and extends an arm toward Stork to protect Court.

Stork never backs down.

Neither does Court.

I stay near the canned fruits. Mulling over what this all means. *Someone died for me.* Three lives for ours. Court says we're not indebted, but I owe them something, don't I? My journal and all my scribbled *owed to*'s are on Saltare-3.

Left behind and unfulfilled. So many debts I never paid, and that remorse haunts me in mindful moments like these.

How do I even repay three deaths? What's the equivalent value to life lost too early?

"They didn't die for us," Court says in a smooth, biting tone. "They died for their cause. For their people—"

"You are their people!" Stork yells, and then inhales a deep, plentiful breath. Tucking loose blond strands behind his ears, he tries to say more calmly, "You. More than even me. *You* are who they want to protect and grow old and create new generations. *You*."

Court is painfully still. "And I should feel guilty. Remorseful?" His arched shoulders are full of authority that lifts my bones as high as his. As powerfully. "These are humans I've never met. A *people* that I've never seen until now. Why don't you go fight for Saltarians? Go fight for *your* people that you know nothing about."

Sighing into a weakened laugh, Stork shakes his head a few times. "You're a blast, mate." He reties his hair at his neck. "You lived on Saltare-3, a planet that remained out of war and conflict for centuries. Which means you have no clue what the majority of Saltarians think of humans. *Of you*."

It's true.

"Let me tell you." He unstraps the sword on his back.

Uneasiness ripples through us threefold. "What are you doing?" I ask, my spine pressed to the shelves. Pulse jumping irregularly.

Stork unsheathes the glinting blade, metal shining but scratched from use. He circles the room until he blocks the door.

Too near. I scoot over to where Mykal and Court stand side by side.

Court clasps my hand and draws me closer to Mykal, who tucks me in the middle, and I hear Court whisper to us, "He's drunk."

But Stork hardly wobbles or slurs. He twirls the sword effortlessly. If he really is sloshed, he's unlike any drunkard back home.

"Scared?" Stork asks. "I can murder you right here, and you will never be able to murder me." And then he tosses the blade. Sword clattering at our feet.

I don't understand him one bit.

"You are pathetic." Stork nearly seethes, iciness chilling his eyes. "*Weak.* So bloody fragile, why shouldn't I wipe you from existence? Let the superior species reign and the inferior die."

Cold snakes down my body, too nippy to speak.

Mykal crouches and grasps the leather hilt of the sword, heavier than I thought. I sense the weight pulling at his muscle.

Stork makes a *come hither* motion. "Fight me. Like I said, you'll lose. Always. Every time."

Mykal snatches the leather holster and strap, and then he sheathes the weapon.

Blade gliding smoothly into its protective case, Mykal tells him, "I'm not fighting my own brother, but I am taking your blade." He buckles the leather across his chest, sword on his back.

Feels even heavier, but Mykal adjusts the weight, able to carry the weapon.

I thought Stork would protest, but he's lost pondering. Until he shakes his head, "We're not brothers. I told you—"

"We share a pa, a ma," Mykal interjects. "That makes us brothers. And right about now, I'd say I'm the older one. 'Cause you're here acting a fool, waving a sword about, trying to frighten us into fearing what you'd like us to fight. But we've already been grabbed with malicious hands, baby brother. You don't need to be evil to show us evil exists."

Court nearly smiles, his pride for Mykal flooding me. Causing my lips to rise.

The three of us—we stand stronger.

Stork rests a hand on his side, like he's a little bit winded. But he lets out a curt laugh. "Look, I wish every Saltarian saw humans how I do—"

"How's that?" I ask, wondering how he pictures humans.

"Strong-willed, resilient." His reddened eyes flit to the floor before rising to us. "And selfless . . . I will never be able to sacrifice my life the way that the admirals just sacrificed theirs."

My brows furrow. "Why would you want to? Why would *anyone* do that?"

Stork tilts his head like the answer is in front of me. "Wouldn't you die to save each other?"

We all inhale.

No thought, no question—just a tremendous feeling.

Yes.

He props his shoulder blades to the door, a tangible loneliness separating him from us. "It's one of the deepest forms of love, and I'm not saying that every human feels it but they all have the chance."

Court goes rigid, unblinking. His joints rusting. "The need to save strangers, is that an innate human trait?"

"For some . . ." Stork says, voice trailing in curiosity. "Why? You asking for yourself? Because I wouldn't peg you as a guy who's overly compassionate to strangers."

Court laughs, the noise almost shrill in my lungs. His eyes well, and he cringes, all sound falling heavily.

Mykal squeezes his shoulder.

I remember easily why Court was sent to Vorkter Prison: he tried to revive people on their deathdays. That time where he was called Etian Valcastle—it perished inside him long ago, and I can practically feel Court scraping the ashes in his palms.

Stork nods a few times in realization. "You're not an Icecastle because you're a thief. You tried to save the dying." He's not asking.

He knows with such little information given.

The wart is smart.

Court locks eyes with Stork. "I'm not that person anymore," he tells him. "I'm not risking my life for strangers, and you can say that your admirals died selflessly, out of some *deep love,* but they died to save three people they need to stop a war. We're just pieces in your game—"

"This isn't a game to me," Stork rebuts hotly. "And it's definitely not a game to the lives that have protected Earth for centuries through fa—" He cuts himself off, rolls his eyes in frustration.

"Through what?" I prod. *What has Earth gone through?*

Stork reaches for the nearest shelf, pushes aside canned mushrooms, and snatches a jug of whiskey. Facing us, he pops the cork. "You're right. We don't just want you." He sidesteps over my question. "The Earthen Fleet needs you. All of you."

He puts the bottle to his lips and swigs. Wiping his mouth, he adds, "I couldn't care less why you want to help. Whether it's for each other, for the admirals who died so you could live, for answers I'll share later, or for humanity—the fleet still needs you."

"Why us?" I ask.

He tucks another lock of hair behind his ear. "Because, dove. You're the only humans to ever grow up on a Saltare planet. Because you have the best chance of blending in on Saltare-1.

Better than even me. The admirals knew that. We all know that."

The mission to retrieve a baby on Saltare-1—their best bet is us helping them.

I owe these people, and it'll be hard for me to say *no*. That suffocating guilt may not fester in Court or Mykal, but they'll share in mine. I hate that too.

"We already agreed to the retrieval operation," Court says suddenly, so resolute that my lips part a little. Mykal carries the same unbending emotion, loyal to this decision. "We didn't need to see your admirals die."

"Executed," Stork amends with a swig, most of us frowning at the new word and at his drinking.

Mykal nods to Stork. "How dangerous is this op-thing gonna be?"

He wipes his wet lip with his thumb. "First, you'll need training. Then, we'll see."

THIRTEEN

Mykal

After some fussing, Franny agrees to bathe first. Our cozy barracks have some kind of planetary appeal that I don't find as glamorous as Court or Franny.

Room shaped like a diamond, four long beds hug each wall. Covered with round pillows and constellation-patterned blankets, too heavy for the suffocating temps. I'd be doing everything in the nude if I could.

Spinning stools surround a circular table in the middle. And lastly, a frosted sliding door conceals a tiny bathroom.

No portholes. No breeze or hoot of an animal.

I only hear droplets hitting tile.

Shower.

What a strange thing. Lukewarm water drizzles on my biceps, steam swathing my body. I roll my shoulders, not liking the sensation.

If I'm not careful, I'm going to start feeling things I shouldn't be feeling. Like Franny's hands journeying over her curves. Privacy is still hard to give with this damned link.

Mind drifting, I struggle.

Franny is tentative at first. Not sticking her head beneath the pour, and as soon as she steps under, water drenches my hair. Soaks my face.

I pinch my eyes.

Bed. Bed.

I'm on one of the beds, round pillow chucked to the floor to make room for Court. His nose is deep in the same *Myths* book while sitting next to me. Our legs stretched out appreciatively.

Without shifting his eyes, he curves his arm around my broad frame. I'm swept up wholly into his senses. Dry. Water gone. His pulse thumps heartily against mine.

Toothpick between my teeth, I smile lopsidedly at him.

He's not looking. But his breath hitches. So he feels me as strongly as I do him.

Shirtless, we're both only in linen night skirts. Too hot for much else. Ink on his thighs and an Altian star tattoo tangled in the thick scars over his heart—he already looks like he's been through war. And I'm not excited to let him face another.

But I vow to protect him. To protect both of them from death. No matter where we go together.

For Court, he's put more pressure on himself with the *where* part. He's worried about leading us in a nasty direction.

It's why I can't steal his gaze from those damned pages.

"How's the book going?" I ask, shreds of fabric on my lap. I ripped up one of the blankets earlier and found a sewing kit with the cigarettes, and I've been stitching a pair of slacks.

Tunics look silly as can be. Like potato sacks.

Court skims a page. "It's two parts ridiculous, one part intriguing."

"A book you don't like." I grin. "I'm liking this book already."

Light passes through his grim eyes. "Aren't you busy sewing something hideous?"

I laugh. "Yeh, and you're gonna love this hideous thing on me." I chew a toothpick and eye the line of his squared jaw. Moodiness in his grave features and feelings, a constant companion that I like greeting.

"Probably," he whispers, his gaze stroking my mouth.

Fire flames my muscles, my yearning, and I toss my toothpick aside. His hand slides up my neck, tugging my hair—I feel the strands gliding between his fingers.

I lean in, untamed eagerness pounding our hearts.

"Mykal." He breathes against my lips.

Court. Not afraid, not hesitant. Not anymore.

I bridge the gap. Mouths melding, we pull together as fast and powerfully as a gun blast. Hands gripping. Kissing, a hunger awakens. Trembling my bones. Aching *closer.*

Closer.

More.

Our knees knock, and I roll on top of Court, my coarse hand to the headboard. Hips to hips, mouths not breaking apart. My other palm slides down his chest. A satisfied noise tickles his throat, but he says deeply, "*Wait,* Mykal." His pulse spikes.

"Court?" I draw back, panting for breath. Our lips stinging. His face is all hard lines. All worries.

Gods bless. I sit on my ass between his spread legs while he pulls himself up. Rigid, jaw tensed. If someone's been halting and hesitating recently, it's been him.

I don't see why. Other than he fears the link is growing stronger, but he didn't mind as much as I did about that.

"Is it 'cause I smell?" I ask. I haven't bathed yet.

He rolls his eyes. "No." He finds his book entwined in the shredded blanket that I'd been sewing.

I rest my forearms on my bent knees. "Is it your brother?"

"What?" Court frowns.

I shrug and stick another toothpick in my mouth. "Kinden didn't like me much. Maybe that's stuck with you."

Hurt clenches his lungs. And I feel that I'm wrong. "I'd never stop kissing you because of Kinden," he confirms, but he stares off at the wall. "And the likelihood that I'll see him again is *small.*"

"You may," I say hopefully.

He doubts. "If there's a future war, maybe I will. And we'll be against one another."

I hadn't thought about that. Saltarians versus humans, and Kinden would be on the opposite side.

Pain grips Court's throat. He swallows a rock. "I don't wish to fight my brother." He's expressed how he feels empty for Saltarians and for humans. I understand that coldness in him. After all he's been through, I know why it's there. Self-preservation is what he's best at.

But he's not all cold.

Court clings to what he loves because what he loves makes him feel more and more alive.

And he loves Kinden.

A world where he has to go head-to-head with his brother, again, will chip more of Court away. I can't have that happen.

"We're not going to war," I say certainly. "We'll be finding this magical baby and all will be right."

He drops his gaze. "We could fail, and as certain as I am that we can run from war and the *Lucretzia,* I don't think she'll desert the fleet. Not after the admirals died to save us."

We both know Franny well. Guilt will be eating at her spirit if she doesn't repay them somehow.

"I won't be able to stop her," Court whispers, "but I also can't fight for them." He grinds his teeth, pained at that scenario.

Queasiness roils my insides. "Don't go predicting the future, Court," I tell him. "It'll be making you even more miserable."

He lets out a sound that's almost a laugh. "Retrieve a baby. Hide Earth," he muses. "Sounds more impossible than entering StarDust and flying to space."

I chew on the flavorless toothpick. "You're the one always chasing impossible things. I'm just along for the ride."

Court almost, *almost* smiles. He taps his fingers to the *Myths* book. Weight bearing on his chest.

I scratch at my neck. "You gonna tell me why you pulled away from me or should I keep guessing?"

His head lowers, hair brushing his lashes.

All right, I'll be guessing. Not minding talking when he's

quiet. I think on how I'm rough. Bedding in Grenpale wasn't about tender hands, and he's been hurt in the past.

"I'll be trying my toughest to be gentle with you," I tell him.

Something bright flutters in his chest. He lifts his head. "I know you will."

"It's not that?" I realize. "The link, then?"

He stiffens.

It has to do with the link.

Court holds my gaze. "On Saltare-3," he starts explaining, "I was never too concerned that people would learn about our link. No one would draw that conclusion. It'd be so far-fetched and illogical. But the Saltare sister planets and Earth—we have no idea the extent of their knowledge yet."

I rub my temple. "Wouldn't they think it's just as strange? I've heard no one on the *Lucretzia* or *Romulus* talk about any sort of bond like we have."

Court thumbs the myth pages. "When Stork gave me this book, he said abilities aren't unheard of, so we can't be certain of anything."

My hand rests on my hot neck. "Can't we just ask Stork if linking exists?"

"No," he says. "It'll give us away, and if someone knows the three of us share emotions and senses, that information can be so easily used against us. Against *you*."

Understanding rushes at me, swaying me backward. "Which is why you've been drawing away."

He nods. "I know no one is around right now, but to be on the safe side, we should be more careful."

I'm not opposing that precaution. Anyone using our link against us would be a sort of torment I don't want to meet. I'm not always good at hiding the frustrations that come with linking, and I never thought someone might catch on till now.

Truth being, I'm not happy about any of this.

I glance at the book in his hand. "What if they have history books on this starcraft? Maybe there's something about linking in them."

Court solidifies at a sudden thought. "That device in the office . . . I think it was a computer. On the way to our barracks, I saw a girl searching some sort of database. It could be a catalogue with information."

I smile. "What are we waiting for? Let's go look—"

A banging crash resounds from the bathroom. Our heads swerve. *Franny.* Her senses are too faint to feel while I'm close to Court.

Something's wrong.

No talking, no lingering, we scramble off the bed and bolt toward the bathroom. Pulses in our throats.

"Franny!" Court calls.

I whip the frosty door to the side. Dark-blue tiles are wet and the showerhead is still spewing water. Franny lies naked beneath the spigot, conked out. Frailer than when I first picked her off the snow.

I squat near her, water soaking me. "Franny." I lightly jostle her arm.

Her eyes flutter.

In response, wooziness tries to pull at my lids. Hurriedly, Court shuts off the shower and then hands me a fuzzy towel. I wrap Franny up and lift her in my arms.

Sensing her better now, a bump throbs at the back of her head. "She must've fallen," I say, carrying her quickly to our room. "You can *slip* in those damned showers."

Court rebuts, "You can drown in a bathtub."

I set Franny gently on the bed and take a knee at her side. "Franny?" I peel a wet piece of hair off her face.

She fights to open her eyes.

Court is quiet for a second, concentrating on her senses. Heightening the link between them. "I don't think she slipped."

My muscles burn. "Someone pushed her?"

Court rolls his eyes. "Can you jump to a conclusion that makes more sense?"

I say a nasty Grenpalish word, never using it before with him.

His grays narrow. "That sounded vulgar."

"It was."

"Don't . . . fight," Franny whispers, stealing our attention tenfold. We shut our mouths, but only speak to ask if she's okay, what happened, and to tell her not to sit up too fast.

She rolls onto her back, towel tucked around her gaunt frame. "One second I was lathering soap in my hands . . . and then the next, I'm groggily hearing you call my name while I'm . . . on the ground."

"You fainted," Court says, nodding. "You need more food and rest."

Exhausted, uncontrollable tears spill from the corners of her eyes. "Fyke," she curses. "I was doing good at the whole taking care of myself thing, wasn't I? It's not my fault. I *care*. You know I care—"

"Heya, we know," I cut in. "We *know*." My eyes burn, and I turn to Court. Because his words will be having a greater effect. His opinion means a lot to us both.

"You're not to blame," Court says in his strict voice. "We were in a prison, Franny."

She wipes at her watery eyes but they keep watering.

A knot is in my chest.

"Just rest here." I comb her wet hair back and then stand. "Court and I will be grabbing some food, and we're going to look into a database thing." We explain the link, all that we need to learn and all that we decided.

She nods in understanding. "Go find some answers."

FOURTEEN

Franny

No luck. We've had *no* luck in snooping for answers. Court and Mykal snuck to the computer without anyone noticing, but it took an hour for them to figure out how to use the machine and access its database system. Finally, when they broadly searched for "linking" or "bonds" between humans, nothing arose.

Even worse, Court tried to find information about Earth, but every time he typed anything related to the planet, an alert popped on the screen that said, *password protected*.

Either the Earthen Fleet always keeps these details secret, or they're just hiding this knowledge from *us*.

Court is on edge, but we go where we're told in the morning. First to the dining hall where kitchen staff hand the crew copper bowls. People eat somberly on benches, heads hung. Voices morose. After we collect our bowls, Stork says we're having breakfast in the library.

He ushers us into the courtyard, balconies largely empty, and he works on opening one of the arched puzzle-locked doors. More sullen faces pass us. Crew lingering in the divine space that now feels haunted with sorrow and tears.

Two girls in military skirts are sitting slumped on the edge of the gurgling fountain. I recognize the red-braided girl as Captain Venita. Eyes bloodshot and hands clasped together, Venita wipes the other's wet cheek and then presses a loving kiss to her lips.

I ask Stork why everyone is so solemn.

The door to the library clicks, but he pauses and gives me a curious look. "It's not apparent to you?"

Embarrassed heat roasts my face. "Should it be . . . ?" My voice travels—suddenly, I taste sweetness on my tongue and notice a faint gag.

Court just ate a spoonful of the yellowish breakfast food beside me. And Mykal is no champion of *fruits*.

I try not to dry-heave or glance at either of them.

I bake twice-over and plant a scowl on Stork.

He looks *knowingly* at my flush, but I'm still holding down the theory that he doesn't know about our link. So the joke is on him.

Stork skims the length of me. Nearly smirking with boastful eyes that say, *what a naïve little dove.* "I guess you wouldn't know." He sticks his spoon in his mouth and somehow speaks clearly. "Saltarians don't grieve death like humans do." Pushing the door open with his back, he also adds, "The crew is in mourning. They watched their admirals die yesterday."

Mourning.

I wonder how long their sadness lasts. If it'll end soon or persist. Death is morbid here, I realize. But I see love in their tears as they weep for those they wished could've lived longer.

Yet Stork isn't grieving like them.

"Where are your tears for the dead?" I ask outright.

He's a bit taken aback. "You're a blunt girl."

"You're a cagey boy."

His smile is briny. And then he proves me right. Not answering back, he pushes into the grand library.

Instantly, Court, Mykal, and I halt, looking down at the squishy ground beneath our feet. Springy green-green grass. Dewy like it's just been watered.

I never thought this could exist on a starcraft. Glittering silver-cushioned benches are clustered in circles so crew can read or study together.

Stork walks backward and studies my awed reaction most of all. "You've never seen grass?"

"Not without snow," Court says austerely, his commanding presence carrying *no* ounce of naivety, despite us being new to this place.

I'm glad we have Court on our side.

Mykal scuffs a chunk with his heel, but the grass is lodged to the ground. "And our grass isn't fake."

Turning his back to us, Stork saunters farther inside. "The roots are hooked into a floor trap so the grass stays alive. Mine is as real as yours."

I cup my copper bowl and look wide and far. Musty-smelling old hardbacks of every size and color stack up high to the domed ceiling. More shelved books curve around the oval room.

One other person is here.

Nia rides a hovering platform, big enough for each sandaled foot. Hardbacks teetering in her arms, she zips to the left shelf with perfect balance. Curls bouncing on her shoulders.

Stork drops his spoon in his bowl and sticks two fingers in his mouth. Whistling. She doesn't hear, so he shouts, "Hopscotch!"

She peeks at us, eyes reddened, and the platform descends to the grass. Gloomily, she slogs the hardbacks over and dumps them onto the nearest bench.

We caused a stew yesterday when Mykal clapped for the dead, and while some crew are still miffed, most seem to aim their hurt toward the *Romulus*.

Nia is the same.

She nods kindly in greeting and comments on our clean state. Though her cheeks crinkle at Mykal, who chose to go bare-chested and dress in patched slacks.

"Hopscotch," Stork says. "Make sure the crew knows the library is off-limits for the week."

She huffs. "I hate reading on the digital tablets." But she nods. "You aren't going to the ceremony today?"

I haven't heard about any ceremony. I pretend not to listen and just push around the yellowish food. Already tasting the gritty substance and sweet bursts.

Court is eating in quiet contemplation.

"No," Stork says, unperturbed. "I'm training these three." He waves his spoon toward us.

Nia marches to a device that resembles an upscale vending machine. "You know, when I agreed to run collections, I didn't think it'd mean becoming a *book overlord*."

He takes a casual bite of food. "What a burden."

She types on the machine's screen and a flat handheld tablet pops out. "Thanks for nothing, Knave."

"Cheers," he calls while eyeing *my* bowl and spoon, breakfast uneaten. Mykal shovels food into his mouth with his fingers, avoiding all the dark-orange berries.

Nia waves back as she leaves, and we congregate around the books she left.

"What ceremony are you not attending?" Court asks and exchanges his bowl for a hardback. We all tap our translators to read the title: *Galactic Encyclopedia: Dis Pater.*

Stork sidles close to me, as though this is the most natural place to stand. When he could literally park his feet *anywhere*. His blue gaze flits to me even more than it does to Court.

Sweat builds under my pits. But I don't break our gaze. "He asked you a question."

"The new admirals are being sworn in today," Stork answers, and before anyone can jump in, he asks me, "Not hungry?" His tone and gradually rising smile indicate that he knows I truly am famished. He has this big-headed air that rubs me hotly.

I lift my chin. "How are the new admirals chosen?"

"Public vote." He watches me *not* eat. "You think I poisoned your food?"

No. "Maybe you did."

He turns fully to me, pauses while our eyes catch, and then

he scoops my sludge with his spoon. Taking a large bite, he swallows and smiles. "See, not poisoned."

Mykal and Court are very tense, their breaths caged. Watching Stork and me. My jaw aches as they clench their teeth.

They shouldn't be so vexed and pissy. Stork unnerves me in such aggravatingly *hot* strides. I feel the exact same as them.

I scoop a spoonful. "What is this anyway?"

"Cornmeal, bonnaberries, pecans, and mashed banana. Affectionately called *fleet grub*."

Chewing slowly, I'm not surprised by the taste or grittiness, but the consistency of fleet grub will take time to grow used to.

"You're not in line to be an admiral?" Court asks him.

From what I've learned, Stork has a high rank. It'd make sense that he'd be considered for the position.

"I'm ineligible," Stork admits.

Court flips through the *Dis Pater* encyclopedia, not even looking over. "Because you're Saltarian."

He pauses. "Mainly, yeah."

I chime in, "But you were raised human."

Stork abandons his bowl on a bench and puts his hands to his sculpted chest. "I'm still biologically Saltarian, dove."

Court lifts his gaze. "We're anatomically different?"

"We all have the same body parts, same organs," Stork explains, being more forthcoming today. Probably to help educate us for the mission's sake. "We look alike, but there are separations."

I sink down on our cluster of benches. Listening keenly, my pulse scampers fast. "Like what?"

"Your DNA. You have a double helix." He tips his head. "I have a triple."

Mayday.

Realizations sway me backward. "The Helix Reader," I mutter. On the *Romulus,* that's the name of the device that declared we were human.

Court looks faraway in thought. "It read our DNA."

Strangely, Stork lowers onto the bench beside me. One is occupied with books, but there are two other free ones in our circle.

I try not to give him attention, but I'm wholly invested in his words.

"A triple helix doesn't change my outward appearance, but my cerebral cortex develops at a faster speed." He unstraps a flask attached to his skirt's band. "Cognitively, Saltarians can do more at a younger age. We're more aware, more adept, brighter—"

"Court is a Wonder," Mykal says, licking grub off his fingers. "Blessed by the gods, he's as smart as they come."

Stork barely glances at Court, unsurprised by Mykal's declaration.

I narrow my eyes. "You know about Wonders?"

Stork nods. "Wonders exist on all Saltare planets. It's a way for society to make use of intelligent Babes and Fast-Trackers before they die. They allow the brightest children to attend school and enter Influential jobs." Court has a stern *I told you so* face.

Mykal makes a noise, still believing our gods kissed Court.

My brows bunch. "If human children aren't as smart as Saltarian children, how'd he become a Wonder over others?" He had to take a test. And at StarDust, Court consistently ranked at the top of the class.

Stork uncaps his flask. "Court is a genius." Before he sips, he clarifies, "An extraordinarily smart human."

Genius. I pocket all these new words.

"Wonder suits him more," Mykal declares. "Sounds prettier."

Court nearly smiles, but his mouth forms a grave line. "What's the average age of human pilots and drivers?"

I drop my head, pulse ratcheting.

"Why do you ask?" Stork questions, looking curiously between us.

He's asking for me.

Court knows I'd want this answer. To make more sense of who I am.

I thought I'd be gushing forth all my stories about driving by now. Even the notion that the retrieval operation *may* involve piloting enthuses me. What I'd give to fly one of those jets parked in the docking bay.

But here and now, my stomach tumbles in nervous patterns. I perspire worse, tunic suctioning to my breasts. I waft the fabric.

I'm less frightened at unleashing this secret for *secrecy's* sake. Mostly, I'm anxious to share this with Stork. Someone who may not understand. Who may poke fun. Driving is such a big part of my old life.

With Zimmer, I blurted out my past almost too easily. He was a Fast-Tracker. Something familiar.

Stork is the opposite, and his unfamiliarity both excites and terrifies me.

Standing side by side, Court and Mykal are quiet, not about to share my old job without approval. Court senses my uneasiness and tells Stork, "No significant reason."

My stomach clenches at the lie.

Stork doesn't prod. "Humans can't be younger than fourteen to drive or pilot."

Fourteen? I was capable of driving *much* earlier than fourteen—maybe all these humans are underestimating themselves.

"You were fourteen when you first sat behind a wheel?" I ask him.

He grins. "An exception was made for me. I started at eight."

Same age as me. I consider telling him, but nerves attack my insides. Shifting uneasily, I pull my feet on the bench.

"What about reproduction?" Court asks.

Stork appraises him in a long sweep. "You were a doctor," he states as plainly as Court did to him about Saltarians not being allowed an admiral position. Mykal and I already agreed that both are too clever for their own good.

Court looks humorless. "Reproduction—"

"Is identical," Stork cuts in. "We all reproduce the same way. Sorry to broach this, dove, but . . ." He rotates to speak directly to me. "The fleet nurses asked about your cycle and you said you didn't understand."

I shrug, confusion compounding with Mykal and Court. "It's an odd question."

Stork thinks for half a second, staring at the domed ceiling. His blues fall to me. "Your bleeding."

He's not referring to my *nose* bleeding. "Right, that. I never had a bleeding in the brig—and *not* because I'm with child," I add quickly. "I've been malnourished." Court calmed my paranoid fears back in the brig. I thought I might've been dying inside; I'd never missed a bleeding before.

No one says anything.

"Right?" I question my rational thinking.

"Did Court tell you about malnourishment?" Stork wonders.

"Maybe . . ." I feel like we're all playing an Influential board game, and I'm the chump trailing behind.

Stork unconsciously touches his sapphire earring, shaped in what he said was a *blue jay*. "Growing up, who told you about bleedings?"

"Are you afraid I've been told wrong? Have I been?" *Stop panicking, Franny.* I bite the inside of my mouth and scowl.

Very softly, Stork says, "I reckon you weren't told a lot."

So I'm not wrong.

Just uneducated.

Court has a pitying melancholy that lowers him onto a bench. Sitting beside him, Mykal leaves his bowl behind and opens a pack of cigarettes, breathing harsh breaths. He's not enjoying our emotions.

"Court?" I ask.

"You didn't know there could be other reasons you missed a bleeding," he reminds me.

"But I knew *enough*," I retort. "My mom prepared me and said it'd come every month and when it stopped, it meant I was with child. At the orphanage, I learned *more*." I point at my chest, defending my decent knowledge that I thought would last me till death. "I knew to drink roselthorn broth if I planned to bed a boy and didn't want a baby. Most FTs did it."

All three boys are silent, letting me finish.

I'm not done yet. Sweltering to a stance, I continue. "My mom taught me *all* she knew. I wasn't supposed to be around for long. Why should I know about sicknesses when I'd die at seventeen years anyway? That's why I know what I know, and I loved my life. So save your pity for the real misfortunate. Because it's not *me*."

Stork tries to shelter a growing smile. He hooks my gaze an extra beat.

Court nods several times; his understanding is one of the best feelings. Like wading in warm waters. I exhale fully.

Mykal raises his hands in defense. "Heya, I never pitied you, little love. Just minding myself here." He upturns my lips most of all.

And I ease back down. Just to double-check, I ask Stork, "is malnourishment the cause?"

"Highly likely," he confirms.

Good.

Since Stork is obliging us for a change, Court shuts the encyclopedia and asks, "Back when both races lived on Earth, did anyone learn what happens when a Saltarian and a human conceive a child together?"

My brows fly off my face. Why in the hells would Court want to know that?

Stork sips from his flask. Licking liquor off his lips, he says, "There's a fifty percent chance the baby would be human or Saltarian. It hasn't been a factor in human population."

Maybe that's why Court asked. I sit up out of a slouch. "Are there any Saltarians still on Earth?"

"I'm the only recorded one." He flashes a bitter smile. "You want to know the main difference between us? The triple helix affects *body chemistry*, and in turn, Saltarians differ when it comes to mortality. We live longer than humans." He raises his flask. "I'll outlive you three. Cheers." He swigs.

Mykal cringes at his drinking. Disgruntled every time Stork puts the rim to his lips.

I've had my fair share of binges, so it's hard to be snappy. And I focus on the life span bit. "So how old can we be?" The *Lucretzia* crew ranges in age, some in their forties or fifties. So I'm not too distressed.

"Early one hundreds," Stork admits.

I smile. *That's old.*

Mykal also wears a lopsided grin.

We all thought we'd die much, *much* earlier. To hear about this possibility is good news.

Stork swishes his flask. "Body chemistry is also why we've been immune to most lethal affronts. Even before deathdays were known, Saltarians couldn't die easily. The invention of Death Readers just made our immunity more of a certainty."

Court processes with another faraway look.

Mykal asks, "You always drink like you're dying of thirst, baby brother?"

Stork lets out a short laugh. "Saltarians can hold their liquor down for longer."

Resting my chin on my knee, I tell him, "I've seen FTs who were sloshed drinking less than you."

He considers this quietly and says something about body mass and alcohol. He reroutes the topic in a flash. "I brought you all to the library for the retrieval op. You all need proper knowledge about Earth and Saltare before we can move forward." He nods to the shelves. "We have a small collection of physical books here."

To us, this is humongous. Court is even astonished at the amount of hardbacks, and he's traveled to all the fancy Influential places.

"At first," Stork continues, "we only held a trillion volumes in the digital databases, but with the threat of Earth being overrun, the Republic of Gaia agreed to send these copies for historical purposes. No one is allowed to remove the hardbacks from the library. You're free to read them here. Otherwise, you'll have to take a digital pad."

Court frowns. "You already lent me the *Myths* hardback."

Stork caps his flask. "That book comes from my personal collection. I like graphic novels and the occasional fable, but to get physical copies, I have to purchase them at auction. I bought the *Myths* hardback about a year ago."

Finished eating, I realize that Stork is saying we should read the big pile of books. Court is already scouring another one, but the thought of perusing these texts pounds my head. I hope they're not too dense.

Mykal seems to be avoiding the mental slog too. Puffing on a cigarette. He's been trying to take short drags of his cig, and Court and I can handle easygoing smoking.

"I have a new plan," I tell Stork. "What if you skip the part where we read and you just tell me what I need to know?"

Court sends me a strict look.

I sigh hard and snatch a book. Not wanting to let him down, but I trust Court to read quickly and verify what Stork says. I've chosen *Earth, 30th Century*.

My lips part. "Wait, you're letting us read about Earth?"

His brows arch mockingly. "Why are you so surprised?"

Court answers first, "We tried to search your computer for information about Earth. Everything was password protected."

Stork massages his own shoulder, tensed. Thinking, he sucks in a breath. "See, here's the thing, mate, I can't tell you about thirty-sixth-century Earth."

Cig in mouth, Mykal mumbles, "Why not?"

"So you're hiding this information just from us," Court confirms.

I think about Nia, Arden, and Barrett. "If we ask the crew—"

"They won't be helpful. Most have no clearance for the scope of information you're seeking," Stork says. "And some have been spaceborne for decades."

Yet they fight for Earth. I turn and face him. "You promised you'd tell us information while we're here."

Stork laughs like I'm joking, but he sees my seriousness. "You haven't even been here for a week."

"Tomorrow, you'll tell us about Earth."

He shakes his head, almost laughing in disbelief. "No bloody chance."

"How long is training going to last?" I question.

"Two months."

"Then in one month, you'll tell us about—"

"When we reach Saltare-1," he interjects but lets his voice drag like he's reconsidering. He pushes forward. ". . . Then I'll share what I know about Earth." He sighs out a tight breath, and I have a feeling this wasn't his original plan.

That's mostly why I nod. "Deal."

He sips his liquor and hands me the flask. "We drink to deal—"

"I remember what you said." I put my mouth to the rim. Slowly swigging to help Court and Mykal with the taste, and the liquor runs sharply down my throat.

Mykal coughs softly into his shoulder.

Before Stork glances at him, I say, "So are you going to tell us about Earth's and Saltare's past?"

He reclaims his flask. "We'd have to start at the beginning. To well over a thousand years ago. Two two twenty-two hundred."

2-2-2200 seems so long ago.

Stork continues, "The day that Saltarians landed on Earth."

"That's wrong," Court says, seizing Stork's gaze. "Saltarians were on Andola before anyone else."

I nod. "I read that in one of our history books too." And StarDust taught us as much.

Stork laughs into a groan. "Terrific." He gathers his snowy-white hair and ties the strands back. "Let's do a training exercise, forget everything Saltare ever taught you about history."

Court glares. "Your history could be the inaccurate one."

"No, see, our version matches forty other species. The one version that stands all on its own is Saltare," he says casually. "We don't rename planets to suit our own agenda. That's what Saltare does. For millennia, they've been *jumping* from planet to planet. Usually uninhabited ones. They stay as long as they're welcome, rename the planet to Saltare, and once they leave, the planet becomes Andola. Why do you think there are five current Saltares?"

Because Saltarians are currently living on five different planets. I never thought that was strange.

I slump forward. Elbows on my thighs. My mind so full.

Stork continues, "Saltarians entered Earth's galaxy and chose to land on the planet *because* of the similarities between humans and Saltarians. It was said to be for research purposes. Humans welcomed them so that humans could learn more about triple helixes, while Saltarians collected information on the double. For the most part, the relationship was amicable." He stares at his flask. ". . . Saltarians and humans coexisted peacefully for over two hundred years. Everything changed in 2414."

"The year deathdays were discovered," Court says, no longer thumbing vigorously through his hardback. He's interested in what Stork has to share too.

"Yeah." Stork nods. "Saltarians invented Death Readers and learned the day we'd die. Humans didn't." He laughs in thought. "To say it created turmoil would be an understatement of the millennia. By 2450, relations between Saltarians and humans were unsalvageable. Saltarians were *banished* from Earth in World War V."

I hug my book to my chest. "Why would they be so determined to take Earth back if it never belonged to them?"

Stork sighs with a solemn shake of his head. "Greed. *Pride*. Earth was the first planet that Saltarians didn't leave of their own accord. We're talking about *billions* of years of Saltare history where a united people peacefully jumped between planets. And here, they were forcibly exiled. It bothered Saltarian leaders, and it's why your history has been warped."

He goes on to explain that some of our language has human origins, even our early history. Woolly mammoths existed only on Earth, not on any Saltare world, and all the extinct animals in our natural history museums were *Earthen* mammals, reptiles, and amphibians. Though Saltarians did transport some wildlife from Earth to the Saltare planets.

Court asks, "How do you know all of this?"

"Because you can read it, listen to it, and watch it. The same event from *multiple* sources," he says. "Our history isn't absolute, but it's recorded much better than anything Saltare has done for its own people."

Brows cinching in deep thought, something nags at my brain. A missing piece to the greater picture. I replay all that Stork shared. Trying to imagine this inconceivable Earth.

I picture a place where deathdays were invented.

How for the *first time* people began to learn the day they'll die. But both humans and Saltarians must've been tested. Stork said that humans never learned their deathdays.

Neither did we.

"Stork," I say with a tense breath. "When humans were tested for deathdays, what happened to them?"

He tucks a fallen piece of hair back. "Clarify."

"Death Readers, the date that shows on the device for Saltarians is a deathday, but what date would appear for humans? What did that day mean?" For me, it was the day I was *supposed* to die. But the next day, I woke up in a dirtied alleyway. Cold. Helpless. And then two boys found me.

They bent down and asked if they could help me.

I said, *yes*.

I often wonder, if that date on the Death Reader is the day a human becomes linked to someone else.

Stork seems to stare right through me, and all I can think is, *does he know? Does it mean other humans are linked too?*

He blinks rapidly and rubs his temple. "Look, humans are no longer allowed to test their deathdays. The Republic of Gaia passed a law over a thousand years ago."

"You didn't answer her question," Court snaps.

"I didn't," Stork agrees. "I don't answer *many* of your questions, and I've also realized that doesn't stop you from asking them a billion and one times. But we all have our flaws." Not letting us edge in a word, he adds, "I told Hopscotch to pull this stack of books from our archive. If you prefer digital, I'll flag a folder in the digital library that covers the topic."

Court shoots me a look that says, *keep pressing*. When we awoke this morning, I mentioned how I'd try to interrogate Stork more. Or as Court called it—*irritating* Stork.

"But you know," I prod further. "You know what the date means for humans?"

A quarter of a smile lifts his lips and he shakes his head slowly. "You're incorrigible."

I should be grating on him, but he looks amused. Pressing my lips together, I stare at him openly, trying to find a crack I can wiggle through.

He studies me just as freely. And then suddenly, *piercing* sirens blare. We all turn. My hands fly to my ears, and blue lights strobe aggressively.

Stork's face folds into seriousness. Swiftly, he's on his feet and running to the door.

We're all quick to follow. Storming after, I yell over the sirens, "What's going on?!" I'm not sure he can hear me.

Stork shoves into the courtyard. More blue lights blink along balconies, and the caustic siren wails more.

I wince and distinguish an automated voice.

"*East Wing Lockdown. West Wing Lockdown. North Wing Lockdown. South Wing C-Jays to the Docking Bay. Code Blue. Code Blue.*"

Stork peers back at us. "Saltarians are on the ship."

FIFTEEN

Court

Stork instructs us to *stay put* in our barracks. For our safety. He leaves us in the atrium.

Pure chaos, sirens blaring, blue lights flashing and glistening off the plunge pool, *Lucretzia*'s crew rushes forward and backward. Some seek solace in their rooms, others prepare for a confrontation. Armoring their chests and heads, their hurried footsteps descend a spiral staircase.

Nothing inside me says to listen to Stork.

To wait.

I've never been good at waiting. Logic, reason, they beckon me to see the fight firsthand. To not remain in darkness in this room. The only interaction between Saltarians and humans that I've witnessed has been an execution of the fleet admirals.

I'd like to see more. To understand more.

Knowledge has always been my greatest asset, and denying myself of that is like purposefully wedging my body in a suffocating cage.

It's settled. Just like that. I can't—*I can't wait.*

But it's a risk, one that I'm not so willing to pull Franny and Mykal into. "You two stay here—"

"*No*," Mykal growls, eyes darkening. He understands what I'm about to do.

"I need to see both sides," I tell him, conviction in my voice. "I need to *see* the differences." *I need to see what we're fighting for.*

Mykal's nose flares. "I'm not letting you go alone."

"We're coming along," Franny says heatedly, "*thank you very much.*"

There is no time to weigh options and dangers and lives. Hastily, I say, "Then we have to be quick." I hurry.

Sprinting, I chase after the clamoring C-Jays in military garb. We pass through the first silver-curtained archway and descend the spiral staircase in dizzying turn after turn, Franny and then Mykal right behind me.

No crew flinches at our presence, all engrossed in this mad dash. All focused on the threat at large.

As soon as we touch the flat tarmac—combat jets and various starcrafts parked in endless rows—I easily spot the C-Jays. Nearly one hundred of them *block* something from view on the docking bay. They stand at the ready. Sporting bronze helmets and leather skirts, weapons are unsheathed and aimed straight ahead.

I can't see the Saltarians, and my only plan is to remain on the outskirts. Get a better vantage, but try and stay unseen. My wish is to watch, not interfere.

Screams ravage from the Saltarian enemies. And then I hear something more distinguishable between the garbled yells.

It's muffled at first.

I can't be sure.

Franny reaches out for my hand and I meet her widened, confused eyes.

I hear it now. A desperate last attempt. A plea.

"ETIAN!"

Heart in throat, I run.

SIXTEEN

Court

E tian!" he screams again. Gutturally. Pleadingly.

Kinden has found us? Impossible, illogical—and yet, my older brother once believed in the unbelievable. He believed that I could be alive when I was supposed to be dead.

I hear him and his unfailing honesty in my mind, as children.

I see him just before we headed to bed, as he said, "Wake me before you leave."

Wake me before you leave.

Crushing sadness builds on top of me and somehow my feet carry me ahead. I run.

Kinden can't die for me, but at StarDust, he committed a crime worth a life sentence in Vorkter, so we could fly off the planet. So I could be free.

There is no bigger sacrifice he could've made.

"BROTHER!" His voice is louder, more caustic and urgent.

Kinden.

His name claws tooth-and-nail to reach my lips.

I run faster.

Coming upon the horde of C-Jays, I push through. Swiftly, I slip between armored bodies and create a pathway.

Mykal is wider and bumps into shoulders. Every *whack* of muscle on muscle, bone to bone, almost ropes me backward. Like the force is from me, but I blink hard out of the sensation.

Franny shoves her way forward.

We draw suspicion and gazes, but no one gropes for Mykal.

No one seizes Franny. No one lays a hand on us, and as we race toward the screams, C-Jays begin to call out, "Knave!"

Stork is the only one allowed to touch us.

A few try to barricade me from the scene. "You shouldn't be here!" a man yells, puffing his chest out. "These are Saltarians; they want to murder you, mate!"

He won't.

I'm tall, but their helmets shield my view.

Screams are mangled with curses and threats—and I imagine my brother beneath the tip of a blade. My chest ignites on fire, blazing with more than just my rampant emotion.

Eyes burnt and neck strained, I yell out, "KINDEN!"

"BROTHER!" His voice is muffled but distinctly who I remember. Who I know.

Every tendon in my body snaps into action. Not slowing, I slip past another shoulder. The Knave Squadron is on the front line. Their backs to us, Arden still wears his weapon.

With unseen hands, I pluck an arrow out of his quiver and unbuckle a strap. Able to slip off the bow. I glide around his towering frame.

Barrett catches sight of me—and then Mykal rams his weight into him. The C-Jay barrels forward and crashes onto his knees.

I breach the barricade.

And like a whip of wind, I spin onto the side. Kinden, the Soarcastle sisters, and Zimmer are kneeling, gagged with cloth, wrists bound with rope, and I place the arrow to the bow and draw the string back.

I aim the iron point at the C-Jays. Almost a hundred wary gazes dart to leaders.

I grit down, "He's my brother!"

"He's Saltarian!" more than one person shouts.

Several vehement exclamations follow.

"He's not your brother!"

"He doesn't bloody care about you!"

"He'll kill you!"

Kinden is on his knees, unable to understand their human language, and even so, he's only staring at me. Glassy-eyed, like he discovered I came back to life for a second time.

"Stand down, Court!" Stork yells, rushing through the nearly arm-locked C-Jays to reach Franny. She struggles to bypass Captain Venita, who uses a metal shield to obstruct her passage.

"They're our friends!" Franny screams. "You can trust them! *Let them go*; let them go!"

Mykal has already stormed ahead. On my side, he drops to his knees and unbinds my brother first. I sense the knotted and frayed rope between his rough fingers.

Padgett Soarcastle has her back to her younger sister. Attempting to untie one another's rope.

Zimmer stays still. Scrawny and shaggy-haired, he looks untroubled. Like he's on a leisure adventure.

"First, lower your weapons," I demand, not raising my voice. Taut string is pressed tensely against my nose and lips, fingers beneath my chin.

I only know archery because of Mykal.

He taught me in the winter wood.

C-Jays protest, yelling, "Don't be dim! They'll hurt you!"

"We know these Saltarians," I say smoothly. "Drop your weapons. They will not harm anyone on the *Lucretzia*."

"He's dehydrated!" a C-Jay shouts. "Messed up in the head."

"This is what happens when they've been starved for thirty-one days."

"It's not their fault."

Gods dammit.

I refuse to question my sanity. These people have none of my memories. None of my history. I'm a boy of eighteen years, but I've lived beyond anything they can possibly comprehend.

Mykal unravels Kinden's rope and runs to help Zimmer.

Hands free, Kinden yanks off his gag and picks himself up

to a self-important stance. Unafraid. Confidence still ringing out in every fiber of his being, my brother saunters over to me.

C-Jays scream so forcefully. Faces reddening and voices cracking in desperate pleas. Begging me to move, to look out.

To protect myself.

Understanding hits me all at once.

I blink back brutal emotion. Choked on a raw feeling.

Humanity.

I always dreamed about a world where people try to save other people. Now I'm aiming an arrow at what I fought for. What I went to prison for. What I would've died for.

My chin quakes, my arms tremble.

Kinden nears, seeing them. Seeing me. And he cups my bicep. "This is breaking you, little brother." He guides my arm down with my weapon. "I'll survive their anger."

I inhale, lashes wet as I blink. And I release my grip on the bow and arrow. Weapon clattering to the ground.

A hush sweeps over the C-Jays. Whispering, their wide eyes drift from Kinden to me and me to Kinden.

My chest hits the ground—*no*, I'm standing. I'm upright.

Franny.

It's Franny.

She just dove beneath Venita's shield. Crawling out toward us, she shimmies her elbows on the tarmac until she rises to her feet.

Stork catches her around the waist—his grip is loose. I sense just how little he holds on, and Franny does too. Questions furrow her brows, and her boil dies to a simmer.

Mykal only halfway unties Zimmer before shooting upward. Fists clenched, he's about to charge—

"Mykal, wait," I call.

Nose flaring, he fumes and treks over to me, concentrating more on her senses.

Kinden asks me, "You trust the one with the earring?"

"Somewhat," I admit.

Mykal splays his arm over my stiffened shoulders and hugs me tight to his side—I breathe deeper in his embrace.

Gently, Stork eases Franny back into his chest. "No one approach or hurt the Saltarians," he tells the C-Jays, and to the three of us, he says in the same human language, "Trust me. The fleet needs to trust *them* before we can move forward in unison."

He's aware the *Saga 4* can't understand this conversation.

He plans to test their loyalty, and Franny comprehends this as well. Still, I worry. Mykal worries, but then she nods fiercely to me. To him.

She's fine.

I hang on to the words. Letting them sink in until my concern recedes little by little.

She's fine.

I nod back.

Our pulses sync in an assured rhythm.

"On the count of three," Venita bellows to the fleet. "One."

Gem and Padgett untangle themselves and wrench their gags to their necks.

"Two."

Gem—the younger and chattier sister—whips her head to me, blond hair frizzed and sticking up. "What are they saying?" Gem pants for breath.

"Court?" Padgett questions.

I have to lie. For their sake. "I'm unsure."

"Three!" Venita yells and launches a spiked club to Stork.

Effortlessly clasping the handle, he lifts the spikes against Franny's throat.

"Heya! You don't know what you're doing!" Zimmer struggles to his feet, tearing at the last shreds of rope on his wrists in alarm. "She can *die*! She's not one of us! *She's not one of us!*"

A pang of hurt rocks Franny back.

In perfect Saltarian, Stork tells my brother and friends, "You want to save her, come fight for her. Otherwise, watch her die."

THE LAST HOPE   149

Zimmer curses at Stork, yelling obscenities, and he races forward, slipping on rope that falls off his wrist. He catches his balance and keeps pace. "Are you mad?!"

Stork moves Franny into Venita's arms, and wearing a protective breastplate but no helmet, he confronts Zimmer.

"Don't hurt him!" Franny shouts at Stork, fear ratcheting her voice.

He drops the club.

Zimmer slams a fist into his jaw, and Stork hardly flinches before returning a blow to his gut. The Fast-Tracker doubles over, and while they both tussle, I look to my right.

The Soarcastle sisters are more methodical. Devising a strategy, Padgett runs to my fallen weapon. "Take this." She scrambles to pick up the bow and arrow. "You know how to use it." She tries to push the weapon to my chest, but I raise my hands.

She freezes. "What am I missing, Court?"

"Release your grip!" Gem yells, sprinting her fastest to Venita, who curves her bicep around Franny's neck.

"Gem!" Padgett shouts, taking one step toward her sister—and then Stork pushes Zimmer hard and he staggers back.

Stork narrows his gaze at the youngest Soarcastle. Probably thinking the same as me. *What is she going to do without a weapon?*

Gem dives.

For Venita's legs.

The Earthen captain is quicker. She kicks Gem, sandaled foot meeting cheek in a hard *thwack*.

Padgett forgets about my unknown intentions, and she lifts the bow and arrow—now aimed for Venita. "Let Franny go. Lest you want a hole in your head."

Stork holds out a hand. "There's no need for that." His voice is casual, unconcerned. "How about we just go with a deal?" His Saltarian is fluent and crisp and the other C-Jays glance to him with utter confusion.

"What kind of deal?" Kinden asks.

My nerves shift, unsettled. Not my nerves . . . *Mykal.*

He doesn't know if this is another ploy.

It has to be.

"We'll let Franny go," Stork says. "If all four of you agree to spend the same time in our brig that your friends spent in yours." *Thirty-one-days.*

No . . .

Kinden glares. "That wasn't *our* brig."

"I need an answer," Stork says. "Five seconds."

This better be another ruse. I won't have my brother imprisoned on any starcraft. But my stomach twists, sickened. This time Franny is the origin. Her eyes ping from Zimmer to Gem. She wouldn't wish what we went through on anyone, least of all them.

"Two," Stork counts down.

"We'll do it," Gem says first. "Padgett and I. We'll go to your brig. As long as you don't hurt Franny."

"Me too." Zimmer nods.

Kinden glances at me, wary. He doesn't want to leave me. I don't want him to either.

Stork sees this. "It's all four of you or no deal."

"Go," I tell Kinden. "I'll see you later." *It's a ruse,* I remind myself. He's not going anywhere.

Kinden pats a hand on my shoulder before he looks to Stork. "Thirty-one days. Not a day more."

"It's a deal," Stork says and then nods to Venita. In the human language, he says, "Release Franny. Take these four to the brig."

Everything moves too quickly.

Color drains from Mykal's cheeks. Bile rises to my throat. Franny is frozen in shock. All three of us, rooted to the ground in confusion. Hands grab at my brother. Hands grab at Gem and Padgett. Hands grab at Zimmer. And all four of them are compliant as they're dragged away.

My head only floats back to my body when I lose sight of

Kinden. The remaining C-Jays disperse, leaving a barren docking bay.

Stork is my first thought. "You bastard," I growl.

"You have to trust me," Stork says, worry cinching his blue eyes.

"You're making it rather fucking difficult," I sneer.

"They're not really headed for the brig . . . right?" Mykal asks.

Stork takes a tight breath. "Just for a day—"

"You lying wart," Franny curses.

"I couldn't mention this part," Stork explains. "The fleet needs to trust them. And a piss-poor fistfight from that scrawny one won't cut it. One *voluntary* day in the brig should do the job, and it'll be enough to prove that your Saltarian friends care about humans. That we're all on the same side."

But Kinden, the Soarcastle sisters, and Zimmer all think their imprisonment will last thirty-one days.

That's the test.

"How do we know you won't keep them in the brig longer?" I ask.

"You don't," Stork says. "That's why it's called trust, mate."

SEVENTEEN

Court

One day passes, and Stork proves he's not a complete liar. My brother. My friends. The four of them are allowed to leave the *Lucretzia* brig.

Stork had also spoken honestly when he said that the *Romulus* released the *Saga 4* on the first day. Over food and drink, Kinden explains that they were tagged as *bludraders* and forced to vacate the premises. Before they left, they were told that Franny, Mykal, and I were humans. They spent thirty-some days trying to intercept *Romulus* communications.

All in an effort to retrieve us from the *Romulus* brig.

Kinden tracked our transport craft to the *Lucretzia*, and Padgett formulated a plan of entry to sneak aboard. And to operate the *Saga* starcraft, they needed *two* pilots. Without Franny, they had to make do with Zimmer. Apparently, he almost, accidentally, flew them into an asteroid.

Twice.

For what knowledge they had, their plan was risky but sound. Gem built thermal detectors onto the starcraft, and the device revealed most of the *Lucretzia* crew congregating toward the bow.

Of course, they didn't realize everyone was gathering in the courtyard for a ceremony. About to induct the new admirals. They also didn't realize the *Lucretzia* has advanced tech. Including motion sensors, which they triggered as soon as they stepped foot on the tarmac.

Before releasing the four Saltarians from the brig, the Earthen Fleet asked them one question:

"Why did you want to free the humans?"

It's occurred to me many more times than I like to admit that they could've abandoned us. That maybe they should've. Sometimes I wonder if, given the choice, would I have abandoned them?

Part of me crumples in shame at the miserable truth.

That possibly, most likely, I would've left them imprisoned on the *Romulus*. Just to save myself and Mykal and Franny, so we could fly to a peaceful planet and leave the chaos behind.

I question whether I'm deserving of Kinden, Zimmer, Padgett, and Gem's loyalty, but for the first time in what feels like forever, I find myself *wanting* to be. And that frightens me more. Mortaring a bleak exterior has always been better, safer, than opening up to the possibility of hurt and betrayal.

Why'd you want to free the humans? I think about the fleet's earlier question.

"They can die at any time," Kinden said.

"And those idiots on the *Romulus* knew," Padgett added, voice silky.

Gem explained how they had only just learned we dodged our deathdays and aren't Saltarian. For the four of them, there's no certainty we would survive, and they'd never encountered people who could kill other people. Who'd even want to kill.

Leaving us in the *Romulus* brig meant we could die by someone else's will. At any time.

"I didn't want a hand in their fykking deaths," Zimmer said. "I've seen some horrific scenes: eyes gouged, jaws blown, fingernails plucked—but no one intends for anyone to die. I didn't think anyone could *kill* people until now."

Gem perched her hands on her wide hips. "We aren't cruel."

After a short deliberation, the fleet decreed the *Saga 4* allies, and they officially welcomed them aboard as equals and friends.

I stare gravely while Franny and Mykal reunite with our friends, smiling. Laughing. Joy fluttering faintly in my chest, and while I'm glad to see my brother—I have to focus on what's next.

The retrieval operation.

I can't betray Stork and forsake the mission to save Earth. Not out of some moral obligation. I just can't fathom deserting Franny and the answers she needs to find.

To come out of this alive, Franny and Mykal have a better chance with Kinden, Zimmer, and the Soarcastle sisters. We've all worked together before at StarDust; I trust their skills and know how valuable Saltarians will be in blending into Saltare-1.

I want them to join us.

With persistence, I convince Stork to bring our friends into the fold. It's not easy, considering the mission is classified and Stork is exasperatingly evasive, but after we eye-roll one another to the next millennium, he sighs.

I glare.

He finally gives in. And he asks his superiors for clearance.

The fleet grants Kinden, Zimmer, Padgett, and Gem access to operation details.

All eight of us stay in the quiet atrium, the rest of the *Lucretzia* crew retreating to their barracks for sleep or helming the bridge. Steam lies on the murky surface of the pool. Frogs croaking softly and stars twinkling overhead from the domed sky port.

I thought Stork brought us here to lay out the crucial steps of this far-fetched mission. Or at least examine the *Myths* book further with our friends.

Important tasks.

Instead, Stork would rather lounge around the pool for a "late-night dip." He supplies pipe tobacco, cigarettes, and bottles of wine and scotch, and for the past hour, no one has been on track.

". . . pig shit, Bartholo still had a chance against Roolin in the iceling championships," Zimmer says while floating on his back, fully clothed in khaki slacks and a black StarDust shirt.

Gem sits primly on a bench that she dragged to the pool's edge. "Nash Redcastle is the *greatest* iceling player of our century," she declares. "And he played for Roolin."

Kinden occupies the other end of the bench and reads a label on a wine bottle with the aid of an EonInterpreter, given earlier to our friends. The silver device behind his ear contrasts against his dark brown skin. "I balk at agreeing with little Gem," my brother says, "but Nash Redcastle was a gift to iceling. I attended the 3052 championships in Yamafort; he single-handedly won for Roolin."

Seated between those two, Padgett puffs on a pipe, observant and quiet. Her brown hair is braided and tied with a magenta ribbon.

Mykal hangs his arm over my tight shoulders, pinching a lit cigarette. He whispers to me, "You enjoy iceling more than I, you realize."

I shake my head once and then go rigid in doubt. Until he left the Free Lands and lived in the city with me, he'd never seen the sport.

We sit side by side on the mosaic tile. I've been gripping my bent knees with an ironbound inflexibility. My knuckles throbbing.

Mykal mumbles in a drag, "I've felt your eyes wandering to games more than once before."

I blink, forgotten memories whirring past me and asking to grab hold. I was six. In our kitchen, mornings before school, Kinden switched our only television to reruns of iceling. Privileged enough to even have a luxury like a television, we ate fresh-baked scones, and I slowly lifted my head out of textbooks.

Young women and men took to the ice on sharp blades and chased after a quilted violet ball, tucked beneath their opponent's arm.

I think it wasn't the strategy I liked. I remember . . . my intrigue was more rudimentary. *Entertained.* By something other than medicine. I had a distraction.

My father would slip into the kitchen and notice me first. "Etian." He smiled benevolently and put a hand to my book, then my shoulder. "Finish your studies."

He chastised Kinden for bothering me, and he turned off the television. Soon after, we'd leave for school.

I never had time to watch a full iceling match. Other priorities always tugged me away.

I wake out of a hazy stupor. Reminding myself that I still have priorities. Ones even more important than when I was a child.

"I knew a group of FTs who snuck into an iceling match a few years ago," Franny admits to everyone.

Mykal and I are dry on the floor—but perfumed water warms my feet, my arms, ankles, legs, and waist.

Franny. Near us, she wades in the shallow pool, the tips of her black hair wet. Her tunic almost floats up, but she tugs the fabric down every so often. "Altia Patrol caught them five minutes into the first quarter, and they spent four days mopping up the bleachers as punishment." She says that one boy only had two days left to live, and he was stuck cleaning.

Gem sighs. "All our time together, I should've known you grew up as a Fast-Tracker. Padgett had suspicions."

Padgett smiles coyly and blows smoke ringlets.

We have no reason to pretend to be other people with my brother, Zimmer, and the Soarcastle sisters. Not anymore. One way or another, we're all outcasts.

Earlier, we revealed some truths we'd kept secret. Like Mykal and his Grenpale heritage and becoming a Hinterlander in the Free Lands.

Mouths fell with an astonishing silence. The idea that a Hinterlander, someone who chooses no country and roams the fiercest weather-beaten terrain, could fit into upper-crust society without being caught was unfathomable to them. After the shock faded, the Soarcastle sisters praised Mykal for his aptitude at StarDust.

For all that he's done and learned, he deserves that admiration and more.

Kinden has been studying Mykal, then me, as though piecing together why I'm in love with him. I could nearly smile at the notion that my brother is seeing more of the boy I know.

For Franny, she had less to share than Mykal. Kinden and Zimmer already knew Franny was a Fast-Tracker and that her name was not *Wilafran,* but the Soarcastle sisters were still largely in the dark until today.

And I was grateful that I didn't need to speak about my past at all. While we were in the *Romulus* brig, Kinden opened up to them about my history. Likewise, Zimmer already confessed his Fast-Tracker status.

With everyone's intentions bare and all they've risked to find us, my sky-high guards have begun to lower. Hopefully not for the worst.

But there is one secret the three of us can't share with our friends or Stork.

The link.

We still keep that hidden to protect each other. And I know I should move away from Mykal, put more distance between us like we talked about. For the sake of hiding the link. But I feel more rigid and unbending today, and his shoulder against mine is a comfort that I can't so easily disregard.

". . . if they paid for their tickets, they could've avoided punishment," Kinden says, my mind dipping back into their talk.

Franny's brows scrunch together. "You know how many bills an iceling match *costs*?"

"Of course." Kinden sips wine from the bottle. "The back rows are less than fifty bills."

Padgett weaves into the conversation. "So says a boy who's likely always had a hundred in his pocket."

"Save your breath, Padgett, and just say I'm grossly rich." With a profounder eye on Padgett, he passes her the bottle. "Tarter than Saltarian wine. What do you think?"

She plucks her pipe out to taste.

"Mom and Dad are flirting again," Zimmer says with a wry grin.

Padgett shoots him a look as she puts the bottle to her lips, and Kinden rolls his eyes.

Gem explains quickly, "Zimmer thinks he's funny."

"Over a month on the *Saga* starcraft with you three," Zimmer replies. "If I didn't make jokes, we'd all go mad." *Over a month.* They've had a long time together, but I can't imagine it was as mundane as the days Franny, Mykal, and I spent in the *Romulus* brig. A month there felt like a year.

My eyes veer to Stork. I no longer expect him to cut off trivial discussions.

Lounging at the head of the pool, he sits on the edge, his legs dunked beneath the water. He smiles into swigs of liquor.

These are the very first Saltarians he's met that he didn't need to fight. *I know this.* But we have such little time. I'm in the same position as him. Surrounded by humans on the *Lucretzia*, the very first humans I've ever met. But I've forgone flippant chats and curious banter for the betterment of the mission.

And this is *his* mission.

His priority.

He's the captain of a squadron, and he's not foolish, as far as I've been able to tell. I want to know what he's playing at. Whether he's gathering information on everyone or if it's something else.

Mykal squeezes my tense shoulder.

"Fifty bills," Gem ponders. "That would've bought me the materials to build a new radio transmitter."

I wait for Franny or Zimmer to say how that money would've fed them for months. Franny has mentioned how Purple Coach wages were low. Countries purposefully paid drivers less and made them survive off of tips.

Neither speaks, possibly not wanting to hurt Gem's feelings, but they exchange a knowing look and Franny drifts toward Zimmer.

Water rushes against her waist as she moves, and Mykal flinches at the strange sensation.

No one can tell we're linked.

It's what I repeat.

A second arm is around my shoulders—*that's not me.* I look back at the pool. Franny floats on her back next to Zimmer, his arm curved around her shoulders.

I tense, cautious for other reasons than secrecy and our fate.

Mykal sucks on his cig, a disgruntled noise in his throat.

"It's so dreary to think we'll never see Nash Redcastle and Eloise Ulycastle end up together," Gem says. "Last I heard, they were rumored to be engaged. Now we'll never know if it was true."

Kinden adjusts his expensive watch. "I already know. The rumor was false. Nash was dating Brauna, the goalie for Bartholo."

I can't believe we're still discussing *iceling.*

"I met him once." Zimmer turns every head.

"Holy Wonders." Gem gasps. "You met *Nash Redcastle.* Did you sneak inside a match?"

"I shined his shoes," he says. "Back at the Catherina Hotel. Buffed them real good and the toad hole paid me a single fykking bill."

Stork clutches his scotch bottle loosely, absorbed at every word and movement. He watches Zimmer casually shifting and linking arms with Franny.

"I've heard Nash was cheap," Kinden remarks, picking up the *Myths* book off the floor. *Finally.* He waits to open the cover. *Kinden.* "But he's still one of the greats, and he's not bad on the eyes."

"No easier way to lose a stiffy than being stiffed," Zimmer quips.

Nash Redcastle was arguably one of the most famous people on Saltare-3. He was a Fast-Tracker who lived like an Influential, and he'll die in four years' time.

All of *that* is meaningless now.

I wonder why Stork doesn't feel the same. How can I trust him to lead everyone safely into and out of Saltare-1? If anyone dies or loses a limb, I'm to blame. Our friends are joining us because I asked. Because for some gods-forsaken reason, they trust me enough to follow my lead.

I settle my hardened eyes on Stork. "What are we doing here anyway?"

"Building morale." He raises his bottle to his lips, unbothered. He nods his chin to Gem. "What are the rules to iceling?"

Gem cheerfully explains the sport, and I contemplate the optimism and unity in the air that I ignored.

I try to ease.

But when she's finished, I ask my brother, "Have you read the myth yet?"

Stork looks me over with confusion. "Wow, have you ever chilled for more than two seconds?"

I blink. "I don't know what that means."

His lip quirks. "Have you ever relaxed, mate?"

I ache to shrug, but my shoulders refuse to budge. Mykal pushes my cheek, and I almost, *almost* smile.

Gem mouths the word, *Wow.* An exclamation I only hear humans use.

"Pardon my little brother"—Kinden sets down his wine bottle and flips open the book—"he was never allowed to have fun." He skims the correct page and reads several lines aloud. "*One day, a baby fell from the sky. She was unlike any other. Born of mystical beauty and power, she alone could bring peace to an ancient land.*" Kinden tries not to laugh.

"I know," I say first, but the myth unnerves me. I memorized the two-page story and I can't place my finger on *why* this absurd tale troubles my mind. "The line about the baby appearing in Montbay on Victory's Sacred Eve is strangely specific, Kinden."

The Saltarian weeklong holiday is two months from today and widely celebrated on Saltare-3. Marching bands and famous athletes parade down popular city streets, and civilians cheer and collect tossed candy.

Padgett takes a quick glance at the page. "What's Montbay?"

"The largest city in Saltare-1," Stork says as he stands, water dripping down his legs.

My brother gives me an uncertain look. "Likely there is no baby, and this myth is just a myth."

I nod, but there is no other path left to take. My gaze drifts to the Soarcastle sisters, Zimmer, and Kinden—all four equally accepting of this venture, even knowing our terrible odds.

"Why help if you believe this is a fool's chase?" I ask.

Gem smiles. "We were always undervalued on Saltare-3, and I want to prove that we can do extraordinary things together." She bumps hips with her sister. "I can't name anything more astonishing than proving a myth to be true."

Padgett plucks the pipe out of her lips. "The myth is peculiar, and I'd like to uncover this peculiarity." She adds, "And I'm not leaving Gem's side."

Floating, Zimmer rests his hands behind his head and gazes up at the sky port. "I've already seen the stars. Thought I might as well add another planet to the list before I die."

Kinden lifts his gaze off the book and rests them on me. "So I'll have more years with you, little brother."

I finally ease, and despite the absurdity in this plan, I'm beginning to feel hopeful.

Mykal and Franny smile wider and fuller.

We're hopeful.

I hang on tight, and as everyone readies for sleep, Stork motions to the seven of us. "Here's how this has to work. I was given strict orders that two of you stay in my barracks. One of the humans and one of the Saltarians."

"What?" Franny balks.

My jaw muscle tics. "I thought you said the fleet trusts the *Saga 4*."

Stork tosses his scotch bottle and catches it skillfully. "That was before they were given critical op details. This is *day two* and to avoid a coup, they want you split up at night. I have no problem choosing, if it's easier." He looks over to Franny.

"I'll do it," Mykal offers, no hesitation.

Stork pats his chest, as though remembering he has no sword. Mykal never returned the weapon. "Except you." He sips his scotch and points the bottle at me and Franny. "Choose."

EIGHTEEN

Mykal

I'm supposed to be interrogating him anyway," Franny whispers to me outside of Stork's barracks. We huddle too near to be overheard.

"You needn't worry about that tonight," I say lowly. After she volunteered, her blazing spirit on some sort of path that neither Court nor I will be smothering, I wanted to talk before leaving her to it.

I recognize, also, that Stork would've chosen me had I not stolen his gods-damned sword. He was sour that I'd taken something else from him, but I promised that I'd be holding on to the weapon while he's drinking himself to oblivion.

Franny peeks over her shoulder, then whispers softly to me, "If Stork is loose-lipped in bed, maybe he'll tell me about Earth."

I chew a toothpick in half and spit the pieces out. "In bed?" I deepen my voice to keep from shouting.

Her heart-shaped face is perpetually hot these days, and not from her mighty scowl. She lifts her chin, appearing taller. "Not *bedding*. I'd never bed a soul just for a bit of information." Hurt pricks her body, thinking that I'd think that of her.

Regret stings me like a winter's curse. I scratch my neck. Not sure how to go about any of this with Franny. She's been a mess of feelings around Stork—feelings that I shouldn't try to make sense of or dredge up. They're hers to feel, and most don't concern me.

Her brows scrunch. "Mykal?"

"I'll be telling you straight," I whisper. "Whoever is in your bed tonight better be treating you like a damned princess."

A faint smile toys at her lips and then vanishes in a thought. "This is the longest I've gone without another body on mine."

Her longing for more affection has caused frustrations. She's missing a need. Court has tried to talk to me about it once, and I wouldn't hear it. Stubborn, I thought *bedding* comes last.

She'll be finding love first. Like Court and I.

Sensing her for so long, I've been feeling how wrong I was and how right Court is. We're all different, and I worry she's been pushing aside this urge because of us. Never thought I'd be the reason Franny would be so unsatisfied.

"Franny," I whisper, "if you need another body—"

"I don't," she says adamantly. "I *don't*. I'm not putting you and Court through that." Because we'd sense the other person . . .

I'm not the one who's been heating her blood. Clawing through each word, I tell her what needs to be said. "Don't be thinkin' about us—"

"That's impossible. You *know* that's impossible." She groans. We both breathe heavily, more defeated, and we've only just begun.

My nose flares, kicking myself for doing this all backward and inside out.

Back in our barracks, Court stands pin straight, his grim concern hanging over our talk.

Franny shifts, her face twisting up. "You'd be okay with me being touched by someone else?"

A beast is gnawing on my ribs. I grimace and run my hand along my jaw. Knowing this isn't about me. It can't be because if they treat her right and she's wanting, then who am I to say otherwise?

"See," she whispers, feeling my selfish emotion that I'd rather crush and hide.

"I said nothing, little love." I rub my hot collar. "You need to be satisfied, don't you?"

"I'm all right." She nods.

Is she?

"Don't worry," Franny says as the door behind her starts to crack. Before it opens, she whispers quickly, "There's *no one* here I'd want to touch me." Her stomach isn't knotting in a lie, but a bout of nerves swarms her insides.

I think she's doing a good job of fooling herself.

NINETEEN

Franny

When I enter Stork's barracks, he makes himself a drink. Captain's quarters are more spacious: a liquor cabinet spans a whole dark-blue wall, thin bookshelf hugging close. Seems silly. Get sloshed and then read.

But maybe those are just two of Stork's favorite things in no real order: read and drink.

Besides the liquor and books, I instantly spot another glaring difference. Instead of four beds, there is only one.

I assess the size. Two bodies could fit without entangling. Three bodies, and limbs will definitely be wrapped around limbs.

Toasty, I waft my damp tunic and blame the heat on the room temps. Nothing about tonight is too strange from my ordinary. Sharing a bed is common for most Fast-Trackers. Though I had my own bunk at the orphanage, I remind myself to do what I'd commonly do.

Claim the bed before someone pushes you out.

I plop down on the end, and the plush but bouncy mattress lets out an uncomfortable *squeak*. I fiddle with my crisscrossed sandal straps, and as Zimmer sidles to me, we're both zeroed in on Stork. Zimmer was the one out of the *Saga 4* who volunteered to spend the night here. I'm glad, seeing as I've already shared a bed with him at StarDust.

Stork pours amber liquid in a cylindrical glass. A little more than half full, he finishes and corks the crystal bottle. I watch him down the drink in one gulp.

Zimmer leans into me and whispers, "He's sloshed."

Still, Stork is far from stumbling or slurring. He carries the same cocky poise that hoists his lip and tips his head, but his gaze is unreadable. All the liquor seems to do is mask a pained sorrow that swims in his blue eyes.

My brows knit and I whisper back, "I think he's in mourning." And he's coping poorly, numbing his grief with booze.

"Whatever mourning is, he's doing a bang-up job of it." Zimmer grips the back of his black shirt and yanks the fabric off his head.

I hone in on his casual movements and half-naked body.

My knees knock together, breath shallow. After dodging my deathday, I had no time to think of doing anything at night other than *sleep*. Now should be no different.

But I can't halt my wandering gaze from traveling down his tall, lanky build. Shaggy brown hair shrouds his eyes while he undoes a button of his slacks, carefree and unrestrained. He pushes hair out of his face, and I catch him skimming my cheeks and bare legs.

Bad heat brews, and I chew on the corner of my lip to cool off and I continue unbuckling my footwear. Quickly diverting my gaze to Stork.

He's looking right at me.

And he untwists the leather binding along his biceps and forearms. Confidence and curiosity teeming off his being. Muscle ripples down his bare chest, and his thighs, strong like the rest of him, peek from leather strips of his skirt.

I retrace my path back to his sharpened jaw and mouth—and his lip hikes up at me. "Need anything, dove?"

"Sleep." I shoot him a scowl, but nerves flap in my belly.

He waves mockingly to the bed.

I kick off a sandal, hoping it'll come close to his face. It thuds miserably at his feet.

Zimmer laughs.

Agitation, I name my emotion. Feisty irritations and frustrations that have *nothing* to do with wanting Stork's hands on me.

I can imagine what his lips would feel like against mine. I can think he's handsome. But I cannot *feel* those things. Court and Mykal will sense hands and legs like they're in bed with us too. Mykal said, *Don't be thinkin' about us.* But his unsettled emotion unsettled me.

Sickness churns at the thought of putting them through that, just for a little bit of pleasure.

Adding distance between me and Stork, I scuttle back to the wooden headboard and wrestle with the bra contraption under my tunic. Why humans *also* wear pointless bras is beyond me, and these ones crisscross and bind like their purpose is to suffocate and torture.

Zimmer steps out of his slacks. "It fykking feels like three hells in here."

Stork unties a pouch attached to his skirt's waistband. "You're a Fast-Tracker," he says to Zimmer, less of a question, more of a casual observation. One that I'm sure he made earlier tonight.

I slow my lousy attempts to remove my bra, more engrossed in Stork. He cradles the leather pouch with such care, and he nestles the little bag between two books on his shelf.

Since he has all the answers, what's important to him is important to me.

The mattress suddenly undulates beneath me, Zimmer jumping onto the bed and lying flat on the other side. "I'd like to think my charm gave me away"—he places his hands behind his head—"but it was the fykking word *fyke,* wasn't it?"

I smash a pillow and barely hear Stork's easygoing response. My attention veers to his movements. How he snatches a taupe linen cloth off a silver hook. Coolly, he turns his back to us, and with the snap of a bronze clip, he removes his military skirt. Buck-naked before tying the linen around his waist.

Stork spins around, facing us again, and my face sears, too distracted from why I volunteered to sleep here in the first place. *Interrogation.* Maybe he won't divulge anything about Earth just yet, but if I press about his life, he could accidentally spill some secrets.

He's about to keep talking, but I interject, "Are you coupling with anyone?"

What.

Did.

I.

Just.

Ask?

Of all the questions in the universe that I could blurt out, I choose one that glimmers his eyes with smugness and brings amusement to his lips.

I blister. "So are you or aren't you?" I'm not retreating.

Zimmer listens in, propping himself on his elbows.

"Why don't you tell me what Saltarian coupling involves, and I'll see if I'm doing it," Stork says with a rising smirk. He kicks back on the wall, nonchalant and haughty all at once.

I've never coupled, but I've driven too many around the snowy city. And I've seen and felt what Court and Mykal share. "Coupling is about loyalty and love," I start.

Stork nods, *mockingly* so.

I hesitate but continue on, "Depending on the couple, sometimes kissing."

"What's kissing?" he teases, his smile overtaking his face.

I catch on and glower. "You already know what coupling is, don't you?"

He scrunches his brows as mine knot. "I never said I didn't."

I groan and chuck a pillow at him, landing a ways off. "You implied it!"

"You assumed it." He laughs once and sweeps my reddened face. "And I haven't 'coupled' before." He wags two fingers on each hand. Seems oddly suggestive.

I swallow hard, pulse thumping low. *Gods, no.*

Not now.

Not him.

I try to extinguish a building swelter. I'm hot from hate. Hate is hot. I repeat the thought over and over again.

My jaw clenches—not me. *Court.* He's sitting up in bed, a book half-opened on his thigh. If I could mutter without appearing strange, I'd mouth words like—*I feel nothing but anger* and *I'm all right*—just so he could read my lips through our link.

I'm not feeding any selfish desires tonight or any night with Stork. Court shouldn't worry. I do my best to send this promise through my emotions.

He's still gritting down.

Nostrils even flare—*Mykal.*

I tuck my legs to my chest. The link is a burden some days.

"Earth to Franny," Stork says loudly.

I flinch. "What?"

He's smiling. "You spaced out."

Zimmer yawns into his bicep. "She does that a fykking ton."

I swear to the gods, Stork is staring right through me. Clasping my gaze with too much *knowingness,* he says, "I bet she does."

"Why?" I ask.

He lifts his brows, opens his mouth, and then shuts his lips with a bitter smile. Gods, some sort of answer is on his tongue. He mutters a halfhearted, "Because why not?"

"What were you like as a child?" I ask.

He loosely crosses his arms, features indecipherable. I blame the booze he chugged. "What was I 'like' as a kid?" He does the two-finger wag again.

Zimmer notices. "Where I come from, you must be asking for someone's knees to drop and hands to—"

"They're air quotes." Stork almost laughs. "Lord, don't overthink it."

Zimmer slouches against the headboard. "No problem for me, Storky. Overthinking is for Influentials."

"Did you always want to be a C-Jay?" I question while constructing a pillow mound between me and Zimmer.

Stork straightens off the door and measures out another drink. "What was your job on Saltare-3?"

I want to answer, but my tongue is tied. Wordless noise in my throat. Maybe his evasiveness pressures me to do the same and safeguard my heart. And all that I love about myself.

Zimmer gives me a strange look. "Why wouldn't you tell him about your job?" His voice and eyes soften, and I doubt Stork heard him.

"Leverage," I whisper, even though this is only a fragment of what I feel. "He's not telling me anything about him, so he won't learn anything about me." Earlier in the night, I explained to Zimmer how Stork knows about me. My birth and all else, but Stork is being tight-lipped so we'll help with this mission.

Nodding, Zimmer bows forward. "Heya, Stork. Who raised you?"

"Why are you asking?" Stork swigs his drink and licks liquor off his lips.

"I like to know the bare minimum about my bedmates. Occupation, deathday—because no fykking way is someone dying in my bed—and parents who raised you, are they dead or alive."

"Dead." Stork raises his glass and finishes off the last sip.

"Question answered," Zimmer tells me with a *wiseass* smile, and then he topples my pillow barricade. Chucking them behind our heads.

"Heya, I put those there for a reason." I retrieve one and pound the pillow back between us, intensifying Zimmer's confusion.

"All that does is shrink the bed," Zimmer says, "and there are three of us—"

"Two," Stork corrects. "I'm not your bedmate, *mate*. I'm taking the floor." He sets his empty glass in his liquor cabinet.

"Why?" Zimmer and I say in unison.

I trust Stork. The thought slams at me. I trust Stork enough to sleep in the same bed as him.

Despite his caginess, the parts of me that screeched, *be wary of him, Franny!* have gradually waned.

Maybe because at StarDust, I feared people learning that we dodged our deathdays—and I was cautious of every candidate, putting all of them at a distance. Even Gem Soarcastle, even Zimmer. No matter how much I liked them, I was afraid they would discover we lived when we should've died and they'd turn on us.

All of that has drastically changed.

Now we're all on the same side with the same goal. And Stork is included in that unifying feeling. He could've sent the *Saga 4* packing. It would've been safer for the fleet to oust a handful of bludraders.

Instead, he let them stay.

As much as he can, he's been trying to work with us and not against us.

Stork is just as surprised by our response as I am. "You'd want me to sleep in the same bed as you?"

"Should I retract the offer?" I question. Sweat drips down my neck, and to ignore the roasting, I try to adjust my bra beneath my tunic.

He smiles softly. "Only if you want to."

Zimmer clears the last of the pillow mound. "Here. The bed is big enough for five bodies."

I gape. "Three at most." He's too used to sleeping on a mattress crammed with people. I try to recollect the pillows, but Zimmer starts throwing them on the floor.

On his side.

"Give that back," I snap.

He fixes himself in place, lying back on his forearms, and his smile is as humored as the one Stork constantly wears.

"You two have slept together before," Stork suddenly states. He's been studying our interactions.

"Plenty of times. Every night." Zimmer shrugs.

"Every night?" Stork whistles, looking impressed.

Why would he be impressed by *sleep*?

My brows furrow. "Sleeping together . . . what does it mean on Earth?"

Stork nears the bed. "It means sex."

Zimmer and I exchange a confused look, and Stork sighs into a tight laugh. "Right." He nods. "I mean *bedding*—"

"What?!" I shout.

Zimmer busts out in full-bellied laughs, falling onto his back. The bed bounces.

I narrow a glare onto Stork. "Why in the hells would people call bedding *sleeping together*? Do humans like being downright confused all the time?"

Stork smiles. "Context is queen, dove." He eyes us. "So you haven't bedded each other then?"

Zimmer controls his laughter and shakes his head. "No, we're better as non-bedding friends."

I wholeheartedly agree, but when I look to Stork, he's staring more intently at me. It unnerves me. Sweltering again all over, and I look away.

I ache below, imagining Stork caressing my body and stroking my skin in a deep kiss that'd push my build up against his. I picture his strong hands trying to tame my frenzied movements.

I'd devour him whole if I could. But . . .

I don't want to. I don't. I don't.

I don't.

I sense Mykal; he grunts gruffly, his frustrations mounting on top of mine.

"You look distressed," Stork tells me, his knee on the edge of the bed.

"I'm not," I snap back. Too hot, my tunic sticks to my chest, and with the layer of sweat, there's no hope freeing my breasts from my bra tonight.

He rounds the bed. Walking *away* from me, he nears Zimmer's side, and then kicks the pillows into a line. "I'm taking the floor tonight."

I relax.

Zimmer sees and gawks at me like I've transformed into a skittish winter hare. "We'd keep to ourselves."

"I didn't think you wouldn't." I'm afraid I'd want more—*I don't.*

I don't.

And who even says he'd be welcoming of the *more* I'd want?

Rolling the heavy blue covers down, I slip under the sheet and lie with my back to Zimmer.

"Franny—"

"I'm trying to sleep," I say, more sad than fiery. Trying to understand why this emotion has suddenly descended is too hard. All I know is that I'd rather feel nothing at all.

Late in the night, I'm wide-awake.

Court and Mykal can't sleep. Tension pulls taut as they force space between their bodies. Hot breath and aching and yearning, and yet they say *no*.

I cover my face with my hand. Trembling with desire. Wishing they wouldn't shelter *their* needs, and I hope and pray to the gods it's not because of me. They did say they wanted to resist their affections so no one onboard would discover our link.

They're resisting almost *too* well.

The thought forces me out of the bed. Quietly, I stand in the dark and tiptoe toward the liquor cabinet and bookshelf.

Stork is fast asleep on the floor, his chest rising and falling in what seems like a heavy slumber. Giving me enough time to search his shelves.

First, I go for the leather pouch. I push aside a book and slip the pouch in my hand.

Easy enough.

I unzip. Slowly, *so* slowly. Holding my breath, I glance back at Stork. *Still asleep.* I peer into the folds and only find two items.

The snow leopard carving and . . .

I'm not sure. I pull it out for a better look. Lying flat on my palm, I inspect the light-blue rectangular object. Thin dark material spooled in two holes. I flip the item over and frown at the symbols.

I touch my EonInterpreter behind my ear and the symbols become words.

Prinslo Tape.

Tinier, hurried scrawl lies beneath that label.

For Stork: play when all is saved, destroy if failed.

I can only make sense of those instructions with some grand assumptions. Based off of what Stork has told us, he can't reveal answers until we've completed the operation. Maybe this tape has the answers to our lost histories, and he can only play it once we've *saved* Earth.

But it scares me to think he's been told to *destroy* the knowledge if we fail.

I hesitate to return the tape. Should I steal it? I cringe at thieving from anyone. And tapes are human intricacies. If I can't figure out how to play the tape, what good is even stealing it?

At ease with my choice, I slip the tape back and set the pouch in its rightful spot. Abruptly, nerves prick in a pleasure—I reach out and clutch a shelf.

It's not me.

Hot tension fortifies, their hands remaining on their own bodies, but friction gathers—I whimper and catch myself too late.

Mayday.

Stork is awake. My high-pitched noise just jostled him from sleep. Out of the corner of my eye, he's already begun to stand.

I cross my legs and bury my face in my arm.

I'm not Court or Mykal.

I'm me.

I'm here.

All of my tricks start to work, but my face is still flush by the time he nears. "What?" I snap defensively.

He smiles weakly, about to speak, but the pouch catches his attention. *Oh, gods.*

I forgot to zip the pouch.

Stork rubs his eyes, almost tired. It's not the reaction I expected. Dropping his hand, he asks, "What'd you see?"

I inhale, able to straighten up. "The Prinslo Tape. What is it?"

"Nothing for you to hear," he says strongly, and even in the darkness, I distinguish a faint redness to his eyes. "Not yet, at least."

I prickle. "Did the admirals write those instructions? Before they died, is that what they told you to do? To destroy the tape if we fail?"

He has his hand over his mouth, processing. Thinking.

His silence is my answer. *Yes, they did.*

"Why would they do that?" I ask, angered tears burning on their ascent.

His hand falls again. "It's complicated, dove." He sees my ire. "Don't hate them."

How is he not enraged? He has to keep so many secrets. He truly is carrying an excruciating amount of weight on his shoulders—because of an order. From *their* order. "Just disobey them."

"Disobey?" He laughs. "Okay."

"Good . . . ?" Can it be that easy?

His brows rise at me. "I was *joking.*"

I sigh roughly.

"Look, I trust in what the admirals wanted," he explains. "You should too."

A rock lodges in my throat. I simmer quietly. He's placed so much trust in his leaders, and now I'm concerned he's loyal to a fault.

Maybe what the admirals wanted is not what we need.

He seems rooted into this purpose. Even when the secret-keeping causes pain, he's still barreling ahead.

"I think you hate this," I whisper.

His chest collapses. "I think you hate me."

"I can't hate what I don't understand," I breathe.

He nods a few times and then waves an arm with more light-heartedness. "What else can we tell each other in the dead of night?"

My eyes drift. And I spy a globe on the bookshelf next to his shoulder. "Is that Earth?" I ask, peering closely at the blue contours and dots of green.

"No," he says. "That's Saltare-1."

Oh. "I should know that," I mutter.

"You'll know more during training," he reassures me. "Like how those patches of green are an illusion to make the planet appear *better* than the rest. Saltarians are a prideful race." He wags his brows, admitting to his own arrogance.

"Wait . . ." I trail off in thought. "If the land isn't real, then . . ."

Stork nods again, and in a whisper, he answers what I'm thinking. "Saltare-1 is a water world."

TWENTY

Mykal

I messed up.

Truth being, I've been messing up a lot recently. With expressing myself to Franny, with making good strides toward my baby brother, and early this morning in the dining hall, I messed up with Court.

We were all right until he sneezed, and the tickle in my nostrils caused me to sneeze. To keep from mimicking me, he forced out a cough. Heads were already turning, *Lucretzia* crew already staring, and I tried to trap breath and growl instead of hacking a lung.

No willpower of mine could restrain the wretched noise. I coughed loudly. I coughed hoarsely. Court and I began a downward spiral of giving and taking senses.

Drawing too much attention, fear pummeled us both like a furious stampede. We left the dining hall abruptly and ended up arriving early to our master Saltare-1 training. Stork said to go to the indoor garden by noon.

No one here yet but us, I pace and pace on spongy grass. Flower bushes and vegetables are planted jaggedly. Water lettuce grows in corners of a deep pond. Some sort of dark-green ivy weaves and tangles up the walls, and fuzzy moss dangles off the ceiling. It's a better sight than metal and space, but this isn't the wilderness I've been missing.

There are no trees.

No snow.

Surely no ice or animals.

And the one person who can make up for the frozen homeland I'm craving is standing at a grave distance from me.

"This can't keep happening," Court says, voice tensed. Nearly choked, his nose flares and gaze burns. "Not in front of the crew." He means *the humans* and *Stork*. Who could know about linking and put all the pieces together if we can't hide these strange synchronicities.

I storm back and forth, back and forth, thinking about how providing for the ones I love makes my life worthwhile. And there aren't many I love in this big ugly universe.

I growl out the rock in my lungs and scuff the base of a blue flower bush. No dirt surfacing. "We've already been trying to be careful around one another," I say aloud. "And poorly at that." I often forget that I can't put an arm around him.

I forget that we can't hold gazes like love endures inside and between us.

I forget a lot of damned things.

"I'm as much at fault," Court murmurs in a tight breath, eyes bloodshot. "You used to hold me even before we coupled, and I like feeling you."

The corner of my mouth pulls upward. I knew he did, but hearing the words is nice. "I think you more than *like* it, you little crook," I tease, but my smile leaves as miserable realities shadow his beautiful features.

Court aches to come forward, his legs nearly jerking beneath him. But he forces himself backward one foot, and then two. "Mykal," he starts, but hanging moss suddenly brushes his cheek.

I swat my face, the bad reflex freezing us both.

It's what can't be happening anymore. Gods bless, it's what I keep doing wrong. If the crew were around, we could be in deeper trouble.

Roughly, I wipe my running nose with the back of my hand, and recognizing what needs to be done, I stop pacing.

I stare at the boy I've loved more than my homeland, more

than wind and the wild. More than the winter wood. His dark-brown hair whisks over his lashes, with intense grim grays and a vigilant stance like he's facing loaded guns at every second. Court is braver than he realizes and stronger than he knows.

"One of us needs to be strong enough and make it official," I tell him. "We have to feel that we're done with one another. That way we won't be slipping up. And we'll be forced to be careful. Everyone onboard *knows* we're coupling because of my loud mouth, and we should've kept that a secret like you wanted. We gotta go backward, Court."

His face twists. "I didn't want to be right about that." Tears well, and agony claws at my flesh, fists my throat. Emotion belonging first to him or me, I dunno. Regardless of our link, I think we'd be feeling the same pain.

I rest my coarse hands on my head. Breathing hard as I keep feet rooted here. When all I'd like to be doing is bridging the gap and pulling Court into my chest.

"I won't be sinking you in a damned *grave* because I love you too much," I promise him, hot tears slipping down our cheeks.

He pinches his eyes. "Is this official then?"

"Yeh." I'm bare-chested, but our hurt stifles me like I'm wearing musk ox furs in the blazing sun. "We're pulling apart, you and I." I say the words that couples use when they end their coupling.

Court nods slowly, in agreement here, but we're both letting this sink like a pit in our stomachs. He'd shove his hands into pockets, but his tunic has none.

I grind my teeth for something to chew. "When we know we're safe," I say, "then I'll be putting my arms around you again."

He doubts. "What if we're never safe?"

"We will be," I say surely, my chest pumping with hope and optimism that he better embrace, even for a short bit.

He shuts his eyes tightly, one last tear sliding out, and then he wipes his face dry. Resolve pushes his carriage higher, standing straighter, and I crouch down by the pond. Gathering smooth pebbles.

Court seems to just be staring up at the ceiling. Thinking hard and long, and while we stay quiet, trying our hand at uncoupling, the door whooshes open.

I sense Franny.

I've been sensing her faintly for some time. All spirited scowls and raging heart. As she treks into the starcraft's garden, she breaks our silence.

"What happened?"

Court does most of the talking. Once she's up to speed, she sighs out a worrisome breath and says there's now more reason than ever to find answers and safety.

She's still thinking about us when we're concerned about *her*.

I flip a pebble in my hand and come right out and say it. "You were mighty hot last night."

"As I said this morning, I was *irritated*," she snaps, lowering onto a silver bench beside a pink blossom bush. Before Court and I left the dining hall, she'd been telling us about the Prinslo Tape she found and how the dead admirals ordered Stork to keep these secrets. "Try sleeping in the same room with Stork and you'd feel the same."

I choke on a laugh. "That'd be some surprise." I chuck a rock into a pond. "Seeing as how I've only felt that way with Court."

Her brows furrow, and she whips her head to Court for explanation.

He pushes aside moss that shields his view of Franny. "Last night, you had affections for—"

"*Irritations*," she corrects too quickly. "And I *felt* you both." She springs to her feet. "You were angry every time I was flustered or my breath was shallow. You didn't want to feel me touching *anyone* else any more than I wanted you two to experience that—"

"No," Court cuts in sharply. "*No.* You are so wrong."

I rise, just as upset that she drew that sort of conclusion last night. "We felt you smothering your desires, and we grew cross."

With a faraway gaze, Franny slowly sits back down. "I have a hard time believing . . . that you wouldn't care if I bedded someone."

I look to Court. Hoping he can do better at speaking than I.

"We care if you're hurt," Court says smoothly. "We care if you're unsatisfied."

"I'm *fine,*" she snaps. "I don't need to go to bed with anyone. I don't need another person to keep me warm. I'm *fine.*" Maddened tears surface.

I rub my eye before any water drips. "You're lying to yourself, you realize?"

"My life has changed." She breathes hotly, pointing at the grass. "I used to love Juggernaut and now that I'm linked, I don't want to take a fykking pill."

Court steps forward. "This is *not* the equivalent of giving up Juggernaut for us."

"Yes, it is!"

"No, it's not!" he yells, pained. All of us, breathing in knives. "You can't push aside passion and love for the rest of your life when Mykal and I are allowed to feel those emotions." He fights a tremor in his voice. We've just barred ourselves from our affections a bit, but that'll be changing in time. I keep hope for us both. Court finishes, "It's not fair to you, Franny."

"It's not fair to you that you *feel* another person in bed." Her voice shakes too, and she rubs her eyes quickly.

"We'll concentrate elsewhere as you've done with us," Court nods, assured.

That works better than my words yesterday.

Franny pants like she's being chased around the garden. She stands still, wide-eyed. "I don't . . . I don't *love* anyone like you're saying . . ." She trails off, mist steaming overhead from invisible spigots.

I whip from side to side, toe to head, searching for the

damned source. A swelter suddenly brews, fake sunlight brightening. And then the door *whooshes* open and in struts Stork.

Kinden, Zimmer, and the Soarcastle sisters aren't far behind, none adopting the human wardrobe. All stay in slacks and shirts found on their starcraft.

Franny flushes and drags her gaze along the grass. While Court is a stone statue, unmoving and unbending, I hike over to the wall and uncover the sword I left underneath a bed of ivy.

Stork ties longish pieces of his hair back, and his gaze darts between us like he can sense something is off. I'm not looking at Court one bit.

He's doing his best to keep wide distance between our stances.

Making no noise about it, Stork tells everyone, "For training, I've set the atmospheric conditions in the garden to Saltare-1's climate."

I buckle the leather strap across my chest. Listening in.

Gem stretches her arms toward the moss and mist. "How peculiar, moisture is in the air."

"Humidity," Stork defines with a dry smile. "Learn to love it or hate it. I really don't care, as long as no one is awkward on Saltare-1. Because once we get there, we all need to pretend like we haven't spent one bloody day off that planet." He waves to the pond. "Everyone, line up."

Franny slips past Zimmer, and hurriedly, she steps to the end next to Gem Soarcastle.

He skims his foot in the pond and kicks water at Franny.

She hugs her arms around her body, confused about what she feels. Mostly.

Zimmer frowns. "What's wrong with you?"

Franny shrugs.

"The three of them had a fight," Padgett says as she sidles next to her sister. "It's obvious in their body language."

I grunt. My body isn't speaking *any* language other than *I hate humidity* and *let's hope this training doesn't involve exams.*

"Was it a bad fight?" Gem wonders.

Kinden narrows a glare onto my head, as though I wronged Court three ways to three hells, and he makes space for his brother at the other end of the line.

I open my mouth to defend my honor.

Court beats me to it. "I pulled apart from Mykal." He goes to stand next to Kinden, and I don't much like how he's taken the fall here.

"We *both* pulled apart," I say strongly but not too proudly.

Court rolls his eyes, frustrated. "It was my choice first."

I expel a rough breath, and I'm the only one who hangs back. Nowhere near the deep pond.

Stork is plucking some of the lettuce out of the water. "You want to talk about their breakup, or should we get on with it?" He wipes his dripping hands on his skirt. "Your choice. I can wait." Stork glances at Franny, but she's staring at her feet.

His humor seems to fade.

"Let's start," Kinden declares, his hand lowering to Court's shoulder. Not a heavy grip, I feel the comfort, but Court isn't easing. He aches to turn his neck. Wanting badly to catch a glimpse of my face. He almost does, strain in his muscle, but his head falls forward.

I run my tongue over my sharp molars.

Gods bless, this is hard.

Stork notices me standing back and trying to dig an impossible hole with my heel. *I hate this dirt-less ground.* "Scared of the water," he states more than asks.

"I just like staring at the backs of heads." I adjust the sword.

He eyes the weapon with a slight grimace. My baby brother can either fight me for the blade or quit drinking himself numb. I gave him that choice, and he said nothing. Just walked off.

Thumbing his jeweled earring, he turns back to the pond. "Here's how this works—"

"I'd like to know something first," Court cuts in. "Before we even *find* the child, we have to make it onto Saltare-1. How do we do that without being seen? I'm assuming the planet has cameras and motion detectors and that they don't appreciate humans."

Stork rests his sandaled foot on a wet boulder. "Saltare-1 has that and more. Every entrance to the planet has ID and Helix Reader checks, and no humans or bludraders are allowed through. Look, you don't need to be concerned about the finer details. The fleet has already mapped out the *hows*."

"Then how?" Court questions.

Stork pauses, but then nods and ends up sharing. "Saltare-1 uses Intergalactic Garbage Disposal. *IGD.* Their trash is robotically shuttled to Rosaline, the closest moon. There are no checkpoints or scans for the bins in or out, and Nia has already hacked the cameras on the shuttles."

"Wait." Kinden holds up a hand. "We're traveling across planets . . . in a trash can?"

I make a disgruntled noise. Wondering how this is safe for anyone.

Stork tries not to smile. "You'll have a full body suit and mask to protect yourself from the atmosphere."

"Mayday," Franny mutters.

Gem clears her throat. "What if an asteroid or projectile hits the trash bins? Debris drifts *everywhere* in space."

Stork gestures to the door. "Nia did the calculations. There's only a fifty-one percent chance one of us could be hit, but see, half of us can't die." He flashes a smile. "And the ones who can will be protected by the body suit."

"We're just floating around in space," Padgett says while she pulls her silky hair back with a ribbon. "Sounds like a stellar plan."

"There's no other opening into Saltare-1. This is it." He shrugs. "Honest, you shouldn't worry about reaching the planet. Being caught as a bludrader or a human *on* Saltare-1 is a capital punishment, and you'll meet a fate worse than death."

He goes on to explain how all the Saltare planets work

congruently with identical governments and laws and caste systems: Babes, Fast-Trackers, and Influentials. Which will make pretending to be Saltarian on a new planet a bit easier on us.

Instead of Vorkter, their prison is called Onakar, and capital punishments are the same: serving life inside a cell.

A chill snakes down Court.

I'm trying not to shiver, but more than anything, I'd like to hug him and whisper coarsely that he'll never be seeing the inside of a prison. He needn't fear.

I'd promise him until I'm blue in the face.

"If the social structure is the same as Saltare-3," Court says to Stork, "then who are we pretending to be? We can't be Babes. We'd already be dead."

No Babe is older than thirteen years, and since Fast-Trackers live to be twenty-nine, we all could pass as an FT or an Influential.

Stork explains, "While we search for the baby in Montbay, we need to be able to walk around without suspicion."

I already know where he's heading. Influentials are nosy. While we were pretending to be them at StarDust, too many ladies and men asked about my knowledge and dealings.

They pay no notice to Fast-Trackers. Ask them nothing about their past or present. Really, most steer clear, and that's exactly what we'll be needing.

"You want us to be Fast-Trackers," Court realizes too.

Stork nods. "Fast-Trackers are basically invisible to most Influentials."

Zimmer lifts one shoulder. "We're wallpaper to their world."

"Cogs in a wheel," Franny says easily. No bitterness. Just stating facts, it seems.

Gem balks. "We're *all* pretending to be Fast-Trackers?"

"Yeah, that's the plan," Stork says.

Zimmer bursts out laughing and points at Kinden on his left. "You really want *him* to be a Fast-Tracker?" He snickers again.

Kinden looks unaffected. "It's not that fykking hard, Zimmer. I just talk like a chump and say the word *fyke* every second while drinking ale and popping Hibiscus."

"Good one," Zimmer says, "you drink and take Hibiscus, and we won't be seeing your egotistical ass for three months because you'll be passed out facedown."

Padgett flips her hair off her shoulder. "I'd flip him over on his back."

"*Pardon*," Zimmer says. "I meant passed out faceup."

Kinden faces him, not appearing offended. "You're just hurt because you know being a common Fast-Tracker means we act in foolish excess."

Franny boils silently and mutters something. I feel her lips form the words: *that's not a bad thing.*

He presses onward, "That means taking irresponsible drugs, smoking beyond limitations, and then there's running around unclothed—"

Something snaps in Zimmer, and he shoves Kinden. He slips back, falling toward the pond, and he fists Zimmer's shirt as they both splash into the deep waters.

Only Zimmer flails, struggling to keep his head above the surface. He gurgles water, and then Kinden easily scoops Zimmer beneath his arm and swims them both to the mossy edge.

Before they climb out, Stork quickly says, "Everyone has to jump in. That's why you're here. You all need to know how to swim."

There are no hot springs or indoor pools in Grenpale or the Free Lands, and unless I wanted to be frostbitten and lose a foot or toe, I wouldn't risk sticking a limb beneath a frozen lake.

Stork asks who can't swim.

I raise my hand, and besides me, only two go up: Franny and Zimmer.

Influentials can afford to swim in warm pools, and even

though Court was a Fast-Tracker, he was a Wonder. Raised more like an Influential.

If I panic in that water, I'll be dragging Franny and Court down, and our link could be discovered. But I hang on to one thought: *this isn't about smarts.*

I know my body well. I'm not gonna be frightened.

TWENTY-ONE

Franny

Before bed, I wring out my wet black hair. Twisting the long strands while I slouch on the edge of the mattress. I'm too sullen to care about creating wet puddles on Stork's floor.

I can't swim.

I can't swim.

Why, gods, can't I swim?

Not even after one month of practice. Day and night, I train in the garden pond, and my pulse spirals like a Purple Coach spinning out on slick city ice. I fear death.

No matter how hard I tell myself, *I don't want to fear death. I shouldn't fear death.* I still fear—and I'm mad at myself. Most of all. I thought I'd conquered this terror, and it reared its monstrous head again.

So easily our link could've been discovered as I coughed on water and panicked, but Court and Mykal always hid their distress by pulling me to land. In the splashing chaos, no one could really tell that they were coughing because of our bond.

"You have a ton of time. An entire month left to practice," Stork says while skillfully riding a hoverboard from one side of his barracks to the other. I believe he's doing it just to infuriate me. The constant *swooshing* sound as he rides past is enough to drive anyone mad.

Despite my irritations, his words ring in my ears.

One month has passed.

One month is left.

I can't see how I'll succeed. In the atrium's shallow pool, I could easily float on my back. I'd done so before in Bartholo's communal bathhouses, but I never tried to swim there. And those waters surely weren't as dark or deep as the pond.

Mykal swam with magnificent, powerful strides the very first day he tried. *The link will help me,* I thought. If I channeled his movements, maybe I could keep my head above the water.

I tried.

Fear capsized me again and again and again.

Mykal's optimism and Court's pushiness haven't helped either.

"That's what Mykal keeps telling me," I mutter. "I have a month left." He'll nudge my shoulder and then knock on my head like I've lost my senses.

Gods, I hate that I'm wallowing. Letting my hair soak my shoulders, I stand and wander over to the bookshelf. I skim the spines with the soft brush of my fingers.

"And you seem to think that's not long enough," Stork says. I can feel his hot gaze on my back as he watches me from across the room, but I make an effort not to turn around and look.

"It isn't."

"And I'd say that's a little odd coming from you."

I snort. Okay, this time, I do turn to face him. "And why is that?" My voice sounds accusatory, like he's called me a wart *and* a toad all at once.

He's smiling. "Because you lived most of your life like a Fast-Tracker. I'd think that someone who thought they'd die at seventeen would believe a month is a long time."

I open my mouth to combat, but shut it fast.

He's right.

That clever wart is right.

A month is an awfully long time for Fast-Trackers. Zimmer would agree. We've both discussed our time in Bartholo, trying to unearth any familiar acquaintances. There was Wyton

Farcastle. A boy of fifteen years who built an entire ice fort in two weeks before he died.

Thoughts of Zimmer remind me that his deathday could be any upcoming week or month. He said he'd rather not share the date of his impending death, and I've found myself, on more than one occasion, wishing he'd live to be twenty-nine: the oldest age of a Fast-Tracker.

It'd give him ten more long years ahead.

Zimmer would believe I could swim an entire ocean by the end of a month.

But I'm just not so sure.

"A month is a long time," I end up saying aloud, agreeing with this fact at least.

Stork rides his hoverboard over to me, and as the board slows to a standstill, he spreads his feet. "Try with me, Franny."

I open my mouth, my pulse racing ahead of my thoughts. Dread coats my skin in a filmy layer of sweat. I'm unsurprised by his request, seeing as how he's already attempted to curb my fear during training.

Back in the garden, Stork tried to coax me into climbing the ivy up the wall. He ascended the greenery, and only gripping the vines with one hand, he hung perilously off and waved me forward. "Climb up." Stork smirked and made a *come hither* motion.

I faltered and inhaled jagged breaths like I do now. Irate at myself, I stormed out. Reckless impulsions used to be a part of me. It used to be *easy*, and I envy his carelessness. Able to shimmy up a vine without thinking, *I will fall and die!*

"Is riding the hoverboard for training purposes?" I outright ask.

"Maybe." Stork rolls back on the hoverboard, and then scoots forward again as if to demonstrate how simple it is.

Maybe.

Maybe could mean a lot of different things. I'm not about to theorize what's floating around in Stork's head. He's a riddle that refuses to be solved.

Gliding closer, he holds out a hand. "On the board."

"I want to," I admit, scrutinizing the floating platform beneath his bare feet. "It just looks . . ."

"Fun, exciting, thrilling—"

"Terrifying." I swallow my speeding pulse. "You know you can't die, but I could fall, hit my head, and be gone."

His brows rise. "Or you could just do it. And worry about what happens later."

"There is no later if I'm dead."

"And you wouldn't even think that if your feet were on this board." He grins. "And anyway, pressed up against me, I'm positive *dying* would be the very last thing on your mind."

I laugh. "How can you be sure I wouldn't want to fling myself off and die and go meet the gods instead? Being *pressed up against you* might have that effect on me."

He smiles wider. "It might. Should we test it, then?" He holds out his hand again.

I take it this time, and he guides me forward.

I sense Court.

Body stiff, his rigid grip tightens on the *Myths* book. I can imagine his stern narrowed eyes. Reading in bed, he pauses on a page. I can't control our link or where my mind wanders, but I shouldn't be dwelling on their disapproval or approval. I'm my own person.

This is my body. Not theirs, but these are just words. Whatever I do, they'll experience faintly.

Court tries to blink, and his breathing deepens and emotions grow determined in a way that tells me he's trying to focus on his book, less on me. But he must still sense me in a frozen standstill because he mouths, *Franny.*

I know.

This past month, I've struggled with letting myself desire

anything outside of training. Who would've thought Court, of all people, would chastise me for working hard?

Mykal said I was scared of confronting what I've been feeling.

I laughed too loud at him and ended up snorting. And then shrugging. Maybe he's right, and as my mind fixates on Mykal, I sense him more strongly.

He whittles a flute, his thumb pressed hard to the dull side of the blade while he chips wood. His nose flares, battling warmth and desires that veer toward Court. Since uncoupling, they haven't slept in the same bed. The powerful urge to crawl to each other and embrace keeps them wide-awake at night.

They've slept terribly. Just when Court had been sleeping well on the *Lucretzia* too, barely tossing and turning. Even without medicine.

"Your feet go here." Stork's voice brings me back to the moment, and I try to forget the lurch of my stomach and my spiraling pulse.

Stork helps me balance while I plant one foot inside his. He holds my hip and places his other palm on the small of my back. "One more step," he tells me.

And then I'm off the ground. Where I could die—I shut my eyes, knocking myself for thinking too much. Bad thoughts be gone.

Clutching onto his back, I put my other foot outside of his. Our legs interlace, and before I can speak—we shoot across the room. Zipping at rapid speed to the door, my lungs catapult to my throat.

"Wait." I panic, my body screaming *abort*. My grip tightens on him, cheek smashing into his chest. *Pressed up against him most certainly.*

"Relax, dove—"

I shift my weight, and the hoverboard screeches, jerking forward and back.

No, no, no.

Stork holds me harder against his chest. "Relax, I have you—" He cuts himself off as the board tilts backward and slips out from under our feet. His spine thuds to the ground, and I crash on top of him.

He erupts in full-bodied laughs, the noise thundering against my belly. My lips upturn as my Fast-Tracker heart sings forgotten songs of thrill and joy. Stork may have never stepped foot on a Saltarian planet, but he's somehow reminding me of home. Of the Franny Bluecastle who delighted in simple pleasures, who never wasted time on fear.

And he's a reminder that I've changed.

I'm different. Court once said that I can still be a Fast-Tracker, but I'm more. I'm my good-natured mother. I'm my long-lost friends, and I know I'm human too—but gods, what does that even mean?

My lips fall. "I wish I were Saltarian." I whisper a sad truth while lying along his muscular build. I'm about to sit up, but his arm curves around my lower back.

"Don't wish that," he says softly, almost achingly. "Your humanity is one of the best parts of you."

My breath slows. Overwhelming feelings bear against me.

The door suddenly *whooshes* open.

Zimmer emerges and then skids to a halt. He smiles wryly like he caught Stork and me lip-locked. But I'm *chastely* on top of Stork, and quickly, I slide from beneath his arm and fumble to my knees.

Zimmer is still grinning.

"What?" I snap.

Stork is not making a move up off the ground.

"Should I come back later?" he asks, his gaze pinging from me to Stork and then back to me. "So you two can finish properly."

My nose flares. "There is nothing to finish. I fell off the hoverboard." Announcing my failure to ride it seems better than declaring some sort of affection toward Stork. We weren't about to declare any love. We weren't about to kiss. Nothing was happening. And that wart does *not* need to think that I like him in any way, shape, or sensual fykking form.

And I don't.

I don't.

"If you say so." Zimmer steps farther into the barracks, and he shares a *knowing* look with Stork. After all the nights Zimmer and I have spent in Stork's barracks, I've noticed Zimmer's and Stork's carefree demeanors seem to mesh well and they rarely, if ever, butt heads like I butt heads with them.

But they're not the same. The deceased admirals strapped too many responsibilities onto Stork, and in life, Zimmer carries close to none.

And if Zimmer hadn't come into the room, *nothing* would have happened between Stork and me. I'm sure of that.

My stomach keeps clenching like I'm lying. *I'm not lying.*

Stork climbs to his feet and abandons the hoverboard on the ground. He walks through puddles from my hair like nothing is amiss, and his sandals track wet footprints on the mosaic tile. "Besides *falling* off the hoverboard, did you enjoy the ride?"

Yes. The answer sits on my tongue. I know I'll be thinking back to more than just the feeling of flying through the air. I did, very much, enjoy being pressed up against him. But those words will never leave my lips.

Stork unlatches the cabinet next to the one Zimmer leans casually against.

In my silence, both boys look to me for an answer.

I shrug, unable to give Stork the satisfaction of a proper response, and then I plop on the edge of the bed.

Stork lifts his brows at me. "Cat got your tongue?" He uncorks an opaque black bottle and swigs.

I scowl. "I don't know what that means."

He ponders for half a second. "You're being unusually quiet."

"I didn't enjoy the ride," I say bluntly. My stomach betrays me and twists, but only two boys can feel the lie and it's not the ones I face. "And a million cats must've *eaten* your tongue because you're quiet on just about everything." I shoot to my feet and approach him.

I'm not afraid of you.

I hold his enthralled gaze, and I snatch the bottle out of his hands.

He lets me. "It's strong whiskey."

"For every sip you take, I take," I tell him, because a sloshed Stork hasn't been forthcoming this whole month, so maybe a sober Stork will be.

He tilts his head. "I'll drink you under the table."

"Then drink less."

Stork laughs hard, like I'm jesting.

"I'm serious," I snap.

"I know, that's why it's funny." He flashes a cocky smile. "You're not much of a gambler if you're telling me to lose."

Ignoring that, I swig from the bottle, the sharp liquor scalding my throat on its vicious descent. I cough a little bit but choke down the whiskey.

Far away, I faintly sense Mykal rubbing at his neck. Disgust lingers, but not as potently as when I eat fruit. I detest the bitter flavor of whiskey much more than they do.

I stifle another cough.

Stork looks less amused.

Zimmer sidles to me and sniffs the bottle. Grimacing. "It smells worse than the piss-water ale they sell on Fowler Street Ave."

"I liked that ale," I defend. "I don't like this."

Stork steals the bottle back. "Don't drink it then."

"I'm doing what I'm doing," I say, not so poetically. But I never had lofty poetic dreams. My eyes roam his cut cheekbones, his dangling earring, and his slicked-back snow-white hair, tied with an elastic band. I'm not just looking because he's handsome. Sometimes I try to see who he is. The Saltarian boy who was raised eighteen years strong on Earth.

The picture is hazy with an unknown landscape and unknown parents, and I only understand more of what he missed.

He was meant to grow up in an Influential city on Saltare-3. He was meant to combat the snow and ice and understand what piss-water ale on Fowler Street Ave. tastes like.

And I was meant to see the world he lived inside.

"Who named you?" I ask.

Stork inhales a sharp breath, as though readying himself to answer. And then he winces into a forced smile. "A person." He swigs.

I jerk the bottle out of his hands when he finishes. "You want to tell us more; I know you do." I barely take a sip before he wrenches the whiskey from my clutches.

"I'd love to tell you more about who I am, but how am I supposed to share the little things when *everything* is connected?" He mockingly widens his eyes, but sadness flashes in them. "The answer is that there is no answer. I wait. *I wait* for when this all bloody ends so maybe you can know me then." He shrugs tensely and downs a larger gulp, staring at the ceiling.

"What's the harm in telling us now?" I ask.

Zimmer adds, "We'll all still do the mission no matter what—"

"It's not about the op," Stork interjects. "The admirals had *one* dying wish, and I swore to them—I looked them in the eye, *knowing* they were about to sacrifice their lives; something I can never do—and I promised that I'd wait to tell you."

I blister. "If their dying wish is to keep secrets from us then their dying wish is cruel." I steal the bottle.

He watches me sip the drink. "It's complicated." He lets me hang on to the whiskey and he waves me onward.

Maybe he's hoping if I'm sloshed, I'll stop harping on about the admirals.

Zimmer snatches the bottle from me, takes a gulp, and passes the liquor back to Stork.

"Who named you?" I ask again. "What if I die on Saltare-1

and I never learn these things about you? What if *no one* ever knows these things?"

While he studies my indignation, a strand of his hair slips out of the tie and brushes his temple. "You think no one on this ship knows who named me?"

Did I assume wrong? He seems lonely, like he's been yearning to share more about his life for eons of time, and with us, he finally has that chance.

But he has to wait.

"Does anyone living know?" I ask.

He shakes his head. "Only me." One sip of liquor and he asks, "Who raised you?"

"My mom," I say without pause. Taking a risk by lowering my guards. I pry the bottle out of his hand. "Just her, and she was *beautiful* and kind, and I watched her die when I was six. Her death was just as glorious as she was." Lungs on fire, I pant like I'm running up a monstrous hill.

He stares into me like he's excavating more of who I am, and he reaches for the bottle—I tuck the liquor to my breast. "I haven't sipped yet." I add, "Who named you?"

"The woman who found me in a pod." He breathes deeper. "On Earth, there's a myth that a bird delivers newborn babies to parents, and she thought the name fit." Before I ask, Stork clarifies, "The bird is called a stork." He grins at my growing smile. "You appreciate that?"

"Very much." The air unwinds, but unleashing more is as grueling as scaling Grenpale mountains. "Did you always want to be a C-Jay?"

"Sip and pass back." He motions for the bottle.

Lips to the rim, I wince before I even swallow, the fierce sting growing worse as we go on.

Once I push the whiskey into his hand, he tells me, "I played with plastic toy spaceships as a kid. I wanted to fly and protect Earth. I thought it was my *destiny*."

I hang on to his use of past tense. "You don't anymore?"

He drinks and licks liquor off his lips. "I reckon I do, but I believe a hell of a lot *less* in destinies. People have choices, and some screw with the lives of others and some help. That's it." He shakes the whiskey at me. "What was your job on Saltare-3?"

I clasp the neck of the bottle. I've held on to this answer for a month, but he's begun to divulge more about his life, so it feels only fair that I do the same. "I was a Purple Coach employee."

"You'll have to be more specific." He has no knowledge of the shuttle service.

I almost laugh at a thought. Of what information exists on file about Saltare-3; Purple Coach never made the history books. My job must not have been important to historians, not enough to grace any page or any computer.

"I was a driver," I say, a bit apprehensive to share. "Whoever had bills to spend, I drove them across cities and countries."

"Bad tips, hostile passengers, dangerous roads," Zimmer chimes in, giving Stork a fuller picture of Purple Coach. "Most FTs never apply for that job. They just take it for the Fast-Tracker benefits."

Stork locks eyes with me, processing.

"I never wanted to be anything else," I say with short breath. "I liked being behind the wheel and having the chance to go places and take people where they needed to be."

I was important.

I was necessary.

I can be left out of history books, but I know my place in that world.

Stork frowns more. "You actually drove?"

"Every day since I was eight." *Up until I was required to retire for the six-week decline.* I chug harshly while amusement glitters in his eyes, and then I shove the bottle into his chest. "It's not funny."

"No, it's incredible." He smiles into a laugh. "If only you knew how weird it'd be for an eight-year-old human to *drive* a car, let alone on the terrain you managed. Does Saltare-3 even have automatic gears?"

My lips part. "There are cars on Earth?" He's talking like vehicles exist, and he's seen people drive.

He swishes the liquor, thinking. "I didn't say that."

"You said something—"

"I can't talk about Earth," he says gently. "We've been through this, dove."

I groan into a sigh. "You can caress those words but they're still aggravating."

He grins while he swigs.

"Why is *knave* your call sign?" I question and tug the bottle midsip. Liquid spills down his chest, and he waits for me to apologize but I just take a showy gulp and cough.

His lip quirks. "How does that whiskey taste?"

"Divine," I snap.

"Must be why you keep choking."

Zimmer grabs the bottle before I stubbornly chug half the liquor, and I sway a little bit into his side. Woozy, I blow out a measured breath.

My shoulders throb, and I only realize now that Court is sitting achingly straight, more cautious than before.

"You never answered," Zimmer tells Stork.

He pauses for a while and rests his shoulder blades against the cabinet. "*Knave* is the human equivalent of what Saltarians call *bludraders*."

His call sign means traitor.

I rock back. "But you fight for humans."

Zimmer cringes. "You let them nickname you that?"

He rolls his eyes in a dramatic arch. "See, I'm what they're afraid of, and I understood growing up that they're just scared of who I am." He smiles more sadly, running his tongue over his teeth. "Honestly, I prayed to be human because it'd be easier."

I can't detach my gaze from his. And again, I notice his use of the past tense. "You don't pray for that anymore?" I ask.

He shakes his head. "The man who raised me sat me down and said not to hate who I am because that's a surefire way to die before you're dead." He pulls the bottle out of Zimmer's hands. "Some kids and teenagers called me *knave* out of spite, and I let the word roll off my back. Sooner or later, people kept calling me *knave*, but out of respect. I like it because it fits. I'm not human, and the Earthen Fleet loves me, not despite being a Saltarian, but because I am Saltarian and I still chose them."

My chest heavies. "You're good and just," I realize.

He smiles painfully. "I'm following an order that is extremely *unfair* to you, Court, and Mykal, and I'm doing it anyway"— he raises the bottle to his mouth—"because if we fail, you get no answers. You get nothing. I wouldn't say that's good *or* just." So he'll comply with those terrible orders until the bitter end, and I hate that he will. But I see that it's already hurting him.

Or else he wouldn't be guzzling the liquor right now.

We only talk for a little bit longer, and I stop drinking before I stumble or slur. Back on the bed, I unbuckle my sandals.

Stork shuts the cabinets and then takes a pillow off the bed for the floor. He's slept on the ground all month.

"Would you rather sleep in the bed tonight?" I surprise myself with the question, but he's shared things that he's tried to keep quiet. We both have. And him sleeping on the floor suddenly feels wildly unfair.

Stork frowns and glances at Zimmer.

"It's up to Franny," Zimmer says, already claiming one side of the bed. If it were up to him, he'd be fine with five more bodies all crammed onto the mattress.

I kick off my footwear and crawl back to the headboard.

Stork eyes me curiously. "Why tonight?"

"You've been less of a wart," I say strongly.

Light touches his eyes like he's smiling before his lips do. "I'll sleep on the bed." He sheds his military skirt and wraps linen around his waist. "But not if you're scared."

I swelter, a glistening sheen on my beige skin, and my tunic already clings to my frame. "I'm not scared."

He approaches, skimming me, and I scoot to the middle of the bed. As Stork rests a knee on the other side, my abdomen cramps like a fist rammed into my stomach.

I grit through a wince and roll onto my belly. *What's happening?* I try to focus on Court or Mykal, but our senses are muddled in razor-sharp panic. Rage. *Anguish.*

"Franny?" Zimmer calls, voice pitching. He hovers over me while I bury my face in a pillow and death-grip the sheets.

Court is yelling, his throat burning raw.

"Franny!" Stork is on the bed, rattling my shoulder. *"Franny."*

I need to go.

I need to help them. "I need to go," I choke out. Mykal cradles his arm around his sore stomach, spitting out nasty curses. He must've been punched. And Court fights hot tears, shouting . . . I concentrate on the movement of his lips that feel like my lips.

He's shouting, *He's not to blame!*

And . . .

I love him!

Water squeezes out of my eyes.

"Maybe it's her bleeding," Zimmer tells Stork.

I had my bleeding last week. I mutter under my breath, "It's not me." My mind is pulled in different directions.

Quietly, Stork asks, "Is it Mykal or Court?"

I freeze.

Why would he ask whether it's them?

Does he know about . . . ?

Gods . . .

He knows about our link. I gasp on cold fear.

Mykal and Court go absolutely still. Sensing my abrupt panic, they turn, and their feet are my feet. Running toward me.

TWENTY-TWO

Mykal

I'm running with no care to glance back at what I've left behind: a riled Kinden Valcastle. He wanted to wish his brother a good night, and what he saw was a watery-eyed Court, despondent from our uncoupling and exhaustion—and Kinden spun on me.

He used some foul words first, and I provoked him before he socked me in the gut. Ever since he knocked Franny unconscious at StarDust, I've been craving to lay a hand on him. But out of my feelings for Court, I didn't touch his brother.

What's happening in Stork's barracks is a different story.

Franny is on a bed with them. Her fear rakes down my bones, and hands touch her hip, her shoulder—my blood boils and my legs pump more forcefully beneath my urgent gait.

Court reaches Stork's barracks, quickly unlocking the puzzle, and I blow past him and barrel inside.

"Get off her!" I growl through gritted teeth, two paces into the room.

Franny hurls herself off the bed and races right into my arms.

I hold her tight, my concern stomping on my anger and banging questions at my head. Skin-to-skin, I sense her more clearly: thumping pulse, apprehensions squeezing her lungs.

She speaks with ragged breath, stumbling over words. "Who hurt you? Are you all right? He knows—he's known all along."

Which one knows what? I lose my chance to ask.

I'm rushing forward—*no.* I'm not the one truly movin'.

Franny and I look up. Court is the slingshot, aimed for Stork, who steps confidently off the bed.

He's taking my place, what I'd do if Franny hadn't flown into my arms. With a lot more grace than I, Court glides across the room in a blink and thrusts Stork against the frosted bath door, rattling the glass.

"Heya!" Zimmer extends his gangly arms between us. "Last I checked, we're on the same side. No need to start a stew."

Boiling inside out with a curdling wrath, Court bears a rigid forearm to Stork's windpipe. Muscle pressing on neck bones, Stork clears his throat in discomfort. Nothing but a tint of bitter sorrow behind iced blue eyes.

"If you hurt her," Court sneers, "you are our enemies."

Her pulse pierces the sky. Franny whips around in my arms, her back to my chest. "Stork didn't hurt me. Zimmer didn't hurt me—"

"I wouldn't fykking *dare*," Zimmer interjects heatedly, surly that we'd believe differently, but this damned link shares no intentions. Just emotions, senses, and all of that combined with the horrors we've been through has made us jump to the worst. We're left assuming too much off only a morsel.

Court narrows his gaze. "Then why?" *Why is she fretting?*

"Stork knows we're linked," Franny professes.

My mind whirls, and I dunno what to think or grasp onto. Court is solid stone, imprisoning breath in his lungs. I wish I could wrap an arm around him. I wish I could whisper in his ear, assuring him, even if nothing is making much sense to me.

Zimmer gawks. "Linked?" He must know less than us.

Stork tries to answer, his voice wheezy. Choked. Court releases some weight off his throat, and then Stork coughs once and says, "We don't . . . call it that—linked, linking."

Court is nearly nose-to-nose with Stork. "I don't give a damn what you call it," Court seethes. "You've known about our connection all this time, and yet you said *nothing*."

"And you'd still know nothing if I hadn't slipped up," Stork retorts with raised brows. "Lord have mercy, I should've kept my mouth shut." He lets out a painful laugh. "But I bloody cared about you and *him*." His icy gaze daggers me. "During Franny's distress, I thought you two were hurt and needed help, and I *slipped up*." He's kicking himself all right.

My mouth almost curves upward.

I'm glad my baby brother cared about us.

I'm glad he tripped up for once, and I'm thinking maybe there is good coming from Kinden's anger toward me after all.

Court leans back off him, just a bit. "Did the dead admirals tell you not to discuss linking with us?"

Stork rests his head solemnly against the frosted door. "No."

Inflamed shock punches my gut, and Franny sways backward into my chest. I must be sensing her surprise. I wrap a comforting arm around her collar, and air fills her lungs. Helping us both breathe better.

Stork meets her blistering gaze. "It wasn't their order. It was my choice."

"I don't believe you," Franny snaps.

His chest falls.

Zimmer is floating mindlessly on a hover-ma-board or whatever the hells it's called, and his head swings back and forth, listening to this unfolding argument.

"This truth," Stork says to Franny, "it's not one I've been dying to tell you. It's not happy. It's not comforting. It pains humans to remember."

"*It pains humans to remember?* So humans know about the link," Franny realizes, voice trembling. "I asked you a month ago." Her fingers curl into fists, containing her temper. "I asked you what happens when humans are tested for deathdays. I asked what that date means on a Death Reader, and you didn't answer me. But you knew then, didn't you?"

Stork nods.

I jump in, "Why didn't we find any of this in the books?" All right, I didn't do much reading, but Court did enough for the whole world and then some.

"What you're looking for was a long time ago, and it'd take more than a month to find the right book," Stork says, having trouble not looking at Franny. "You could've done an advanced search in the database, but none of you know how to work our computers that well."

Zimmer rocks from side to side on the hover-ma-board. "Someone care to clue a wise FT in?"

Franny scowls. "You're more of a chump if you need to be clued in." She mutters, "Like the rest of us."

He touches his heart. "Beg your pardon, I meant a wise*ass*."

Humor is far out of reach for the three of us. His smile drops at our collective silence, and he floats on the board over to Stork. "What do you know that they should know?"

"Everything." He inhales, as though preparing to unleash hells. "Right now, they're referring to the point in history when deathdays were first discovered. Back then it wasn't illegal for humans to test their deathdays."

Court takes another step back. Giving Stork enough room to stand straighter.

Tying the cloth tighter around his waist, Stork continues on, "Saltarians and humans believed deathday testing would work for both species. There'd be no divide between us. We'd all know the day we'd die."

Franny's heartbeat *thump, thump, thumps* against my forearm, still wrapped tight along her collar. She clutches onto my arm like she's clinging desperately to a hopeful outcome.

Storm clouds hang over Court. Unbelieving, doubtful, pessimistic, and moody, and I try to see the good for them. So we'll all be standing upright at the end of this.

Court frowns. "But only Saltarians learned their deathdays. It never worked for humans."

"Right." Stork nods. "The Death Readers showed a date for

humans, but they never died on that day. You three didn't die on your alleged deathday. See, the prongs on a Death Reader are coated in a teal pigment called *nylide*. It's what reads a Saltarian's body chemistry to determine deathdays, but Death Readers don't read a human's body chemistry. They change it."

Silence drapes over the barracks.

Stork says, "Humans who were pricked with the same exact Death Reader became what is known in history as lifebloods."

Lifebloods. Funny thinking how Court and I named our bond with a simple sort of word—the *link*—and all along, there'd been a prettier-sounding name out there, something that feels fuller and as intense as the raw sentiments we share.

"Lifeblood?" Franny mutters.

Stork wets his lips like he's trying to lick up liquor, and after a short beat, he says, "Court is your lifeblood. Mykal is your lifeblood. And you're theirs."

Zimmer wobbles on the board and braces himself with a foot on solid ground. "What makes them lifebloods exactly?"

"Our emotions," Court says in a deep whisper, lost in thought.

Slowly, Franny releases her clutch on my arm. "So the date on the Death Reader . . ."

"Is the day your body chemistry changed," Stork answers. "The day you became tethered to your lifebloods. The three of you share emotions and *three* senses: touch, taste, and smell."

Zimmer is wide-eyed. Staring like we've gone and sprouted antlers.

"How do we reverse it?" Court asks promptly, his urgency a familiar beast. So is his guilt and self-loathing, gnawing on my muscles. I crack a crick in my neck, and I wish I could be nearer. I'd be whispering in his ear.

Telling him not to hate how we're forced to feel his misery. His sufferings.

Because then I'd never feel the roll of his eyes. Or the flutter in his chest when he looks at me across a room. Or the strength he musters just to smile, and his tearful surprise when he recognizes he can and he does.

"Reverse it?" Stork repeats with the shake of his head. "You can't go back . . . it's permanent."

His nose flares. "No. There must've been someone who found a solution. Over a thousand years has passed since then."

"It's also been over a *thousand* years since lifebloods existed," Stork rebuts. "Like I said, testing deathdays on humans is illegal. No one wants to return to what happened in 2414."

Franny braves a step forward. "What happened? All the lifebloods just died out?"

"People didn't understand that Death Readers were the cause of lifebloods. Not at first. So humans unknowingly used the same devices." He leaves the frosted door. Nearing Franny. "You're only tethered to two people, dove. Think about a time where someone had fifteen, twenty, a *hundred* other emotions and senses from a hundred other humans in them. It led to hysteria, chaos, anarchy—and millions died . . ." He stops in the middle of the room, voice trailing.

Something's scratching at his mind.

Sinking dread shackles Court at the ankles, unmoving. I suppose he knows why Stork faltered. Very quietly, Court asks, "If I die, what happens to my lifebloods?"

The air sucks out of the room.

"We'll all be dying?" I question. Never did I think we'd all perish as one.

"Gods," Franny inhales.

Stork shakes his head with a wincing smile. "No. The way it's described in history . . ." He lets out a sad laugh that rings out like an apology. "It sounds worse than death. They say if your lifeblood dies, you lose a part of your soul forever. A . . . hollowness is left that can never be filled."

Eyes are burning. Overcome with something I can't explain, welling up my gaze. I exhale a coarse breath, grumbling, and I rub at my face with a callused palm.

Silent tears track Franny's cheeks.

Court has shut his eyes. Sinking and sinking, and I ache toe to head to heave them up out of this grief, but I dunno how.

It's a good thing Zimmer is here. He asks a question I think we'd all forgotten. "So humans know about lifebloods. It's in the history books, but does the *Lucretzia* crew know about Franny, Mykal, and Court?"

Have we been walking 'round all this time, trying to hide something that didn't need to be hidden?

"The crew has no idea," Stork says. "It's above everyone's clearance level." He watches Franny wipe her cheeks. "To be safe, I wouldn't tell anyone you're lifebloods. Not until the op is over and we're on Earth."

"How come?" Franny asks.

He nearly smiles at this part. "Historians say that at their best, lifebloods were the very *essence* of humanity. What you three have together . . . there is no definition that can sum up the pure empathy and compassion. You know more than I do." He pauses again, finding the right words. "But lifebloods are more vulnerable than a regular human. The crew would never hurt you, but they may distract you from the op. I have a feeling you'd be bloody paranoid if they found out beforehand."

We already have been. But I suppose it'd be worse if we yammered about being lifebloods to the whole starcraft. I wouldn't trust anybody afterward.

Court has opened his eyes. "Do other Saltarians know about lifebloods?"

"Saltare-1 does, yeah. I can't be sure whether the *Romulus* knew about you three. They never mentioned lifebloods when we negotiated the trade to free you from the brig."

That's good.

Court feels uncertain.

"Let me sort this out," Zimmer says, hopping back on the hover-boardie. Feet belong on the fucking ground.

Or mountainside.

"You two"—Zimmer skates to the middle of the room, halting beside Stork, but he motions to Court and me—"you can *feel* whatever Franny feels?"

Franny is on fire.

"Like it's our own body," I say. "Yeh."

"My body is not their body," Franny clarifies quickly. "We are all three bodies. Three minds. We just . . . feel."

I nod, glad she's better at speaking than I. That way someone can untangle the mess I make with words.

Court stares hard at Zimmer.

"So you knew Franny was straddling Stork then?" Zimmer realizes.

Franny's eyes bulge. "It was *not* that kind of straddling."

Stork smirks into a laugh and turns toward the cabinet.

"We ignored it," Court says smoothly.

Franny spins on him. "You ignored *nothing*. Because there was nothing to ignore."

"She's right," Stork says casually from the cabinet. "It was nothing."

My stomach sinks in disappointment, and immediately, I know it's Franny. Maybe she wanted it to be more.

Zimmer glides on the board, closer to Franny. "I know what I saw, and it was textbook Fast-Tracker straddling." Him yammering about Franny and Stork only puts more of Franny's sinking feelings in my belly.

Zimmer begins to pass me, and I shove his shoulder. He trips off the silver board. Stumbling. "Every time." He dusts off his slacks, not offended. "I'll take that as a Grenpalish affirmative."

I give him a ruder gesture. "This is more like it."

Court rolls his eyes, but his lip aches to lift.

"We're all a strange sort," Franny says quietly, but light brightens in us. We're making greater sense of what we share. What others like us once shared.

Stranger, even, to think we're all that's left now.

The last three lifebloods.

"You're forgetting something," Court suddenly says, more weight descending on his chest. He's staring at Stork, who fills up a damned glass with liquor.

Sighing, Stork rotates to Court. "Am I?"

"If lifebloods are only created by using the same Death Reader," Court says. "How did all three of us use the same device and end up in three different places?"

Yamafort.

Bartholo.

Grenpale.

Stork smiles bitterly. "It's all connected, mate. I told you there was a reason I kept this secret. It's all *connected*. And here we are. You, wanting answers. Me, protecting a dying wish." He kicks back against the cabinets. "Tell me, which matters more? Your greed? Or their sacrifice?"

We all glance at one another, unsure.

Stork opens his arms. Tears cinch his eyes. "I'm waiting."

TWENTY-THREE

Franny

S imply put, don't fall in the water, and you won't drown,"
Padgett says while I push fleet grub around in my bowl.
At 5 o'morning, the warmly lit dining hall is hushed,
early risers chewing on cornmeal and berries.

More militant than StarDust, there are no velveteen chairs
or crystal goblets. Just a piping-hot buffet spread, benches
wrapped around bronze circular tables, and framed picture
screens on leafy-green walls.

In a corner next to a potted fern, Padgett, Gem, and I eat
breakfast together and talk about the retrieval operation.

We leave the *Lucretzia* tomorrow, and after two months of
trying and trying, I botched every attempt at swimming. Lately,
I've thought less about being a lifeblood and more about staying above water.

I dig a bonnaberry out from the mush. "I was hoping humans
were majestically buoyant as a natural survival instinct." Turns
out, I'm the opposite of buoyant when panicked.

I sink.

Anyway, I only learned about buoys and sailboats and sea-
faring things from our two-month Saltare-1 training, but talking about the ocean is different than seeing it.

Gem takes dainty sips of orange juice. "Humans do have
floatation jackets. I read about them in a safety manual."

I straighten up from a slouch.

"*Human* floatation jackets," Padgett emphasizes, stirring her grub. "If you wear that on Saltare-1, they'll know you're not Saltarian." And then I'd be sent to Onakar Prison.

I try not to mope. "I guess I just better pray to the gods that I don't fall in." I eat a spoonful, the gritty texture easier to swallow since my first day here.

"Chin up." Gem cups her glass with two hands. "Between the three of us, we'll overcome all odds. I also put in a request that we share the same trash bin to Saltare-1."

We all laugh when she says *trash bin* like it's a Purple Coach and we're just leisurely being driven to a new planet.

"A request with who?" I ask. "Stork or Court?"

"Both."

Padgett adjusts a pretty pendant at her throat, the pink jewel complementing her brown skin. "Most likely, you'll be in a trash bin with Court and Mykal. I think they'll want to keep the humans together."

"Or they'll split them apart," Gem predicts. "They'll have less chances to die if we use our bodies as shields—"

"No," I say, eyes flashing hot. "Don't do that."

"It's just a theory," Gem muses.

"Incoming," Padgett says silkily.

I hardly see what she's noticed until a confident and bookish Nia waves to us, spiral-bound texts tucked under her arm. She places the haul in front of Gem. "Found all your requests."

"Holy wonders, this is brilliant. Thank you, Nia." Gem smiles and taps the title to show all of us. "I plan to build one in my lifetime."

I peek over and read, *How-to Kit: All About Cars & Manual Transmissions.* My lips part, and I ask Nia, "So there are cars on Earth?"

"There have been in past history, but currently? I wouldn't really know." She's about to depart.

Padgett is quick to ask, "Why wouldn't you know?"

Walking backward, Nia tells us, "I was born on the *Lucretzia*. Never stepped foot on Earth in my life."

At this, she turns and leaves, and I notice Court at the buffet line. Grub bowl in hand, he wavers on approaching our table, stepping forward.

Stepping back.

Nervousness clams his palms, and the more I concentrate on him, the more I feel bitty pieces of metal in his sweaty hand. One end sharp, the other smooth and familiar. I recognize what he's clutching.

My heart swells, and I motion him over.

TWENTY-FOUR

Court

I hesitate to join the girls at breakfast.

They laugh together, and my austere presence is a reminder of practical matters: the mission tomorrow, the dangers.

And then Franny waves me over.

My feet move beneath my rigid body before my brain catches up to speed. Sandals clapping on mosaic tile, I approach and unclench my fist while I slide on the bench. I set my grub on the tabletop.

"Good morning, Court," Gem greets, polite and cheerful.

"Gem." I nod, joints stiff. My lips hoist—just a feeling. I touch my mouth to be certain no smile crests my face. This one belongs to Franny on my left. She senses the metal in my palm, but I'm not certain she realizes what I hold is for her.

Beside her bowl, I place three silver pieces of jewelry. For an eyebrow, lip, and nose piercing.

Overcome, like her past suddenly rushes back and crashes against her chest. Pressure falls on my breastbone and then washes away with her stronger breath.

She pinches the hoop ring, meant for her lip. "You remembered?"

I can't forget.

How I met Franny with messy green-and-blue dyed hair, three piercings, and inked FT tattoos. How I told her to pretend to be an Influential—to be with us, she needed to take out the piercings.

I try to answer, but I can't form the words. Swallowing, I say, "They weren't difficult to find. I asked around the starcraft." Humans wear piercings too.

With the heels of her palm, Franny rubs her glassing eyes. "You found these for me—"

"It's nothing." I shake my head. "Just preparation for the mission." I'm not kind like Mykal. If we weren't trying to pretend to be Fast-Trackers tomorrow, I doubt I'd hand over the piercings, but gods be damned, something inside of me is crying out, *you know it's more.*

You know you're more than survival.

Or maybe I'm just wishing I were.

Of what I've studied about our sister planets, their way of life is largely similar to people from Saltare-3. Down to the stereotypes of Influentials and Fast-Trackers. The former is elite class, often overdressed and proper, while the latter is hedonistic, pierced, and tattooed.

"Tomorrow, we all plan to look the part of a common Fast-Tracker." I remind Franny of this.

"You didn't have to bring me these three piercings," Franny says in a scorching whisper, like she's trying to set fire to the bleakness in my mind. "But you did."

I did . . .

I nod several times. Not arguing.

I did.

The girls return to talking about cars, hair dye colors, and trash bins. Laughing again, even though I'm with them, and Kinden struts over with a glass of pear juice.

"Soarcastles, Franny," he greets. "Little brother." He sits on my right. "You're all smiling now, but tomorrow, we'll be flying to a trash moon, and I'll laugh when one of you trips in someone's soiled underpants."

"You're a juvenile," Gem rebuts.

"You're a juvenile," he mimics, his impression of Gem's high-pitched voice nearly spot-on at this point.

Gem huffs.

Padgett motions her spoon at Kinden. "You just proved Gem's point."

"I prove many points right, Padgett." He unbuttons his champagne-colored blazer. "It's a gift."

"And a flaw," she says easily and takes a casual bite of grub, but she's pursing her lips to restrain a smile.

I sense him.

Trudging into the dining hall, Mykal scratches the back of his head. Wheat-blond hair threading his coarse fingers. Sweat pricks his bare chest, no cold slap of the wind or wet snow against his ankles. Discomfort grips his body like a belt five notches too tight.

He's ready to be out of a starcraft and on land.

I want that for him.

Instead of just sensing, I look over at the buffet. Watching Mykal take a bowl and pick out the bonnaberries with his fingers. He tosses them back into the steaming vat of grub and grumbles under his breath.

Suddenly, he goes still, and then his head whips over his broad shoulder. He locates me, fixating on my mouth.

I realize only now . . . I'm smiling.

He felt my smile.

His lungs expand. Chest elevating. Just as the corner of his lip lifts, realities bear on me and him, and at the same time, our mouths form lines.

We need to be uncoupled so no one thinks we're lifebloods. On the starcraft *and* on Saltare-1.

Mykal grunts out a gruff breath. Raking his hand harsher through his hair, and my jaw muscle tics. He jerks his head toward the door. Telling me he's about to leave.

He's been eating breakfast in the library. Not always alone. Franny spends every other day with him and me.

"Mykal," Kinden calls, raising his voice to be heard. "Eat with us." He digs into his blazer pocket and holds out a package of cigarettes for him. His peace offerings this past month have come in the form of wood, tobacco, thread, and fabrics.

He's understood quickly what Mykal likes.

Mykal grinds his molars, uncertain.

I'm about to make an excuse for him, but Kinden clamps a hand on my shoulder. "You're both being obtuse. Clearly, he still likes you, and you still like him."

If only it were that simple. "Just last month you thought he broke my heart," I remind him, "and now you're advocating a recoupling like it's the only wise thing to do." I don't mention how he punched Mykal. Kinden has apologized profusely for their confrontation.

Not because of anything I said. I would've screamed until I lost my voice. Just to make him understand how much Mykal is not to blame.

How much I care for him.

How much I'd die for him.

How my life has no pure meaning without him.

Kinden squeezes my shoulder before letting go and whispering to me, "I was only focused on your heartbreak. I never saw his." He picks up his pear juice. "Not until later that night."

The night they fought.

The same night we learned we were lifebloods. My older brother wanted me to sleep in his barracks, and it hurt to leave Mykal. But we agreed to pull apart, so I willingly left.

I stormed ahead of Kinden, and I didn't see my brother lingering behind. He heard Mykal crying through the door.

I sensed him. Feeling his heart ripping apart, while mine shatters, has been excruciating. To say the least.

The more Kinden fixates on our uncoupling, the less he or anyone else has suspected we have a strange bond. One day, I plan to tell him that Mykal is my lifeblood.

I could almost smile thinking about that moment, but it can't come until we're safe.

In the dining hall, Mykal decides to join our table after Kinden's persistence. My older brother even slides over on the bench. Freeing a space so that Mykal can sit next to me.

He takes the spot beside Padgett.

Kinden glares but pushes the cigarettes to him. "You could've sat next to Court."

"I like this seat better because Court's not on it," Mykal teases, his lopsided smile slowly fading as I tense.

He lowers his head.

I'm sorry.

He growls under his breath as soon as he senses my regret.

Franny massages her shoulder and tells me, "You have less than a day to master the art of slouching."

Most Fast-Trackers *slump.*

I don't loosen my shoulders, but I bow forward in a casual posture. I rest my cheek on my fist.

Everyone mentions how I appear exactly like a common Fast-Tracker, and it helps that I already have tattoos.

"You could've been an actor," Franny muses.

Mykal nods. "He's more than pretty enough." He curses, our necks hot from his compliment.

"Have you coupled again?" Gem wonders.

"No," we say together.

Standing, Mykal picks up his bowl. "I'll be leaving."

Kinden whispers for me to walk him out. *I can't.* My older brother suggesting what I crave is pouring salt in the wound.

Mykal messes Franny's hair, then pushes her cheek. "May the gods be in your spirit."

She pushes his shoulder. "And I in your heart."

I almost lock eyes with Mykal, but he diverts his gaze to the door. While I watch him exit, in my peripheral I notice Stork and Zimmer near the buffet line. Speaking hushed, both carry little amusement in their closed stances. Severity tightens their gazes, and Zimmer nods repeatedly.

He looks over at Franny.

They both do.

She's unaware, caught up discussing human music with Gem. "It's called rock and roll," Franny says. "I'd never heard anything like it." She talks about how Stork has miniature speakers for his ears, and he'll fall asleep listening to guitar riffs.

I catch Zimmer handing a folded paper to Stork.

The probability that the paper is about the mission is low. Stork has kept me in the loop for the entire retrieval operation, going as far as asking for my interpretation of the myth and seeking advice on Saltarians.

The paper is personal.

Unimportant, my mind screeches at first.

No time.

No room to ask and pry.

Unimportant.

I blink slowly, my soul humming off in the distance. Waiting for me to find the courage to open up again.

And again.

And as Stork leaves the dining hall, Zimmer walks over with a lighter gait. Plopping down backward on the bench, he takes the spot that Kinden left for Mykal. Zimmer braces his elbows on the table and smiles. "What'd I miss?"

Chatter reignites.

Ask him.

What if he'd rather I not know about the paper? What if I make him uncomfortable?

Just try. I seize my confidence, and as the conversation pauses, I ask Zimmer, "What was the paper you handed Stork?"

"That little thing?" Zimmer uncaps a saltshaker. "It's not about the mission, if that's why you asked."

"It's not why." My hand is frozen on my thigh. "I just wanted to know."

His smile reappears, and I release my tight grip and breath. Zimmer spins toward me, straddling the bench. "You've heard of a Final Will?"

Of course. I nod.

"Well, I have one."

The table quiets. Overhearing.

Final Wills are sealed until death and a relative or trustee will open them on their behalf. All Influentials have Final Wills since the document states where or to whom their property and wealth will be distributed. Ensuring the prosperity of generations. They're also useful for Fast-Trackers and Babes, but less so, as family lineages are shorter.

Mykal's pa had a Final Will. He left his hut, weapons, and furs to his son.

Mykal had a Final Will. At eight years of age, he left his possessions to his whole village.

I had no Final Will. At ten years of age, I became a criminal and thusly all my assets were taken by my country.

Franny—she had no Final Will. At seventeen years of age, she had no belongings to give.

"You have a Final Will?" Franny frowns, her shoulders drooping at talk of death and Zimmer. "What for?"

"I have something, *one thing*, that I'm going to pass on when I'm gone." Zimmer mouths to Franny, *don't be sad.*

"I'm not sad," she lies. "Death is normal."

"Clap for me." He smiles wryly. "Loudly."

"You're not dying today—"

"I'm not." He nods. "Who knows when I'll die?" He laughs since he hasn't told anyone his deathday. "Could be in a few years."

Franny asks, "Then why'd you leave your socks to someone?"

"Not my socks."

Kinden sips his pear juice. "No one wants your baggy floral shirts after you've died. My brother of six years had better style than you."

I stare far away at the mention of Illian. Our little brother. A Babe.

Zimmer laughs.

And then Padgett slips in and asks, "You gave your Final Will to Stork?"

He dumps salt in a mound on the table. "I initially planned to give the Final Will to you." He glances at *me*. "You're the most responsible one, but I realized . . ." He pauses, drawing in the salt mound. ". . . what good is a Final Will if it's left on another planet? I can't be sure you'll make it out of Saltare-1 alive."

The air strains between us, and Franny takes a shallow breath.

Death is uncertain.

But how can you be fearless despite that uncertainty? I don't know. Because I sense her fear. I feel mine. We're about to land on an enemy planet that wants us dead.

Fear seems like the only sensible emotion.

TWENTY-FIVE

Franny

Eyes still heavy-lidded and mind slowly buzzing to life, I thought I'd wake to nerves. Today, we're finally leaving the *Lucretzia* and flying to the moon. Fear and worry is instilled in my future, but right now, in this moment, I'm bathed with sheer content.

Like I had the most *miraculous* sleep in all my life.

Soft breath leaves my lips, and I hug closer to the pillow I've been curling up against. *Wait...*

My arms hold something firmer than a pillow, and my legs slide against something rougher than the sheets.

Oh...

Gods.

My eyes shoot open.

The pillow is Stork. White-blond hair tousled from slumber, his arms are threaded with mine. His eyelids are shut—*thank the gods.* Chest against chest, comfortable, warm heat brews between us. It feels too good. I must've rolled over to his side of the bed in the middle of the night.

Zimmer is still soundlessly asleep on the left, and I don't look over and risk bringing attention to this . . . situation.

Maybe I can feign sleep and just naturally roll away.

Roll away.

Just *roll away,* Franny.

"You're awake." Stork's soft voice is a whisper, but it blares in my head like a horn. His eyes fall open and his lips rise.

I'm immobile. Too nervous to move and wake Zimmer. So I bring the heat through my eyes.

"And how long have you been awake?" I whisper.

He smiles wider. "Long enough to know that you liked sleeping in my arms."

I did.

I can't deny that.

Even now, there are parts of me that ache to move closer. To remember what it was like for a body to be on mine. But I can't have that—I don't think . . .

My nose flares. Court and Mykal must still be fast asleep because neither of them are alerted by my emotions. *Good.*

Let this moment go to my grave.

"Your body is surprisingly comfortable," I tell him as I untangle from his legs. "That's all. Nothing more."

His brows rise and he lifts his arm off me. "Of course. Nothing more." Those words hurt just as much as they did the last time he agreed with me.

I sit up, slowly, careful not to draw attention from Zimmer. He's practically passed out, his two arms cuddling a pillow like I thought I'd been doing all night.

Stork rises off the bed.

I glance to him. "Thank you." The words tumble before I can catch them.

He looks back, frowning. "For what?"

Last night might be the very last time I go to sleep. I could very well die today. On the ride to Rosaline or on the trash bins to Saltare-1, or on the enemy planet that wants me dead.

Last night was truly the last time I might ever feel safe.

And it was glorious, peaceful sleep.

I don't know how to say these words, but Stork has seen my fears during training. He knows what lies ahead. And he's a clever wart.

He nods, like he understands. But then humor touches his eyes, and his lips lift again.

"Don't," I start, already sensing his charming quip.

"Next time you want to cuddle, dove, just ask."

And there it is.

I snort, chin raised. "Maybe I will."

"Looking forward to it."

He walks out of the bedroom to bathe, leaving me roasting toe to head.

TWENTY-SIX

Franny

Fast-Trackers everywhere would never bet on my odds. I lived to be eighteen years of age, when I was supposed to die at seventeen, and I made it to a moon.

The easiest part is reaching Rosaline, a chalky, rouge, crater-covered sphere. We take a jumper-starcraft and park on a flat landmass.

Dust kicks up and whirls around all eight of us, shrouding our sight. I can only distinguish jagged boulders a few paces off, and an outline of a humongous garbage heap.

Gravity drags me down, about ten pounds heavier on this moon. Every arm movement and footstep is slower than the next.

This is fun.

I'm not trying to trick myself. I'm trying to remember that my old Fast-Tracker self would've enjoyed moon-walking.

This is fun.

There is fun in fear.

Right?

Thanks to Court and Stork, we aren't chumps floating around without good planning. We're all well-prepared.

Our burgundy Saltare-1 jumpsuits protect us from the dust and low oxygen, made of polyester, nylon, and genoforla. A snug-fitting helmet is attached to our spacesuits, microphones in our ears to speak to each other and the Knave Squadron. Nia, Arden, and Barrett remain on the parked jumper-starcraft. They're to fly the small ship back to the *Lucretzia*.

After that, there'll be no other way off the Rosaline besides the trash bins.

"Good luck, Knave," Nia says. Static layers on top of her voice through the microphone. "And the rest of you. Stay sharp."

Stork turns to the jumper-starcraft and raises a hand. "I'll see you three soon." Confidence encases every word, and even I try to hold on to it.

"Don't miss us too much," Arden replies. "Taking off in three . . . two . . . one."

The jumper-starcraft grumbles and dust billows from underneath the vessel before it lifts off and zips away.

With the starcraft gone, the rest of us cluster together, all looking identical in our protective gear.

"The assembly line is this way," Stork says, voice echoing through my mic, and he points to the left. He leads us through the swirling dust, darkness enveloping us.

My breath is too loud in my helmet.

"Whoever is panting, you're exploding my eardrum." Kinden calls me out.

I swallow hard, and a hand drifts against my palm. Someone clasps my hand, and I can't tell if it's Court or Mykal or someone else. Like Zimmer.

With gloves on, we have no skin-to-skin contact, so the life-blood link wouldn't heighten.

I turn in slow motion.

And through the glass visor of his helmet, I see Court. He nods as though to say, *you're doing fine.* His reassurance means everything to me.

His new eyebrow piercing reminds me that everyone looks more like Fast-Trackers. Before we left, everyone dyed their hair or pierced their face, some a combination of the two.

My black hair is streaked green and blue. And all three of my piercings are in place.

I'm not trying to be who I was before I dodged my deathday.

I know that's impossible, but I want to be some version of both.

All of who I was and all of who I am.

We drag sluggishly toward the assembly line, and I hear the groan of machinery. Court and I let go when we notice the graveyard of empty dumpsters. Eight feet tall, but some are too narrow for more than one person to fit inside.

"Far right!" Gem says with mic static. "I see an oversized trash bin."

I can barely distinguish the first row of dumpsters. I try to waft away the dust.

"We'll all be able to squeeze into that one," Kinden says, trekking slowly forward.

"Good find, Gem," Court tells her. "Let's hurry."

We try to quicken our pace.

Mykal is the only one able to move with no setback. I bet he could jog if he wanted to. This gravity must feel only a little different from the weight of an animal on his shoulders.

The groans grow louder, and the robotic shuttles I'd seen pictured in textbooks are suddenly up close. Materializing through the dust.

Each shuttle is like a jetpack. Engines blast and keep the shuttle airborne while their monstrous claws shut the lid of an empty gray dumpster. Once the robotic arms grab hold, the trash bin is secured and the shuttle soars off the moon. Heading to Saltare-1, so the dumpster can be refilled with garbage.

This is fun.

So much fun.

I blow out a measured breath, and the tallest help boost the shortest into the sturdy dumpster. Court is among the tall, along with his older brother and Stork.

Mykal easily climbs over on his own, and once we're all inside, we press our backs to the firm sides. Cramped, I'm between Court and Mykal, and I'm barely an arm's length away from Stork and Zimmer across from me.

Remember the plan, Franny.

I unclip a handle attached to my jumpsuit's belt and press the ends to the wall of the dumpster. It suctions, and I grasp hard for support.

I hear the *pop* of suction from everyone else's handles. We kick back our ankles and a sticky grip on our spaceboots adheres to the wall.

"Now what?" Zimmer's voice crackles with more static.

"We wait for a shuttle," Stork replies.

I shut my eyes. Trying not to repeat the worst-case scenario: *an asteroid hits our dumpster.* Or more terrifying, the *Romulus* intercepts the trash bin.

Fear snakes down my spine, and I can't tell if I'm sweating since the spacesuit wicks away perspiration.

Technology is a beauty.

"It smells rank in here," Kinden complains.

"That's just *you*," Gem says, nestled beside her older sister. Bangs cut blunt across her forehead and dyed a periwinkle shade.

"Poor . . . insult." His voice breaks, bad connection. "Seeing as . . . we're . . . a trash . . ."

Something slick is stuck to my boot. I let go of the handle and crouch to the bottom of the bin. Moving so, *so* slowly.

I can do this.

I better do it without hyperventilating.

Lifting my sole, I make out a flyer in Saltarian. I read aloud, *"And so let the God of Victory bless us and unite us on this Sacred Eve, for now, for always."*

Everyone grows quiet.

Court rolls his eyes.

Mykal hangs his head and mumbles huskily, his prayer unfamiliar to me.

The mechanical groan is suddenly above us.

"Here we go," Stork says, just as the lid *bangs* shut. We're in complete pitch-black darkness. In a quick moment, Stork snaps a plastic stick and drops it at our feet.

Blue light glows. Illuminating all of us while the dumpster rumbles. Rocking from side to side, I grip my handle like my life depends on it.

Gods, my life does *depend on it.*

No one speaks.

We can't see outside the dumpster, but my stomach lurches like the claws have grabbed and lifted the bin.

The walls rattle.

We must be rocketing through space.

Spending months in StarDust, in all those gravity simulators, has paid off for us. No motion sickness touches me or Court or Mykal, and the *Saga 4* seem just as content.

Stork is used to space flight as a C-Jay. I didn't think he'd be the one to botch this trip.

Soon, we must hit a patch of debris, as the dumpster quakes violently.

"Hold on," Court tells everyone.

My arm bangs into Court's arm. Mykal's elbow digs into my side—and then the dumpster careens forward and back in a whiplash *snap.*

Only my neck moves, my head slinging forward. The same happens to Stork, and in a perfect collision, our helmets crash together.

Crack.

Crunch.

As my head slings back to the wall, I'm disoriented. Confused, panicked, concerned . . . terrified—tripled senses veering in several directions.

"Franny!" Court's voice pitches in my ear. Everyone is speaking. Yelling. I hear my name from five different people.

Stork shakes the dizziness out of his head, his glass visor crunched in the corner but not broken.

Why is a red light flashing inside my helmet? I focus . . .

No.

No.

A slender fissure runs through my glass visor. It seems small, but it's a gaping *hole*. The dumpster is sealed shut, but it can't protect me from space. Who knows how much oxygen crept inside this bin before the lid shut?

Holy hells . . . I'm going to die. *I don't want to die.*

I don't want to die.

Gods, I don't want to die today.

"Stay calm," Court snaps at me, static softening his stabbing voice. "Take shallow breaths, Franny."

Zimmer lets go of his handle and is about to pull off his helmet—

"No, *no*," I almost shout, my eyes frantic.

He could die. Today could be his deathday, and he's not dying in this fykking dumpster.

He's not.

He deserves a better death than that.

Zimmer falters. "Today . . ." His voice breaks. ". . . death . . ." He must still see the warning and fear in my searing eyes because he grabs the handle. Backing up from me.

"Conserve air," Court cautions me. "Do . . . scream." I think I must've missed the word *not*.

Do *not* scream.

I hold my breath, my pulse lodged in my throat.

Mykal tries to breathe for me, but his strong inhales are only a sensation. It's not real.

Though it comforts me.

Stork lets go of his support, unsticking his feet, and before the turbulence tosses him like a doll, he clutches my handle with me. Body pressing up against mine, he assesses the damage of my helmet up close.

And then his hand rises to the buckle of his helmet.

I shake my head. "You can't wear my cracked helmet!" I'm not sure how much he can hear through the spotty signal.

He holds up one finger.

And then five fingers.

And then makes a zero.

One hundred and fifty.

He will die at one hundred and fifty years. He's saying he'll survive this part, and since he acts more like a Fast-Tracker than an Influential, I know he cares little about injuries.

I ease back, and his lip quirks before he unbuckles his helmet and pulls it off his head like he didn't need one in the first place.

"Hold . . ." Gem says.

". . . breath . . . hold," Padgett tells me.

"Don't . . . bre . . ." Kinden instructs.

I hold my breath and pop the buckles of my helmet. Using both hands to remove it.

Stork pins me to the wall with his muscular body, and quickly, he situates his helmet on my head and locks it onto my suit.

I breathe a lungful.

Mykal and Court relax back, and Zimmer nods in thanks to the gods or Stork. I can't tell which.

Stork fits my cracked helmet on himself, and I try to catch my hot, ragged breath.

He knocks lightly on my glass visor to grab my attention.

I'm all anger and guilt.

His face glows red from the emergency lights. "I . . ." His lips move, but I hear nothing else.

"I can't hear you!" I shout. "Save your breath!"

He tries again. Yelling, "I can't . . ." I see the shape of his words: *I can't die!*

"You can be injured!" I remind him, and after frustrating communication back and forth—where many of us tell him to stop talking—I understand his next response.

Stork says, "Better me than you, dove."

I'm human. A vulnerable, fragile human, but he treats my life with more importance. I'm someone who can be kept safe.

His life isn't less important than mine because he can't die.

The dumpster rumbles again.
This is fun.
I inhale sharply. *So fun.*
Stork smiles at me, not moving back yet.
My lip so badly wants to rise.

TWENTY-SEVEN

Mykal

I choke on the thick, muggy air and toss my helmet aside with the rest of the garbage heap. Behind me, the others crawl from the trash bin on all fours, unstable, like creatures leaving a cave for the first time.

My eyes burn from the sun, brighter than I'm used to. Cupping a hand above my gnarly brows, I examine the new landscape.

First impression: it's the strangest sight I've ever seen.

Water surrounds us. Endless blue-green with tops of white foam. I turn around and every which way, I'm met with the same colors. Waves crash hard like they're thundering snowstorms from the skies. The small pond we practiced in is nothing in comparison to *this*.

We're all silent for a moment.

Taking it in.

Even Kinden, Zimmer, and the Soarcastle sisters are hushed by the vastness of a warm ocean.

Court is the first to break the quiet. Sliding to my side, he says, "We have to make it over there." He points toward more water. But then I squint, and I can sorta see a faint outline of skyscraping buildings. Taller than the ones back in Bartholo *and* Yamafort. Some seem to even disappear into the clouds.

My gaze rotates to him, and I can't help but stare. Not only did Court pierce his brow, but a strand of his brown hair is dyed gray. It suits him well. Matches his eyes.

Even pretending to be a Fast-Tracker, he's beautiful. He fits in.

Better than I.

The tips of my blond locks are fire-red and don't look nearly as good. I have no tattoos, but I did agree to a small silver stud in my ear.

"What?" Court asks, catching me gawking.

I dislike, very much, being uncoupled from him. But those words don't do us any good on the crest of this mission. So I just shrug, and his own riled sentiments crash into me and he bears down on his teeth.

"Toss your jumpsuits *under* the trash," Stork says, and I turn to the task at hand.

Everyone sheds their outer layer like a skin. Underneath the jumpsuits, we wear ripped shorts and frayed shirts. Not as graceful, I step out of the jumpsuit only having on a pair of torn jeans and a shirt that looks like it's been clawed by a mountain lion.

Apparently all the fabric rips and tears is the silly fashion style of Saltare-1. Strings on my shirt fly about in the wind, and I yank them off in frustration.

Franny kicks her jumpsuit underneath a heap of crushed cans.

"This is the hard part," Gem says, narrowing her eyes out at the ocean. Her periwinkle hair blows in a gust.

My stomach twists in knots, and I realize it's not me at all. Franny bounces on her heels, and looks to the water with complete dread. She still can't swim.

But we'll be doing fine.

I have to believe that for them both.

"Remember what we practiced," Stork says as he pushes to the front of our group, near the edge of the island. He holds a handheld device that's shaped like a gun. The first time I saw it during training, I thought we were being outfitted with Saltare weapons.

Turns out the damned thing isn't even a weapon.

Or a Saltare device.

Franny bounds to my side. "There are oceanic crocodiles in the waters," she whispers to me. "I read about them." She swallows hard as her nerves mount.

"Shoulda done what I did." I nudge her shoulder. "No reading. No worrying about whatever's deep in these oceans."

"At least you can swim."

"You're gonna be fine, little love." I tap her head for good measure, and her spirits fight to rise.

"I can do this," she mutters under her breath.

Court and Stork stand side by side and they whisper for a second before Court appraises the rest of us with a quick sweep. "We've done this a hundred times," he reminds all of us. His eyes stop on Franny. "You don't need to know how to swim, Franny. Because you're not going to fall in."

Confidence blazes his words, and I feel it in my bones. She must too because she nods strongly in acceptance.

Court motions to Stork. "Let's go."

Stork holds the handheld device out to the water. He clicks the button, and just like in training, a small translucent platform—no bigger than a rung of a ladder—appears inches above the water. He said it was a "solid" hologram. One that could carry our weight. It shimmers in the sunlight and is only big enough for a single boot. Stork will keep clicking the device, creating plank after plank, to make a walkway above the ocean.

Even bringing the *human* device here was a nasty risk, but according to Stork *and* Court, there was no other way to cross the wide ocean from the trash island to the mainland.

So here we are.

Crossing a whole damned ocean with nothing more than hologrammies.

"Watch your step!" Stork yells over the growing waves.

We'd been training for this part of the journey back in the *Lucretzia*'s pool, but there weren't any waves. And I see now that a small pool is nothing compared to the vast, turbulent body of water before us.

No need to think about that.

I'll be thinking about safely crossing and reaching solid ground. Once there, Stork will be pressing another button and the hologrammies should disappear.

Out in front, Stork clicks the device and continues to create the shimmery planks. Each time he clicks one, he steps forward. Court goes next, and I fall in line behind him.

In a single row, we walk.

Franny is situated between me and Gem. Then Padgett, Zimmer, and Kinden bring up the rear. The journey is quiet as we all concentrate on stepping. Warm wind bathes me, heating my skin, and sweat starts to uncomfortably build.

Court glances back, eyes pinging to me. It's not the first time, and I'm fearing it won't be the last. "Look where you're going," I say, worry cresting. "Or I'm going to push you off myself." *I'd never.* But he understands the threat all right.

Concern. Worry. It mounts like a thousand bricks between the three of us. I think we're more distressed about the possibility of each other going in the waters than ourselves. Being in this damned single-file line and walking without being able to see eye to eye is unnerving is all.

"Did you know that there are exactly one thousand steps from the island to the mainland?" Gem says, loud enough to be heard over the waves and the wind. "Nia and I did the calculations yesterday."

"We know now," Kinden says like he wished he didn't know and then he lets out a curse.

I glance over my shoulder to see the rear of our line.

Waves behind Kinden and Zimmer grow taller and angrier. They crash harder into the ocean, creating more white foam.

"Heya! Move faster!" Zimmer shouts over the swells.

We all pick up our pace, but the shimmery planks have grown slick from the water rushing over them. I concentrate, eyes focused on where I'm stepping, making sure I don't accidentally lose traction.

My pulse speeds, and something in my stomach dives like a rocket speeding straight into the ground.

"GEM!" Padgett screams.

I swerve around to see the youngest Soarcastle sister slipping forward, teetering, not able to catch her momentum. She knocks into Franny and the last thing I see before both girls plummet into the ocean is the look on Franny's face. Wide eyes, opened mouth. And then she's gone.

Just like that.

Water rushes around me like I'm the one under, but I hold onto my own panic. "FRANNY!" I scream, lungs set on fire. I'm about to jump in after them, but both girls suddenly bob up to the surface. Choking on water.

"Thank the gods," Kinden says in relief. Franny kicks and paddles with panicked breaths, not safe yet. Her fear stabs me left and right.

Gem does a better job at swimming over.

Padgett and I, the closest to both Gem and Franny, bend down and reach out for their hands.

"Hurry," Court calls out, watching the growing waves behind us.

Stork starts to backtrack, creating new planks beside ours for a closer vantage. He stops next to me.

Only a few feet away, Franny stretches out, trying to reach, but our fingertips barely brush. She swallows a mouthful of sea.

I grimace, the water tasting salty and going down harsh. "Grab here," I call out to Franny and extend my arm farther.

We clasp hands, and then suddenly, both Gem and Franny are tugged down by an invisible force. Her palm is ripped out of mine.

"FRANNY!" I holler.

I can't see them. I can't see anything but white foam and restless waves. My ankle begins to sear. Overwhelming pain.

Stars blink in my vision.

"Padgett!" Kinden is yelling. She looks to him and he throws her something. The long stick—it's a depowered electrowand. A Saltare weapon. As soon as it's in her hands, she dives in a clean arc and vanishes into the deep, dark water.

I make a move like I'm gonna step off the plank into the ocean. Find her. Grab her. Bring her back.

"MYKAL!" Court cries out in panic. Stork is already grabbing me around the waist, stopping me.

I struggle beneath him. "Let me go!" I scream through angry tears. Pain lances my back. My ankle. Water rushes into my lungs. I feel like I'm choking and dying on fear. *Her fear.* My fear.

All three of us.

She's going to die down there and we're just gonna let it happen?!

"We can't risk both of you drowning!" Stork yells. "You know what would happen to Court if you both died."

Tears burn my eyes. I can't think of that future. I can only think of the possibility where I go into the waters and come out alive. Whatever's clawing at her, I can fight it.

"Trust Padgett," Kinden tells me.

"Mykal." Court calls my name. His grim eyes sear into mine, saying, *I can't lose you too.* I shake my head harder. I can't live with myself doing nothing. Letting her go.

Stork is the only one close enough to clutch onto me. His fingers dig into my neck like I'm a wolf pup. Court touches his chest. "The best thing we can do for her, Mykal," he says, "is stay calm."

I relax suddenly.

He's right.

If she's feeling my hysteria, it's not going to help her one bit. And if I'm underwater, that may even be worse for her.

He's right.

I realize that this whole time, he's been trying to be calm for her, and he's doing a better job than I.

I'm messing it all up. I go limp in Stork's hold but I let out an uncontrollable sob.

"Just breathe," Court tells me, silent tears running down his cheeks.

Zimmer shakes his head, eyes glazed on the water. "They should be up by now," he says. "That's it. I'm fykking going in." He's about to jump, nobody stopping him.

But suddenly, three bodies breach the surface.

They all gasp for air.

A pool of red blooms around Franny, Padgett, and Gem like it's staining the ocean. Padgett supports both girls the best she can and kicks over to us. Franny grabs one plank and Gem grabs the other. With Stork's and my help, they both manage to rise fully onto the solid holograms.

Blood streams down the right side of Gem's face. She groans in pain. Padgett's usual cool exterior fissures. Her chin quivers and she holds her sister tightly to her chest.

Franny winces, eyes stinging with tears, and I can feel the gnarly wound on her back. It blazes like a thousand hells. Blood soaks the fabric of her shirt and drips from her back to her legs to the plank she stands on.

"Can you walk?" Court asks, sensing her wooziness.

"I think so . . ." She teeters, unsteady on her feet. "Those crocodiles . . . they aren't like the ones in the Saltare-3 museum." She pants, out of breath, and then coughs up a bit of water.

Gem holds a hand over her right eye and when she lifts it up, I see the mangled socket where her eyeball should be.

Padgett hugs her tighter and says, almost breathless, "They were long-armed, and they used their claws."

The waves crash hard behind us.

"We have to move," Court says, caution shading his gaze, but I feel his relief. Tenfold. Just glad Franny's alive. He can patch her back up later. "The waves are growing."

"She won't be standing for long if she keeps bleeding," I tell

Court, and I'm about to suggest carrying her, but they both send me a look that says, *you can't, Mykal.*

Because I'd feel her wooziness, and if I trip, we both could end up in the ocean.

"You can ride on my back," Stork suddenly tells Franny. "I'll carry you."

She nods without hesitation.

No one wastes time arguing, and Stork's eyes pin to her wounds in deeper concern. "Let's get off this bloody ocean."

TWENTY-EIGHT

Franny

Horrific screams pitch the night sky, and then muffle in a trembling moan.

Gem. I hug my knees. Listening to her agony while Court cauterizes a deep gash where her eyeball used to be.

Before reaching the city, we came upon a crumbling, abandoned structure. Roof destroyed, the ocean laps against the mossy stone walls, the flooring damp beneath us. I imagine this must've been a house once upon an era, and over centuries, the thunderous sea took the home, and the family left for the calm mainwater of Montbay.

The mainwater is far in the distance. I only spy glimmering glass buildings that tower in the night, and electric lanterns swinging on the bows of ships. Casting a glow along gentler sea.

Tomorrow, we'll go farther into the city, but for now, we're staying among the unruly waves. Hopefully the ocean drowns Gem's wails and no one from the city can hear.

We're trying to blend in and be invisible. Not stand out and be questioned by the country's Patrol.

Please, no one find us.

Please let us be safe through the night.

Please.

I shake, trying to forget the violent waters and being swept below. Tumbling with no control. Choking on briny sea. My throat is scratched raw.

"Squeeze my hand," Padgett coaches her sister, their voices carrying. Walls block my view of them.

We've all split up in the driest parts of the house. Deeper inside, Court is with Gem. He's been using a piece of steel that Padgett found washed up inside the dilapidated house. The metal is heated with an industrial lighter that Stork brought.

He also packed a small supply of painkillers in a med kit, but the medicine doesn't rid all the pain. I most definitely know this.

My back is stinging madly. Like I've tripped on ice a thousand-and-one times. Away from most everybody, I'm tucked in a small alcove. What I imagine could've been a fancy wardrobe closet. With rich garments full of oceanic splendor. The picture almost makes me smile.

I'm not all alone.

With antiseptic and cotton balls, Stork lightly dabs at the cuts that rake down my back, from shoulder blades to hips. I sit between his legs in the tiny space.

Moonlight from Rosaline brightens our surroundings, and I often look up at the starlit black night.

Cloudless.

Smokeless.

A beauty made to revel in, but pain flares and I forget to be grateful for the sight.

Court hasn't had the chance to check on me yet. I all but shoved him toward Gem. She needs him more. My wounds feel shallow.

Mykal wanted to be here beside me, but it's better if he's farther away. It'll save him from experiencing the pain, and if he's closer to Court, it'll help keep them both agony-free. That way Gem has Court's complete focus.

Zimmer just left me a moment ago to wash bloodstains out of my ripped shirt. We didn't bring a change of clothes. Even torn to shreds, I can fashion the fabric into a top, but the blood would catch unwanted attention.

Before he left, he held my cheeks and he said, "You're alive."

I'm alive. I managed a tearful smile. Not dying is a feat that I've come to appreciate.

The memory drifts with the slap of a wave. Mist showering me and salting my skin. *I'm alive,* I repeat over and over to keep fear at bay.

Stork wipes a biting slash near my hip. I wince into my knee-cap and hold my legs closer to my breasts.

"Sorry, dove. I'm almost done." Still behind me, he gently strokes hair off the nape of my neck, his fingers trailing down my collar.

That feels good.

He repeats the soothing motion, and I find myself tilting my head. Allowing Stork more access to the soft flesh of my neck. He draws a feather-light line across my collarbone and then slowly . . . so . . . so slowly down the length of my arm.

Until his fingers brush over my fingers that are death-clutching my legs.

"Are you scared or are you in pain?" Stork breathes, just barely audible over the crashing waves.

The question takes me aback. I've been with Court and Mykal for such a long time now. Boys who can feel what I feel. They jump to the *whys* first. Why am I afraid? Why am I in pain?

I forgot what it's like being around someone who doesn't know my emotions for certain. "Mostly, I'm scared," I admit, my voice raspy from gurgling salt water. "And I really don't want to be."

I've never felt more like a chump.

My cheeks burn, and before he speaks, I ask quickly, "What does the tattoo on my shoulder look like now?" I've tried to crane my neck behind me, but I can't see the ink.

"Half of a . . ." He sucks in a breath. "A squirrel?"

My lips lift. "It's an ugly fox," I correct. "Is that all?" I'm about to peer over again, but he answers fast.

"Yeah, your ink next to the fox will be a scar." A gash must've run through the tattoo of Mal's tree.

I smile wider, *thank the gods.*

Stork shifts and catches sight of my smile. "Least favorite tattoo?" he wonders.

"Something like that." I tell him the story about the Fast-Tracker tattooist who wanted our toes, more forthcoming about my life. By the time I finish, he has stood up and then sat back down. Facing me.

Same snow-white hair, no new piercings, Stork just kept his sapphire earring for his Fast-Tracker disguise. It's odd seeing him out of Earthen clothes, and the Fast-Tracker garb in Montbay is a *washed ashore after a shipwreck* look—but he wears frayed shorts with no signs of discomfort.

His legs are parted again, and I fit between them. Not much room, his knees are bent on either side of my build.

My breath hitches, nerves flapping. Especially alone in the night. But I'm more used to his limbs brushing my limbs now since he'd been sharing a bed with me and Zimmer for a month. And I try not to think about the morning I was nestled in his arms. Unintentionally. That was a little more than our limbs *brushing*.

I keep my arms wrapped around myself and listen to the smack of sea against stone behind me. Sometimes I envision the water arching over the wall and drowning us, but I've already been under.

I know the taste of an ocean, the feeling of water rushing down my lungs. I know what it's like to be dragged so deep beneath that the world around me darkens.

Knowing what drowning and near-dying feels like should bring me comfort. There's less unknown in the sea. But I'm unsure if I could survive again.

The waves crash—I flinch.

Stork watches me, no smirk or mocking brow arch. His amusement is in short supply tonight.

"Have you ever been scared?" I ask him. I try to envision something Stork could be afraid of, but I come up blank.

"Once." He pats at his waist where he'd usually find a flask.

His pockets are empty. Ridges of his lean muscles peek through his tattered shirt, his skin clammy. Sweat soaks the armpits, and his face is pallid.

He's stopped drinking. A girl in my orphanage went through withdrawal, and she had awful sweats like him.

I can't tell if he's quit purposefully or not. "Are you looking for your flask?"

"Reflex." He forces a half-smile. "I didn't bring it with me."

Strange. I thought I saw his flask in the bag. We brought the lightest piece of luggage with us, and Stork and Court were in charge of packing necessities. So if it wasn't Stork, then *Court* must've brought the flask.

I try not to question why he would. He thinks so far ahead. I'm sure he has his reasons. Maybe he knew Stork would grow ill without it.

"Why didn't you want to pack it?" I ask.

"I don't need it."

My brows jump. "You haven't gone without a sip since I met you."

He laughs. "That's true. Terrible, but true." He sighs out the laugh. "But this mission, it's more important than my pain." He flashes a brinier smile.

His pain. So he is numbing something.

"It's not physical pain, is it?" I ask. He's been in mourning, but I still don't fully understand what that feels like or means.

He takes a moment to think as though considering what he should or can tell me. He balances his elbow on his knee, in a position where he could so easily reach out and wrap his arms around my frame.

Yet I'm balled up, and he's hesitant. Space and history separating us.

"I thought it'd stop hurting." He laughs lightly, eyes reddening, and with a deeper breath, he tells me, "The admirals. They weren't just my superiors." His gaze lifts to mine. "They raised me."

My mouth slowly falls open.

He's laughing again. "And I don't know why I'm telling you. It makes no bloody difference. You can't possibly understand. You lost the person who raised you and you were *happy*." He edges back and kneels, about to push himself to a stance.

"That's not fair," I spit back.

I may not have mourned my mom—I may have known the exact day when she'd die so I wouldn't be sad—but I still miss her. And I can imagine losing Mykal or Court and crumbling beneath the weight of their absence.

Even *thinking* about their death is a punishment I can't bear. He says I can't possibly understand, but I can try to.

Stork pauses on one knee. "Nothing in life has ever been fair. You were raised on a planet that treats death like a celebration. I was raised on one that treats death like despair. The funny thing is, right now, I can't tell you which is worse." He lifts his brows at me.

"I'm sorry you lost your parents," I say, a knot in my scratchy throat. "I really am, and I know my words probably mean so little, but I feel *terrible* that I had a hand in their deaths."

I owe them.

I owe them so much more than I can give.

He takes a seat again, but he holds his legs like me, only with a looser clutch. "They weren't my parents."

I frown. "They raised you—"

"They never called me their son."

I bristle, eyes narrowing.

He shakes his head at the sign of my protective glare. "Don't hate them." He's told me that handfuls of times. *Don't hate them.* "And the trade wasn't your choice."

But they still died to free us from the brig.

All this time, Stork has been around Court, Mykal, and me knowing that we're the very reason the people who raised him are gone. They could've been alive instead of *us*.

I'm sure he wishes that.

Stork eyes my nose and lip piercings and the green-and-blue strands of my hair. His smile gradually rises. "It fits you—"

I startle at a rough wave, rumbling the stone beneath us. And I huff at myself, mad that I startled in the first place.

"I wish I had a way to help you," Stork says. "So you can be unafraid."

To be unafraid of death. I thought I had mastered that. But then I learned I was human. Then I learned about lifebloods. It feels almost like an insurmountable fear now. And more than anything, I hate that my death won't be kind.

If I die, I tear out a piece of Court's soul. Of Mykal's soul.

"Sometimes I think I'll always fear, even if it's just a little bit," I tell Stork. "And I'll just have to figure out how to focus on what makes me less scared. But it's hard *here*."

"When you're on a planet where everyone wants to kill you, yeah, I wonder why?" He flashes a smile that settles my pulse.

I hear Gem screaming louder, and the *swish-swash* of the sea silences her sobbing, and this time, I'm grateful for the rush of the waves.

Stork is quiet again, and I wonder if he knows what I'm about to ask.

We've made it to Saltare-1. He has to tell me about Earth. *He promised.* And after talking to Nia before we left and hearing how she was born on the *Lucretzia,* a disparaging thought has hounded my mind.

And so finally I ask, "Is Earth gone?"

His forehead crinkles with the spike of his brows. "We're on an op to *protect* Earth. If there was no Earth, why would we be here?"

"For laughs."

He actually laughs, light sparkling his eyes. "Bloody hell, I want to live in your head."

"I'm not a chump," I defend hotly.

He smiles more. "It wasn't a slight."

I simmer down. My arms slacken around my legs. "What about Earth then?"

Stork frowns up at the stars, thinking for a long while. "I'm not even sure where to begin."

I have so many questions about the planet. All we've learned about has been an Earth from the past, and the Earth of 3525 could be so different.

A question barrels in front of all the others. *Are there trees on Earth?* I mean to ask for Mykal, and I open my mouth and I waver uneasily.

If Stork says *no,* then I'd crush Mykal's spirits for the rest of the mission. I can't do that.

I find another one. "Are there cars?" I wonder.

He cocks his head. "For you to drive?"

"Yes," I say. "I'd like to drive a human car."

He looks me down and up, as though picturing me driving a human car. Thankfully he doesn't laugh like it's silly. He's smiling. "I want to see that."

"So there are?"

"No and yes; they're not cars like from Saltare-3." He explains, "Your cars are on the ground. Cars on Earth are in the air."

"Flying cars?" I like the sound of that.

He eyes my rising lips. "We call them aerovans. And there aren't many of them." He pauses and grimaces. "There aren't many . . ." He rubs his forehead. Struggling. His face contorts in a series of tormented emotions.

"It's all right."

He lets out a signature brisk laugh that fades solemnly. "No, it's not." His throat bobs. ". . . there aren't many people left."

I listen closely.

"Earth has gone through six World Wars, three Armageddons, including *famine* and pestilence. Seven catastrophic natural disasters and four interstellar conflicts. Humans have suffered, but they've endured."

I try to picture Earth and I see a desolate war-torn wasteland. "How many people are there?"

"There used to be billions of humans in the world." Stork searches the stone walls like he can find liquor, but he continues on without a drink. "Now, there are only two thousand left. One thousand are currently registered in the fleet and another thousand are still on Earth. That's it."

I'm stunned cold.

Two thousand people.

There were more than two thousand on the *Romulus* alone.

There were a little under two thousand just at the start of StarDust.

Two thousand people.

The whole human race.

"Are you sure that's it?" I ask.

"Unfortunately, yeah." He nods. "Some have sought refuge on other planets, but those are few. Maybe another hundred, if that."

Two thousand lives. A people who are uncertain of death. Who weep over the ones they love and selflessly sacrifice all they are for all their people are.

"So it's even more important," I realize. "To save Earth."

He gapes, wordless for a moment. "I thought . . . I thought you'd see it the other way. So did the admirals." He frowns deeper. "There aren't a lot of people left. Easier to just throw your hands up and let Saltarians take Earth and watch the human race die out. That's what Court would do."

"You underestimate him," I say out of defense, but I share Court's emotions, and I do know there is a cold part of him that could prove Stork right.

Stork thinks this over. "Maybe . . ."

"Does Earth have oceans?" I wonder.

"Just one," he tells me. "There used to be more. But waters rose and the islands and landmasses started sinking underneath.

Now there's just a single continent: Gaia. One land. One ocean. One people."

It sounds more unified than Saltarians, who've divided themselves upon five different planets. "What else?" I ask.

He thinks for a second before speaking. "Our armor and clothing—the tunics and linen skirts," he explains. "Humans didn't always wear them. There was a time when our style was a lot like the Saltarians'. Pants and boots and even heavy armored vests for war. But when Saltarians were banished from Earth, humans tried to cling to the things that reminded them of the times *before*. So they began to adopt styles from the ancient eras, and after more centuries, it evolved and stuck."

I try to imagine humans from the *Lucretzia* in ripped shorts. It's a fuzzy picture, but I do have a good view of Stork in a pair.

We drift closer, knees knocking together. "Do you think I'll like it? Earth?" I ask.

"I hope so." His words are filled with a tender conviction, and I almost don't hear them over the growing waves.

Our eyes latch. Heat blossoms everywhere, but neither of us looks away. I take the opportunity to trace the lines of his jaw and the sculpted arc of his nose. Light bathes him like the moon knows he's beautiful. But even more than that, he's bared more for me than I ever thought he would.

In his vulnerability, I feel compelled toward him. He has an unflinching responsibility and a heavy burden that he can't share with anyone.

We're not lifebloods.

We're not linked.

But I've begun to empathize with his impossible situation. Head and heart scream at me to run in his direction, even when I try and stumble away.

He leans forward, just enough that our knees thread and his hand rises up to brush a flyaway hair behind my ear.

An unnamed sentiment *swells* so big inside of me, and when

he turns to look at me, it's as if our lips find each other before our eyes do.

His mouth deepens the blazing kiss, and his hand cups my cheek.

Inhibitions releasing, my hands roam.

Three off-kilter pulses thump my veins, and I try not to waver. *I'm not hurting Court or Mykal,* I remind myself, but Stork pauses as I hesitate.

"Is this okay for you?" he whispers.

Yes. Gods, yes. But why is it so hard to give him the satisfaction and make my emotions plain and clear? Maybe because it's taken me this long to admit them . . .

"I want you . . . I mean I want *to,*" I murmur. *I'm messing this up.*

"Franny," he whispers against my lips. "I want you too." His soft lips press back to mine. I breathe into the kiss like I'm ripping through restraints, only feeling my body against his body and this emotion—*gods, this emotion*—that explodes with every *thump, thump, thump* of my heart.

I've never kissed anyone like I kiss Stork. With this unbridled feeling swimming around in me: nerves and giddiness and affectionate thrill.

Going to bed with no-names and somewhat friends, I only had the heat and the pleasure. I loved both of those—I still love both, but this is new.

So new.

His hands tangle up in my dyed hair, and I dig my fingers into his shoulders. Lip-locked, I grind my hips against his waist. He keeps pace with my needy aggression and nips my lip.

I expect Court or Mykal to come out any minute and interrupt us.

But they never do.

TWENTY-NINE

Court

It takes three days to travel into the city. We wade through knee-deep marsh and ride abandoned canoes through the canals. All the while bailing water from the leaks. When night falls, we catch rest in the tunnels. I attempt to sleep, for Mykal's and Franny's sake. But it's difficult to close my eyes when I know what awaits the closer we get to the city center.

People.

More and more people.

On the fringes, we can blend in better. In the city, we'll be surrounded by Saltarians who could see underneath our disguises and turn us in. It's a greater risk. But I also yearn to be in the middle of Montbay because once we're there, we're closer to finding this baby and being off the planet.

Being safe.

It's all I want.

When we finally approach shops, Stork won't allow me to steal anything. The risks are too high on Saltare-1 with their advanced tech. If I'm caught, this whole mission could be exposed. But I know my skills. I spent *years* being taught how to steal in Vorkter by the best criminal in the world. Thieving feels natural to me.

Still, I'm shot down, even when Mykal vouches for my talents.

The farther we venture into Montbay, the more Stork treats Mykal, Franny, and me like little porcelain figurines. Franny getting hurt—it shook him in some way. And after the night they kissed, his affections and protectiveness toward her has only grown. Both Mykal and I tried our best to ignore them, and we were both given a taste of what she's been doing for us all these months.

It's not easy.

But I'm glad that she's beginning to open herself up to passion again and not letting the link interfere with her desires.

On the fourth night, we finally make it into the heart of the city. Hugging the walls, we walk along the slick stone path near the canals.

I hear the music first.

Large drums bang and people sing at the tops of their lungs. They celebrate Victory's Sacred Eve by hanging streamers outside windows and on their small wooden boats. Some have sails. Others are no bigger than a canoe.

A Fast-Tracker paddles atop a floating wooden door and screams, "Happy Victory Week!"

Mykal grins and I can feel his eagerness to join in the party. They're celebrating his gods, and for a second, I do try to relish in that happiness.

We turn a corner.

Up ahead, glittering buildings tower in the clouds. Algae and barnacles crawl up the base of the structures, but the glass still glistens from sunlight. Holograms blink in and out in the sky like advertisements. Without even knowing for certain, I'm aware that's where the Influentials live.

Around us, shadows darken the shorter buildings. Some nailed haphazardly together with wood, others made of the same metal as the skyscrapers.

This decrepit area stinks of mold, and the metal structures have rusted. The wood is decaying, more worn and neglected.

But the people still sing. An orange-haired FT bangs on a drum and another plays a flute. Their friends throw their arms over each other's shoulders, pints of ale in hand, and they belt out an unfamiliar tune.

Have you gone and fought today?!
Don't be a chump. Don't run away!
Throw up your fists and take a swing!
This week, the God of Victory is king!

They all stomp and cheer and laugh. Out of the corner of my eye, I notice a drunken FT dancing without care, edging toward our group. Swiftly, I grab onto Gem's elbow before she bumps into him. He wobbles as he slurs the words to the song and passes us without a care.

Gem gives me a grateful smile that's half-tensed. A blue scarf covers her eye socket. The gash is closed and healing nicely. Though she's not concerned or troubled by the injury. Her upbeat energy turns a little anxious the more die-hard Fast-Trackers surround us.

She's out of her element.

I'd say I'm the same, but I'm confident I can blend in well.

Franny and Zimmer cup their hands around their mouths and cheer with the Saltare-1 Fast-Trackers. We catch on and make a show of raising our fists in the air. My muscles feel like they need oil to loosen, but I manage to force a smile and a half-hearted yell.

"The God of Victory is king!" Kinden screams the loudest. A bright-orange-haired FT raises her pint to him.

My patience for the festivities wears thin, but we finally find a Fast-Tracker hostel around the corner. On the east end among the shadowed, dank structures.

This is our only choice. But for some reason neither Franny nor Zimmer is thrilled about spending time in the hostel.

It costs a couple bills per person to enter. Stork had to go into a vault on the *Lucretzia* to grab a small stack of Saltarian money. He acquired the bills through auctions and deals on other planets. I learned that Saltarian currency is rare. Most Saltarians only live on Saltare planets and never venture elsewhere.

Even though we have bills, we don't have enough. Not nearly

as much as we should have for eight people. The price of the hostel cuts our stack in half.

We're ushered inside the dark and musty building. Humidity clings to my skin, my clothes, and the smell of mildew is more potent.

A rusted sliding door creaks open and cigarette smoke wafts out. Hundreds of scarves and suit ties hang from the ceiling in different colors, separating the mattresses and areas where Fast-Trackers sleep. Limbs twined together. Some groups appear to be as large as ten.

Young men and women chat loudly as we meander slowly through the hostel, careful not to bump into anyone. Crowded and raucous.

A bar in the back of the room is filled to the brim, and more than a few dazed girls and boys sway to the soft background music. Eyes glazed from drugs.

I watch as people pass small containers back and forth. Some with powder. Others with pills.

Even back on Saltare-3, I never entered a place that was solely dominated by Fast-Trackers. I was raised like an Influential. School. The hospital, work. Being here, it reminds me of the life I might have had, had I not been adopted. Had I not been a Wonder.

Then again, I'm human. I shouldn't have even been on a Saltare planet. All I know for certain is that my history is mine, and nothing that happened—no answer that Stork breathes from his lips—will change the fact that I was a Wonder. I was adopted. I grew up on Saltare-3 like a Saltarian.

Nothing changes that.

Gem hugs her arms close to her chest like she's scared to touch anything. "Was Bartholo's hostel like this?" she whispers to our group. We keep walking through the large space.

"Yes," Franny and Zimmer say together.

"I never liked it," Zimmer adds, stepping over a passed-out boy. "They had too many rules."

"No music after dark," Franny says.

Zimmer smiles. "No hard drugs."

"No guns," Franny says.

"That rule, I did like," Zimmer replies and then nods to the left of the room behind draping purple scarves. "That mattress is empty."

We make our way there.

Stork says, "We should relax here and wait for another spot to open up." Gem crinkles her nose at the stained mattress. There are no better accommodations.

In my heart of hearts, I don't even want to stay here.

I don't want to sleep.

We don't have time to waste, and this feels frivolous. All of us could so easily spend our time out *there*. Looking for the baby.

It twists my stomach, choosing this option. Even though I understand the sensibility in it. Franny's muscles are sore, and Mykal's empty stomach knots painfully. Padgett gratefully sinks onto the mattress with a soft sigh. And Stork has been going through withdrawal since we arrived on Saltare-1. Color has only recently returned to his face, but I still catch him trembling when he thinks no one is looking.

"Court," Franny breathes, feeling my nerves ratchet up. I don't want to be this way. I want to let them relax and offer compassion in the wake of a four-day trek to the mainwater.

But it's like pulling at the bottom of a well for those emotions. Trying to trudge up something that doesn't exist.

I catch Mykal staring at me on the other side of the mattress with a knowing look. Like he understands the battle inside me. A purple scarf brushes against his cheek, and then his stomach lets out a low groan. I feel it, but everyone else hears it.

None of us have eaten since yesterday.

Thus far, we've survived on fish that the Soarcastle sisters were able to catch. Their youth was spent in Maranil, where they learned some basics in fishery, despite loving and yearning for engineering. While Montbay doesn't have the iced waters they're accustomed to, they still managed to catch some small trout. When their luck worsened, Mykal hunted for snakes and frogs, and tonight I sense he'll go out and search for more.

Franny yawns, and her exhaustion pummels me, weighing down my bones. *This is what they need.* Rest.

I want to be at peace with that.

With stiff muscles, I lie down and close my eyes. But my mind is reeling, unable to stop. Tomorrow we look for the baby, and I remember the line from the *Myths* book by heart. *Tucked away in Montbay in the year 3525, she's the only newborn to arrive at the orphanage on the first day of Victory's Sacred Eve.*

The author never mentioned the baby's name in the book. She's the only newborn to arrive in a Montbay orphanage this week. That's the only concrete fact we have.

But after studying Saltare-1 for two months, I'm aware that there are five orphanages in the city. Each a possibility. And there's only one way to search all of them in enough time.

We have to split up.

THIRTY

Franny

Your brother was not happy," I tell Court. We hike along the dark sewage tunnels, the rancid smell something I've unfortunately grown accustomed to.

"Kinden will survive not spending a day with me," Court says. It's just him and me in the tunnels. To save time investigating the five orphanages, we paired off. Mykal immediately slapped a hand onto Stork's shoulder. He mentioned this morning about wanting quality bonding time with his baby brother. But I know that Mykal and Court's uncoupling has played a hand in their decisions.

Court chose me, much to Kinden's disgruntlement.

I think it's easier to be around someone who knows everything—like being lifebloods. No secrets between each other. No need to hide. It's simpler. Freer.

I imagine Stork doesn't have a clue what that feels like, and parts of me ache with pity. The day I dodged my deathday, I'd have been a chump to leave Court and Mykal. But I almost did. The greatest motivation to stay with them was the knowledge that I wouldn't be alone with my secrets.

We stop in the middle of the empty tunnel, and Court unfolds the crumpled piece of paper. I click open a lighter to see.

Ink blots the page with directions to the Lulencrest Orphanage. Zimmer's handwriting is legible for an FT, and he drew a little knight in the corner. When we trained on the *Lucretzia*, the Montbay orphanages weren't marked on the maps of Saltare-1. So Zimmer spent most of today drinking in the hostel and pretending to party with the Fast-Trackers to gain information. Locations.

Whatever Fast-Tracker told him about Lulencrest, they specifically mentioned the fastest route is through the sewers.

"The tunnel should branch up ahead," Court says, refolding the paper. I pocket the lighter, and my boots splash in the puddles. *Don't think about what's in the puddles, Franny.*

I focus on Mykal. The warm sun bathes him . . . *me.* I can feel the cool breeze brushing against my cheeks and the smell of salt water in the air. He's taking the pedestrian bridges to the Gandwich Orphanage, and I know he much prefers to be outside.

But I'm not used to Court and Mykal being so separated all the time. It's weighing on them . . . and me.

"We should talk," I tell Court. My lips already lift into a smile.

He eyes me. "You're always so pleased when you say those three words."

"Because I know you'll actually talk to me," I reply. "It's a good feeling." It's been a long time since Court refused to truly open himself up to me, and I don't take any day with him for granted.

Rushing sewage invades my nostrils again, but I don't much care. I skip over a wide puddle and my peeking smile fades as I say what I mean to say. "I hate that you've uncoupled."

Pain stabs and wrenches my insides just at the word *uncoupled.* Emotional distress belonging to him.

He tries to be stoic. Eyes cast ahead, marching without misstep. Both of us are already adjusting to the darkness of the tunnel, only light streaming through crumbled holes and cracks in the ceiling.

"Court?" I say. "You may look all right, but I know the truth."

He blinks, his defenses crashing down as he inhales a tormented breath. "I hate it too," he whispers.

"Then stop," I say. "We can take the risk—"

"I can't . . . we can't," Court retorts, and more sternly, he adds, "Franny, Saltarians will use *it* against us."

It being the link . . . being lifebloods.

My eyes sting, too dry to cry. "Then we need to get this all over with, and fast." I'm adamant, more determination in my steps.

I don't want to waste another second on Saltare-1. I want to be where Court and Mykal are in each other's arms and happy. So *deeply* happy.

There is no other choice: we need to find the myth baby and make it to Earth. Done and done.

Sewage slushes as we slog along, and I'm surprised when Court breaks the quiet to ask, "Have you pictured life after this?" He speaks so faintly, like these are newborn words. "Have you imagined what our lives will look like if we reach some sort of peace?"

I think he means once we're on Earth, but he can't mention the planet here.

"Sometimes." I nod. "We're all happy, firstly."

Court stares far away, our pace slowing.

"Can you see our happiness?" I wonder. He always focuses on survival. For Court, there is no *when* we reach peace. It is always *if* and *not now*.

"Almost," he says tightly. "I'm afraid to picture it and then lose it." His eyes redden, and he snuffs out the hurt that pricks his gaze. Blinking a few times.

The longer they're uncoupled, the more restrained Court has become. He used to find solace in Mykal's arms, and I can feel him aching for that embrace again.

Even being Court's lifeblood, I'm not equivalent to Mykal.

But as his friend, I do what I can, and I reach out and cup his palm.

He takes a breath, clasping firmer.

We pick up our pace, and to distract him from Mykal, I end

up asking, "Do you prefer Zimmer or Stork?" One is my friend. The other is something else. I don't have a word for Stork yet, even if we have kissed.

Softly, Court tells me, "If you ask Mykal, I'm certain he'll go on and on about which one he prefers more." He nearly smiles thinking about this, but his mouth forms a line.

Botched it. So much for a Mykal Kickfall distraction.

I already know that Mykal prefers Stork since they share the same pa.

"You prefer Zimmer?" I wonder.

Court stuffs his other hand in his frayed shorts pocket. "Are you asking who I like *with you* or in general?"

Now I'm curious, even though Zimmer and I both agreed we're best as *non-bedding* friends. "With me."

"I prefer your happiness," he says smoothly. "But I worry about one of them."

"Stork?" I'm guessing since he's still keeping secrets for the admirals.

"No, not Stork."

Zimmer?

My brows pull together. "Why Zimmer?"

Court gives me a strict look. "You care deeply about him. And he's going to die young."

I try to shrug. "Everyone dies. It's normative." *It used to be.* And then I remember the way the humans sobbed for the dead admirals. I remember the pain in Stork's eyes the night he couldn't drink his hurt away.

One day Zimmer will just be gone. And that thought crushes my chest.

Court swallows. "I shouldn't have mentioned it." Guilt sinks low, but I shake my head.

"I should prepare. You're right—" I cut myself off as our hands break apart. Court has come to a complete halt.

His head whips left to right along the dank tunnel. "We should have come upon the branch by now."

I flick my lighter, but the flame only illuminates a portion of the passageway. Unable to peer down its dark depths.

I hear the splash of sewage and the pitter-patter of lively footsteps. Maniacal laughter echoes closer and closer.

Fyke.

"Court, run," I say, not trusting whoever has decided to creep down here.

He spins around swiftly. We're both a breath from sprinting back the way we came. And then a second shadowed figure approaches. Obstructing our exit, he stomps a metal pole into puddles. The boom reverberates off the walls.

My pulse speeds.

We're being boxed in.

I step backward and bump into Court's firm chest. His back is pin-straight. Carriage poised, confidence emblazons every muscle in his body.

I pull back my shoulders. I'm used to warts, and they can't be too different than the ones I've met on Saltare-3.

"I'm glad you're here!" Court shouts to the approaching shadows on both sides. "We're lost in this fykking tunnel. We're trying to meet some friends at Lulencrest." He hunches his weight onto his right foot like he's an unconcerned FT.

The Fast-Tracker on our left emerges from the darkness. He's older than us. Maybe by five years or so. Bald-headed, dirt and grime smudges along most of his pale skin. He reeks fouler than the sewage.

Holding my breath, I watch him grin, a few front teeth missing, and he twirls his long metal pole.

He sidesteps around us to join his friend and frees one side of the tunnel.

Can we run for it?

I try and take a step back—

"Ah ah ah." He wags a finger at me in disapproval.

I glower. "Who made you king of the fykking tunnels?"

Court stiffens more than he should as an FT.

The bald-headed boy snickers and he unpockets a glowing orb, the soft light illuminating his equally dirty and sniveling friend. He has spiky pink hair and a half-bitten ear, but Court and I are more focused on what he holds.

A rusted . . . mechanical device, something more suited for Saltare-3. A screwdriver, maybe?

"I know, she's a beauty." The pink-haired boy grins. He raises the rusted object and kisses the metal edge. "Bought her on Saltare-4. They call it a *nail* gun over there."

They both laugh shrilly again.

I shoot them a scowl. "Do I look like I care about your nail gun?" Court's pulse hammers harder in *my* veins, but I continue, "I'm not into pain. I'm into *pleasure*. Like my friend said, we're headed to the Lulencrest—"

"Only chumps would use the tunnels to get to Lulencrest," the bald boy tells me. "Everyone knows that it's only accessible by boat."

Court grinds his teeth into a grimace.

The pink-haired boy snickers louder. "Freddie must've given you the wrong directions. He does that sometimes."

The bald one spins his pole and retraces his steps. Blocking us in again on the other side. "He knows we have a tally to reach before we die."

I cringe.

"We're at one hundred and thirteen," the pink-haired boy adds. "You two will make it one hundred and fifteen."

"We can count," Court says flatly. "What do you want?"

He lifts his nail gun. "Pay the toll for walking through our tunnels. One in the hand for each of you."

My stomach somersaults.

"And if we refuse?" Court asks.

"It's called a toll for a reason." He laughs. "You can't refuse."

THIRTY-ONE

Mykal

The Gandwich Orphanage is a four-masted sailing ship. Enormous. Dozens of thick ropes tie the vessel to a rickety dock, and it sways gently in the crammed harbor. Boats brushing up against more boats. Two glass towers flanking the wharf.

I don't know where to rest my eyes. Up above, wooden bridges crisscross dizzily from one building to the next and swing in the breeze. Cheap and free. Unlike the glass railways and elevators that cost bills.

I've gone from the stark emptiness of snow and ice.

To the quick hustle of stone-and-brick Saltare-3 cities. Where people kept warm inside.

To the rowdy and crowded water world. Where everyone and their damned friend leisurely yammers away in the sun. Like they have nothing else to do.

Stork at my side, we've come out from the stuffy bottom of the ship. Standing on the front grimy deck, nails stick up from uneven planks of wood and green mold grows on the ropes.

The country has taken no care to tidy up this ship. Streamers and seaweed garlands—decorations for the weeklong holiday—hang off rusted rigging and torn sails.

Little boys and ladies pay no notice. Climbing up the mast, they play a game where one chases and the rest flee.

Stork and I just spent a hot hour down where the orphans

sleep. A lady flipped through a registry of the newborns. According to the fairy-tale *Myth* book, the baby should've arrived in Montbay by now.

But the Gandwich Orphanage hasn't had a newborn in a whole month. Which means the *Myth* baby has to be in one of the other four orphanages.

I haven't lost hope. We'll be finding this baby. When Court puts his mind to something, he makes anything possible. And he's as determined as ever.

Stork has been largely ignoring me. He watches the orphans play. Partly lost in thought, he unconsciously pinches the skin at his temple.

The corner of my mouth rises. "Our pa used to do that."

His head jerks to me. "What—?"

"Heya, mister." A bony boy of five years tugs on my frayed shorts, his curly, sun-bleached hair matted at his shoulders. "I like your hair." Tips of my blond locks are dyed fire-red. "How'd you get all those scars? Why is your nose crooked? Can I touch your muscles?" He pokes my thigh.

"Leave me be, or I'll be throwing you overboard."

He giggles.

I roar at him like a beast in the mountains.

He shrieks, darts to his gaggle of friends on the bow, and giggles again.

"Our pa," I say to Stork. "He used to pinch the flesh by his temple when he was thinkin'—like you just did there."

Stork smiles into a wince and nods a few times. "Next you'll tell me how we looked just alike?"

Our pa had a narrower jaw and thinner lips than Stork. "I think you must've looked more like our ma—"

"I was being sarcastic," Stork says with a short laugh, audible even over the clanking ship noises and hollers across the harbor.

"You're craving to know more, or else you wouldn't have kept that damned carving." *The snow leopard I whittled.* Franny said he put it on a bookshelf in his barracks.

Stork inhales but stays on the ship deck. I watch him wipe sweat off his brow. He's been queasy the past few days. More hurt fissures through his features, and he puts his hand on his hips. Winded.

He looks like he needs somethin'.

I lower my voice. "I'll be giving you your sword back." I didn't bring it, but first thing when we're back on the *Lucretzia,* I'll be passing it to Stork. He's no longer drinking himself away. And I'm glad to see he's no longer sweating through his clothes or shaking like a tree in a snowstorm from the withdrawals, as Court called them.

"You took it, keep it," Stork retorts.

I glower. "Why do you have such a nasty attitude around me and only me? You can be bright-eyed around everyone else—"

He takes a pained step closer and beneath his voice, he says with conviction, "Because you're too *kind.* You keep trying to tell me everything about where I came from while I'm telling you *nothing* about your life."

I scratch the stubble along my jaw. "I was alone for eight years before I met Court, and then Franny came along, and I had two people I could talk to. You were the *third* damned person I could share stories with, and maybe I was a bit overeager. But I get more out of talking with you than you realize. You needn't tell me anything in return."

"Heya, misters!" the gaggles of children yell.

We glance over at the bow and they giggle like they caught us undressing.

Stork tries to smile but cringes. Watching the orphans, he tells me, "I reckon I've wanted to know about you and Grenpale since I first saw you." He reties loose pieces of his snow-white hair, pushing strands out of his face. "But every time you talk, it reminds me of what I'm denying you." He turns and flashes me a half-smile. "The end."

He's about to pass me, but I catch his shoulder.

And I say, "I'll be waiting to tell you about our pa, if you just stop shoving me away."

Stork considers this, and then the children bellow, "Fight! Fight! Fight!" at the two of us.

I grunt out, "You don't fight your brother."

Stork is smiling with less bite, and he sighs out and looks to the sky. Maybe speaking silently to his Lord.

"Kiss! Kiss!" a few yell.

Gods bless. "You damned well don't do that with your brother neither."

Stork laughs hard. "Stay in school, kiddos." He nods over to the ship's ladder. Our exit.

I follow at his side, and the children shout back at him gleefully.

"What's a *kiddo*?"

He's been casual with slang, often tossing in a random word no one's heard of before. Not as cautious as Court about slipping up our disguise.

"We're not allowed to go to school, you wart!"

Stork gasps. "No kidding." He already knew Fast-Trackers and Babes aren't formally educated.

I wear a crooked smile, and before we head down the rope ladder, we glance over at one another—we're both smiling the same kind of humored smile.

And he nods to me. "You know, I was never going to spar you for the sword. I couldn't be sure how badly it'd hurt them if I hurt you." He's referring to the lifeblood link. Court.

Franny.

We've all sparred enough that there's no harm, but now I know he thought about their well-being. It meant more to him than his blade.

I'm liking my baby brother more and more. "I would've won anyway."

He laughs. "Yeah right." As we descend the ladder, he mentions how he had me pinned the first time we met.

I'm explaining how I was underweight, and I've wrestled creatures three times his size to the ground. We drop down on the rickety dock, the sailing ship about twelve feet high beside us.

I sniff. Sewage stench bombarding my nostrils.

Hairs stand up on the back of my neck. Court, Franny—both are in the sewer tunnels. I'm sensing them more strongly.

"What's wrong?" Stork rounds back when he notices I'm not budging.

"I dunno . . ." My breath cuts short—Court.

He's holding his breath, and a fiery growl tickles Franny's throat.

Stork watches me with a keen eye. "Is it Court and Franny?"

I nod. Concentrating on them, I taste bitter iron. *Blood.* Franny's nose is bleeding. I sense a prick of fear, but I'm unsure about the origin.

Is the nosebleed frightening her?

"How bad is it?" Stork asks, concern cinching his brows.

I dunno. Frustrated, I expel a harsh breath between my sunburnt lips. "We gotta go find 'em—"

"You two." A lady interrupts us. "Come here." She peers over the railing of a pristine two-masted boat, vessel polished and sails proudly displayed with the painted words: TOSS ASIDE YOUR TRICKERY! GIVE BLESSINGS TO VICTORY!

The dock dead-ends to our left, and her sailboat is tied up about four vessels to the right of the orphanage. We left our dinghy somewhere farther down that pathway, and to return to it, we'll have to be passing this lady.

Getting our tiny boat had been our luckiest deed. A man with a pint wanted us to cheer with him about the God of Victory. We sang a few songs and he let us borrow his dinghy.

"Let's act like we didn't hear her," Stork whispers as we head down the rickety dock.

Wood creaks beneath our tough strides.

"You two," she coos, her jeweled ring glinting in the sun. She holds on to a hat shaped like a boat, a yellow feather sticking out of the corner. More feathers are sewn onto the hem of her dress, and seashells curve along her neckline.

Two more steps, and her sailboat with the name *The Montbay Majesty* is next to us—and someone suddenly heaves their body off the damned thing.

A hefty boy of twenty-some years drops down.

Creeaaak.

A board breaks under his weight, and the dock quakes. He has about two-hundred-odd pounds on me.

Instantly, I extend my arm over Stork's chest. Pushing my baby brother back.

He won't let me.

Stork swings his arm over my shoulder. Staying locked right up against my side, he whispers to me between his teeth, "I won't die." He shoots a fake smile at the boy and shouts, "Heya! Move your ass."

The Fast-Tracker lifts his hairy chin. Crossing his arms over his burly chest. Dark-purple hair is wrapped in a bun on his thick head.

"Or we'll be making you," I threaten.

"He's with us," says the lady on *The Montbay Majesty.* "Our security guard won't bite unless he has to. Now, come here, boys."

We turn our heads. A man weaves his arm around the lady. Wearing a silly hat with a feather, brass buttons run down his velvet vest.

"My companion didn't stutter," he snaps. "Come aboard." He motions to the metal ladder attached to their boat.

I grind my molars. My pulse hammering. Sweat dripping down my temples, and I wish it were me.

Touching my face, no sweat has beaded up.

Court.

Franny.

I wipe at my nose—*not me.* She's rubbing and pinching her nose.

Stork laughs at the Influential couple. "We're not interested in whatever you want. Go bother someone else and tell your gu—*boy* to move." He clears his throat, catching himself from saying *guy* fast enough.

I keep my eyes on their security guard. So he won't be hurting Stork.

"We're taking you both," the lady announces, paying no mind to all that Stork said. "For the *night.* Three hundred bills apiece. If you prefer pills, we have those as well. You'll do and say whatever we want from here on out."

Stork mumbles under his breath, "You've got to be kidding me."

Her eyes undress him slowly.

The man isn't looking at me too kindly either.

"Put your eyeballs back in their sockets before I rip them out," I growl.

He laughs. "I like that one."

"Mmm," the lady coos in agreement. "The other is more handsome."

I'm glad to be considered ugly in her eyes. She's uglier in mine.

Stork waves a hand at them. "How about you *ask* before you take?" he says with a raise of his brows. "And the answer is *hells no.*"

"You'll enjoy it," the lady says smoothly.

"Wow, you must be a mind reader—"

I elbow his side. Never did I think I'd be scolding someone for tripping on dialect. If Court were here, he would've been talking us out of this mess much better and sooner.

"Wow?" The lady frowns.

The man is fuming a bit. Impatience curling his lip. "If you don't come aboard, I will drown you in the harbor. You will cough up salt water for *years.*"

My gnarled brows knot. "*You* will be drowning us? Not your security guard?"

The man is scrawny. Not as broad as I. Not as muscular as I. Easily, I could fight him and win.

He pulls at the frilly white sleeve of his shirt. Revealing shimmering metal and gears where his arm should be. Wires are tendons of his muscle.

There aren't any robotic prosthetics on Saltare-3.

"This is the latest model of the Power 3400. It has the strength of *fifteen* men." He grins. "Let's try this again, shall we? Come aboard or drown—"

Pain attacks me. I scream through my gritted teeth and stare wide-eyed at my quivering hand. Something stabs my palm— *his palm.*

Court.

I scream angrily. A fierce puncture throbbing my flesh. *His flesh.*

"Mykal." Stork has a hand on my back. "Hold on."

Gods dammit, I gotta go find 'em—I peel out of Stork's hands and I charge at the security guard. I punch his gut.

He hardly flinches. Doing nothing to me. Just standing there like a rock on a dock.

I'm strong. I'll be shoving him down. I push.

Nothing.

Nothing.

I twitch as fear rakes down my back.

"What's wrong with that one?" The lady inhales a disgusted, uncertain breath.

I'm in a tunnel.

Stench all around me. Sharpness impales my palm again—*no.* Tears prick my eyes. "RUN!" I growl into a scream. *You better be running. You better be moving.*

Court mouths to me, *it's fine.*

I shake my head over and over. They're not all right, and I'm too far away.

"Something is not right with him, Florian," the lady tells her companion. "I don't want him, and the other is too peculiar."

Florian sighs. "Fine. We'll find another."

She lets out a disappointed breath. "What a waste."

THIRTY-TWO

Court

Today has been terrible.

I pull out the nails and bandage our hands with fabric from our shirts. The rest of the night we search for Lulencrest by canals. Once we find and enter the rusted metal structure, Franny and I meet bleak news. No newborns. As we make our way back to the hostel, I feel as if I failed us both. Pain sears in both our palms, not even having enough time to stop and suture the gashes closed.

"Can you stop?" Franny mutters, feeling my guilt mount up in her. "It was the only way, Court. They had us blocked in, and we couldn't have overpowered them both . . . they had weapons." She pulls at my shoulder to make me stop and face her. "I'm serious."

"There could have been another way," I say. Maybe if I had more time. If I could have thought of something better. If we just didn't go down in the tunnels to begin with.

Franny's brows knot. "No."

"That's it?" I snap.

"That's it," she agrees. "So stop fretting over this before I start a real stew. It's just a silly wound." She waves her bandaged hand. Blood dotting the cloth. "The nail is gone."

"You can't close your fist," I remind her.

"Tomorrow, maybe I can," she says determinedly and then pushes her way to the door. I trail behind her, trying to let her words sink in. There's a good chance that if we tried to run or even fight, the Fast-Tracker would have pointed the nail gun at our heads. He wouldn't think it'd kill us. But it could.

I hold on to that.

The hostel bursts with excitement, people chattering and drinking, and we weave between the young bodies to find our familiar place. I spot Padgett and Kinden first, lounging on the mattress and chatting quietly. Then I see Mykal. He shoves his way through the crowds, panicked blue eyes flitting to me. Worry bursts in my chest. *His* worry.

I know he felt us. I'm not sure how long, or how strong. But by the ragged breathing and the carelessness with which he pushes a little girl away from his path, I'd say he felt a lot.

Immediately when he's at our side, his hands fly to my cheeks. Cupping them as tenderly as he can. It's the first time he's really touched me in weeks. And for a strong moment, his emotions double me over. "What happened? Who hurt you?" His voice is coarse with concern.

"It's nothing," I say, shaking him off. It hurts to do.

His hands fall to his sides, and pain wrenches between us. For some reason, it aches more than the dull throb in my palm. I suck in a tight breath, wanting nothing more than to fold into his arms.

Mykal grinds down on his teeth, but with his eyes, he searches for my hands. He can feel where the pain is coming from. *He knows.* I hold my hands behind my back, so he can't see.

Mykal shoots me a look like *you're being a real crank.* Then, quickly, he turns to Franny and snatches her wrist, lifting it up to inspect the crimson-stained cloth. He slowly removes it and reveals a deep, bloodied hole in her skin.

"Funny story," Franny starts.

Mykal glowers at the word *funny,* and Stork sidles near us to listen. He ties his blond hair back with a ripped string from his shirt.

I try to direct the conversation somewhere else, so I ask

Stork, "How did you and the others do with your orphanages?" Though I already know the answer. They'd all be in much better spirits if they found the baby.

Stork shakes his head. "No luck." Then his gaze lowers to Franny's hand and his eyes flash with a pained wince. "What happened?"

Franny continues, "The directions to Lulencrest were a ruse. The tunnels had FTs that wanted us to pay a toll." She pauses and muses, "I guess a nail through the hand was better than a toe."

"You've got to be shit—" Stork stops himself short from saying a human phrase and then he smiles bitterly. "Fyke," he says to cover himself.

I don't think anyone heard.

It's too loud in here.

Mykal swings his head from left to right like he's looking for something, and then he storms away without another word. We all frown.

"That's not like him," I say. He barely comforted me. And I know we're uncoupled, trying to be apart, but he didn't even argue to see my wound.

I watch as he pushes aside a hanging scarf and bends down near Zimmer. They chat for a quick second, and then Zimmer points to a short, dusty-brown-haired boy across the room.

"No." I breathe. Mykal's intentions start clicking. I'm too slow, and Mykal is too determined. I watch him cross the room with angry, furious strides.

He yells loudly at the boy, who can't be older than eighteen. "Heya!" Mykal screams. "Eggen Orcastle?"

The boy appraises him with a laugh. "Maybe. Who's asking?"

It's so quick.

"Me," Mykal growls and shoves the boy into the wall. I don't even see Mykal take out his knife before it's halfway in the boy's palm, stuck into the plaster behind him.

The wail is sickening.

People shout. Eggen's friends start to push at Mykal. Bottles break. The last thing I see is Mykal wrenching the knife out of the wall. Out of the boy's palm. When I lose sight of him, I scream, "MYKAL!"

"We have to go." Zimmer has come to our sides. "*Now.*"

Not until—

Mykal emerges from the crowd, unscathed. He takes my good hand, icy blue eyes already set on the exit.

THIRTY-THREE

Court

What do you want for it?" I ask the Fast-Tracker. We're on the west side of Montbay. The rough waves unsettle a rickety wooden structure that bobs up and down. A FOR RENT sign hangs on the front door of the house barge. Calling it a *house* is utterly kind. It's more of a structure. But there's a roof and privacy, two things our group badly needs.

We don't know how long it will take to find the baby—or if this baby is even real—and we can't spend our nights on the streets.

After Franny and I struck out in the tunnels today, we had to find a boat to row through the canals. The abandoned ones were along the west side of the mainwater. So as we searched, we both noticed the FOR RENT sign on this house barge.

But nothing can be simple.

The problem—Fast-Trackers all seek something different. And I can't be certain this one wants bills for rent.

Colorful tattoos ink the FT's flesh, gliding up along his neck. He glances back warily at the house barge. "My Influential mother just died in it," he tells me. "I'd say with that kind of luck, it's worth more than you've got." He looks between each of us in our group. The others stand back, letting me talk. Out of everyone, they believe I can convince him the best. Let's hope they're right.

"Bills?" I question.

"Two thousand," he demands.

My stomach sinks, but I think the emotion stems from

Mykal, since he's the one who put us in this position. But I don't blame him.

"Two thousand bills? For that thing?!" Kinden says in disbelief, pointing a finger at it. Padgett leans into his hip and whispers quickly, probably telling him to keep his mouth shut.

The FT lifts his chin. "Like I was sayin', it's worth *more* since my mother died there. Take it or leave it."

I swallow hard. "What if I had something of equal value?" I question.

The FT laughs and looks me up and down. "You're pretty, but not worth two thousand—"

Mykal lunges forward, already hot-blooded from today. Swiftly, Stork grabs him by the shoulder and pulls him back to his side. Pieces of blond hair fall into Stork's face, and Mykal lets out a low growl.

The Fast-Tracker takes a step back. "Heya, keep that one away from me." He sets a grimace on Mykal.

"Do you drink?" I ask.

He full-belly laughs. "Are you a chump? What kind of question is that?" He laughs again. "Do I drink?" He touches his chest. "Have you not heard the stories of Bollow Bormcastle? The Fast-Tracker who lives on the west sea line and can drink any FT to the ground, all the while keeping the contents in his belly during the *roughest* storms? I'm a fykking champion."

Great.

This might actually work.

"What if I told you that I had the world's best liquor? It's like drinking gold."

Stork whips his head to meet my gaze, eyes wide. "No," he snaps angrily. "That's mine."

Confusion pinches every part of me. I know Stork loves to drink, but I didn't think he'd be possessive of it right now. Mainly because he didn't even pack the flask.

I did.

Not only that, but he'd always planned to stop drinking as

soon as we touched Saltare-1. It's what he told me. For the mission, he wasn't going to numb his grief any longer. He'd be focused. Clear.

But maybe he's tempted by the flask. I'm not linked to him. I don't know how far his cravings run.

"I'm the one holding it," I remind Stork.

He glowers and releases his grip on Mykal. "Do you know what I did for that?" He sneers. "No, I don't think you do. It's not yours to give away, Court."

Bollow swings his head from me to Stork and back to me, lips slowly lifting. Enthralled by this exchange.

I clench down on my teeth. "If it can acquire a roof for us, it's worth—"

"I'll never get another bottle," Stork interrupts. "It comes from President Freycastle's stash." Those words are a signal, one that I catch.

Stork's liquor is a human scotch.

While I don't know where he acquired the flask, I do know that President Freycastle governs over this country in Saltare-1, and Stork has never stepped foot onto this planet until this mission. There's no possibility he stole it from Freycastle. I recognize the lie.

Stork's anger is a fabrication to make the liquor appear more valuable. *Clever.* I play along, my mouth falling open in shock. "How?"

Stork rubs his lips. "It was a gift. In exchange for being entertainment for the night. A Fast-Tracker dartboard. Her guests loved it."

Bollow lets out a long angry noise. "Influentials have no right . . ." He stares at the flask, a little more interested than before.

I hold the flask up, feigning sympathy. "I'm so sorry," I say softly. "I'm going to have to retract the offer. I can't give this to you." I go to pass the flask to Stork.

"Heya! Wait a second," Bollow says quickly. "Let's not make any rash decisions."

"It's worth more than two thousand bills," Stork seethes.

Bollow crosses his arms over his chest. "Two days," he counters. "Heya, that's better than one night."

"Four days," I counter. That'll keep a roof over our heads for the rest of the holiday.

Bollow lets out an agitated sigh. "Fine. For the *entire* flask."

"You have a de—"

"Wait." Bollow narrows his eyes at me. "How do I know that flask isn't filled with piss or ale . . . or both?"

I hold it out. "Take a sip, see for yourself. It's nothing like you've ever tasted."

He reaches for the flask. "Well, I've never tasted piss," he says and takes the drink. Putting it to his lips, he swigs.

I watch as he frowns deeply.

He licks his lips and then stares at the flask with a pinpointed gaze. "What'd ya know. It tastes like gold." He laughs loudly and then nods to me. "You've got yourself four days."

I watch as he skips off, singing to the gods as he downs more.

My pulse finally settles to a normal rhythm, and Stork says to me, "Glad you finally picked up on it, mate."

"I'd have been quicker if I thought you were capable of a ruse."

Stork smiles. "Sounds like an insult, but I'm going to take that as a compliment."

It was one.

As the others enter the house barge, I tell Kinden to hang back.

That I have to talk.

The waves thrash against the nearby rocks and wind whips through my hair. I can taste the salt in the air and smell the mold as Franny and Mykal walk farther into the house. She knows what I'm about to do.

Mykal doesn't.

But he'll be okay with it.

I know he will.

Kinden looks me up and down like he's slowly discovering more of who I am. Court Icecastle. Not the Etian Valcastle he used to know. "Little brother," he says. "That was quite the deception. You brought that flask all the way here just to barter it."

I nod.

He grins. "They didn't deserve you."

They.

He's talking about Saltare-3. Our world. What used to be our home.

His faith in me never waned, and even now he carries a torch, bright and burning, leading the way for me. How lost I've been. How much I needed him. *He's here now.*

And yet, I am playing the ultimate deception on Kinden. He doesn't know I'm linked to Mykal and Franny. He has no clue we're lifebloods.

And this is eating me apart.

I'm just not certain how to begin. Kinden always makes it easy, though. He rocks on the backs of his feet and tilts his head, waiting for me to speak.

It takes a harsh beat. "I've been keeping something from you," I say. "And I can't any longer."

He's here on Saltare-1 for me. To make up for lost time. But how is he supposed to know the real me without knowing this vital piece?

Kinden glances out at the sun that begins to slowly dip below the water's edge. Colorful oranges and pinks bathe the sky. "I should be offended you've been holding back from me," he says, "but I'm unsurprised. I knew there was something else." He looks to me again, strength battling his brown eyes. "You know, you carry yourself like you have a thousand secrets."

I do believe only he'd be able to see that.

"Just one more."

He smiles and then his lips slowly fall. "Why now?"

Telling Kinden about the link is a risk. It allows one more

person to know our secret. One more person who could accidentally spill it. So I've been waiting to explain everything to him until we're safe.

But what if that day never comes? Back in the tunnels with Franny, we could have been killed. So easily, our luck could have turned for the worst. It seems more and more likely we won't make it off Saltare-1. That's what struck me most of all.

I may die here.

I've accepted that today.

What I can't accept is leaving Kinden without knowing me. *All of me.*

The boy who spent five years in a cold prison—influenced and taught by a criminal. Who was forged from misery and pain only to be brought back to life by this unseen force.

By Mykal.

By Franny.

My lifebloods.

He has to know before I'm gone.

"I need you to know why I can't be Etian anymore," I say. "I need you to know . . . before I die."

He nods strongly. "Okay."

I tell him.

Everything.

From the day that I met Mykal. How we came to fold our arms around each other in the winter wood. To the moment Franny woke up in an alleyway, and I could sense the cold, frozen snow falling on her cheeks. The ice that bit her lips. I could feel her pain like it was my own.

I tell him it all while holding back tears and snot and I watch as his own eyes glass. He's quiet. Only asks questions when he needs more pieces. And once the picture is filled in, once it's all said and done, he wraps his arms around me in a brotherly embrace. One filled with years of love.

And until my dying day, I won't ever forget the words he spoke.

"It's good to finally meet you, Court."

THIRTY-FOUR

Mykal

I suppose you'll be telling me I was wrong to touch your face," I say to Court while I scout our private room for the night, the rich interior of the house barge surprising the lot of us. Considering the outside was rightfully hideous. But this boat had previously been owned by an Influential, keeping the inside clean and decorated.

We divvied up the three rooms. Our cozy corner in the stern has an oak vanity and a double-sized bed, the gold-threaded blanket wrinkle-free. All varnished wooden floors and walls. A fishing net is strung across the ceiling and cradles dozens of nautical-stitched pillows.

More than anything, I like how the good-working walls deaden noise. No yelling Fast-Trackers from outside can be heard, no hostile hollering or railway sounds.

Just the hush of water softly pushing against the barge.

Court leans stiffly against the closet door, his spirits high. Less pressure on his chest, more confidence hoisting his carriage. Earlier, he explained to me how he told Kinden about our link. And then he gave his brother permission to clue in the Soarcastle sisters tonight. There's a burden gone there, and I'm glad for it. I don't mind others knowing our secret if Court thinks it's all right. And he's more than all right.

Even free from burden, I thought he'd be gravely serious since we're down to only one orphanage.

And because I touched his face while we're uncoupled.

No regret gnaws at me. Truth being, I'd do it again.

"You put a knife through someone's hand," Court says with the arch of a brow, "and you think the problem I'd have is with you holding my face?"

A smile pulls up the corner of my mouth, and I rest my ass on the vanity across from him. "Yeh. You like when I protect you. Makes you feel all warm inside."

He rolls his grim grays, but they land strongly on my hard-hearted eyes. "I also love when you hold me."

Our cracked hearts mend on each powerful thud.

And thud.

And thud.

No anguish tethered between us, and my smile widens. There's no one around that we have to hide our connection from.

"I'll be touching your face then," I say. "Right now." I wait to feel his emotion.

Brightness floods his lungs, and I step off the vanity.

Thud.

Thud.

Court comes forward. We meet in the middle, eager energy teeming my veins. His veins. I tap his foot and our legs knock together.

He breathes deeper.

The Grenpalish in me takes over. I nudge his cheek. I lightly push his shoulder.

His head sways like a breeze, and his lips lift in a beautiful budding smile. Swelling my heart to the size of mountains.

And then I cup his face between my two callused hands. "I don't want to be pulling apart any longer," I whisper huskily. "Do you?"

Court clutches the nape of my neck, our breath at the same heady pace. He shakes his head. "I *never* wanted that, Mykal . . . but it felt like the only way." He swallows hard. "We can be together again, now that my brother knows. We'll just be careful while we're in the city."

I'm smiling.

His lips begin to lift and then our foreheads press together. Sharing senses all at once. We're like that for a long moment. Before he breathes, "Do you feel that?"

I close my eyes for a second.

It's a feeling.

Deep in my blood. A stillness and serenity like I'm floating around in bliss. Doubled. Both of us basking in it. I open my eyes and sink into his. "Why are we feeling this way?"

His chest rises. "We've been living for tomorrow, for the next month, the next year. Living to survive instead of living to just *live*." He pauses. "I, more than you, have struggled with that." His lips near my lips. "I think we feel this way because finally, we're both living for today. At the exact same time." A freeing tear rolls down his cheek.

I feel the wet track drip off his jaw, and we pull into a soul-bearing kiss that explodes light inside of me. His soft lips smile against my chapped ones.

Thud.

Thud.

Breathing. Needing. I hunger forward, our chests melding, and we excitedly shed one another. Shirts off, shorts off, all clothes gone. Hands exploring ridges and carves, stoking a roaring fire.

I kiss him to the bed. Not pushing him down—I'm gonna soften my roughness as I promised I'd try. So together, we climb onto the gold-stitched blanket, and I roll on top. Feeling his excitement match mine.

Our lips swell from the force, and I comb his dark-brown hair out of his face. Court hooks his ankle with my calf. Tangled up in each other, I whisper in his ear, "You'll be all right if I take the lead?"

He's more experienced than I, but Court makes me feel like all we do together is more right and never wrong.

"Yes," he murmurs against my neck. "I'd be more than fine with that."

I pat his cheek twice, and our hands go lower. We are heat. Melted ice and melted snow. He helps me where need be, and I don't feel shy asking if he's all right now and again. He confirms, and I go on with Grenpalish stride.

Rocking against him. He clutches my shoulders, and the deep noise he makes bursts me alive. I breathe harder, soaking up how he's living in this very second. This very moment. Overcome tears squeeze out of the corners of my eyes.

Bliss shatters us and builds us whole. I hold him in my arms afterward. Hugged together like there is no better place than here. And now.

I'm still with him in every thudding heartbeat.

THIRTY-FIVE

Franny

Gods, let this be it.

We only have one orphanage left. One possibility. If the newborn isn't here, we're all out of hope.

Stork, Zimmer, and I take the lead while the others wait outside Rovenview Orphanage. The wooden, algae-covered building is situated on the north end of Montbay. Five stories high, the orphanage is an eyesore, built right in between the gap of two pristine glass skyscrapers.

We walk carefully along the swinging bridge over the still canals and reach the front door.

Once inside, the air is stickier and orange flowers bloom off vines that snake up the walls. I'd think we were still outside if I didn't spot the wooden administration desk and dizzying hallways right behind.

I hear children's laughter, screams, and the banging of doors opening and closing. The sound is different but familiar. I've never ached to return to my time in the Bartholo orphanage, but sweeping nostalgia suddenly overtakes me.

"You wart!" someone shouts, and I spot the tail end of a thievery. A girl in braids screams as another child runs off with her satchel. "You'll pay for that!"

"Hush, Eleanor," an older woman chastises. "Inside voices. If you want to scream, do it on the bridge."

The little girl bellows in protest, and the woman points a finger. "I will drag you by your ear—"

Eleanor slams her little foot onto the woman's toes and then dashes off as the woman yelps in pain. She's about to race after the girl, but catches sight of us.

Letting out a long sigh, she meanders to the desk. "I apologize for that. During this time of day, the younger ones tend to be more restless."

Zimmer leans a hip against the desk and sends me a wiseass smile.

I assume he's picturing me as that little girl, upset over a stolen satchel. Of course it's happened, but I never stomped on anyone's foot.

Stork says, "It's all righ—"

The woman claps her hands, interrupting him. "Ah, a Fast-Tracker couple." She shimmies her shoulders in excitement.

At first, I'm unsure of who she's referring to. Zimmer and Stork. Zimmer and me. Stork *and* me? All three of us?

Heat shades my face, and I scowl. Zimmer is laughing underneath his breath, and Stork even grins. Am I the only one not humored by this?

Her gaze finally dances from Zimmer to me and then back to Zimmer. "How nice, you both looking to adopt before you die? Such a sweet thing to do. We have Babes and Fast-Trackers who'd pair up nicely with you two, I think."

Zimmer's grin reaches cheek-to-cheek, and he slings a lanky arm over my shoulders. "She's always wanted a child."

That couldn't be more false. I have never even thought about babies until this *Myths* book. I was meant to die at seventeen. Taking care of a child wasn't in my future.

But I play along with the charade. "It's been a goal of *ours* to help raise a little one before we die."

The woman touches her hand to her chest, and then glances at Stork. "And are you here to adopt as well?"

He motions to Zimmer. "I'm their friend."

Her mouth forms a perfect *O*. "Right. Yes. I've seen this arrangement before. Friends coming in with couples." She swings her gaze from Zimmer to me. "Which of you is dying soon?"

Oh.

She's assuming Stork will be helping to raise the child after one of us dies.

"That'd be me," Zimmer says before I can. He flashes a brighter smile. "It's been a good life, but a little baby will make it a *great* one."

His words feel like needles poking holes in my heart. I don't understand this sudden ache. I wish it'd go away.

Zimmer lets his arm fall from my shoulder, his fingers gliding down my forearm to my wrist until his palm is against my palm.

What is he doing?

He laces our fingers, and he squeezes my hand, as though to remind me, *we're pretending to couple.*

I try to relax, and I watch the woman type on the desk. Soon, a hologram springs up with faces of babies . . . children.

My breath hitches.

I wonder if my mom did this. Obviously, not with a hologram. Saltare-3 had large photo albums with each of our pictures tucked inside. Did she skim her fingers over my face? I was just a baby, but she chose me. Felt something then.

My eyes speed along the faces, lost for words.

Stork barely glances at the hologram. "We're looking for a newborn," he tells the woman. "A girl. She'd have arrived within the week."

"Let me see . . ." The woman peruses through the hologram quickly. It dizzies my head, and I'm already a ball of nerves. Zimmer runs his fingers through my hair gently, still playing up the part that we're a couple.

I try not to be a stiff board, and I hold on to his arm. Somewhat sinking into his waist.

"Hmm . . ." She tilts her head. "No . . . we haven't had a newborn in the past few weeks." *No, that can't be.* "Not unusual during this time of year. It's Victory's Sacred Eve. The gods favor death over birth. A lucky week, I'd say." She gives Zimmer and me an apologetic smile. "But not so lucky for you. I do have some six-month-old Babes, if you'd care for a look."

Numbness infiltrates with disbelief. We have no other options . . .

Stork clears his throat, his eyes reddening. "Can you check again?" he asks. "It's a fykking newborn. Maybe she slipped through the cracks."

The woman shakes her head. "There are no cracks here. Rovenview Orphanage is the most prestigious in all of Montbay."

"*Please*," I beg.

She scrolls through the faces again.

Three more times.

"I'm so sorry," she apologizes when she reaches the end of this list. "How about this young FT? She's four years old and makes *everyone* in Rovenview double over laughing. Quite a comedian."

Stork turns around and runs a hand over his hair. I don't have to be his lifeblood to know he's distraught. Zimmer is as calm as ever, like maybe this doesn't surprise him at all.

I try my best not to look at the little girl's photo. My heart has already fractured in two today, I don't need it completely obliterated. "Our minds were set on a newborn," I tell the woman. "We'll wait. We have time."

She smiles. "Splendid." A crash in the hallway pulls her attention, and she slips away, hollering at the children who scream shrilly.

"This can't be right," Stork says. "There has to be a mistake."

"Or," Zimmer says, shaking his hand out of mine, but he slings it back onto my shoulder. "This *Myths* book is wrong. It's just a fykking fairy tale, Storky."

Stork isn't in the mood for Zimmer's humor. He flashes a half-smile and makes a rude Fast-Tracker gesture that *Zimmer* taught him.

"That's just nippy," Zimmer mutters.

"Or," I cut in. "We read the instructions wrong."

"We didn't," Stork says. His head is swinging so much that his hair frees itself from the tie. The string falls to the ground. Frustrated, he bends down to pick it up. "Think of something else. Anything else." His words are soft and he remains squatting, gaze on the floor in thought.

"I'm thinking . . . the answer isn't down there," Zimmer tells him.

"That's not helping," I say.

I'm surprised Stork hasn't given up. Called it quits. But maybe he just can't come to terms with the fact that this might be it. No other options for Earth but war. And with only two thousand humans left, the possibility of an entire race of people dying out is . . . inevitable.

I shiver.

Zimmer raises his hands. "All I'm saying is that maybe whoever wrote that book just wanted us to go on a great big adventure. Maybe it was a die-hard FT wanting to provide others with some thrills."

Stork stands suddenly, hope glimmering in his blue eyes. "The author. That's it. We find Sean Cavalletti. We ask him where the baby is."

Zimmer groans. "No, fyke. That's not what I meant. I'm done with the scavenger hunt. It's been fun but I don't much like all the water and mold." He motions to his nose. "It's botching my sense of smell."

"It's not about you, mate." Stork walks toward the door.

Zimmer snorts and looks to me. "How many times have you heard that phrase in your life?"

"Too many," I say.

Stork falters a little as we step outside, apologies shadowing his eyes. "I didn't mean it like that, Zimmer."

"No, yeah. I get it." He laughs bitterly. "Heya, I'm just here for the ride."

They argue on the steps of the orphanage, and I hold a hand

above my eyes, shielding the sun. Across the canal, Mykal, Court, Kinden, and the Soarcastle sisters stand on the wide wooden pedestrian bridge. They're not facing the orphanage like I'd thought they'd be. But I am glad to see Mykal holding on to Court, his arm slung up over his shoulders.

At least something is going right. Them being coupled again—it's a bright spot.

I focus harder on their feelings and then I finally see what they're all staring at. High above the main canal, a hologram is lit up. It broadcasts a news station to the whole city. The reporter's lips move but no sound comes out.

I've seen this before . . .

I search around for one of the many bulletins, large metal structures that hover near the bridges. Gem theorizes that they're held up by magnetism. Flyers and messages are pinned, and there's a button on the side. I press it.

The reporter's voice suddenly sounds from the slender speaker along the frame of the bulletin. Zimmer and Stork quiet in an instant and turn their gaze to the hologram.

The reporter stands near an oversized starcraft that's grounded on a tarmac, stilted above rushing water.

The *Romulus*.

It's *here*. On Saltare-1.

My breathing quickens with a tripled sense of panic.

Commander Theron cups his hands in front of him and stares at the screen—at us. "After five years in the stars, the *Romulus* has finally come home. For celebration on this Victory's Sacred Eve, we're proud to announce that the Andola admirals are dead."

People in the city cheer around us, but it's not the type of joy that usually accompanies celebrating deathdays. These fists in the air and loud hollers feel more sinister, crueler.

The reporter grins. "In other news, we've been given an exclusive video from a Fast-Tracker. Let's go to the tape."

They cut to a shaky video, like someone was recording while moving.

It's fuzzy, but I recognize it immediately. Eight bodies step onto shimmery planks. The person in the front creates them from a handheld device. A *human* device.

Someone spotted and recorded our trek from the garbage island to the mainwater.

Fyke.

I feel the pull of my neck, but it's not mine. I glance over and see Court swinging his head quickly away from the video, looking for us. When his eyes land on mine, he waves me over to the main pedestrian bridge. He's scared. Of being separated. Of being caught.

Of prison.

For him, it will be the third time.

I'm rooted to the ground.

The hologram pans back to Commander Theron, and he says, "Three humans and five bludraders are currently living in Montbay. Our processing team is working on retrieving clearer images of their faces. Reward for turning them in is set at one million bills for each of the humans. One thousand for each of the bludraders. Good luck."

I blink, dazed.

We're wanted criminals in a city *filled* to the brim with people. All who would gladly turn us over for *one million* bills.

Dear Gods, please help us.

"I can't believe I'm only worth a thousand," Zimmer says, trying to lighten the mood. "No, wait, yes, I can." He frowns suddenly. "Franny."

Something pitches my ear. At first, I think it's a dream.

But then I hear it again. Cries.

A baby's wails.

"Franny!" Court yells my name across the other side of the canal. He sees me turning away from them, edging back toward the orphanage. His panic is full-on seizing my insides. He walks toward the unstable, swinging bridge that separates him from me.

I'm focused on the structure ahead. A bridged alleyway snakes in beside the orphanage and the building on the right. I wonder if it goes *behind* the buildings too. This whole place is like a maze.

The alley is narrow, but large enough to squeeze through, and it wouldn't make sense not to build the orphanage flush against the other building if there wasn't something in back.

Faint cries pitch again.

"Do you hear that?" I ask Stork. I don't wait for him to answer. The cries sound for a third time, and maybe I'm going mad, but with the news of being a wanted criminal, there's no time to waste.

I run.

My feet carry me, and I hold in my breath to squeeze between the buildings. It narrows before widening up into a bigger alleyway. I stumble over a rotted floorboard, and five stories below, water glides along the canal. Fyke, I prefer the Saltare-3 alleyways that were on the ground.

I take three more steps and then my leg goes barreling through the bridge. A plank breaks off and crashes into the canal below. Someone grabs me around the waist before I face-plant and break my leg in two.

"Careful, dove." Stork breathes along my neck, his chest rising and falling heavily against my back.

The cries grow louder.

He looks up at the same time I do. "You hear that too," I say.

"Yes." Hope fills his voice like a thousand balloons lifting straight into the air.

Zimmer appears beside us after squeezing through the narrowed part of the alley. He raises his brows at me, my leg halfway through the bridgeboard. "Already breaking things, Franny?"

"I hate this place," I mumble.

"You and me, both." He bends down and braces me underneath my other arm. With Stork, they both swiftly but gently pull my leg out of the hole. Freed and together, we race toward the sound.

Rounding a corner, I see *her*.

Swaddled tightly in a blanket. And in the arms of a Fast-Tracker. A teal uniform matches the blue swirling tattoos that cover his arms. I squint to read his name tag on his breast. THE PREMIERE HOTEL. RIKTOR.

The baby screams shrilly as if he's hurting her, but he's doing nothing more than holding her in his arms. Suddenly, he pulls out a small pouch that looks like it was tucked inside her blanket.

"Is she yours?" Stork asks as we stop near the FT.

He meets our gaze. "Found her right there." He nods to the ground beside the wall. "Just looking to see if she has anything of value on her." He smiles and shakes the pouch.

"Thief," I growl.

He frowns and pockets the pouch. "Heya, it's mine. I found it first." He looks between us, fear flitting in his eyes like he thinks we might steal it from him. Three to one. The odds are in our favor. But then, as a diversion—he drops the baby and runs.

Zimmer is the fastest. He dives for her, and catches the baby in his outstretched arms. She cries harder and louder, and since we're currently wanted by all of Saltare-1, roping attention onto us is the last thing we need.

But I can't think about that right now.

We have a newborn, and this might seem like our saving grace, but we can't be certain she's the same baby from the book.

Zimmer cradles her, and she continues to wail. "She's not happy," he says.

I turn to Stork, who's approaching the baby like she's a small bomb. "She wasn't in the orphanage like you said." I'm haunted by that fact.

"She was outside the orphanage," Stork refutes. "That's close enough."

Zimmer and I share a look.

Is it?

Stork pulls back the blanket, revealing a pale baby with bright green tufts of hair atop her head. Short, but *green*. "A Fast-Tracker dyed her hair," I say. "She's an FT's child. A Saltarian." She's not of a different species. And more importantly, this baby could have parents in the city who just set her down for a minute.

"You're jumping to conclusions, dove."

"Her eyebrows are *brown*," I counter angrily.

"The book said she's of a new species," Stork says. "She was probably born with green hair."

Zimmer shakes his head. "This is bizarre."

I take a deep breath, trying to collect my thoughts. "Okay, let's say she is of a different species," I say, testing that theory. "How did she end up on Saltare-1? Why is she just sitting *behind* the orphanage in an alleyway? That means she has parents somewhere. People who brought her here."

I agreed to take an *orphan*. Not a child with parents. It makes a difference to me. I imagine what it'd be like for someone to rip me from my mom's arms in the cold Bartholo snow. I can't do that.

I can't.

Stork turns on me and the baby wails harder in Zimmer's arms. He tries to rock her with no avail.

"What do you want me to do?" Stork says, his voice breaking. "Leave her where we found her?" He touches his chest. "I know what it's like to be taken from my parents—do you honestly believe I *want* to do that to someone else?"

I don't know.

For Earth, maybe.

When I don't disagree, his face breaks into a pained, choked laugh. Zimmer frowns. "Since both of you are too emotionally invested in this . . . situation," he says, "I'm going to make the decision." He shifts the baby in his lanky arms. She cries again. "She can't stay in the alley. If she doesn't have parents, she's going to starve or get stolen by a worse wart. We take her back to the barge and decide things there."

Stork nods, and I also agree to the plan.

Nearby sirens wail, but they're coming from the opposite direction of Court and Mykal and the others. But it's a reminder.

It's only a matter of time before our faces are plastered across this city. And when that happens, with or without the baby, our window to leave Saltare-1 will have closed.

THIRTY-SIX

Stork

One thing is bloody certain.

She's the correct baby. She disappears every few seconds, causing all of us to look around the house barge in tense anxiety. Until seconds later, she reappears on Court's lap.

She's been doing that all night. Cuddled contently in his hands. He's the only one who can hold the newborn without her crying.

Got to give it to the kid, she knows how to make a joke. See, of all people she could have preferred, she chose *Court*. The guy who's stiff as a board and cradles her like she might combust in his arms. Honestly, he doesn't look that comforting or soft.

Anyone else would have been a better choice. If I were a baby, I'd have chosen me, but not all newborns can be as smart.

Quietly, she sucks on her thumb, happy for now. We don't even know if she's hungry or if she drinks milk like newborn Saltarians and humans. Not that we have any.

I sit atop the wooden dresser in the main living area, my gaze plastered to the baby. Franny's earlier words have infiltrated my head . . . my heart. And Franny is right. If that baby has parents here in the city, it changes everything.

The *Myth* book never mentioned her parentage, and I'd always felt right about taking her from an orphanage. It's why I never brought up this scenario. I didn't think it'd be possible to find her in an alleyway. That she could have family in the city. People who love her. Want her. I myself was stripped of a father.

Knowingly doing that to a child is something I'm trying to grapple with. Something I'm not sure I can actually go through with.

But if we don't bring her back to Earth . . .

Lord, I don't know what to do.

"Maybe she was *inside* the orphanage and teleported her way into the alley," Gem offers as explanation. Cross-legged on the ground, she tinkers with a portable fan and tries to disassemble it.

Padgett folds a paperback over her thumb, having picked one off the tilted shelves in the barge. "That's a good possibility," she agrees.

"Maybe she was always in the alley," Kinden refutes. "Fast-Trackers do stupid things like leaving their children alone in the city."

"Heya." Zimmer points a finger. "I'd never leave a baby in an *alleyway*."

"I didn't say *you*," Kinden says.

Court cuts in, "You've been horribly quiet about all of this."

I don't realize he's talking to me, until the silence grows. I meet Court's stern, narrowed eyes like he can see through me. He's too observant for his own good.

"What do you want me to say?" I ask into a sigh.

Court glares. "This is *your* mission."

I laugh. "And here, all this time after training, I thought we silently agreed that we'd both bear the leadership role." Or was it just in my imagination that we had been working well together? It was nice for some time. To fake-believe someone else was carrying some of this responsibility.

Court frowns, but he doesn't reply.

Mykal stops sewing for a second. He told us he was making the baby another blanket. I can't feel their emotions. I don't know what they're sensing between each other, but even Franny is glancing over with worried eyes. She picks at the frog leg, the slowest to eat dinner tonight. No appetite.

Lifebloods—I'm trying so hard not to be jealous of what those three share. Franny has told me more than once about all the negatives. How it feels like a curse sometimes.

But there are moments in my life where it'd be nice not to have to explain what I'm feeling. For someone to just completely, wholeheartedly *understand* me.

Court finally speaks again. "You're the one that knew the admirals," he says. "What would they want us to do?"

"Does that even matter, mate?" I shrug. "None of you were doing this mission *for* the admirals. You all have your weird reasons. And I'm not an idiot; this baby could feasibly have parents in the city and that changes things for some of you."

"What Court's asking is," Franny says to me, "does it change things for *you*?"

I don't have a flask, so I reach for the closest thing to me. A metal cigar tin. "And if we put it to a vote, mine won't make a difference." I open the tin; nothing is inside.

Zimmer looks me down and up. "I think you don't know what to do."

He's right.

I don't. There's more to this situation than just my feelings. There's a history involved with taking babies from their rightful birthplace and bringing them to a foreign land with foreign people. A history that belongs to Court, Franny, Mykal, and myself.

But I'm the only one with the brutal knowledge. And they deserve to know. Every piece of it, they *deserve* to know.

Tell me, how am I supposed to go against the admirals' dying wish? They raised me. Cradled me as a baby and loved me—even though I was their enemy. They gave me a place to rest my head and taught me all I know: ships, flying, and languages. How to be a good man, even when I failed at that.

Not a day passed that they didn't remind me that I had a choice. Earth or my people. I chose their planet. Their home because one day, I thought it'd feel like mine.

And then without a second thought, they gave their lives for these three people in this room.

How . . . how do I just turn my back on that? For what, my own guilt? My own pain? They believed I was strong enough to carry this burden. But I am weak and selfish, and all I want is to rid myself of every last word.

And then, I can't.

I just can't.

"I don't know," I mutter.

"Fyke," Franny curses. She pinches her nose and leans her head forward, blood rushing out of her nostrils. Mykal rushes to her side with some fabric to staunch it.

My eyes burn as I watch her growl in frustration. Something heavy weighs on my chest like it's being compacted down by cinder blocks.

Guilt.

It's been screwing with me for months.

But right now, all I want to do is sprint toward it. Not away like I've been doing.

"Franny," I breathe her name. Too soft, she doesn't hear me.

I run a hand at the back of my neck. Hot all of a sudden. I know why she's been getting nosebleeds, and I've been sitting with this information since I met her. Telling her hasn't been possible. It's connected to too many other secrets that the admirals wanted to be kept.

But I can't just sit by and watch her get more nosebleeds. Not when I know she'd calm down with the answer.

I have that power, and I'm allowing a human to suffer. Something I promised I'd never stand beside and let happen.

I can't do this anymore.

I can't.

Lord . . . help me.

"Franny," I say louder, restraining tears, my eyes stinging harshly.

She turns her attention to me, holding the bloodied rag to her nose.

I lose every ounce of resolve when her fiery gaze meets mine. *She's going to hate me.* A silent tear falls down my cheek. "I'm sorry."

She replies back, but the rag muffles her voice.

"She said, *what do you have to be sorry about?*" Mykal tells me, close enough to hear her clearer. Seven pairs of eyes lie on me like I'm under the hottest spotlight.

I sniff and rub at my cheek. *Get it together.*

There's no going back after this.

I take a tighter breath. "I know why you get nosebleeds," I say. "I've always known." I flip the cigar tin open and closed, my fingers trembling. "It's hereditary. Your birth dad had the same benign condition." I smile painfully at a memory. "He always used to carry a handkerchief in his pocket . . . just in case. And every day he'd change it to a different pattern. When I was a kid, I used to try and grab them from him, to see what the pattern of the day was. Polka-dot. Chevron. Banana-print." I shut up, not knowing why it's all coming out like this. It's like opening a dam, and I can't shut it closed. "I'm sorry."

My throat swells like a thousand bees stung my esophagus. I shift uncomfortably on the dresser. The quiet strains the air.

Franny removes the rag from her nose, the bleeding stopped. Confusion laces her eyes. "Why are you talking about him like you know him well?" she asks. "Is he still alive? Was he on the *Lucretzia* this whole time? What about my birth mom?" She fights her own tears.

"Just give me a second." I can't look in her eyes. Again, I focus on the cigar tin. Open and close.

Open and close.

Click.

Click.

Tear droplets ping the tin. I need something to drown this

pain. I need the scotch. I need the mission. I need *anything* else. But I have nothing but the truth. And it's time.

It's time.

"He's dead," I say abruptly. "He died." I raise my head, owing it to Franny to meet her gaze to deliver the rest of this news. "I knew him well . . ." I choke on a sob. "He raised me."

"No." Franny shakes her head, connecting the pieces.

I wipe the tear streaks beneath my eyes. "Admiral Voss was your birth father," I tell her. Then I look to Court. "Admiral Hull was your birth mother." Finally, Mykal. "Admiral Moura—"

"Stop," Mykal growls.

Court is in silent, grave contemplation.

"It must make more sense." I breathe. "Why they'd give their lives for you. You three weren't just strangers to them."

Franny narrows her reddened eyes at me. "You said *look away*."

"What?" I frown, not following.

"When they were murdered," Franny explains. "You told us to look away. Because you knew . . ."

I pause, choked. "I didn't want that to be your only memory . . ." I shake my head and swallow hard. "I wish I could have given you the choice. Told you all then." I laugh out a sharp sigh. "I shouldn't even be telling you now."

"Why are you then?" Court asks. "Why are you telling all of this now? We're not on Earth yet."

I'm not sure we're going to make it there, and even if we do, there's a chance this baby isn't going to come with us. We'll find her parents. Leave her with them. And I can't carry this information any longer.

I've failed the admirals.

But I don't want to fail myself. I turn to Franny. "I agreed to their dying wish—keeping all this information from you— because I thought I was offering kindness in the face of their certain death. But I realize now they asked . . . *too much* . . ." I choke on those words.

My abdomen cramps and I have to stand up, shaking out my limbs. Bile rises to my mouth, but I've come this far without puking. I need to stomach the rest.

"*Please,*" Franny says. "We want all of it. The truth."

"I'm going to give you that, dove," I tell her strongly. "I promise."

"Tomorrow?" she asks hopefully.

"Right now." I give her one better. I've opened the gates. Why wait? There's no going back from this. "But this is a story that you're going to want to take a seat for."

Franny settles next to Padgett on the couch. I'm thankful that Zimmer, Kinden, and the Soarcastle sisters have been quiet. Making it easier.

Because it's only going to get harder from here.

This time, I start the story from the beginning.

The *very* beginning.

Almost two decades ago. I tell them about the Battle of Drodinia. Admiral Moura used to show me hologram reels of that day, videos of the wreckage. Each morning, she'd make me breakfast—fresh apples, cinnamon, and oatmeal—and I'd spread out the battle plans on the oak table. I memorized the strategies. Combed through every last detail. Our cottage was in the countryside, the sky so clear you could see every single star. I'd lie on the grass, stare up, and visualize the battle.

It was Earth's single biggest casualty.

Strategically, the fleet had been cornered by Saltarians. In a blink of an eye, the *Romulus* took out Earth's largest warship. It happened like a snap of a finger. One minute, the ship was there. The next, pieces of the metal . . . and the bodies were just floating in space.

The Summit of Alcoara came next.

Our cottage still has the photograph where the admirals, captains, and strategists stand in a towering arena on the planet of Alcoara. Some were from the Earthen Fleet, others were our allies across the universe.

Not all were human.

I'd point to each face and ask Moura to name them. Some had blue skin, others had gills, and some were floating five feet in the air. It was an eclectic group. All with a singular purpose.

Save the human race.

At the summit, they were to devise alternative strategies. Ones that wouldn't pit fights with the Saltarians. It took fifteen days.

Everyone agreed they needed a long-game strategy, something that would benefit them later. Intelligence *inside* a Saltarian planet.

Spies.

When Moura said that word, *spies,* it almost doubled me over. Even as a kid, I understood the weight. To send humans to a Saltarian planet would be certain death. Even if they could pass as Saltarians, they'd make it weeks, maybe even less before being caught. Most of the Saltare planets have advanced surveillance and mandatory Helix Reader screenings every month.

Her next words always ring in my head. She countered with, *not Saltare-3.*

Even studying Saltare planets day and night, I'd almost forgotten about the isolated world. Saltare-3 is a footnote in history books.

A single paragraph. A location on a map.

It'd been frozen over and deserted by its sister planets. But Moura and the other admirals feared the challenges of blending in. There's little knowledge surrounding the customs of Saltare-3. And being able to perfectly pick up the dialect on *any* Saltare planet . . . it seemed impossible.

Those at the summit came up with a solution. A very controversial solution.

For the best chance at survival, the spies would need to be embedded on the planet at infancy. There they would grow up. Learn Saltarian ways. Adapt seamlessly.

The admirals called for volunteers.

They needed parents to part with their newborns. Send them to this big frozen planet in hopes that one day, they'd grow old enough to serve the Republic of Gaia and bring peace to their true home.

Moura always told me that the room went into the coldest silence she'd ever *felt*. It was like all the air drained from the atmosphere. The risk was too big.

No one came forward.

So the admirals did the only thing they could—they gave up each of their future firstborns for the mission.

Moura told me stories about Mykal. She never named him, but she'd call him the boy she lost. The one she had *for* Earth. *For* humanity. He was born first of the three. On the *Lucretzia,* Moura gave birth in the atrium overlooking the stars.

She said he wailed and cried in her arms and only quieted when she sung him hymns.

And then she broke the law to test his deathday. Pricked the bottom of his heel with a Death Reader, and when she saw the number, she knew it wasn't good. *His deathday.* The Saltarians would think he'd die when he was eight. A Babe. It was a problem, but one they would deal with in time.

Court was next.

Admiral Hull gave birth two weeks later on the *Lucretzia.* Not more than a day old, he was swaddled in blankets with Mykal and flown to Saltare-3.

"Who flew the jet?" I asked Moura. That's what I was most interested in. Who was this great, big, brave person that single-piloted the jet onto a Saltare planet? *Hero.* I always thought in my head.

"Captain Prinslo," Moura replied. "She was pregnant at the time. With the girl."

The girl.

The one I'd later come to know as Franny Bluecastle.

Prinslo was supposed to be the liaison between the spies and the *Lucretzia*. Her role seemed anything but simple. Embed the babies on Saltare-3 and then hide out in the Free Lands until the children turn eight years old. Then, she'd give each of them the details about their parentage. About Earth. The spies would remain on Saltare-3 to gather data before venturing to the bigger, more advanced Saltare planets. All the while, blending in and feeding information back to Earth.

Everything hinged on Prinslo. And when a whole operation is weighing on one person's shoulders, there's bound to be mistakes.

Moura let me listen to the early communication recordings that Prinslo was able to send from Saltare-3. She told me that originally it took three days to break the encryption.

In the house barge, I remove the Prinslo Tape from my shorts' pocket. I've been carrying the tape and an old player with me, ever since Franny found it in the bookcase. I never meant for them to hear the recording until we were on Earth.

But here.

Right now.

I pop the tape in and press play.

"It's Day One," Prinslo says. Hum and static fill the background. Her voice is like gravel, and it becomes worse and worse in each recording. Until the very last, I always have to strain my ears to pick up each word.

The wind. The cold. It was painfully scarring her vocal cords.

She continues, *"I've just landed in the Free Lands. It's colder . . .* much *colder than we originally thought. I'm struggling to make it into Grenpale. But I* must.*"

Originally, the plan had been to leave Mykal in Bartholo, but there was still that problem. Mykal was a Babe. He would dodge his deathday at eight years old. Too young to have that happen in a crowded city. So Prinslo did the only sensible thing: she took him to the villages where there weren't any Influentials around.

But she faced another problem.

There aren't any orphanages in Grenpale.

There was nowhere to leave him without drawing even more suspicion.

"*Day Two,*" Prinslo says in the recording. Slight pain drips along her voice, and she chokes on certain words. "*I had to swap the babies. Moura's child for a little boy in the village. His own mother just died. Kickfall . . . was supposed to be his last name . . . I heard.*" She sniffs, but not from the cold. "*The Saltarian baby—I couldn't . . . I didn't want to take him to the city. He'll serve a better life on Earth. My escape pod, the one I have for emergencies . . . for myself. He's inside. I set the coordinates for Earth for . . . the cottage on the hills. M should know what that means. I'm sorry . . . I'm so sorry.*"

Moura's cottage.

I arrived there.

Moura used to give me ancient comics, ones with super-heroes. She'd tell me that I was like Earth's superhero. An alien who appeared on a planet, come to save the human race. But it was something to make me feel good. Because my birth home wasn't destroyed. My father hadn't died. I didn't just end up on Earth by coincidence. I was sent there.

Yet I still fell in love with the people.

Still wished to fight for them.

"*Day Seven,*" Prinslo says. "*I've finally made it into the city. I dropped off Hull's baby boy in Yamafort. On the steps of an orphanage. I waited out of sight until I saw a young woman open the door. She took him inside. He's safe. I know he's safe.*"

After that, communications with Prinslo became less active.

"*Day Ninety-two.*" Her voice is hoarse. "*I'm still in the Free Lands. It's safer here. No one around. I don't think I could last undetected in the cities or villages. But it's cold . . . less* casia. *I can't see the stars. The sky.*" She cries.

Moura told me that homesickness plagued her. Among other things. Loneliness. Isolation.

"*Day One hundred and thirteen. I can feel her kicking in my belly. She's* strong. *I won't be able to make it to Yamafort this time. I'll have to leave her in Bartholo."*

I traced the cities on a map. A rough sketch of the Saltarian countries. Earth only had intelligence of a handful of the cities, and Moura scolded me when I embellished some of the drawings with extra trees. *You don't know that belongs there,* Moura reminded me. *Make it right or not at all.*

I made it right.

"Day One hundred and fifty," Prinslo rasps. *"She's beautiful. My baby girl.* She's beautiful. *She's gone."* She cries harder this time. *"I left her in Bartholo . . . an orphanage. The birth went well. I cut the umbilical cord myself and kept her warm in the hut. She'll be okay. I think she'll be okay."* Static clings to the recorder, and the first time I heard it, I always thought she cut out. But minutes later, her voice is back and deeper: *"Now begins the waiting. I'm going to check up on them every three hundred days. Year Eight, I'll find Moura's boy in Grenpale. He'll be the first I talk to and I'll tell him the truth. Of his purpose. Then we'll go from there."*

It seemed easy. Hide out in the Free Lands. But I can't even begin to imagine what she endured out there.

"Day . . . Two hundred . . . sixty-one." Prinslo's voice is barely distinguishable over the hoarseness and guttural rasp. *"I can't . . . seem to catch . . . it's . . . so . . . cold."*

That was the last recording.

After a year with no communication, she was declared dead.

Court's and Mykal's birth fathers were both C-Jays and volunteered to carry out the rescue operation for the three children. But they never made it to the planet. A Saltare-2 battlecraft intercepted their approach, and they were shot down in the galaxy.

After that, Moura told me that too much risk was involved. No more rescues. No more attempts to even send someone else down to be a new liaison. The Earthen Fleet had already lost too much.

It was decided within days.

The three children were failed assets.

Moura said that they could have used different Death Readers when they first pricked their babies, but they purposefully used the same device on all three. Knowing this act would permanently change their kids' body chemistry.

In the event that Prinslo died—in the event that their children would be abandoned and lost—they knew there was a chance, a *very* small chance that their kids would find one another after they dodged their deathdays.

Becoming lifebloods was the last hope of their survival.

Numbers.

They needed numbers. And three was better than one.

Years went by, and I sometimes returned to the recordings to remind myself that I wasn't alone. There were . . . had been . . . maybe still are three people who've experienced the same as me. Growing up on a foreign planet, surrounded by people different from me.

But most of the time, the story of the three lost children was just a forgotten memory. Something that passed by without notice. Because the chances of survival after they dodged their deathdays—it'd be too small, too inconceivable.

If someone didn't find them and kill them for it, they'd die from the madness of not knowing *why*, or the harsh cruelty of the weather.

To find them alive.

That was the biggest surprise of all.

THIRTY-SEVEN

Franny

hey left us to die on an enemy planet.

Failed assets. Chills keep nipping my body at those two words.

Failed. Assets.

I botch most every plan I've ever made, but gods, our parents botched this one good. I still hear Prinslo in the pit of my ears. Raspy and dying out, my mother's voice stolen by the cold.

"She's beautiful. My baby girl. She's beautiful. *She's gone."*

My eyes glass and sear, not understanding if I'm sad or furious or just relieved at finally knowing the truth. And I imagine a time where we were on the same planet together. Me and her. So close, but only for a little while.

Now I understand why the admirals were scared of us learning this. Why they'd made Stork promise to keep their dying wish right before they traded their lives for ours. They were worried we'd hate them if we knew the truth, and if our loathing was strong enough, there was a chance we wouldn't even want to save Earth.

If they're with the gods, at least they can rest knowing those fears didn't come to fruition.

I can't dwell solely on the past, not now at least. What the eight of us do next will decide everything: our future, the future of the human race.

And the future of Earth.

I was a Purple Coach driver. I was a nobody to most, and

now I'm about to make a choice that affects two thousand human lives and the life of this baby and all of us.

We all know that we have two painful choices. Continue the mission as planned and bring the baby to Earth. Saving a planet and its people. But ripping a child from her parents and home.

Or we find the baby's parents and leave her in their care, committing Earth to inevitable invasion. And possibly annihilating the human race.

We think silently on our own. We also think among each other, trying not to start a stew. And when we take a vote, the decision is made.

Not unanimously.

When everyone goes to bed, I hole up in the quiet wheelhouse of the barge. Unable to sleep, I sit on the velveteen sea-blue captain's chair and skim my hand over the wheel's cylindrical wooden spokes. Shaped more like fancy balusters.

Nobody on the docks can spot me. An abundance of gold-painted seashells are strung along the glass windshield as a curtain.

I look next to me at the co-captain's chair, and I whisper, "Do you think we've chosen right?" A dresser drawer lies on the velveteen seat, the newborn nestled inside and wrapped in a woolen blanket that Mykal sewed.

She stretches her teeny tiny arm with a squeaky noise. I wish that were a resounding *yes*.

Her empty bottle rolls on the ground as the barge gently rocks. Using the very last of our bills, Kinden and Court snuck out earlier and bought milk meant for newborns. She didn't have a bad reaction to the Saltarian milk, and she sucked the bottle dry.

Peering over the drawer, I run my thumb over her soft cheek and tufts of green hair. "You're beautiful," I murmur, and then a lump knots my throat.

"*She's beautiful.*" I hear my mother again. "*My baby girl. She's beautiful. She's gone.*"

I lean back and try to concentrate on Court and Mykal, who have managed to fall into a slumber.

It matters little to them. Their parentage. Their history. Because they didn't believe it'd have a real bearing on their future.

They only wanted answers for me. So I could be at peace with the knowledge. And really, I think Court was afraid of the truth. Afraid that it'd hurt more to know, and maybe it has.

Our parents sacrificed their lives for Earth and for us, but they also left us on a foreign planet without giving us a choice and I know their guilt must've been insurmountable.

Tears sting.

The baby lets out a soft cry.

"Shh," I whisper—like a blink, the baby vanishes with the drawer. She was only next to me for a few minutes anyway. She must have teleported back to Court.

"Can't sleep?" Stork asks, quietly walking into the wheel-house. Eyes still bloodshot and swollen. He takes a seat, and leans back, the co-captain's chair squeaking. "It's not like the weight of a literal world isn't on your shoulders at all." He sports a halfhearted smile.

"It's on your shoulders too," I sling back.

"Must be why I'm awake with you." His smile softens, and we share a tender silence with so much less strain.

Stork would've been in pain no matter if he broke or kept the admirals' dying wish. But letting us share in his burden has lessened a brutal tension. And he was finally able to tell me exactly why the admirals never referred to him as their son. He said that Moura, Hull, and Voss each had a child, ones they left to die. He was something else to them. Not something more or less. Just different.

We hold each other's gaze for a long beat, and he asks, "Do you wish I never told you about Prinslo?"

"No," I say strongly. "*No*. I'm so glad you did." I blink back tears.

"Do you really think Court is right?" Stork asks.

During the vote, Court had one final remark. He stood up and said that he had given up on people, after his country imprisoned him.

He wouldn't risk his life for anyone's cause, and then he told us, "But I'm here. I'm on a Saltare planet, and it's not for me. I've been here for you." He looked to me with no trace of anger or self-hatred.

I felt him, and it was as though he accepted that he could be the person he longed to be, and that slowly, without really realizing, it was already happening.

"I want to be here for them," Court professed. "We have the chance to save people. Thousands of people, and this time, it will mean something when we do."

He's not all cold and dead inside. So much of Court is very, very alive.

In the wheelhouse, I keep my eyes locked on Stork. *Do I think Court is right?* "I think you're both right in your own way."

While Court voted to save Earth, Stork voted to find the baby's parents.

I think at the start of this, we'd all predict the opposite vote. Even Court and Stork would too.

Stork bends farther back on the chair, his eyes swimming softly against mine. "I can't repeat history."

I know.

He said as much. I still remember what he told everyone before he voted. "I had a good life on Earth. I was loved, and I know she will be there, but I look back in time . . . and I was *stolen* from my mom's arms. A mom who died giving life to me . . . and what good did it do? What good did dropping you three on a foreign planet actually do?"

I don't want to make the same mistakes as our parents.

I don't want to botch it as badly as they did.

And I was torn between both choices. I still am, even after

deciding. Maybe I always will be, and I wonder if our parents had the choice, if they'd do it all differently again.

Keeping a hand on the wheel, I turn my body more toward him. "Really, how big is the chance that we find the baby's parents and they let us take her to Earth?"

He tilts his head. "Big enough for me."

It was big enough for Padgett, Gem, and Zimmer.

Mykal and Kinden voted with Court to just leave now, and I was left to choose Stork and the baby or to choose Earth with my lifebloods.

Thunk.

The drawer meets the wooden floor.

Stork and I glance down at the space between our chairs, the baby cooing softly and slowly smacking her lips.

And I whisper to her, "Stork Kickfall doesn't want us to steal you away."

He smiles in real amusement, looking at me as he tells the baby, "Franny Bluecastle wants to steal you out of your drawer."

I voted to save Earth. Court is here for me, and I'll be here for him. With my vote, there was a four-to-four tie. We have no time to convince anyone to switch sides, and so when Stork tossed a coin, we agreed that we would be all-in on whatever the gods, or luck, chose.

The baby wiggles her toes.

"Don't fret," I whisper to her, "we're going to find your parents."

To find the baby's parents, our only clue is Riktor. The Fast-Tracker who stole a pouch from her blanket. We hope the pouch has some information about her origins.

I remember that Riktor's name tag said THE PREMIERE HOTEL. We depart quickly for the hotel at 5 o'morning before the sun crests the mainwater.

We're unsure how long we have before Commander Theron

posts *clear* images of our faces, and when that happens, we need to be off this planet. Hopefully the baby will be with her parents by then.

Right now, she's strapped to Court in a makeshift sling. Gem had taken several purple scarves from the hostel, just to carry some broken gadgets she found lying on the docks—and Mykal used the fabric to secure the baby to Court's chest.

He isn't complaining about being in charge of the newborn. I think he's grown attached, more than he lets on. Court rubs her little back often. Sometimes I sense her tiny hand grabbing on to his finger. And then his lips gradually tic upward.

None of us dawdle. Together, all eight of us locate the Premiere Hotel, a glass building lost in fluffy clouds. The main entrance is twenty stories high, and we can't take an elevator up and traipse inside like we're Influentials.

We have no bills, and we all look like FTs.

"There should be a backdoor entrance on the first floor," Zimmer tells us. He'd know better since he worked in hotel hospitality on Saltare-3.

Algae and barnacles shroud the first few floors of the hotel, and a dock wraps around the base of the building. Sailboats and canoes tied up. We walk along the slick pathway, water sloshing on the wooden planks—*just do, don't think.*

I breathe in.

Breathe out.

Listening to the here and now.

And we find an EMPLOYEES ONLY door.

Once inside, I realize the Premiere Hotel is startlingly beautiful. No gold finery or oil paintings, but glittering sea glass in wondrous shades of green and blue dangle from the ceiling. Chiming melodically as they clink together.

And this is just their hallway.

"There should be a locker room for staff," Zimmer whispers. We file down the hall and find the locker room easily.

Slipping inside, wooden cubbies with electronic passcodes

line the room in long rows. Some Fast-Trackers hurry like they're late for work, and others leisurely chat and take their time dressing.

No one recoils at our sight. I wouldn't either if new people sprung up at Purple Coach. I'd keep my head up and worry about my day. Not anyone else's.

Zimmer picks a row where a short girl of thirteen or fourteen years buttons a teal uniform: short-sleeved formal shirt and thigh-cut shorts.

Her eyes ping to each of us, and she brushes a curl off her tan cheek. "New hires?"

"Yeah. We start today." Zimmer peers around. "Which chump wants to give us the tour?"

She chuckles. "No tour. Baxley likes to throw the FTs in cold. You'll just pick things up along the way. If you're a bellhop, take the elevator to the lobby. Sweepers, grab a cleaning cart in the supply closet and ride up to the guest rooms. Only go in ones with VACANT signs." She points to a dresser. The surface is an electronic screen. "Master keys are in the second drawer, uniforms in the third. If you're new hires, your handprints will open up the dresser to get them."

Mykal mumbles behind me, something about hating technology.

Court steps in, propping a casual arm on Mykal's shoulder. "Heya, do you know if Riktor still works here? He's a friend of a friend. Thought I'd say hi."

And thieve back the pouch that wart thieved.

"Sure, he's senior staff," she says. "He cleans out the elegant suites. You'll find him on the top floors."

Zimmer nods in thanks, and as we go, we're about to forget the master key and uniforms. We only need to find Riktor. But Gem and Padgett falter before we leave the locker room.

"It'll be useful to have a keycard that can access all rooms," Padgett says beneath her breath.

Gem stares excitedly at the dresser. "We can try to open it, and then we'll meet you upstairs." She reties a scarf around her stitched eye socket.

Stork looks to Court and tells him, "We should split up anyway to cover more ground."

Court agrees.

I worry the Soarcastle sisters will be caught tinkering with the hotel's electronics. "What if someone sees them?"

Court tells Kinden to stay here, and his older brother takes the task of lookout with arrogant grace. Letting us all know there is no one else better for the job.

We leave them in the locker room, and the five of us that remain find the glass elevator. We rise up to the elegant suites. On the buttons, the two highest floors are marked with an *E*.

"How are we splitting up?" I ask Court.

He instantly glances at Mykal, who already has his muscled arm over Court's shoulder. Coupled again, they're in great beautiful spirits—so much so that my chest swells and swells.

But silence falls because their strengths may be better suited apart. Zimmer knows hotels the best, but he's admittedly the scrawniest. Mykal can protect him from anyone that tries to slow him down.

"Franny and I will take the floor above you," Court tells Mykal and Zimmer. "Stork can keep a lookout between the two."

We can't pay Riktor off, so I ask, "What do we do when we come upon Riktor?"

"Break his neck." Mykal grunts.

Court rolls his eyes. "We threaten him."

Mykal outstretches an arm. "Exactly what I said."

The elevator dings and slows to a halt.

We're here.

THIRTY-EIGHT

Court

I don't believe in any gods, and so to me, leaving the fate of Earth to a coin toss is impossibly ridiculous.

But I believe in Mykal and Franny. I believe in my brother, the Soarcastle sisters, and Zimmer. I even believe in Stork.

And I believe in myself. We can find the baby's parents. One step at a time, and I focus on the present.

Franny and I knock on VACANT doors and wait to see if anyone shouts.

My thirtieth door, a boy yells, "I'm cleaning in here!"

The sleeping baby stirs against my chest. I put a stiff hand to the back of her head. She never seems to mind my rigid affection. "Riktor?!" I shout back.

"He's not with me!"

I move on.

Franny raps her knuckles on the other side. Opaque portholes are screwed to each sleek door, and sea glass clinks together above us, disturbing the baby.

She rustles a little more, and I let her grip my finger.

"We're just trying to find our mat—*friend*," Stork says with earnestness. My head swerves. Down the hall, Stork tries to stop an older man in a frilly-sleeved shirt and black vest from charging over to us.

The Influential glares. "If you're not a guest, you can't be up here."

Gods be damned.

"We *are* guests," Stork says casually, walking backward. Distracting a hotel owner, he bides us time.

Hurrying, Franny and I skulk forward and knock on doors, listening for responses from sweepers.

The Influential tells Stork, "I need to see your identification right now."

Stork flashes a half-smile and pats his frayed shorts and shirt. "Must have left it in my room."

"If you're a Stormcastle—"

Stork launches an elbow at the man's windpipe. He chokes, grasping his throat, and then Stork head-butts him.

The man's eyes roll back and then shut. Stork catches his limp body and lays him on the floor. His calculated movements look trained and militant. C-Jays must learn how to disarm Saltarians in hand-to-hand combat.

Franny frowns at me. "The Influential thought we were Stormcastles?"

Stormcastles are the Saltare-1 equivalent to Icecastles. Criminals who've served time in prison. If we appear that threatening, then we really have no time to waste. "Keep going," I urge.

We knock on several more doors.

Franny bangs angrier on one beside me.

"Heya, I'm cleaning!" a boy shouts.

Stork hears and immediately runs over to us. He mouths, *that's him.* He recognizes his voice.

"Riktor?!" Franny asks, her pulse thumping faster in my veins. Stork and I join her side.

"Yeah? Who's asking?" he says.

I cut in, "Baxley sent us!"

"You chumps must be new! This floor is *mine.* I earned it! You can take the lower—"

"We're not here to clean!" I shout. "A couple left you a tip, and Baxley wanted us to give it to you! He was too busy downstairs to do it himself—"

The door swings open, and immediately, Franny bangs Riktor's chest with two palms. Pushing the buzzed-haired Fast-Tracker backward, she shouts, "Give us the pouch, you baby thief!"

Stork smiles at Franny as we slip in behind her, and I lock the door. The rich suite has nautical flair: all polished wood and golden boat décor. The bed comforter is downturned, mid-cleaning, and on the ceiling, more sea glass hangs in harmonic clusters.

"I'd have to take the fykking baby to be a baby thief," Riktor retorts. Teal ink washes down his arms like waves. His eyes dart to the newborn braced to my chest, and then he laughs at Franny. "Seems to me *you're* the baby thief—"

"Shut up," I sneer, but Franny is still hurt by the comment. Her nose flares, swallowing hard.

Riktor grins. "Not as feisty now, are you—"

"How about you stop telling me what I am, you *pouch* thief." She holds out her palm. "Give it to us."

Riktor tosses his cleaning rag at her face. Cloth brushes her cheek. I feel the fabric like he threw the rag at my body—but greater than that sensation, *hostility* springs inside me.

Mykal is sensing Franny, but he's not running back here. I can only assume he's encountered a hotel owner like we did or different trouble. *He's fine.*

He's fine.

I try not to cage my breath. I trust that Mykal can handle an Influential like Stork just did, and before it reaches that point, Zimmer can try to talk them out of a confrontation.

"Your boss is unconscious in the hallway," Stork tells Riktor. "You throw any shit at her or try to jump us, and your lights are out next."

Riktor lets out an uncertain laugh. Not understanding all of what Stork just said.

Let me try. "We'll break your neck." I think of Mykal. Always.

Riktor hoists a hand and backs up into his cleaning cart. "Heya, no need for that kind of violence. But that pouch is mine. I'd only part with it for a cost."

I roll my eyes, and the baby wakes more, squealing playfully. "Shh," I whisper, rubbing her back. *Sleep.*

"What do you want?" Stork asks.

Franny crosses her arms.

Riktor skims her up and down. "You seem fairly skilled with your mouth. An hour with me and the pouch is yours."

I clench my jaw.

"Gods." Franny cringes.

Stork flashes the most biting smile I've seen from him yet. "Counteroffer. An hour with me, and you'll learn *exactly* what I'm skilled at after I'm done with you."

Riktor is still eyeing Franny.

"My mouth is good for *spitting*," Franny retorts. "You want to find out just how good?" She prepares to spit at him—

"Heya, I'm well-liked in Montbay," he rebuts, shifting against the cart. He's not scared of us, so why is he so fidgety? "If you start a stew, you'll have worse hells to pay out of that door."

"I'm shaking," Stork says, sarcasm thick.

Riktor peeks over his shoulder at the cleaning cart. *He's blocking the cart.*

"The pouch is on the cart," I say.

Riktor points at Stork who takes a step closer. "There's no value in the pouch. Joke's on you. It's just a rock!"

Like Mykal is with us, Stork disarms the Fast-Tracker in two blows. One elbow to the throat, and then he rams his head into the wall.

His body thuds to the floor, unconscious.

Franny and I reach the cart. Packed with bottles of antiseptic, fresh towels, a bowl of mints—I find the pouch next to a bar of soap.

"I have it."

They gather around, and I remove . . . a small black stone. Smooth along all sides and lightweight.

"Is there anything else?" Franny asks, worried. Her stomach is knotting mine.

"No." I pass her the pouch.

She reverses the folds. Empty.

I glance over at Stork, and I freeze. His hands are on his head and eyes tightened on the stone. Looking whiplashed.

"You know what this is?" I ask.

He nods strongly, and his hands fall to the back of his neck. "It's a UHR, a Universal Hologram Record." He licks his lips. "But it doesn't make any bloody sense."

"Why?" Franny asks.

"It's a human device, dove."

My frown deepens. I flip the stone over in my left palm, the baby clinging to my other hand. "How could a human device end up on Saltare-1?"

"It couldn't have." Stork stares off in thought, trying to find *reason* in this impossibility.

"Well, how do we open it?" Franny asks.

"You can't." Stork lets out a broken laugh. He sinks down on the unmade bed and kicks a pillow, thread stitched in a pattern of breaking waves. "UHRs are one of the most encrypted devices. Only the owner's fingerprint can open one."

And we have no way of finding the owner.

Franny searches the cleaning cart to see if there's anything else.

The baby shrieks gleefully. Catching our attention. She wiggles against me and stares up with glittering blue eyes.

Life is precious. I was never taught just how much *lives* are worth our sacrifice and devotion and love. On Saltare, life means something different, but there is a world out there waiting for us and for new generations. A world still worth fighting for.

I narrow my stern gaze at Stork. "Earth can't become another Saltare."

He watches the restless baby and sighs, conflicted.

She tries to rattle my hand, and I drop the UHR out of my other. It slides across the waxed floorboards toward Stork.

He reaches for the stone. "If we take the baby—" His voice dies as the device *clicks*.

He opens his palm, and the stone is glowing bright green.

"That's not possible," Stork says, mouth ajar as he rises off the bed. Standing and nearing us.

"It's opening?" Franny asks, just as a hologram projects from the UHR like a film screen. I tune out my surrounding as I fixate on the video.

Wait . . .

Wait.

I sway back at the image. Blinking in a daze, as though this is a dream. In my logical, reasonable mind, there is no conceivable way this can be real.

What I see is . . .

Me.

But it's not me. Not really. My jaw is a little wider and wrinkles crease the edges of my bloodshot eyes. I'm older. Thirties, possibly. Bronze armor shields my chest, the Earthen emblem etched on the breastplate.

I cradle a baby against my armor, my hands coated in blood. The baby is tightly swaddled, blankets stained crimson. Green tufts of hair puff off her little head.

This can't be real.

Standing here, staring at a version of myself—my face older and scarred, and eyes eerily blank—I feel as overcome with madness as the day I lived past my deathday. When I hungered and starved in the Free Lands and nothing made sense except for the boy a country away. Feeling and hoping and screaming for me to keep going.

The recording has sound.

"*I don't have long,*" he says, glancing over his shoulder. Noise cracks behind him. Banging, violent booms. It sounds like war . . .

Looking forward again, his voice is deeper than mine but just as grave. "*If you're hearing this, it means you've found her. And you must have many questions, Stork. If you're with Franny and Court, then I know they must have even more.*" Crashing resounds in the background, and he speaks more urgently. "*I'm going to explain everything as quickly as I can.*"

"What is this?" Stork asks softly, slowly shaking his head. Lost in disbelief.

Franny gapes at the hologram, her brows furrowing while we watch an older version of myself check cautiously over his shoulder . . .

And then it hits me.

"The future," I breathe.

This is our future.

The hologram flickers like static interference. He speaks hurriedly. "*The three of us—Franny, Stork, and myself—came up with a plan as soon as we learned of the child's abilities. We knew we must send her back to Earth.*" He glances at the baby in his arms.

I look at the baby in mine.

They're identical, and returning my focus to the hologram, the baby in his arms lets out a soft whimper. "*Little one, you're safe.*" His dull gaze lifts to us. "*Time travel is a complex business and will be discovered in a decade from your year. So as not to spend the next century agonizing over this, Court. Understand, this was the only way. We only had enough power for two time jumps. One for the book. One for the baby.*"

The book.

"No," I whisper. "I didn't . . ."

"*The author of* The Greatest True Myths of the 36th Century *is Sean Cavalletti.*" He nods, like he understands that I've already put the pieces together. But he tells me anyway, *"An anagram for Etian Valcastle."*

My birth-given name. I knew the book held a strange familiarity, but I never would've imagined it was because they were *my* words. Something I could've written, if given the chance.

He tucks the baby closer to his armored chest, the hologram flickering again. *"We chose the auction that Stork attends, and we knew he wouldn't pass up that title."*

Next to me, Stork lets out a soft breath.

"It's safer separating her and the directions. Our greatest fear is that someone else will find her—but if you never reach Saltare-1, if you never locate the right orphanage, or if she moves herself and you never listen to this recording . . ." He takes a long pause. *"She's resilient . . . we've known that for some time. She'll take care of herself."* He looks down. *"At least, that's what we're going to tell ourselves."*

He glances back again. More crashes and yells and gunfire.

I don't understand.

Something isn't adding up in this overall picture. If we needed the baby for the purpose of cloaking and transporting to Earth, then . . .

"Why not just send her directly to Earth?" I ask aloud.

Stork shakes his head, unknowing, and Franny says, "Is someone behind him?" Pinging lights flood the hologram. Screaming, and then the banging of a door.

We watch an older version of Stork rush over to the older version of me. His snow-white hair is cut much shorter, and blood drips down his armor and stains his pale cheeks. He still wears his blue-jay earring, but there is a noticeable difference about Stork and it's not old age.

"I lose an arm in the future," Stork says matter-of-factly.

From bicep to his fingers, his arm is a bronze prosthetic. Made of the same lightweight metal as his breastplate. *"Is it done?"*

"Almost," the older version of me replies. *"Do we have ten minutes?"*

"*Five.*" He glimpses at the baby and instantly chokes on a sob. "*I'm so sorry.*"

The future Court focuses on us. "*You're going to ask why we didn't send her to Earth.*"

Yes.

"*The way this works, I would need the current location of the planet. And Earth is . . .*"

"*Gone,*" the future Stork finishes. "*Destroyed. Years ago. The Lucretzia is all that's left of the Earthen Fleet. Seventy-five souls aboard.*"

Franny rocks back.

"*In minutes . . .*" He's crying, tears streaking his bloodstained cheeks. "*. . . that'll be gone too.*" Their baby wails, and future Court strokes her head until she hushes.

A void hollows his eyes. He seems to be drifting. Not talking. Not really present. Like he's dying.

No.

Like he's already dead.

"*Court.*" Future Stork snaps and waves his hand in front of his face, and then he taps his cheek twice. A Grenpalish gesture.

My tears flood uncontrollably as I watch—as I know. Mykal is dead in the future, and I'm something worse than miserable without him. I'm empty. Filled with nothingness.

"*Come on, mate. It's just a little longer.*" Stork jostles his arm until he lifts his head higher.

"*Mykal is gone,*" the future Court says numbly.

Franny wipes her wet cheeks—I turn my head. Mykal, *our* Mykal is running toward us. I sense his strong stride and burning tendons.

He'll be here soon.

I calm.

He's not gone.

"*Sometimes the Grenpalish gesture focuses Court,*" future Stork tells us. "*But when Mykal died, a part of Court died with him.*" The hologram flickers badly.

The older version of myself is back speaking in haste. *"The baby. You should know her abilities by now. Once on Earth, she'll make the planet invisible. Our enemies will not understand what happened, and this gives you time you desperately need."*

Why do we need more time?

He barely pauses. *"She won't have the intelligence to teleport Earth to a galaxy of your choosing. Not yet. Wait a few years and then she'll be able to teleport the planet safely where it needs to be. This also gives you three years to find a new galaxy that Earth can call home."*

I pocket every instruction.

"Stork, tell them her name." They both look down at their baby—and their baby is our baby. But I have a difficult time comprehending how this little peaceful newborn in my arms has seen and heard and been held in a battle-torn, bloodied future.

In the hologram, future Stork rubs away his tears. *"I'd like to introduce you to the darling light of my life, Zima Bluefall."*

Something wet touches my cheek. Franny drops her head, stepping back like a punch to the gut, and the hologram stone is as unsteady as Stork's quaking palm.

Bluefall.

This is Franny's baby. But if her child is a fall . . . and not a castle—it means Franny died in childbirth. I stare at the older version of myself. His crimson hands, the hands of someone who tried to save a life. He helped deliver the baby, I think.

He watched Franny die.

I stand stoic. Trying to remind myself that Franny is right beside me. Breathing. Alive. I am not him.

He is empty.

And so very alone.

Future Stork tries to speak, but his words break into a sob. He fights to raise his grief-stricken gaze, and he says clearly, *"I love you, dove. One day, you'll know how much."*

Another boom, and he runs out of sight. Leaving my older version and the baby.

Franny has her hand partially over her eyes. Distraught, her pulse like a knife unknowing where to cut and stabbing haphazardly.

Stork is watching her with concern, and then looks to the hologram as future Court speaks.

"*No one knew this would happen,*" he continues quickly. "*Not until she was conceived. Zima is the first child born of a Saltarian and a lifeblood. When Franny was pregnant, Zima's abilities started emerging. The green hair was just as unexpected.*" A gun blast pops in the distance. He holds her closer. "*You both wanted to name her after him.*"

"Zimmer," Franny mutters his name, pain twists her stomach.

"*Stork and Franny, if you're listening, you need to know— you did not make this choice lightly. You never imagined sending her to a foreign planet. Franny, you did not want to do what our parents did to us.*" He checks over his shoulder. "*If the baby stays here, she will die. We will all be gone soon, and by sending Zima, you knew she'd have a chance at life and to extend the lives of thousands of others.*"

The hologram sputters out, and then rapidly blinks back. More gunshots popping.

"*I have no more time left. Once you find Zima, do everything in your power to make it to Earth. It's then you'll know you've succeeded, and you'll have changed our future.*" He pauses to say, "*We never made it. Mykal, Franny, and I—we never saw Earth.*" Gravely, he tells us, "*May the gods be in your spirit.*" He looks down at the baby. "*And she in your heart—*"

The hologram sucks into the stone, the video vanishing.

My head suddenly whips to the left—a blow to my jaw. *Not my jaw.* "Where is Mykal—?"

I duck, metal crashing down on my shoulders, *his shoulders.*

Before he can make sense of what's happening, he's kicked to the ground.

I'm kicked.

I kneel—*gods dammit*. I stand up. He tears at limbs, his rage surging, and I hear Franny and Stork beside me. Screaming my name, but their voices are distant to his overwhelming senses.

His wrath. And pain, ripping through me.

"Mykal!" I cry.

I can't lose him.

I can't let that future be ours.

THIRTY-NINE

Mykal

Six *Romulus* cadets.

That's how many it takes to restrain me in the hotel suite.

They've shackled my ankles together with some sort of metal ring and chained my other hand to the leg of the bed. All the while poking me with an electrowand.

I grit my teeth in pain and boiling ire. Spit spews between my furious lips, and I struggle to escape. Growling and wrestling against the restraints. I tug and tug, the bed creaking but not moving.

They laugh like they finally caught their prey.

Another zap to my thigh, and my muscles spasm. My shoulders fall back against the shiny wooden floorboards. Lying face-up on the ground, a steel-pointed shoe stomps on my opened palm, each little bone snapping underneath the weight.

I release a gritty scream, and then a boot suddenly crushes my throat like a mountain lion sits atop my windpipe. *Get off.* Instinct grabs hold, and I ache to tear this boot off my neck.

But I can't lift my left hand out from under the steel shoe. And so I jerk my right wrist against the chains. The leg of the bed starts cracking. Wood splitting.

The cadet presses harder on my throat.

Air is stuck in my lungs, and tiny spots blanket my vision. *Don't give up.*

I wrench with all my force, the metal chain digging into my flesh—but the wooden leg is starting to break.

I can feel my eyes rolling back in my head. And my wrist goes slack.

"Heya, he's going to pass out," the bossiest cadet snaps. "Lift your boot."

The tall, freckle-faced cadet complies, and I choke on air. Gasping. My throat swells in pain, and they laugh some more.

Wretched luck. It's what I focus on—my poor, ugly luck—while sweat slips down my temples and my tongue is thick in my mouth with snot and spit. Or else I'll be thinking about Court and Franny, and I can't think of them without fear punching my gut.

I pray to the gods that they're not feeling this torture.

I'm not sure how the cadets found us. If there are cameras outside the hotel, or maybe we were spotted in the east wing. But just as Zimmer and I were checking on an empty suite, we heard footsteps banging up the stairwell and the door whooshed open right beside us.

Six *Romulus* cadets emerged in burgundy StarDust uniforms, and the looks on their faces—like they'd just discovered the rarest and most prized bear among all the lands—is not something I'll be forgetting easily.

They grabbed at Zimmer first. Just tossed him like a sack of potatoes into the opened suite.

Seven shocks with the electrowand and they had me subdued enough to shove me right behind him. Then the door swung closed.

Locked in.

Without the boot on my throat, I yell between my teeth and fight against the metal clasps on my ankles and the chain on my wrist. When I try to rip my hand from underneath the shoe, a bossy, short-haired lady cadet holds out her hand to another. "Adrian," she snaps. "Pass me the electrowand."

Adrian is the one stepping on my damned hand. His voice is shrill, and his barbed eyes gleam wickedly. "You lost yours, Henna. You can't have mine." He's bulkier than the others, and he leans more of his weight on my opened palm.

I growl, "You—"

He zaps my side, and I shut up all right. Muscles burning, I shake violently, as helpless as a tree limb in a snowstorm.

I hear the sound of splashing water, a vicious struggle coming from the bathroom.

"Leave him be!" I holler, my pain subsiding to a dull throb. I don't have eyes on Zimmer. A younger boy dragged him into the bathroom, and the only thing I've been hearing is that water. They're hurting him. I don't have to be a Wonder to know that.

Henna smiles a nasty smile. "Don't worry about your bludrader friend. He's being dealt with."

I scream harsh obscenities, my throat rubbed raw and my voice gnarled.

A third, much older cadet—gray wispy hair above his lip and nestled on his chin—squats near my face and presses his electrowand to the flesh beneath my eye. "I wonder," he muses, voice deep and hollow. "What would happen if I shocked your eyeball. Would you lose sight or just die?"

"Probably die," Adrian says, unknowingly releasing some of his weight off my hand. "Think about it, Igor. He's weak. Jolee could slice him right now and he'd just pathetically bleed out."

Jolee, I realize, is the leering lady with piercing green eyes and a mane of golden hair. She's seated on an elegant blue chair and swings a battle-ax back and forth.

Just sitting. Just watching. Like a vulture on a branch, waiting to dive onto the carcass.

That ax—I recognize it from the *Lucretzia*. By the leaf emblem forged on the blade, it must be a human weapon. Not something anyone can find on a Saltare planet.

Her lip quirks as she catches me staring. "You like this?" she asks and inspects the ax with a fondness. "Plucked it straight off your precious Admiral Moura's back." *My birth ma.*

I glower, wrath suffocating me. Stealing my voice.

"Commander Theron let me have it. You want to know why?"

I'm about to yank my limbs every which way and growl until all noise dies out. But I remember Court. What he'd tell me to do. *Calm down, Mykal.*

My aggression quiets as I breathe and remember.

I may not be able to feel Court, not while I'm in this much pain, but we're more than this strange link. He is still with me. No matter how heightened or how faint this bond becomes.

He's still with me. Guiding me.

Stay calm.

Jolee twirls the battle-ax. "I'll tell you why I was bestowed with this beauty. I've murdered more humans than I have lived years. It's an accomplishment that had to be rewarded."

I take advantage of her yammering and try to slip my hand free from the chain on the bed. Twisting and turning the cuff.

The tall, freckle-faced boy catches me and *slams* the end of a long iron rod onto the top of my hand. I scream in agony.

They laugh louder.

Energy starts draining from my body, but as pain fades and light wells in my head, I start to sense something . . .

I feel his heart in my chest.

Beating rapidly.

His lips . . . are moving.

Court is mouthing, *Mykal.*

Mykal.

Mykal.

Please don't be feeling this, I want to tell Court. Please let this pain be mine alone.

He keeps repeating my name. Over and over. And soon, I realize that Court is trying to help me stay awake.

I blink. Hot, exhausted tears stinging down my cheeks. I focus on keeping my eyes open and conserving my strength.

The quiet freckle-faced cadet checks his watch like he's waiting for something. Someone.

I imagine they did their jobs and called the commander, let him know they've wrangled and caught a human and a bludrader.

Everyone turns their head as the youngest cadet exits the bathroom. A tattooed hornet inks the side of his cheek, and he drags a limp body by the wrist. Strands of wet hair hang over Zimmer's heavy-lidded eyes. Soaked from toe to head, wet tracks trail him along the floor. The young boy pulls Zimmer behind him, like he's nothing more than a tree chopped down for wood.

I lay a nasty glare on the cadet. "You lay another finger on him and—"

Smack.

Steel-shoe makes contact with the side of my head. I dizzy something mad. The world around me spins, and they all start screaming at each other.

Stay awake.

I blink out the fuzzy lights.

"Don't kill him!"

"Not yet!"

"We have to wait!"

"His lifebloods will be here any minute!"

What . . .

I think I dreamt that last one. Heard it all wrong. They can't know that I'm tethered to Court and Franny. Right?

Adrian bends and taps at my cheek. "Wake up!" he yells. "You're useless asleep."

What are they even *using* me for?

I feel like I'm falling behind. Not catching on. I spit a wad of blood on the floorboards and pant for breath.

"Where are your lifebloods?" Henna barks. "They have to be feeling your pain."

My jaw falls.

How could they have known? How long? And more than that, I understand what they've been doin'. Beating on me so that they don't even have to go searching for Court and Franny.

They're waiting for Court and Franny to come for me. I'm not their prey.

I'm *bait*.

Sickness rises to my throat, burns.

Henna glares. "I asked you a question. Where are your lifebloods?"

Another kick to the gut.

My breath hitches.

Igor strokes his gray-haired chin. "Did you think we didn't know about your tether?" He lets out a husky laugh. I must be looking startled. The God of Victory is spitting on me.

Jolee passes her battle-ax from hand to hand. "We were watching you for thirty-one days while you were on the *Romulus*. You were the best entertainment the crew has seen in over three hundred years. The first time you tried to grab the electrowand from the guard—" She chortles. "You twitched around like a big, idiotic insect caught in a trap. And you know what we all saw? Your lifebloods stumbling around. Looking disoriented. *In pain*. I wonder why that could be?"

They've known about our link for that long, then.

Adrian grins. "The only thing that could have made it better was if you three didn't whisper so much. Audio quality was lacking."

Henna nods in agreement.

I lose it.

Furious, riled emotions push forth, and with energy restored, I wrench and wrench my wrist against the bed. Trying to break the whole damned thing apart.

It lasts for three seconds before a blow to the chin knocks my skull back into the floor. "Adrian!" They all yell at him. "Gentle."

He snorts. "His lifebloods aren't coming. Maybe they just don't care—" He cuts himself off and spins around. Near him, a sea glass lamp is floating in midair off a glossy table. How is a lamp levitating like that?

Gods bless, I hit my head so hard, I'm seeing things. I blink. The lamp has disappeared.

Adrian laughs uncertainly. "Did you all see—"

Thwack!

Adrian's eyes roll back, the unseen force colliding with his head. His legs buckle, and he crumples into an unconscious heap. Finally pressure releases off my broken hand, but I can barely clench my fingers into a fist.

Henna gapes. "What the . . ."

Adrian's electrowand suddenly rises off the floor, hovering. And then the weapon just vanishes like the lamp.

"Who's in here?" Jolee shouts, strengthening her grip on the battle-ax.

Realization strikes me now. Someone else is in the room. Invisible—but here with us.

The only person I know who can cloak themselves is a teeny-tiny baby. Last I saw, she was strapped to Court.

Court.

Blood rushes back to my head, and then Henna drops to the floor in a seizing fit. The other *Romulus* cadets shoot to their feet and try to stalk an invisible enemy.

One second later, Igor's head twists brutally, and he slumps to the ground. Out cold.

Court is fast and lithe with his attacks.

Just three left.

The tall, freckle-faced cadet.

The tattooed boy who hovers near Zimmer.

And Jolee.

She starts swinging the battle-ax aimlessly in the air like she means to hit Court. My nerves ricochet and I yank hard at the metal that chains my wrist to the bed.

The wooden leg cracks and breaks cleanly in two.

As soon as I free my hand, the freckle-faced cadet edges back to the wall. He hoists the long rod out in front of his tall frame.

No one is touching me.

I fumble with the metal locks on my ankles. Trying to unlatch these binds.

Jolee is still swinging her ax, and with enough force, Court's head could be rolling clean off if she slices through his neck.

Urgency clings to me. Fear claws at me.

I'm not letting him die here.

Not for me.

Not like this.

I bellow, enraged spit flying and tears combining with snot. *Snap.* I look up at the harsh noise.

A body has hit the floor.

Not Court, please, not Court.

I quickly spot the boy with the hornet tattoo, slumped against an ornate dresser. Eyes shut.

"Demon!" the freckle-faced boy screams, the only word he's spoken. He opens his mouth to yell again, but suddenly, a shard of sea glass appears in the side of his neck. Blood spews, and he chokes and falls to the floorboards.

"Show yourself!" Jolee screams, her mane of blond hair whipping as she spins around with the battle-ax.

She's the last remaining cadet.

. . . and then I see Court.

In the corner of the suite, he appears from thin air, standing with the baby strapped to his chest. His hands are stained crimson and his carriage rises and falls heavily. He whispers to the infant. As though coaxing her to make them invisible again.

Jolee is about to spot Court.

"HEYA!" I spit, and she whirls toward me. I scoot my body up against the bed, and my fortitude grips her attention. I taunt, "You think you're so mighty?"

She stalks closer.

Court is still whispering to the baby.

"You're all alone now." My lip begins to curve upward. "Where I'm from, you'd be no one and nothin'—not even the God of Victory would waste breath on your ugly spirit."

Jolee grimaces and with one last twirl of the weapon, she presses the cold metal up against *my* neck. I stiffen, feeling Court's distress spike my pulse.

He is screaming inside, but outwardly, he's more urgent. Forcing himself not to yell my name.

I'm all right, Court.

I try to feel at ease, but Jolee has the battle-ax flush on my skin, the force strong enough to nick the flesh. Blood trickles.

Fear like nothing I've felt before rushes into me with a sickening darkness. It's not just mine. Court.

Franny.

Jolee whips her head around—and Court disappears in a blink before she can see him.

I expel a breath.

Her eyes blaze with a panicked fury. "Show yourself! Or I take his head!"

The door to the suite swings open. In a flood of panic, Stork and Franny storm inside without a second thought.

"MYKAL!" Franny screams.

The pressure on my neck intensifies, and I reach out to grip her wrist. To pry the damned weapon from her hand, but she swings the blade back—and she's about to cut my neck cleanly.

"NOOO!" Franny cries out.

Just as Jolee whirls the ax at my head, Stork dives out in front of me. Wet, cold blood sprays my face as the blade slices through his arm. *My brother.*

Stork tumbles to the floor, his arm chopped right off—and at the same time, an invisible Court stabs sea glass into Jolee's windpipe.

She gurgles, the ax slipping from her hands. She touches her throat and falls to her knees.

Stork groans in sheer, unadulterated agony, and I slide to him with bound ankles. I tear off my shirt and use the fabric to help stop the bleeding.

"Court?!" I call out, panicked. He needs a doctor. My baby brother needs a doctor. His face is losing color fast.

"MykalMykalMykal," Stork says in a staggered breath. "I can't die."

Franny snatches up the ax and hurries to me. "Mykal, your ankles."

I show her the clamps, and she swings and breaks the metal lock.

Freeing me completely.

Court is checking on Zimmer. The skinny Fast-Tracker moans and coughs up a bit of water. I think they were drowning him in the bathtub. He assesses him before going to Stork.

Someone will be needing to carry Zimmer. I pick myself off the ground, my bones shrieking. My hand hurts the worst. I reach Zimmer, and with aching muscles, I heave him up in my arms.

"They'll wake up soon," Franny reminds us, her eyes darting to each of the fallen *Romulus* cadets. Strewn limply around the suite.

They're all Saltarian. Nothing can kill them. Not even sea glass to the throat.

"We have to get out of here," Court agrees as he rips a blanket off the bed. He bends and ties it around Stork's gnarled wound. Franny looks to Stork's severed arm, the one lying detached on the ground.

"Leave it." Stork groans as Court helps him stand.

"Are you sure?" Franny wonders. I imagine she'd carry it for him. For however far and however long. She'd do that. I know she would.

"Leave it," Stork repeats. "Let's go."

The five of us step out into the hallway, and just as we move toward the stairwell, the door bangs open. Kinden sprints with intense urgency. Like he's been searching for us. We turn back to follow him, and he waves his hands. "Not this way!"

Hurriedly, Padgett and Gem emerge from the stairwell behind him, and the sisters slam the door shut. Boots thud on the stairs like a roaring army. The Soarcastle sisters must've been able to break into that electronic drawer because a slim keycard is pinched between Kinden's fingers.

Quickly, with the master keycard, we're able to open the nearest vacant suite, and we all slide inside. Kinden locks the door behind all eight of us.

My pulse is racing and my arms ache with Zimmer's weight. Our silence is strained with panting and heavy breathing. Padgett removes a mechanical cube from a satchel on her hip. I recognize it instantly. It's the device that she and Gem had been tinkering with and creating back in the barge. She presses the cube against the small sliver of space where the door meets the wall. It makes a whirring sound and locks in place. No one had bothered to question what they'd been building.

But it's looking useful.

"What is that?" Court asks.

"A better lock," Gem says with a grin and a nod.

"But it won't last long," Padgett tells us.

The footsteps grow louder and then someone starts banging on the door. The suite is small. Four walls. One door. Rushing to the window, I look out at the city below. My stomach sinks.

Hundreds of *Romulus* cadets are storming the entrance to the hotel. Others barricade the building, pushing back people from getting too close.

It doesn't take long to realize . . .

We're trapped.

FORTY

Franny

Court, Stork, and I don't have time to explain what happened in the hotel suite. Time travel. Zima. We're running out of seconds. The eight of us fall into tense silence, all of us thinking of an exit. An escape. And maybe even coming to terms with what might actually happen.

We're going to die on Saltare-1. Court, Mykal, and I. We're going to die here, and our friends will be sent to a fate even worse than death. A prison out in the middle of the ocean. To serve a lifetime sentence.

And this baby . . . my baby . . .

I'm not sure what will happen to her. I think that scares me the most.

The air isn't nippy, but my skin chills and sinking dread heavies me. Court carefully passes Zima to me, and I hug her close to my chest. She reaches up with her tiny hands like she wants to grab my nose.

She's mine. And Stork's.

It hasn't sunk in yet. I don't know when it will.

"They're everywhere," Padgett says, angling her head to the window. "We're blocked in."

Gem has gone pale at the sight of Stork. He's drenched in blood, eyes fluttering. The sight of blood has never made me queasy, but my belly twists seeing him in such agony.

Court quickly tends to Stork's wound, trying to tie the blanket tighter. Stork grimaces and lets out a low yell between his

teeth. His reddened eyes catch mine and then drop to the baby.
When he looks up at me again, he mouths *ours*.

Ours.

She's ours.

Tears sting my eyes.

"I can . . . stand," Zimmer says weakly.

Mykal keeps Zimmer in his arms. "Not yet. You're barely
even speaking the words." He has immeasurable grit and an
iron-willed heart, and even drenched in sweat, muscles strained
and aching, even with a broken hand—Mykal is able to hold another person upright.

The noise outside becomes caustic. Banging. Sawing. "OPEN
UP!" someone screams.

"We can't go through the window," I say. "So what else is
there?"

"Maybe we can reach the roof?" Kinden offers a solution,
staring up at the suite's ceiling. "There has to be a way up."

"Or we can use her," Padgett says pointedly, eyes on Zima.

Court follows her gaze and nods. "She's teleported me once.
She could do it again. But we need to be touching."

The eight of us huddle together. I'm in the middle, holding the
baby, and everyone has at least one hand or finger on me. Stork's
good arm is thrown over Court's back, and I can feel Stork's
weight like I'm carrying it myself. All along my shoulders.

Stork's fingers lightly brush the top of my head.

"Okay." I breathe and glance down at the baby. "You can
teleport us now."

She yawns and then smacks her lips.

Fyke.

Kinden glares. "She's useless. This is a waste of time."

"Give her a second," I snap.

"Take us to Earth," Stork tells our daughter. "*Please*."

"Wait." Padgett frowns deeply. "We voted. We have to find
her parents first."

"We already did," Court replies.

Zimmer tries to keep his eyes open. "They're allowing us to take her?"

"Yeah, they are," Stork says, looking at me.

Wood splinters, the door cracking, and the voices on the other side become clearer. "All eight of them are in there, sir." Light streams underneath the frame.

Panic bubbles, and we all fixate harder on the baby in my arms. *Come on, Zima.* I don't know how her abilities work exactly, but we have no other solutions.

"Court, you should ask her," I tell him. The baby was fond of Court in the future, and maybe she'll only listen to him.

Court takes a tight breath. "Little one," he says in his softest voice, which isn't very soft at all. "Teleport us to Earth."

My world spins.

Everything around me swirls and dizzies like blood rushes from my head too quickly. It's a worse sensation than coming down from a Juggernaut high. I blink hard a few times, trying to right myself. Warm light illuminates harsh steel walls.

Gods, this isn't right. Earth can't be made of metal.

"Bloody hell," Stork murmurs as he looks around. "She teleported us inside a ship."

He's right.

Lights flash on the dashboard, and I recognize the two-person cockpit. The entire starcraft layout is what I memorized all those months ago at StarDust. It looks exactly like the *Saga,* which is back on the *Lucretzia* in the docking bay. While not Earth, that's the second-best place she could have teleported us.

"We're on the *Saga,*" Kinden says, thinking the same as me.

"No," Court refutes. "Look." We all follow his gaze to the tinted windshield. Outside are hundreds of parked starcrafts, the sun radiating on the vessels.

We're on a launchpad, and as ocean slaps against cement and the *Romulus* crew crowds around battlecrafts, my stomach sinks.

We're still on Saltare-1.

After we look around, we come to the conclusion that this starcraft is the same layout as the *Saga*, only an updated model. Gem pops up the database on the MEU station, and we learn that it's called the *Nebulus*. A smaller battlecraft that has a retractable third cockpit for weaponry.

We're parked toward the middle of the launchpad, but we can't easily fly out. There are too many *Romulus* crew walking around, and near them are massive artillery starcrafts. If they caught a rogue battlecraft starting up the thrusters, we'd be immediately blown to bits.

The best we can do is wait until night falls and the crew go to sleep. When the launchpad is clear, we'll fly the *Nebulus* away from Saltare-1.

It's a solid plan.

But Court hates waiting, and I feel the tense, nervous frustration like it's my own. After we change into the clean Star-Dust shirts and slacks onboard, we agree to be as quiet as we can and take seats on the ground for extra precaution.

I find a comfortable, quiet spot near the extra jumpchairs and storage compartments. With a clear view of Court and Mykal at the MEU station, I watch them whisper quietly to one another.

Court has Zima tucked to his chest, since she quiets the most in his clutch. And he already bandaged Mykal's broken hand. With his good one, Mykal threads his fingers through Court's thick brown hair.

I can feel the soft strands like Mykal's fingers are *my* fingers. Court nearly smiles, and those sinking, nervous feelings suddenly lighten.

The three of us are lifebloods, but I know what they share goes beyond this connection. It's something more, and no matter what happens, I'm so deeply happy for them.

My eyes well and lips begin to rise.

Across from me, Zimmer and Stork are murmuring, too hushed for me to hear. We found the med kit onboard, and Stork seems more content now with medicine. He leans into Zimmer's shoulder and breathes deeply.

I turn my focus to Gem and Padgett. Near the captain's chair, they both flip through a paper emergency manual for the *Nebulus*. I'm unsure what would have happened if they hadn't come along. If we'd even make it this far.

They were here to prove something to the world, and I don't know if Earth will understand the enormity of what they did. But I do. And if I live through all of this, I vow to make sure they're in Earth's history books.

"Franny," Zimmer hisses, humor dotting his eyes. I'm not sure what they've been whispering about, but by the raise of Stork's brows, I know it's either going to embarrass me or unnerve me. Or both.

Zimmer says, "You and Stork bedded each other in the future, and you weren't going to tell me?"

Well . . . Stork told him about the baby.

My face roasts. "I think the more important takeaway is that there's time travel in the future," I point out.

Stork wears a wry smile. "Can you not imagine it, dove?"

He means us bedding each other.

And I can picture that. We've already kissed. I've imagined more.

Which is why the baby doesn't surprise me. I've always been drawn to Stork, and now knowing our histories, there is so much more that has existed between us. It's as though we've been wrapped around one another from the very start. As though we were intertwined by the gods.

And even if we never met, if I had died on Saltare-3 like I

was supposed to, we'd still have this unseen string, tying us together.

But I dodge his question by saying, "Time travel, yes, I can imagine it."

He licks his lips into a wider grin. "I meant bedding me."

"I know what you meant," I say hotly.

Zimmer stares around the starcraft like he's trying to etch each face into his memory. His lips lift, and I wonder if he thinks this is the greatest adventure a die-hard Fast-Tracker ever took.

"Did Stork tell you her name?" I ask Zimmer.

Stork wipes sweat off his brow. "I left that part for you, dove."

Zimmer meets my gaze with a deep frown. "What's special about her name?"

"In the future," I tell him, my heart swelling. "We named her Zima."

Zimmer's eyes glass and he wears the largest grin I've ever seen. One that dimples his cheeks and fills me whole.

Even in the future, however much time passed since Zimmer died, we loved him enough to name our daughter after him.

That means something.

A tear slides down his cheek. "Never thought for a single day that I'd have a legacy," he whispers. "Those are for Influentials, you know."

I know.

I nod strongly and he wipes at his cheeks. "Also, what godsforsaken reason could you have not just called her Zimmer? It's a better name."

We laugh and cry and I do something I shouldn't do. Something so irrational that no one ever thinks it.

I still don't know the day Zimmer will die, but I pray to the gods to give him more time.

FORTY-ONE

Court

An hour passes and the crew still haven't left the landing port. I fear they're never going to leave.

But I'm trying not to think that way. Because if this is truly the last few hours I have with Mykal, I won't spend them horribly focused on surviving. I've survived enough.

I just want to start living again.

He makes a silly face at the baby, and she quietly blows spit bubbles at him. Mykal glances up to meet my gaze. We simply look at one another for a long moment. Sharing emotions, passing them back and forth.

Love flows between us like a featherlight wind. Soft. Tender. And then strong all at once. He smiles into a crooked grin and whispers, "For as long as we live, never stop looking at me that way."

"I'll never stop," I promise.

He leans forward and cups the back of my head. Our lips find each other in a kiss. When we break apart, I spot my brother nodding from the other side of the room. Alone. He's kept his eyes on the windshield all night, waiting for the perfect moment to leave.

"Go." Mykal nudges me forward.

I cradle the baby in my arms as I leave, not wanting to pass her along and risk her crying.

When I reach Kinden's side, he shifts his gaze off the windshield. I sit beside him and tell him something I should have said long ago. "Thank you," I breathe. "For staying by my side. All this time."

He wears a rich smile. "There is no better way to spend my long life." He stares at me like he can see right through me. He used to do that when we were young.

I wait for his unbridled honesty. I yearn for it.

After he places a hand on my shoulder, he says, "I don't think they're going to break you anymore, little brother."

Tears gather. In both our eyes.

"They won't," I agree. There's strength deep inside me. I've been trying to reach it for so long, and I'm finally grasping it. Pulling it free.

Finding a place for myself in this world.

"What are you going to do?" I ask him. "When we reach Earth?"

"If," he reminds me. "And I have plans . . ." He looks toward Padgett, who's quietly letting Gem braid her hair. Padgett glances up, and they lock eyes. Smiling inside their gazes.

Someone is unsteady, making more noise than the rest of us. I look over and see Stork trying to right himself up to a stance with just one arm. Zimmer and Franny help, and when he's on solid feet, he aims for Mykal.

FORTY-TWO

Mykal

My baby brother is a mess. Pale and sickly and stumbling about. I have to catch him before he goes careening into the MEU station.

We both sink down to the ground, resting our backs against the paneled wall. "You coulda waved me over," I whisper to him. "Instead of standing and walking about."

"Yeah, but I wanted to speak to my brother alone." He flashes a smile at my confusion. He's never called me his brother. Never admitted to our relation out loud. "And just so you know," he adds, "I'm technically younger, but not by much."

I shake my head, letting my lips lift. "You don't act only a bit younger than I. You're still more of a *baby* brother."

He laughs lightly. "I lost an arm protecting you."

"Yeh, you have a point." I glance at his bandaged wound, more gruesome than any injury I've had. *Protecting me.* I'll never be forgetting. "Are you all right?"

Stork takes a bigger breath. "It feels like . . . I will be." He swallows hard. "But I didn't come over here to argue with you about who's older." Carefully, he reaches into his pocket and pulls out a small earring identical to the sapphire blue jay that dangles from his own ear.

"This was Moura's," he tells me. "Your birth mother's. She gave the pair to me when the trade was agreed on. She told me to keep one and give the other to you when we reached Earth."

I frown. "We're not on Earth, you realize."

He smiles. "I know."

How many of us on this starcraft are actually saying good-byes and I don't even know it? Somethin' strong pulls in my stomach, an ache that I don't want. "Keep it," I say. "Give it to me when we're on land."

"Mykal—"

"I said keep it," I growl. "We're gonna make it there."

We have to.

Blond hair falls into his eyes and he nods. "Okay."

FORTY-THREE

Franny

We spend five hours in hushed quiet on the *Nebulus*, waiting for our opening to arrive. The Saltare-1 crew haven't vacated the launchpad for bed or a break like we expected.

Kinden rises to his feet, roping in all of our attention. "We can't wait any longer in the hope that they clear out. Hope is not a strategy." He's about to move toward the communications panel, but he stops himself short. His gaze sweeps us. "Does anyone have an objection?"

Padgett's brows arch in surprise. "You're actually asking us, *Saga 1*?"

He almost grins. "I'm not about to take this risk without all of you."

Court stands and approaches the captain's chair. "What's your plan?"

Kinden quickly explains his idea, and it's riskier than even flying to the trash moon. Riskier than stealing the *Saga* starcraft and flying off Saltare-3.

He wants to blow up the tarmac. Along with all the battle-crafts sitting around us. It will give us a way to escape without Saltarians following, but there are a thousand and one risks.

"What if we blow up in the process?" I ask. It seems like a probable outcome.

"We'll already be in the air, and hopefully far enough away from the explosion," Kinden says.

"You just said hope isn't a strategy," Stork argues.

"It's not," Kinden agrees. "But hope happens to be a small, minuscule factor in every single plan I could think of."

My nerves increase tenfold, but it's Mykal who blows out rough breaths, pressure mounting on his chest. He's not fond of this plan. I pace toward the cockpit to try and rid his feelings.

Court glances out the large window. "Gem, can you calculate how far up we'd need to be to avoid the blast?"

Gem shakes her head. "Not without knowing the exact amount and type of ammunition in the other battlecrafts."

Padgett adds, "Trying to implode all of them is incredibly dangerous. We'd be better off brainstorming a better idea."

Zimmer backs up from one of the monitors, eyes wide. "Looks like we're not going to have a choice."

We all follow his gaze to the screen. It's a prime view of the area behind the *Nebulus,* and currently *hundreds* of *Romulus* cadets are sprinting toward the tarmac, like they mean to gear up for battle.

Either they've found us or they're about to. Zimmer is right . . .

We don't have a choice.

"Stork," Court says, urgency deepening his voice. "Can you command the artillery?" We all scrutinize Stork's sickly complexion and the blood-soaked bandage on his bicep. Hand and arm gone.

"With one hand, I'm all yours." Stork nods, his confidence verging on cockiness. But in all honesty, it feels good to have someone so sure of something on this ship. He's already settling into the third chair in the cockpit.

We all take our positions like we're in another simulation from StarDust. Padgett and I strap into the pilot chairs, mine right next to Stork.

"Prepare for liftoff," Court commands. "*Quickly.*"

Zimmer and Mykal strap into jumpchairs near the bridge door.

Gem switches on the engine from the MEU station, and the battlecraft rumbles to life.

"Heya! They're getting fykking close!" Zimmer yells, eyes still on the screen.

"Engaging the thrusters," Padgett calls out and then looks to me. We don't even count down. Both of us maneuver our joysticks and the triple-barreled engines let out a more aggressive roar.

The ship doesn't take off.

It doesn't even move.

Fire blasts out of the engines and does *nothing* but rumble our ship and create a giant target on us. We might as well have hung out a sign that reads WE'RE RIGHT HERE!

I start to perspire underneath my armpits.

"Gem, what's going on?!" Court yells.

She's typing hurriedly. "It looks like a safety lock is on for this starcraft. It's been in a maintenance mode that these newer models seem to have."

"Can you disable it?" Court asks.

"It'll take me some time—"

The radio on the comms dash blinks and a voice fills the *Nebulus*. "*Nebulus*, this is *Arclight 4*. Your thrusters have been engaged. Is that an error, over?"

"Reply to him," Court tells Kinden. "Lie."

Kinden adjusts the microphone on his headset. "*Arclight 4*, this is the *Nebulus*. It seems like we have a malfunction onboard. We're trying to take care of it. Over."

We all wait to see if they bought the lie. The only sound in the ship comes from Gem, who types quickly.

Static from the radio seeps in our vessel, signaling incoming communications.

"*Nebulus* crew, please kindly exit your battlecraft. Over."

"No fykking way," Zimmer curses. "They can *please kindly* shove that directive up—"

"Got it!" Gem says.

"Engaging thrusters," Padgett and I say in unison. We maneuver our joysticks and this time, the roar of the engines is accompanied by liftoff.

The pressure on the straps of my chair intensifies as we shoot up.

Gem shouts over the noise. "You'll need to be at least twenty kilometers away before you can unleash artillery! It's my best guess."

Mykal pales at the word *guess.*

"We're currently ten kilometers." I read the panels.

Stork can see them clearly from his vantage point as well. His eyes are trained down below at the tarmac, and his hand squeezes the joystick. He controls the interstellar artillery, and the heavy weaponry groans as he moves it into position.

Court continues to shout commands.

We fly higher and higher.

"Seventeen," I call out so the others know. "Eighteen."

As soon as we drop the explosives, we're either going to be charred alive with the *Romulus* cadets or we'll make it out unscathed.

There is only one certainty in all of this: Mykal, Court, and I are the only ones who can die today.

"Nineteen." My pulse hammers. "Twenty." I hold my breath.

Stork clicks a button on his joystick in fast succession. *Click. Click. Click. Click.* And the battlecraft shakes violently. Seconds pass before a glaring light breaches our windshield. Heat.

Gods, the heat nearly chokes me.

Explosives detonate on the tarmac, and I can only hear the blistering, all-consuming thunder. My senses are overpowered. Suffocating warmth cocoons me like I'm brewing from the inside out, and the battlecraft keeps pushing off from the blasts below. Flying away from Saltare-1.

Shooting faster and harder with explosions at our rear—at any second the fire and flames could engulf our vessel and send us backward.

I just keep focused on my job.

Forward. Up.

Don't stop.

The water world falls behind us as we rise and rise.

And then, we breach the darkness of space. We speed away from the largest Saltare planet. It almost feels unreal. The sudden quiet outside.

Spots of light dance in my vision, and my ears ring shrilly.

Kinden flips a few switches on the comms panels. "I'm going to try and send a signal to the *Lucretzia.*"

Stork calls out a radio frequency for the Knave Squadron. Nia, Barrett, and Arden are the ones meant to help us with the return passage.

We all work in silence. Holding our breaths, waiting to be chased by enemy starcrafts that survived the explosion, on the chance that we botched the plan. But the universe is dark and still, and Saltare-1 fades into the background, a speck in the distance.

Thank the gods.

I exhale, my hand sweating on the joystick between my legs.

"I can't believe that worked," I say, stunned, my gaze planted on the windshield.

"Of course it did," Kinden says. "It was my idea. I'd call it a success."

"And we also just subjected hundreds of *Romulus* cadets to third-degree burns and years of pain and suffering," Padgett says, eyeing Kinden. "What would you call that?"

"An unfortunate casualty."

Stork spins around in his weaponry chair. "Look, we need to hyperdrive to Earth's galaxy, but Kinden has to radio the *Lucretzia* and let the current admirals know. Or else the Earthen Fleet will blow us up upon arrival."

"What?" half of us shout.

Court is the one to answer, "We're flying a Saltarian starcraft."

"Bingo," Stork says, confusing us all again, but we have no time to ask about his choice of word.

The starcraft rumbles violently.

"Gem?" Court asks.

She hurriedly presses buttons on the MEU station. "We have a problem."

Mykal curses under his breath. My shoulders jostle in my straps. Pain blooms from Mykal's aching limbs that are tossed around in the jumpchair.

Court grips the armrests of the captain's chair. "Are we losing engine power?" We all tense.

"We will." Gem unstraps herself to reach up to another button and switch. "The hyperdrive fuel pump is leaking, and to compensate, the starcraft is using the engine's reserves."

We can't hyperdrive, but what's worse: if we lose engine fuel, we'll sputter out and drift uncontrollably in space. We could collide with debris, craters, asteroids, or even a moon—we'll all fykking explode.

Court inhales strongly. "What's the best solution?"

"The only solution is to fix the fuel pump." Gem slows, a dread weighing her movements. "It's on the outside."

"The outside?" Mykal frowns.

I fly the starcraft around a jagged asteroid, and Padgett decelerates to a crawl. Conserving fuel.

"The fuel pump is on the outer shell," Gem says, sinking back in her chair. "These starcrafts were built to fix fuel pumps on the ground. Not in space. In emergencies, the starcraft uses the main fuel supply so we can immediately land and refuel."

I wipe my palm on my leg and grab the joystick. "Can we refuel anywhere?"

Gem reads out all the energy gauges, and Stork and Court leave their chairs and study the coordinates to the nearest Saltare planet. We're not out of the Saltarian galaxy because we can't hyperdrive.

We're supposed to be going to Earth, and my stomach lurches at the idea of rerouting our course. *We're so close.*

We're so close.

We're so close.

Stork mentions Saltare-4.

Zimmer unclips himself from the jumpchair. "I'll do it."

"What?" My voice spikes above the rest.

"You can't fix the leak in space, Zimmer," Kinden tells him. "Gem just said it's impossible."

"I never said it's impossible." Gem frowns. "I said the star-crafts weren't built for it. He could, theoretically, fix the fuel pump in space. But once he connects the valve, the force will blast him away from the starcraft."

My pulse is in my throat. "And then we'll pick him up," I say hopefully and look right at him, convincing myself more than him, I think. "I'll fly the starcraft and pick you up."

Shaggy hair in his eyes, Zimmer smiles fondly at me. "It's time to see the stars, Franny."

And I know.

Today is his deathday.

"This soon . . . ?" I ask.

Zimmer nods, and everyone starts moving into action for this midspace repair. We either lose Zimmer Creecastle and go to Earth or take the biggest risk and land on Saltare-4.

His mind is already made up. Zimmer slams a fist at the wall, opening a paneled compartment where a bodysuit and helmet hang. Gem rattles off instructions.

I lock my joystick to keep the starcraft stationary, and I un-clip myself from the cockpit. My stomach is in knots, and my mouth is chalky and dry. I don't know if I'm ready.

Maybe I'll never be ready.

Once he has the skintight spacesuit halfway up and under-stands the instructions, Zimmer starts saying his quick good-byes to everyone. He hugs Stork and they whisper a few soft words, and then he turns to the next person. Each one bids him farewell. Even Court surprisingly wraps a stiff arm around Zimmer. They pull into a warm hug that floods my body.

I watch them break apart, and then Zimmer places a soft kiss on the top of the baby's head. Zima coos and wiggles her toes.

I'm the last person Zimmer nears.

He stretches his gangly arms above his head, as though feeling what it's like to move them. One last time. "Today is the day, Franny." He smiles like a wiseass chump, but it fades to something softer. He holds my cheeks and brings my face closer to his. "And I've lived hard and fast . . . and full."

Tears burn my eyes. My mom used to say those words to me. He knows that. I've told Zimmer once or twice or more during our long nights together.

He tugs me in a tight hug. For a goodbye.

I'm not sure how to say it anymore.

"Clap for me." His breath warms my neck. "Laugh for me." He kisses my forehead. "I'm not scared. It'll be the *grandest* death that any Fast-Tracker has ever had. I'm going to die among the stars."

I'm happiest, truly happy, knowing Zimmer will have the greatest death. Tears streak my cheeks, and my ribs shrink around my lungs in a stifling emotion.

I whisper that I love him. I whisper how I'm honored to have met him and shared my time with him. And the last words I manage to say are words he'll want to hear. Something familiar. Something to remind him of the home he left.

"May the gods be in your spirit," I breathe.

"And I in your heart." Zimmer rubs away my tears and his tears. Hurrying, he sticks his arms through the fabric of the jumpsuit and zips it up to his neck. He grabs his helmet. "I'm going to tell my moms about you when I see them," he says. "They're going to love you."

I breathe stronger.

I try to, at least.

Everything happens fast. Zimmer fits on his helmet and disappears through the bridge. He has to take another exit.

Ringing fills my ears, and my head dizzies. Once he reaches the shell, I watch through one of the portholes. Zimmer waves and gives a signal that he found the hyperdrive fuel pump.

After a few minutes, he speaks through his headset. "Live and love, you chumps." He connects the valve, and his audio cuts out, a silent blast pushing his body back into the starry-canvassed universe.

I smile for him. I clap for him. We all do.

And I do, also, cry for him. Wiping my eyes, I realize almost everyone is sniffling and wet-cheeked.

Gem clears her throat. "The hyperdrive fuel pump is activated."

"He did it," Stork says.

I return to my pilot's chair, just as Kinden shouts, "I have a signal!"

Stork reaches the comms station. Kinden is fluent in four human languages already, but Stork has the clearance level to speak to the admirals after Nia patches him through.

He talks loudly, and I recognize the words *Lucretzia* and *baby*. Without an EI behind my ear, I can't comprehend much else.

Kinden lowers a headset. "We're clear, little brother."

Court straps into the captain's chair. "Prepare for hyperdrive to the *Milky Way*."

"Preparing for hyperdrive," Padgett says, initiating the thrusters.

"Preparing hyperdrive," I chime in and reach up for a switch. Thrill thumping in the wake of my sorrow. The joystick rumbles, asking me to clutch it and hold tight.

"Three," Court counts, "two . . . one."

FORTY-FOUR

Franny

A planet is outside our windshield. One with swirling white clouds, deep oceanic blues, and one single green landmass.

Earth.

Last time we let ourselves be happy when we thought we found peace, we were pulled into the *Romulus* starcraft. Court, Mykal, and I seem to cage our breath just a little longer. Though smiles peek, and a powerful excitement trembles in our core.

We should reach Earth in twenty-four minutes.

I lock my joystick in the right direction, and I unclip my straps. Before I stand, Stork walks over and places his knee on my armrest. Towering above.

"*Excuse* you," I snap.

I expect a mocking lift of his brows, but he takes a sharp breath. "We have to take care of his Final Will."

Breathing takes more energy than usual. Like rocks are in my lungs. "You've been carrying his Final Will around all this time?" I watch him unfold a stack of papers that could've fit in his pocket.

"I knew he'd die today," Stork confesses. "He told me a while ago. So yeah, I carried it here."

I try to inhale deeply but it cuts short.

He notices. "You loved him. So it hurts worse."

I understand now. What he means. *Grief.*

And mourning. All along, this is what Stork has been feeling. He hands the papers to me. "His only possession. He wanted *you* to have them. He said you'd 'get it.'" Stork does the two-finger wag, air quotes that Zimmer made fun of him for. It seems fitting right now.

I wipe at my face with a rough hand and inspect the papers. My mouth drops.

Pages and pages of torn scraps. All along them are doodles, little drawings of knights and princes and princesses. Of adventures and dreams. Spaceships and rockets.

I flip more—there are so many. Scrawled over every spare inch. Boats and pirates. Fairies and goblins. Fantasies he read from books. Castles dot the edge of a page.

I peer closer, noticing a partial word.

And my handwriting. It reads, *owed to.* These are the drawings that he used to ink onto pages from my journal. Back at StarDust. I never even knew Zimmer kept them.

I rub harder at my face, and I tell Stork, "Thank you." He will never know how much this means to me. For him to carry it here.

I hug the papers.

We were the same. Zimmer and me. Fast-Trackers from Bartholo, and even when we were pretending in StarDust, even when we left Saltare-3, being with him felt like being home. The only difference between him and me was that I was human all along.

He couldn't escape his deathday.

"Franny," Stork says, wrangling my attention again. "Can I ask something from you?"

"Anything." And I mean those words.

"When we land on Earth, I'm not going to have a mission. I reckon the admirals won't give me another one for a while after this." He touches the blue jay that swings from his earlobe. "And without a mission, I can't find any reason not to drink again." He takes a tight breath. "Would you help me?"

"To not drink?"

He nods once. "I just need someone to care. Support. That sort of thing, dove."

My eyes almost glass with his. "Stork, I already care about you." I tell him words that have never been truer. "And I'll try to be the best support in the entire . . . *Milky Way*."

Just hearing Earth's galaxy again hoists both of our lips. In the future, we were coupled. We had a baby together. How long did it take us to fall for one another so completely that he confessed his love for me?

I smile wider.

Because I have time.

Glorious *time* to wait and find out.

Kinden calls Stork back over to the radio, and I continue on toward the captain's chair where Court and Mykal talk quietly. They both keep glancing out the nearest porthole, a direct view of Earth. The planet seems to grow larger and larger as we approach.

Court cradles Zima, the baby conked out like she's been through three blizzards tonight. Though I never imagined I'd be a mother—I know Zima won't just be raised by me. Court has already told me as much. If we were to reach Earth, they wouldn't put the responsibility solely on my shoulders. She'll have Court and Mykal and Stork.

She'll be so very loved.

"Franny, do you remember when we found you?" Court asks. I glance up at both of them. Mykal rests his bottom on the armrest of the captain's chair and then slings an arm around Court's hips, pulling him closer. Their lips rise and rise.

"That's not a day I can easily forget," I tell Court.

"I know it's one of the worst days of your life," Court says. "But it's one of the best days of mine." Tears prick our eyes. I'm not sure who's the source. I'm not sure I care.

Mykal adds, "And mine, little love."

My heart swells. I never truly understood love and friendship until I met them. "But you're wrong," I tell Court. "It's not one of the worst days of my life. Not close. Not anymore."

He tries hard not to cry more by pinching the bridge of his

nose, and after a second, he says, "I know what I want to see. On Earth."

Mykal and I share a look of surprise.

Court hardly ever knows what he wants outside of goals and missions and survival. Mykal is simple. He wants the trees—if there are any. Maybe that makes me simple too because I want to see the human cars. To fly in one.

For Court, he never really told us. Of course we guessed, but guessing for him is different than hearing him say the words.

"And what's that?" I ask.

"Spring." He glances between us. "I read that's when the snow just begins to melt."

We each begin to slowly smile again. And I feel their heartbeats in my chest.

Humming at the same lively rhythm as mine.

FORTY-FIVE

Mykal

Truth being, I've had plentiful opportunities to ask Stork about Earth. Once he's been freely spouting facts, that is. But I never spoke up.

I knew and I'll be knowing that ugly surroundings can't frighten me away. I'm used to ugly, and no matter where we go, the happiest I'll ever be is with them.

Reaching Earth together is the mightiest victory. Everything else is just an extra blessing.

I hold Court's hand, and I step out onto the earth. A crisp cool breeze brushes our faces. Gentle and kinder than the cold. We stand on the grassiest greenest hill that my two eyes have ever seen, and I stagger—I'm staggering to a tree.

Sliding down the sturdy trunk, I sink into the soft grass and Court is watching me stare out at the forest-blanketed hills and valleys. Snow-capped mountains edge across the horizon. A bird flaps through the melted blue sky, and not far from our place, an antlered animal grazes in the peace that I'm feeling. Children's laughter catches the wind, Stork's cottage back behind us.

"Just for a moment," I tell Court, not aching to leave any-time soon.

He sits next to me, his arm up against mine, and as his beautiful grays meet my awed eyes, he tells me, "We have longer than a moment."

My lopsided smile rises, and I hook my arm over his shoulder. "That we do."

FORTY-SIX

Court

Three years later

To live and not just survive. I never imagined I could stop and breathe and simply look at the trees that Mykal loves so immensely.

But I have for three whole years. I have seen and felt and breathed all of Earth's four seasons, some shorter than others, some more pleasant. But even the hottest days and the coldest months, I would not trade.

And today, on the first day of spring, I'm in the earthen woods.

All around me, towering firs and spruces rustle in the gentle wind. Snow melts off vibrant green leaves and drips melodically off branches. Droplets falling to the mossy ground and smooth rocks.

Glowing orbs drift in midair and cast warm blue light in the woods. The sun hasn't risen yet, but we wait for dawn, as Grenpalish tradition decrees.

Nerves flap inside my stomach, and I straighten out my leather jacket that Mykal stitched, my favorite piece of clothing he's ever made me.

I'm standing in front of a beautiful, strong-willed Hinterlander with a crooked smile more powerful than seven suns.

Mykal stands in front of me, a twenty-one-year-old man who has light in his gray grim eyes.

Music is already in the crisp, spring air.

Our life is here on the countryside. Where we first landed the starcraft. Where an overgrown forest sweeps a picturesque valley and animals graze along rolling hills. We're a short hike from the cottage: a massive marble-columned structure that serves as a home for us and many others. It's a communal space with draped archways, a courtyard, and even a shallow pool.

We quickly realized the interior of the *Lucretzia*, which we'd spent months on, was replicated to resemble Earth's cottages. In case the planet was lost, the admirals wanted the people aboard to feel at home.

So three years ago, when I first stepped through the archway and featherlight curtains brushed my cheek, I looked down at the mosaic tile and everything felt so familiar.

And now, the cottage and this land do feel like home.

I take a readied breath. My eyes skim the man I've loved— the man who is about to be my husband.

Light fox fur drapes along his broad shoulders, and his winter wheat hair lies as messily as the first day we met. Mykal holds a river wreath in his hand, one he made with plump red berries, twigs, and ferns. Crafted crudely in his large callused hands, but it resembles everything I adore about him. Simply, it's gorgeous.

The wreath in mine is more methodical. I went to the babbling brook he loves and plucked wildflowers along the bank. I spent weeks weaving.

He eyes the wreath for the first time, and his breath deepens as his chest swells.

Our friends are gathered in a circle around us. Each one rattles a stone in a wooden cup, the sound belonging in nature, but it's created for Mykal and me.

I can feel Franny smiling already. Out of the corner of my eye, I see our lifeblood shaking a cup with a face full of happiness. She has flown an aerovan. Many times, and yesterday Franny said that she's less afraid of death. Each day is easier, better.

And we are safe. All of us.

Thanks to the baby. Zima Bluefall has grown quickly, and

in three years, she looks like a sprightly green-haired child but she's intelligent beyond her age. We all dote on her and offer wisdoms passed down from those who raised us. My future self was correct in the hologram. It took time to find the coordinates to a safer galaxy and gain permission from neighboring planets to reside there.

Just last month, Zima teleported Earth to the *Lalli Kai* Galaxy. When she's older, she'll know just the enormity of the role she's played. Until then, she is just a child bouncing in the woods. Playing with a wooden bird that Stork poorly whittled and rattling a stone in a cup at his feet.

He curves his arm around Franny. The fleet has given Stork time to rest for a few more years, as he should. His other arm and hand, a bronze prosthetic, grips a wooden cup and stone. He makes music with many more who are circled around us.

My honest brother. Kinden is smiling, brimming with pompous arrogance and also encouragement. Padgett rattles the cup beside him, their hands clasped together.

Young Gem has an arm around Nia, and beside them, Arden and Barrett play flutes while a little girl strums on a fiddle. They each spent three months learning the instruments and Grenpalish songs.

Mykal grins wide as the tune carries with the wind and birds chirp overhead, all in harmonious unison with the shaking of stones.

There are more friends around us. More people that we've met on Earth. People that Mykal says are too good to hate.

Love flutters inside my chest, and Mykal blows out a lungful, his heartbeat racing in anticipation.

I only look at him.

He's only ever had eyes for me. Even when I couldn't appreciate myself, even when I lost all belief in everything. He still loved me.

I wipe a tear that drips down my cheek.

He laughs and rubs beneath his eye. "Gods bless, yer gonna

make me start cryin' already." The more he smiles, the more my nerves subside.

I wanted today to be perfect for him, and I already feel that it is and it's only just begun.

Melted snow squishes underneath my boots, and I capture Mykal's hard-hearted blue eyes again. They fissure through me. Pure joy swirls through him. But the emotion is mine too.

"Just like you imagined?" I ask, only a foot away from him.

His lopsided grin overtakes his face. "More." He nods to me as light starts to bleed from the sky, the sun rising. "You ready?"

I nod back. "I'll go first, then."

"I imagined that too," he says. "You know what that means. Yer still predictable."

"But never as predictable as you," I quip.

Fondness passes strongly and beautifully and wholeheartedly between us, and as the sun crests, I take the next step.

"Mykal Kickfall," I say and watch him kneel at my feet. His homeland runs in his blood, no matter how far away we are from Grenpale. There is only one way I wanted to wed him, and it's the way he knows. "With my heart. My spirit. My strength and my soul. I will love you through eras. You're mine, as the gods see it, as I feel it, as you will it."

He rubs a fist at his cheeks.

I place the crown of wildflowers atop his blond hair, and then as he rises, I kneel at his feet.

The berried wreath is still in his hand. He takes a big breath. "Court Icecastle." He says my name with so much pride.

My throat swells.

"With my heart," Mykal tells me, "my spirit. My strength and my soul. I will be loving you through eras. Yer mine, as the gods see it, as I feel it, as you will it." He sets the berried wreath on my dark brown hair.

Tears sting my eyes, my heart overflowing. I rise, and our friends begin to walk around our bodies and let soft ribbons fall to the earth, creating a colorful circle along the ground.

Everyone sings, "Heya, heya, you're together! Heya, heya, you're forever!" Merriment flourishing, and the music fills the woods.

Mykal and I draw into each other's arms where we're safest, and as our lips meet, our bodies pull together in a powerful kiss. Emotion ripples between us like an endless river. I clench his hair between my fingers, and I feel his smile against my mouth. I feel my smile rise in kind.

I feel as though his lips are my lips and my lips are his lips. Dizzying and brightening and loving.

We are together.

We are one, and we are two and then three, and finally, we have found real, everlasting peace.